Qualinesti lies prostrate under the armies of the bandit king, Lord Samuval, where the lingering curse of the great dragon Beryl poisons the heart of the land. Cast out of one desperate situation, the Lioness is delivered first into Qualinesti, then into the hands of brutal slavers where she experiences first-hand the oppression of her homeland.

Unknown to her, another lost soul has come to Qualinesti. Inspired by an unlikely mentor, this mysterious figure leads a handful of Kagonesti foresters against a bandit army numbering thousands. Superstitious enemies—and allies—call him the Scarecrow. When the Lioness meets him, she will know him by another name.

Far away, the elves in exile struggle to leave Khur and reach the hidden valley of Inath-Wakenti. The nomads, consumed by dreams of vengeance, won't let them go in peace. Adala, the chief of the Weya-Lu, drives her people on, with only one goal in mind—the complete extermination of the the elves in Khur. Opposing her, Speaker Gilthas has only pride and promise to keep his faltering people on the unmarked trail to safety. The question is which will give out first, the Speaker's life or the quest for Inath-Wakenti.

The rebellion in Qualinesti smolders, then explodes. Cities fall, armies fail, and the elusive elves pass on through the angry countryside, fanning the flames of revolt. A forgotten queen, a loyal scout, and a lovelorn soldier cast their lot with the Lioness and her enigmatic leader. But will they follow the Scarecrow into the lan

ALSO BY PAUL B. THOMPSON & TONYA C. COOK

THE ERGOTH TRILOGY

VOLUME ONE
A WARRIOR'S JOURNEY

VOLUME TWO
THE WIZARD'S FATE

VOLUME THREE
A HERO'S JUSTICE

THE BARBARIANS

VOLUME ONE
CHILDREN OF THE PLAINS

VOLUME TWO
BROTHER OF THE DRAGON

VOLUME THREE
SISTER OF THE SWORD

ALLIANCES

ELVEN EXILES
VOLUME TWO

PAUL B. THOMPSON &
TONYA C. COOK

ALLIANCES

©2006 Wizards of the Coast, Inc.

Cover art by Matt Stawicki
First Printing: October 2006
Library of Congress Catalog Card Number: 2005935536

9 8 7 6 5 4 3 2 1

ISBN-10: 0-7869-4076-X
ISBN-13: 978-0-7869-4076-9
620-95615740-001-EN

U.S., CANADA,
ASIA, PACIFIC, & LATIN AMERICA
Wizards of the Coast, Inc.
P.O. Box 707
Renton, WA 98057-0707
+1-800-324-6496

EUROPEAN HEADQUARTERS
Hasbro UK Ltd
Caswell Way
Newport, Gwent NP9 0YH
GREAT BRITAIN
Save this address for your records.

Visit our web site at www.wizards.com

DEDICATION

Thou has left behind
Powers that will work for thee; air, earth, and skies;
There's not a breathing of the comon wind
That will forget thee. Thou hast great allies.

—William Wordsworth, "To Toussaint L'Ouverture"

shadows

Shadows gathered around. No amount of light would dispel them.

Kerianseray, seeking death, vanished in the blink of an eye. So too had the elves' tenuous peace disappeared, like water spilled on the hot stone streets of Khuri-Khan. Gilthas Pathfinder, Speaker of the Sun and Stars, had tried to maintain peace as long as he could, but it evaded his grasp. His wife gone, concord lost, the Speaker's only thought was to save his people. So he chased a shadow called Inath-Wakenti.

Adala Fahim, chief of the Weya-Lu tribe of Khurish nomads, pursued vengeance. The loved ones of her tribe had been slaughtered by a shadow which she saw in the shape of elves. So great was her anger, it took on a life of its own, a name of its own—*maita*, fate—and commanded the loyalty of numerous tribes.

Prince Shobbat plotted to replace his father, Sahim-Khan, on the throne of Khur. He made pacts with sorcerers and fanatics and traveled deep into the desert to see the shadows of the future. The Oracle of the Tree gave him the glimpse he craved, and it was far more than he had bargained for. The shadows entered his soul. In the fertile field of the prince's treacherous mind, the shadows grew and multiplied until the light of reason was nearly extinguished.

A master plotter in his own right, Sahim-Khan bent the disparate elements of his kingdom to his will to preserve his

1

unhappy guests, the elves. Sahim dreamed of great days for Khur, of triumphs on the battlefield, in the council chamber, and in the vibrant souks, where all manner of goods and services were sold. The seed of these dreams was the treasure the khan extracted from the Speaker. When shadows gathered from many sides to endanger the continuing supply of this treasure, Sahim dared the wrath of the elves' enemies to safeguard their exit from his city. In such ways are heroes made, even heroes with the blackest hearts and basest motives.

Across the world more shadows gathered. A grieving queen would not give up the search for her lost king. An ambitious child sought to exceed the fame of her bloody father. A loyal warrior searched for the Speaker's lost consort. A peerless bounty hunter stalked a hidden criminal. And entangled in the ghostly expanse of the Silent Vale, a scholar courted madness by trying to fathom a secret left behind by gods.

Of all these shadows, the longest and darkest was cast by a faceless, nameless being, delivered to death's very doorstep. Cursed with a life he loathed, he must choose between oblivion and blessed obscurity, or glory and the endless terror of discovery.

Finally, one other had gone abroad to meet his destiny. Older than the trees, he followed in the footprints of the gods, striving to decipher the shadows they left behind five thousand years earlier. He intended that no one and nothing would stand in his way. Kingdoms and nations, the lives of thousands, were nothing compared to his final goal: eternity itself.

The sun rose. Only the deepest shadows could remain.

1

No breath of breeze stirred among the trees. A dense canopy of leaves, parched by summer heat until they were brittle as glass, cast a perpetual shade on the forest floor. Although excluded, the sun made its presence felt. The air in the forest was stiflingly hot and still as a tomb. Birds did not sing, and nothing moved that could avoid moving.

A trail no wider than a horse's hips was worn through the underbrush. It wound up hills and down hollows, following no discernible path. At an uncommonly straight stretch, the path ran along the foot of a hill, between a pair of lofty ash trees. The hill comprised shelves of broken slate, terraced down like a timeworn staircase to disintegrate at last into the dust of the narrow path.

A person occupied the last of the slate steps. Covered in a monkish robe despite the heat, he sat with his forearms resting on his knees, hands hidden in the robe's capacious sleeves. His head was completely covered by a ragged cloth sack, loosely tied about his neck. Holes were cut out for his eyes. Rips and tears too numerous to count dotted the robe's faded brown surface, each neatly darned or patched.

He had been sitting there, unmoving, unspeaking, for a very long time. Where his robe touched the ground it clung, matted by leaf mold. Some who passed took him for a scarecrow. Others saw the stick thinness of his limbs, the knobby shape of his

3

joints, and decided he must be a corpse. One or two, thinking to relieve the dead fellow of his purse, approached. They saw his eyes.

Staring from the sack, the eyes were not dead, but neither did they belong to a sane or peaceful being. The whites were shining and damp, as with tears, but the corners were as dry as dust. Set in them were pupils as hard as gems. When the eyes did blink, their lids were revealed to be mottled red, without any lashes at all.

Upon beholding those eyes, the would-be scavengers fled, calling on long-ignored gods for protection. Word spread that the lonely, ancient path was haunted. It was said the spirit of a murdered priest kept watch at the slate stairs, a man doomed by an unknown transgression never to rest. Soon enough, those few who trod the forest path abandoned it, finding other ways to their destinations. The trail had never been a popular one. It came from no place special and led nowhere worth going.

The one they feared no longer knew how many days he had sat there, enveloped by a stillness only the ignorant could mistake for tranquility. Neither man nor ghost, he was an elf. Silent and immobile as he appeared to the world, his mind was a maelstrom, boiling with memories of the journey that had brought him there.

*   *   *   *   *

Had it hurt to be burned alive, to feel the flames consuming his clothing, skin, hair, flesh? There were times he couldn't remember. The burning seemed a thing apart, sometimes as immediate and vivid as the dreams that sent him screaming into wakefulness, and at other times remote, a thing that had happened to someone else.

For an eon he had known only pain, coupled with an intense desire to live. He crawled away from where he'd fallen, at first using only the tips of four fingers and a few toes. Three sunsets passed before he'd dragged himself ten yards. Every grain of sand, every bit of leaf he slid over, was a knife, shredding his outraged flesh. He kept going until he fell into a shallow, clear-flowing brook. There he was born again. Chill water dampened the raging fire in his body and cooled—but did not extinguish—the fever in his mind.

He arose from the brook in the grip of an undeniable compulsion to go east. Home lay eastward, and he had to go home. There he would find succor. There the fire would be quenched at last.

He crawled out of the stream like a newborn salamander and turned to the rising sun. Living as an animal in the forest, he ate whatever he could find, whatever couldn't crawl away fast enough. As his damaged body couldn't bear the slightest touch of clothing, he went naked, garbed only in mud and leaf litter, or rain and air.

All that existed was the journey eastward. He grew strong enough to walk, but a new horror took shape in his mind: that others might see him as he was—mutilated, disfigured, destroyed. The very thought brought a shame so great he could scarcely breathe. No one must see him, not friend, foe, or stranger. He tried to steer clear of settlements and travelers, but his senses, ruined by the fire, no longer served him as they once had, and he learned then what shame really was.

One morning he was looting carrots from a garden when a dog found him. It circled, growling deep in its throat. He had never been afraid of dogs before, but slow and crippled as he was, the approach of the mongrel filled him with dread. When it drew too near, he flung dirt in its eyes. It shook off the grit and began to bark.

Down the hill from the garden was a cottage, a solid homestead built of stone and thatch. Gray smoke spiraled from its chimney. As the dog barked, he heard the cottage door bang open and a youthful voice call, "Wolf! Wolf, where are you?"

He backed away on his hands and haunches, keeping his face toward the dog. It followed, head down, ears laid back, barking. His fingers found a rock just under the surface of the tilled earth. He pulled it free of the soil and hurled it at the dog.

The effort made his arm and shoulder muscles sing with pain, but the stone found the dog's forehead. Yelping, it ran down the hill to the farmhouse.

He staggered to his feet, a half-chewed carrot still in his teeth, and made for a nearby canebrake, pushing through the wall of green. Bladelike leaves scored his ruined skin in a dozen places, the wounds like fresh fire. Dropping into the cover of the tall cane, he choked back sobs.

Rapid footfalls announced the arrival of Wolf's master. He glimpsed a shock of sandy hair, a homespun tunic, and tanned bare feet. With two fingers he parted the cane a little wider.

"Is someone there? Wolf, what is it?"

The youth was an elf, with the sharp chin, narrow nose, and upturned ears of a pure-blooded Qualinesti. The boy was a fine-looking lad, and despite the caution ingrained over the untold weeks since the burning, he was moved to speak.

"Forgive me for stealing. I was hungry."

Actually, those were the words he intended to say. All that came out was a series of loud, dry croaks.

The young elf heard. Shouting for Wolf, he lashed out with the staff, laying open a gash in the cane and revealing the intruder crouched within. Shock and horror twisted his fine features.

"Goblin!" he cried. "Stay back! Wolf, help!"

He tried to reassure the boy, but his scorched throat wouldn't form words, only inarticulate grunts. He held out a hand, meaning to show the boy he intended no harm, but the young elf recoiled, screaming, and tripped over a furrow. Wolf rushed forward and buried its fangs in the outstretched arm.

Indescribable agony jolted through him, equal parts pain and fury. He jerked his arm, hauling the dog close, and grabbed it by the throat. He would have throttled the animal had not the boy begun raining blows on his shoulders with the staff.

New pain raced through his body. He hurled the dog aside and reeled away, deeper into the scissorlike cane stalks. The elf boy ran down the hill, shouting for help.

Deeply wounded in body and soul, he fled to the deeper woods, resolving never to show his face to the world again. In the days that followed, he was chased by his own kind, harassed by flies and mosquitoes, and treed by a wandering panther. Where insects bit him, boils erupted. He covered the wounds with mud and kept moving. The urge to go home died, destroyed by the elf boy's reaction and by the glimpse he caught of his own reflection in a pool of water. The monstrosity that stared back at him was so horrible, he actually recoiled from the sight. The reaction was instinctive, but his was a nightmare from which there was no waking.

The day finally came when his hunger could no longer be denied. Berries, beetles, and snails were not enough. His healing body demanded more. One day deep in the woods, far from any habitation, he smelled the fecund aroma of bread baking. Like a marooned drunkard sniffing wine for the first time in a month, he sought the tantalizing odor, braving discovery.

The aroma drew him to a clearing. He hid behind a thick elm tree and studied what lay beyond. The center of the clearing held a crude hut constructed from rough-hewn trees—a human habitation. It was their way to build shelters from freshly killed trees. Besides, the fire hadn't stolen his senses completely; he smelled the humans before he saw them.

There were three in view, male and bearded. Were their beards not of different colors he doubted he'd be able to tell them apart. Judging by the row of axes leaning against the hut, the three were foresters. A smoky fire burned in a ring of scavenged stones. The red-bearded man tended a flat iron pan by the fire. The smell of bread rose from the pan. However, the sight of the humans caused something other than hunger to twist in his belly: hatred. These three were invaders in his forest.

"Who's there?"

Without realizing it, he had allowed himself to be glimpsed by the red-bearded man. He moved as quickly as fire-ravaged muscles and taunt, scarred skin allowed, crouching in a dense thicket. His grotesque shape was barely concealed as the other two humans approached.

"What's wrong?" called the one on the left, yellow bearded and younger than the others.

"I saw something," Red Beard replied, standing up from the fire.

"Man or beast?" asked Black Beard.

"Maybe neither."

Black Beard snorted. "What, again? You see elves behind every tree, Gaff. I told you, the only ones in forty miles of here are in Olin's slave pens."

"You don't know that for sure. I heard a bunch of Wilder folk raided Aymar's camp just two nights past."

Yellow Beard agreed. "He's right. We don't know what might be out here." He retreated to the campfire. "I'll be glad to get the job done and get out of here."

"Not me," said Black Beard. "I haven't seen this much virgin timber in ages. There's a fortune all around us—"

"Three fortunes," put in Yellow Beard pointedly. "But we have to be alive to enjoy them!"

The two humans persuaded their black-bearded comrade to abandon the camp. Sunset was not far off, and they'd be safer at the logging camp, where there were soldiers.

The three shouldered their axes and departed. He had no trouble following their heavy-footed progress through the forest. He emerged from hiding and crept forward in a stoop, his fingers touching the leafy ground lightly. Beneath the grime, each hand was a mass of fibrous scars, the nails black and hard as talons; he still could not make a tight fist.

The men had dumped the bread in the ashes, taking the pan with them. The bread was underdone, black with soot, but he'd never tasted anything so wonderful in his life. He finished every ash-covered bite.

In the hut he found a half-eaten fowl and two wizened apples. After stripping the bird's bones of meat and eating the apples whole, he searched for clothing. A pile of rags in one corner proved to be a robe. It was heavy, made of coarse brown cloth, and ragged at its hem, but he pulled it on quickly. Sized for a human, it easily covered his slighter frame from neck to heels. He hiked the trailing hem up so he could walk without tripping and cinched the sash tight. The garment's deep cowl was a gift from the gods, but he supplemented its concealment with an old flour sack. With two ragged holes for him to see through, the sack made a fine mask.

Tired as he was, he left the clearing quickly. The loggers might return, might bring soldiers.

He followed a narrow stream until the water suddenly vanished. A few yards farther on, he came to the edge of a ravine. Descending, he found a cave perhaps twelve feet deep and eight high. The stream dripped down from the ceiling, pooled on the floor, and flowed out the opening to continue on its way.

Heart hammering, he curled himself into the deepest corner of the cave. The makeshift mask filled his head with the dry odor of old flour. That, and the unaccustomed heaviness of the food he'd so rapidly consumed, caused his stomach to rebel. He crawled to one side of the little cave and was thoroughly sick.

When his stomach was empty and the heaving had stopped, he dragged himself to the other side of the cave and lay on his back, staring into the darkness.

* * * * *

Birds alighted on him, unaware they perched on a living being. Troops of forest ants, black as polished jet, marched over the twin hills of his feet. Still he did not move, only remembered.

* * * * *

Hunger had again driven him to desperate measures, and he was digging through a refuse pile on the fringes of a human village when two women drew near. Their approach nearly sent him fleeing back into the predawn forest, but they ignored the ragged, cowled figure squatting beside the trash. They continued on their way and never interrupted their conversation.

"They bought *another* one?" said one, disbelieving.

The other woman nodded vigorously. "Emalen and her husband bought another slave, an elf who was actually in Qualinost when it was destroyed! He can read and write, so they set him to keeping the tavern books. He ran away once so Brand had to hamstring him. . . ."

The two women passed out of earshot. For a long moment, he couldn't move, frozen by the casual, callous horror embodied in those few sentences.

He forced himself to approach a dwarf peddler and ask of Qualinost. The dwarf's laconic account of the city's destruction took his breath away. Had he heard it from anyone else, he would not have believed it, but dwarves did not exaggerate. Qualinost was no more.

He needed to see with his own eyes the fate of his city. And so he did. From a hilltop a mile away he looked down on the place that once had been his home and saw its mutilation as the crushing mirror image of his own. Gone were the towers, the elegant homes, the vibrant greenery. Lost were the lives of countless elves, extinguished in the very instant of liberation. Qualinost had been freed, only to face its doom. What remained was submerged beneath a foul lake, with the rotting corpse of a dragon at its heart, like a poisoned blade in a sunken grave.

* * * * *

The light beneath the trees changed subtly as another day drew to a close, the sun descending in the west. A fat cicada droned down the empty path, weaving from side to side on unsteady wings. Exhausted, it landed near his left foot. The insect was enormous, twice the size of the elf's thumb, with wet, gauzy wings folded awkwardly across its back. It struggled through the dry moss, heading inexorably for his foot. When the cicada was an inch away, the elf moved. He lifted his foot and held it steady as a stone, waiting for the turgid insect to crawl beneath.

ALLIANCES

"Don't!"

To his left stood an old man leaning on a tall blackthorn staff. He wore the remnants of priestly garb—robe, sash, and stole all grimy with age and inattention. His short white hair stood out from his head in all directions. He pointed a stubby finger at the foot still poised to crush the cicada and repeated, "Don't!"

Without turning his masked head, the elf said, "Why not?" in a voice as dry as the litter covering him. "It's dying anyway."

"Its life is not yours to take."

The old human came closer, walking slowly with the aid of his staff. "That cicada has spent seventeen years asleep below the ground. It's been awake only a few days, but in that time it found a female, fought off rivals, and mated. Having fulfilled its purpose, it can only die."

"Then why not kill it? Further existence now is pointless." The cicada was just entering the footprint etched into the moss. The foot still hovered above it.

"Stay! Every act has a consequence. Can you know what will happen if you kill without cause?"

He hesitated then lowered his foot behind the struggling insect.

"Another useless life spared."

Grunting loudly with effort, the old fellow seated himself on the slate ledge. "No life is useless. Each is a gift from the gods," he said, smiling.

"You talk like a priest."

The old man inclined his head, acknowledging the truth. He produced a hide waterskin from his robe and offered it. Receiving no response, he refreshed himself.

"You've been here a while. Are you waiting for something?"

The elf was indeed waiting for something, for the same thing that soon would find the exhausted cicada. His lack of response did not discourage the priest. The old man took another swig and asked another question.

"Where does this road go?"

"Nowhere."

A droplet of red wine clung to the corner of the priest's mouth. "I thought it led to Qualinost."

For the first time the elf's granite façade was breached. He flinched as if struck. "There is no Qualinost! Nothing remains but a fetid lake of death!"

"That must be a sight."

The elf laughed, a painful, throat-tearing sound. Yes, it was a sight, a sight to turn the heart to stone and shrivel the stomach with despair.

He pushed away those thoughts and tried to retreat again into unfeeling immobility, but his attention was caught by the cicada at his feet. It had been found by the ants. They circled the ailing behemoth, tapping it with their antennae. It ignored them, struggling onward. Satisfied by the cicada's lack of hostility, the ants seized the larger insect by its legs, each tugging it in a different direction. The result was stalemate; the cicada twitched in place, neither advancing nor retreating. The situation did not persist. Organizing themselves, the ants swarmed over the still-living cicada and dismembered it. They severed the wings one at a time, passing them to comrades, who discarded them in the litter beside the path, then fell to butchering their prey, snipping off its legs and peeling open its soft belly.

"So much for mercy," he sneered.

"You take the wrong lesson. Crushed underfoot, the cicada would be wasted. This way, it will feed the ants for many days."

The priest's voice had changed. Gone was the genial, fatherly objectivity. So different was his tone the elf finally turned and took a good look at him. A chaplet of leaves rested on his head. Brown things clung to the front of his moss-green robe. They looked like leather pouches—until they moved.

"Consider the ants, not the solitary cicada," the priest went on in the same instructive tone. "They are tiny but many. Birds and spiders reap them by the score, but their colony survives. Working together for a common goal, they overcome far larger enemies. Only when they lose cohesion, with each pulling for its own sake, do they fail."

ALLIANCES

The elf shifted position, sitting more upright and folding his arms across his chest. Between gloved hands and robed arms, his wrists showed wasted, scarlet skin.

"Who are you, human?" he demanded. "Do you know me?"

"We've never met."

"But you lecture me as though you have some right!"

The old man smiled disarmingly, showing stained, crooked teeth. "Perhaps I do." His friendly expression hardened into something sterner. "But it hardly requires magic to recognize your state. You stink of self-pity and despair. You came here to brood and die, didn't you?"

Goaded at last into action, the elf sprang to his feet. The debris of many days fell in a dusty rain at his feet. By reflex, his hand went to his hip but found only air. His sword was long gone, a melted strip of scrap metal.

"It's no business of yours! Leave me be!" he rasped.

One of the brown things clinging to the front of the priest's robe stirred, spreading small leathery wings—a bat. His chest was covered with live bats. The human stroked the tiny animal with the back of one finger. His manner undergoing yet another lightning shift, he inquired kindly, "How long since you ate or drank?"

The elf couldn't say. The priest reached into his robe and withdrew a packet wrapped in waxed parchment. He parted the flaps. The packet contained a heap of pearl-colored disks, each thinner than the parchment enclosing them.

The elf breathed in sharply, astonished. The small disks were honeydew wafers, impossibly delicate sweets made from honey produced by the silver bees of Silvanesti, mixed with crystal dew and flower pollen. The confections traditionally were eaten at weddings, births, and other festive occasions. None outside Silvanost knew the secret of their creation. He had eaten them only once before in his life. Not only did the decrepit human have honeydew wafers, but they looked and smelled freshly made.

"Take them," the priest urged.

Like a striking viper, the elf's gloved hand shot out, tearing the parcel from the old man's grasp. With trembling fingers, he laid a single wafer on his tongue. The disk melted at once, releasing a rush of flavor. The crystal dew in the wafers was collected one tiny droplet at a time from the leaves of plants and flowers all over Silvanost. The life's breath of the plant was captured in every drop, and every plant imparted a distinctive flavor. Even more unique was the earthy savor of pollen. Rose was always unmistakable, as were violet and nasturtium. This particular pollen had come from sunflowers. The elf's mouth was filled with the golden soul of summer, as if sunshine had been turned into fine powder.

"Consider the ants," the priest said. "Though small, they are mighty in unison."

Clutching the packet of wafers close to his heart, the elf watched his benefactor rise and depart. The priest's back was covered with the same small brown bundles as his chest, bats that squirmed against each other as the old fellow's heavy footfalls jostled them. The elf realized the chaplet of green leaves wasn't resting on the priest's head. Its woven tendrils emerged from the skin of his brow.

The priest paused and looked back. Lifting a hand, he said, "Farewell, Porthios. You have yet a part to play."

In that instant, the elf knew his mysterious benefactor. He dashed forward as the priest shuffled around a curve in the path and was lost from sight. Porthios wasn't swift—his legs were stiff from disuse and his burns—but the priest was out of view for only a few seconds. Yet when Porthios reached the bend in the road, the old human was gone. The dust clearly showed the prints of his bare feet ending a yard ahead.

Porthios stared dumbly down at the abrupt end of the footprints. The single wafer he'd eaten caused his stomach to knot with raging hunger. He put another wafer in his mouth, waited until it dissolved, then retraced his steps to the waterskin the priest had left behind. The contents tasted like Qualinesti nectar, which surprised him. Nectar was clear as water, yet he had seen the old human drink red wine from that same vessel.

Why should he be surprised? A god could do anything.

Porthios took another drink, capped the waterskin, and slung it over his back. Cinching his rag sash tight, he started down the path, in the same direction the priest had taken. The hopeless torpor that had enveloped him was gone, even as the oppressive heat had subsided with the sunset. He had been given a message, one he could not ignore. Whatever lay ahead, he had a powerful ally. Many more would be needed before the wrongs of recent days were righted, but he would find them.

Putting his back to no place special, he made straight for nowhere worth going.

2

The world changed in a flash.

One moment Kerianseray was riding to her doom against a swarm of Khurish nomads; in the next instant she was swallowed by a sphere of light so bright even clenched eyelids could not keep it out. After the flash, she saw nothing, heard nothing, and, aside from a slight sensation of coolness, felt nothing.

I am dead, she decided, struck from behind by a cowardly nomad. It was just as the old saying had it: you never see the blow that kills you. Kerian was surprised but not alarmed by death. Leaving her comrades behind and going off to face the nomads alone had been her choice. Life did not seem so dear with Gilthas turned against her. By removing her from command of his armies, he had not only demeaned her abilities, he had impugned her honor. Worse, his continued distrust wounded her pride. She couldn't bear to remain with a partner who trusted her so little.

The notion death had claimed her vanished as feeling returned. She felt herself tumbling, air rushing by her face. She could again feel her arms and legs. Given that she'd been mounted on horseback, the fall was unnaturally protracted. Long after she should have crashed into the parched sands of Khur, she kept falling. Her useless eyes streamed wind-driven tears, so she closed them. On she fell, tumbling head over heels through damp, chilly air. Bards often sang of what lay beyond death, but never had she heard of an afterlife like this.

Gradually she became aware of light against her eyelids. She opened them, blinked several times, and realized she could see. No sooner had sight returned than she wished fervently to be blind again.

She was high in the sky, plummeting through broken white clouds toward the distant ground. The knowledge was so astonishing that at first she couldn't breathe. When she could, she took a deep breath of cloud and screamed.

It wasn't fear erupting from her throat. Fear was an old adversary Kerian had bested long ago. Hers was a shriek of pure rage. Her instantaneous shift from the battlefield outside Khuri-Khan to this lofty point could have been accomplished only one way: by magic. Someone had interfered with her last stand.

Her scream died away, smothered by iron will and the tearing wind. By spreading her arms and legs out from her body, she managed to halt her dizzying tumble, and ended up facing the ground. Her armor was gone, how or why, she couldn't say, and her sweat-stained hacketon rippled and billowed as she plummeted.

The clouds thinned and she saw the ground clearly for the first time. She was not falling toward the desert kingdom of Khur, that much was certain. Beneath her shimmered a body of greenish water, a lake perhaps or a broad river. Leafless treetops jutted from its surface, as did broken pinnacles of stone. Moss clung to them, and vines trailed from treetop to spire to water like rotting shrouds. Everything was deeply shadowed, though the sun was still above the western horizon. She could see little but turbid water and desolate ruins. The rest was obscured by mist.

The stench of decay filled her nose. This was no crystal spring beneath her. She was falling near the western shore of the lake or river. A wide mudflat ringed the water's edge, connecting the fetid water to the forested shore. It was confusing, seeing it all from such a height, but the terrain didn't seem familiar. Stumps of stone towers, mottled by lichen and dull green moss, poked through the water here and there. Their tops were shattered as though lightning-struck. Remnants of a broken causeway connected some of the towers.

As the ground drew nearer, Kerian was suddenly aware of the speed of her descent. Fetid water, broken towers, and moss-encrusted trees all were rushing toward her at an alarming rate. She drew her knees to her chest and hoped the water was deep enough to contain her plunge.

Gathering herself mentally for what was to come, she saw Gilthas's face. He'd betrayed her, disowned her, and yet it was him she saw on the cusp of death. Pushing thoughts of her fickle, still-loved husband away, Kerian closed her eyes and tucked her head into her arms.

Suddenly her fall was arrested. Her hands and feet flew out, and her teeth clashed together so hard that she saw stars. She found herself borne up by unseen forces, as though something had seized her by the scruff of her neck and brought her up short, thirty feet above the water. She descended slowly for the space of a few alarmed heartbeats, then the restraining force vanished as quickly as it had come. Feet first, the Lioness hit the scummy green water.

The air was driven from her chest, not by the impact, which had been scarcely harder than a fall from a galloping horse, but by bone-numbing cold. Although high summer mantled the land, the water was as frigid as the gray seas off Icewall.

She sank, stunned, into the murky depths, weighed down by her hacketon as surely as she would have been by her armor. When she finally came to herself, daylight was only a pale green oval far above. With no knife, she attacked the lacings of her heavy clothes with bare fingers. She couldn't budge the swollen leather ties. Her lungs burned and the compulsion to inhale was becoming unbearable. Her head thundered. Frantic, she abandoned the lacings and tore at the quilted cloth itself. Weakened by sun and sweat, the material gave and she was able to wriggle free of its killing embrace. She toed off her boots and kicked hard for the surface.

She erupted at last into the air and inhaled with a great gasping shout. When the roaring in her ears and the red veil over her vision had faded, she made for the nearest shore. It was a thin rime of sand beyond which spread a flat sheet of mud. It felt as though hours had passed before she felt mud under her feet. The ooze was charcoal gray and stinking, but Kerian dragged herself out of the water and fell upon it as if it were the finest silk rug in the khan's palace. After a few grateful breaths, she rolled over and faced the sky.

By the time the quaking in her limbs eased, the light had metamorphosed from late evening to dusk. On her feet she staggered drunkenly. Her entire body felt as though she'd taken a beating from an enthusiastic ogre wielding a heavy stick.

A whooshing sound from behind her galvanized Kerian's instincts. Despite stiff joints and bruised muscles, she dropped instantly to her belly. Something large had flown overhead. She'd not seen it, but the sound of dragon wings was unmistakable. For two full minutes she lay still as a corpse. Her Kagonesti senses, long battered by the arid, unrelenting furnace of Khur, still served her, and she used them to search her surroundings for signs of danger. There was nothing. If a dragon had flown by, it was gone now. The water behind her was as smooth as a mirror.

Narrow trees grew like a rail fence beyond the mudflats. Whatever might lay beyond, the trees called to the forest-bred Kerian. She sprinted for cover. Her bare toes left clear marks in the mud, but there was nothing she could do about that. Clad only in cotton smallclothes, she was unarmed, unprepared, and alone.

Among the trees she immediately felt better. They were water-loving willows and cypress saplings, none more than four years old, but the shelter they offered was familiar and long missed. She looked back at the water. Must be a lake, she decided. A river would have currents, but the surface of the water was as smooth and unmoving as a slab of polished stone. The shore curved away into the gloom north and south. It was a large lake, several miles across at least. The far shore wasn't visible even to her keen eyesight.

Alert for the slightest hint of trouble, she moved deeper into the forest. The living trees were all young saplings. When the occasional larger tree appeared, it was never more than a limbless shaft, its top blasted away high up from the ground, its bark sloughed off like skin, exposing the gray trunk to the clammy twilight. Something cataclysmic had happened here, and not so long ago.

A gleam of white, vibrant in the gathering darkness, drew her attention. She headed toward it.

It was one of the ruined stone towers she'd spied during her heart-hammering drop from the sky. The remnant of a mighty spire, the tower was a full thirty feet wide at its base, and its deeply fluted sides rose another thirty feet from the vine-choked ground before ending abruptly. The column was solid stone, marble of the whitest species, yet its upper portion had been snapped cleanly away. No seams were visible. The entire thirty-foot width of marble was formed from a single block of stone.

The tower was elven. No one else could shape stone with such precision and delicacy. Was this Silvanost, a city destroyed by the minotaurs? Her knowledge of the elves' first home was sketchy, but she couldn't recall it containing a lake such as the one before her.

Moving around the base of the shattered marble spire, she found an inscription. The letters were monumental, carved deep, and had once been inlaid with solid gold. Someone had hacked the metal away, but traces remained here and there, glinting pathetically in the twilight.

Kananath Kithri Nesti N'Loth Sithelan Sannu, it read. *Kith-Kanan, son of Sithel, built this.*

She wasn't in Silvanost, but in Qualinost!

Her head snapped around, and she stared at the now-black lake glimmering between the weedy trees. Somehow she had been plucked from the battlefield in Khur and thrown into the nightmarish ruins of Qualinost. The green dragon Beryl had fallen to her death there, destroying the city founded by Kith-Kanan. The beast's impact created a huge crater into which rushed the White Rage River. Nalis Aren it was called: the Lake of Death. Kerian's life had not been spared. Her death had merely been deferred, transferred to a place far worse than the hot sands of Khur.

Like the vile dragon before her, Kerian had been dropped onto Qualinost! Well, she would not share Beryl's end. She would not die in this dreadful place. She would survive.

When the stars appeared, she used them to navigate away from the noisome lake. The woods were alive with buzzing mosquitoes that swarmed around her exposed limbs. Squat alligators, armored like draconians, lay watchful in shallow pools. She skirted more than a dozen of the lethal reptiles. Their blank eyes followed her, but the animals did not move.

Her thought was to head west, through the great woodland of Qualinesti, then south to the Kharolis Mountains. Qualinesti might be her old home, but it was infested with bandits, brigands, and Knights of Neraka. The mountains contained fewer enemies, and she'd be able to rest and restore herself. As for what she would do then—that would require some thought.

She knew she was in a land beset by anarchy, where evil lived in every town. To the east, Silvanesti was in no better shape, trampled beneath minotaur invaders. Hundreds of miles away, far to the northeast, her comrades in arms were fighting for the survival of their race against the nomad hordes of Khur. Gilthas, her noble, steadfast, *stupid* husband, had a wild scheme to lead their people to Inath-Wakenti, a fabled valley said to be located in the mountains north-northeast of Khuri-Khan. He had sent Kerian and five hundred warriors to learn whether the mysterious valley really existed. It did. But although the valley's climate was mild and damp, just as legend held, Kerian's explorations revealed many dangers hidden within it.

Accessible only by a single pass at its southern end, Inath-Wakenti would be a deathtrap for the last free elves in the world. They could be blockaded easily by their enemies (of which there were many). The valley also was cursed in a strange and mysterious way. In all the time Kerian and her soldiers had spent there, they never found a single living creature. Plants aplenty, yes, but not so much as a fly or bird dwelled within. Something about the valley was hostile to animal life. By night specters wandered the valley's faceless stone ruins, and weird lights, possibly intelligent and certainly malicious, pursued her warriors, causing several to vanish without a trace.

Kerian tried to make Gilthas understand, to see reason. Their people didn't need that uncanny valley. They needed to stand and fight! She argued passionately for a new war against the invaders who had taken what rightfully belonged to the elves. Yet Gilthas would not be dissuaded from his dreamer's notion, even by her report of the dangers of Inath-Wakenti. He insisted their people must make the treacherous desert crossing and conquer the valley.

Kerian halted, realizing she was drenched in sweat. As her mind had raced, so too her pace had quickened through the willow thickets. That was not smart. There were too many enemies about for her to behave so irrationally.

Fireflies sparkled around her. Since her experience in Inath-Wakenti, she had become wary of phantom lights in the night. These proved to be nothing more than luminous insects, sad reminders of the lost serenity of summer nights in Qualinesti.

She was exhausted: first a battle in Khur, then a fall from great height, a near-drowning, and a trek through the wilds around the Lake of Death. It was past time to halt for the night. Food was a problem that could wait, and she'd trained herself to need less water than most, but rest was absolutely necessary. An exhausted soldier was soon a dead soldier.

She wedged herself high up in an elm, above the clouds of mosquitoes. As she had done so many times before, Kerianseray slept in the arms of a tree—a leafless, blasted tree, it was true, yet it would keep her safe, at least from the lesser predators of the forest.

The stars above her were the same ones that sparkled over Khur. She stared at them and allowed herself to wonder what had happened after she'd vanished. Had the nomads beaten her people, or had the children of Kith-Kanan taken the day? Did her comrades survive? Did Gilthas still live?

Only to that last question did Kerian have an answer. As surely as she still drew breath, she knew her husband was alive. Some ties were not easily broken, despite the damage they sustained.

She rested her cheek against the elm's rough bark. A cool wind eased over the woods, drying the sweat on her face. She trembled a little from the night's caress, then succumbed to a deep and dreamless rest.

* * * * *

For two days, Kerian dodged many dangers. Qualinesti was dotted with outposts of the Knights of Neraka, and freebooters led by the human Captain Samuval ravaged the roads and cities. Bands of goblins and other vermin infested the countryside, robbing and killing unopposed. Small bands of draconians might pounce on the unwary. Rogue sorcerers were on the loose. She sensed dragons too, patrolling shifting enclaves of their own.

Despite the wounds of recent years, Kerian's soul could not but rejoice in her return to Qualinesti. She was an elf, and her heart spoke to trees and growing things. The sun and sand of Khur had almost leached the wildwood from her veins.

This was another point of contention between her and Gilthas. She tried to make him see that if they abandoned the forest to live in distant lands, very soon they would cease to be elves. With her bare feet once more traversing the mossy glades and leaf-littered hillsides, Kerian could feel a new strength filling her heart. This was the land of her ancestors, the land to which she and her kind had been born. She would never give up the fight to regain it. Here was where the elf race belonged!

She fashioned a crude knife from a flint shard and made two spears from windfall limbs. Thus armed, she felt better able to face what might come, with one glaring exception. What she could not seem to find was food, despite all her craft. High summer was on the land. There ought to be berries and roots, small game aplenty, but there was none. She blamed the proximity of Nalis Aren. Its miasma of death infected the land for miles in all directions. Trees and bushes grew in abundance, but all were subtly *wrong*. Limbs were twisted, growth stunted, green leaves tinged with brown and yellow. Of birds, rabbits, and squirrels there was no sign, though insects thrived.

A stream crossed her path. The odor of the water told her it was tainted. Drinking it would mean sickness or death. However, it did provide some useful mud. Liberally applied, that offered some protection to her limbs from the swarms of mosquitoes. It would also aid in concealing her identity. There were likely still some in Qualinesti who might recognize her, enemies who would rejoice in the capture of the Lioness.

To further conceal her identity, she pulled her thick hair into a horsetail and began to saw at it with her flint knife. In moments her all-too-recognizable golden mane was gone. Clay concealed the color of her hair and left it sticking up in spikes all over her head. She doubted even Gilthas would recognize her.

By her second day in the forest, however, even the Lioness's stamina was sorely tested. She couldn't remember the last time she'd eaten or drunk. Leaping another tainted stream, she nearly fell on her face on the other side. The emptiness of her belly made her head swim. Yet there was nothing for it but to keep moving. If she were to survive, she needed to get clear of the shadow of Nalis Aren.

Game animals obviously had fled to more healthful surroundings, and the same seemed to be true of her own kind.

ALLIANCES

Many Kagonesti had not joined the march into exile, choosing instead to remain in their beloved forest, occupied though it was. She expected to detect some traces of them, but in two days of constant searching, she had found none.

At midday of the second day, a scent came to her on the wind: goblin. The odor was unmistakable. She cast about briefly, determined the direction, and moved carefully toward the source.

A band of goblins was camped around the ruined trunk of a gigantic oak. Kerian despised the malodorous creatures. They were notorious cowards, yet hired themselves as mercenaries to the Nerakans. The Knights treated them as sword-fodder, but the goblins didn't seem to mind as long as they could loot when the fighting was done.

Unsurprisingly, these goblins were thieves. The clearing was filled with obviously ill-gotten goods. Luxurious carpets and tapestries lay alongside heaps of battered metalware; brass, copper, and silver were sorted into separate piles. Furniture lovingly shaped by Qualinesti skill sat in the weeds, the once-fine upholstery filthy. Over everything hung a pall of bluish wood smoke, a smell of cooked meat, and the sour odor of spilled wine.

Five goblins were camped at the oak. Two slept, snoring like bullfrogs. Two were engaged in a noisy argument over a muddy tangle of clothing. The last poked the smoky campfire. Next to the campfire sat a delicately wrought metal table, its top holding wine jugs, bread, fruit, and various other foodstuffs. Kerian's stomach cramped at the sight of such bounty.

She had to have food. More than that, she could not bear to slink away and leave these villains to continue their plundering. The flint knife she'd made would be useless against the goblins' armor. Her spears might be more successful against their eyes and faces. One way or another, she would attack. Wasn't that exactly what she'd told Gilthas they should be doing, attacking those who'd dared invade their lands? Any blow against the enemy, no matter how small, was worthwhile.

An idea took shape. Perhaps she could lure one away, relieve it of its weapon, and use that against the rest. Even if she couldn't kill them all, she could at least make off with some of their provisions.

Silently she climbed a tree and crouched on a branch, balanced on her toes, ready to pounce. She swallowed several times—her throat was parched—then gave a high, whirring call, the song of the cloth-of-gold pheasant. No goblin could resist the chance to obtain the largest (and rarest) game bird in Qualinesti.

The goblin by the campfire was closest to her. He turned toward the sound. Kerian called again. The goblin dropped its stick and came toward her, moving with a ludicrous attempt at stealth. She called once more. The arguing goblins never noticed their comrade's departure. They were too busy with a tug-of-war over a two-handled silver urn.

Kerian waited until her prey was directly beneath her. Then, like a bolt from the sky, she dropped behind him. She gripped his chin with one hand, and with the other drew the flint blade across his throat. Blood poured from a severed vein, and he fell without a sound. She relieved the dead goblin of his sword. It was crudely made, but she felt better with it in her hands.

Gruff goblin voices interrupted her triumph. The two had ceased their argument over the urn and were looking toward the campfire and calling for their missing comrade. Before they could rouse the two sleeping goblins, she cupped her hand to her mouth and made the pheasant's call again. The goblins exchanged a look and came clomping over on the double.

Silent as a shadow, Kerian moved away from the dead goblin, her calls leading the other two deeper into the woods. She worked her way around so the two became separated by a dense briar thicket. Thus she was able to dispatch them one at a time, taking each by surprise.

Back at the clearing, the last two goblins continued to snore on, undisturbed. Kerian thanked her ancestors for this blessing. Her limbs were shaking from exertion. As long as they did not wake, she would spare them. She made straight for the campfire and the table of provisions. She slung two waterskins over her back and picked up two loaves of bread.

Just as she was lifting a small wedge of cheese, one of the sleeping goblins sat up, roused from sleep by she knew not what. His eyes went wide as he took in the clay-caked elf standing by the table. With an outraged shout and a hearty slap, he woke his companion. Then he was on his feet, drawing iron.

She dropped her purloined goods and hefted the sword in both hands. The blade wobbled and she firmed her grip. With two goblins coming for her, she widened her stance, weight evenly distributed, ready to move in either direction. The lead goblin was still several yards away when she saw its gaze flicker past her. At the same time, a blow landed on the back of her head, knocking her to the ground. Vision swimming, she managed to roll to one side. Her sword was jerked away.

The foe towering over her was no goblin, but an ogre, eight feet tall, muscular, with dull yellow skin and shaggy black hair. The piercing shrieks of her attackers had completely masked any sound of his approach.

The huge creature bent and seized her by the throat. Lifting her so her feet dangled above the ground, he cast a ferocious glare at the two goblins.

"Not waste elves!" he growled. "Capture!"

His thick fingers tightened. Darkness rose up and dragged Kerian into its depths.

3

From the parapet of the log fort called Alderhelm, Breetan Everride, Knight of the Lily, watched the dirt road from the fort's gate to the hazy woods, about two hundred yards away. Alderhelm was located in a remote district of the former kingdom of Qualinesti. Situated halfway between Gilthanost on the coast and Ahlanost at the foot of the Anviltop range, it was among the smallest of the forts built by the Order since the fall of the overlord Beryl.

Heat made the road shimmer. The sun behind her was low, and Breetan lifted the visor of her helmet, but no matter how long she stared, the result was the same. The patrol was overdue.

She called down to the guard on duty, "Where is Lord Freemantle?" The guard claimed he didn't know. "Well, find him, lout! Go!"

The guard jogged away to the earthen casement at the center of the fort. The laces of his boots flapped in the dust. The quality of recruits here was pathetic. Most of them were Samuval's castoffs, driven out for being too lazy or too stupid to serve the freebooter chief. Alderhelm seemed to attract the sorriest ones, and its commandant, Midgrave Freemantle, hired them all. It was his way of making up the losses his garrison was suffering.

The guard returned and called up, "The commandant is in the keep, Lady."

Doing what? she wanted to shout but did not bother. It was far simpler to go there herself.

She dispatched the guard with a message for Sergeant Jeralund, one of the few professional soldiers in the garrison, then descended the rough-hewn log steps to the bailey.

Around the inside of the stockade were assorted shanties of logs, planks, and canvas. They belonged to the civilians allowed to dwell under Lord Freemantle's protection. They were a picturesque lot, the usual scum and scrapings too inept or weak to survive in the bigger towns. Breetan didn't mind gamblers, quacksalvers, and purveyors of strong drink. She did despise third-rate ones.

On her second day here, she had to make an example of one of them, a nasty little procurer called Three-Lips for the large scar just below his bottom lip. Touring the fort in civilian clothes, Breetan met Three-Lips at the entrance of his establishment. He made overtures she found offensive, and she knocked out two of his front teeth with the bronze knuckles she carried. Furious, and still unaware she was a knight, he sent two hired blades after her. She beheaded one and disemboweled the other. Three-Lips she had hung from the flagpole atop the commandant's keep.

She climbed the mound at the center of the fort and entered the keep. Five paces inside she found Lord Freemantle struggling into his armor. He was a stout man, and in summer wore steel only when the situation demanded it.

"I know, I know," he said irritably. "The patrol is overdue."

"Another six men lost."

"Maybe not." Freemantle gave up on his pauldrons and shoved them back at his beleaguered manservant. "They might only be delayed."

Breetan laughed, a sharp, mocking sound. "The pattern is plain," she said, planting hands on hips. Unlike the commandant, she was at ease in her three-quarter plate, enameled in sable, as befitted a Dark Knight. "We'll find them with their throats cut, just like the others."

For the past three months, someone or something had been whittling down his troops. One here, three there, soldiers went missing only to be found with their throats cut. Freemantle's reports to the Knights' citadel in Gilthanost had resulted in the arrival of Breetan Everride. Her task was to put a stop to the slaughter.

For six armed men to disappear together was unusual, however. No group of that size had gone missing before. The patrol had been on its way to reinforce the sentinel post at the Shattered Rock crossroads. Twice in the previous three months, the sentries' relief had arrived to find the two men slain or, more disturbing, simply gone.

"I'll ride out with a company and see what we find," she told Freemantle.

"Don't go far. There's little daylight left."

She almost laughed at him again. The commandant was afraid to go out after dark? What were things coming to out here?

Sergeant Jeralund and twenty men were waiting for her at the gate. Breetan's horse had been brought from the stable. She mounted and rested the butt of a cocked and loaded crossbow on her thigh.

"Sergeant, we have ground to cover. At the double, if you please."

Jeralund drew his sword and thrust it in the air. "All right, you donkeys! Time to be war-horses! At the double!" he roared.

This late in the day, only a few travelers remained on the road. They dived for the ditches when Breetan's column approached. In ragged order the mercenaries lifted their booted feet and jogged behind their elegantly mounted leader.

Breetan was a member of a select organization within the larger Knights of Neraka. According to reports compiled by its headquarters, the Black Hall, the only elves remaining in the province were slaves. Breetan believed the reports were wrong. Who but rebellious, forest-bred elves could be at the bottom of all the trouble?

All seemed normal in the forest. Alert for ambush, Breetan saw only squirrels scampering from branch to branch, heard only birds singing in the treetops. Her dark red mantle hung limply from her shoulders. No breath of breeze stirred the air. Beneath her helmet, her sun-browned face was flushed from the heat.

Dusk had fallen by the time the column reached Shattered Rock. The soldiers tensed as they neared the crossroads.

Shattered Rock had earned its name from a great boulder on the southwest side of the intersection. The sharp-edged block of gray granite, roughly cube shaped, resembled none of the native rock in the vicinity. Local lore held that it had been dropped by a giant in centuries past.

Opposite the boulder was the sentinel post, a thick-walled, flat-roofed stone hut. The windows were covered by stout planks, with loopholes for archers. Out front, an iron tripod perched atop the ashes of a cold campfire. At Breetan's command, the company broke ranks and surrounded the hut.

No one answered Jeralund's calls. The brass-strapped door was bolted. Both windows were shuttered and like-wise fastened from the inside. It required two men with war axes many minutes to hack through the heavy door. While they labored, Breetan ordered a large fire laid where the roads met. By the time the battered panels yielded, darkness was almost complete and the bonfire's light was welcome indeed.

Jeralund brought a brand from the fire to light the way, and Breetan entered, crossbow at the ready.

The missing men were not inside. The single room was a shambles. Everything in it, from the two cots to the bowls that held the sentries' provisions, had been smashed. The soldiers' bedding had been trampled into the muck on the floor.

The ladder to the roof trapdoor had been torn down. The trapdoor itself, like every other opening, was secured from the inside. Jeralund had himself boosted up. He threw the thick bolt, pushed the panel upward, and levered himself onto the roof. It was bare but for a scattering of leaves. The hut's walls continued up past the roof, creating a two-foot parapet. Jeralund turned to survey the crossroads and the woods beyond. He exclaimed hoarsely.

"What?" demanded Breetan from below. "What do you see?"

Jeralund's face appeared in the trapdoor opening. "Bodies. In the trees!"

From his vantage point, with the light of the bonfire to aid him, Jeralund had seen what no one on the ground had been able to: corpses hanging from high tree branches. The dead were lowered to the ground and identified as the members of the overdue patrol, plus the two guards assigned to the sentinel post.

Breetan glared at the bodies, now decently covered with their own cloaks. More than the Black Hall must know of this outrage. She would have to send word to the Knights' headquarters in Jelek. Unfortunately, her return to Alderhelm would have to be delayed until morning. A night march through hostile territory was too dangerous. They would have to pass the night here.

The decision was not popular with the men. Numbers and a stone stronghold hadn't saved their comrades. They clamored to return to the fort at once, but Breetan wouldn't consider it. She ordered half the company, led by the sergeant, to stand guard while the others rested. The fire would be kept burning throughout the night and, an hour after midnight, the sleepers would relieve those on guard.

Breetan placed her bedroll below the east face of the great boulder, so the first rays of the morning sun would wake her. She set her helmet and crossbow within easy reach and settled in. It wasn't the first night she'd bedded down in full armor. The bonfire and alert eyes of the watchers eased the worry of ambush. Bright embers drifted skyward with the smoke. Breetan fell asleep watching them wink out like dying stars.

She had positioned her bedroll just right. The light of the rising sun, filtered through the forest, fell on her face. As was her way, she went immediately from sleep to wakefulness. The smell of wood smoke hung heavy in the muggy morning air. Above, the sky was cloudless and blue as a robin's egg. Birds trilled in the trees. What Breetan did not hear was the bustle of a soldiers' camp coming to life. The rough voices of her company were completely absent.

Carefully, she stretched out a hand and felt the stock of her crossbow. She eased the weapon to her but suffered an unpleasant surprise. The bowstring was cut, the bolt gone.

She rolled to her knees, groping for her sword. Her scabbard was empty. Astonishingly, her black-handled dagger had been taken from her boot sheath without awaking her. Her helmet was just where she'd left it, but it sported a new decoration: the bolt from her crossbow pierced it.

With a curse, Breetan jumped to her feet and put her back against Shattered Rock. Jeralund and her twenty men were gone. The clearing was littered with blankets, utensils, and dropped weapons. A confusion of footprints covered the road, giving no clue to what had happened. Even Breetan's horse was gone. Every living soul had been spirited away in the night and she had heard nothing, though she had always been a light sleeper.

"Yes, you're alone."

The male voice, coming from behind and above, sent her whirling away from the boulder. Atop the landmark rock stood a weird figure. A patched and faded brown robe covered his thin body. His head was enveloped by the robe's hood, and his face was further concealed by a close-fitting cloth mask that covered everything but two eyes, light in color, but cold and hard as a draconian's.

"Who are you?" she demanded.

"A ghost. Who might you be?"

"Breetan Everride, Knight of the Lily!"

"Any relation to Burnond Everride, by chance?"

She blinked, surprised out of her hauteur, and claimed the kinship. The masked man said, "A bold and fierce campaigner. He never would have allowed himself to be taken like this."

The taunt angered her, but she reined in her emotions. His cultured voice and knowledge of her illustrious warlord father meant the fellow was no illiterate forest bandit.

Breetan saw no sword or other weapon on him and considered rushing him. With a running jump, she could reach his ankles, drag him off the boulder, and thrash the impudence from his voice. The memory of the dead soldiers hanging in the trees caused her to hesitate. One person could hardly have wreaked all that havoc. The wretch must have followers nearby. Why else would he be so confident?

"What do you want?"

He gestured with a gloved hand. "You. I knew if I made enough trouble, the humans would send someone like you. Not a warrior, but an enforcer."

She scowled at him, but her thoughts were racing. The humans, he had said, so he wasn't human himself. An elf then. Perhaps a Qualinesti not driven out with the rest of his kind.

"I want you to deliver a message to your masters," he added. "A simple one: The forest is mine. From here to Ahlanost, where the trees meet the mountains, it is mine. You and your Order will depart or be destroyed."

She laughed. "A few rogue elves with a Qualinesti lordling at their head? The Order does not flee from trash like you!"

Her shot yielded fruit. For the first time, her words penetrated his shield of amused condescension. Thrusting a finger at her, he spoke in a loud, trembling voice. "Do not befoul the name of Qualinesti or speak to me of trash! You, with a lineage like a mongrel dog, aren't fit to judge even the least of my kind!"

Careful to let nothing show on her face, Breetan stored the small jewels of information he'd let slip. He was indeed a Qualinesti elf, and a well-born one at that, judging from his voice and vocabulary.

"I will deliver your message. It will be your death warrant."

He was master of himself once more. "Murder affects only the living. You cannot kill the dead."

"Very well, dead elf. Until we meet again."

She picked up her useless crossbow and ostentatiously turned her back on him. Head high, she walked away, west toward Alderhelm. She crested a slight hill and disappeared beyond it.

When the Dark Knight was gone, Porthios slid from the tall boulder to the ground. He clapped his hands once and the bushes on the east side of the clearing disgorged eight Kagonesti. They were covered from head to toe in borrowed greenery. Their faces and hands were smeared with malachite paste, staining them dark blue-green. Even standing in plain sight, they were hard to recognize as persons and not foliage.

"She'll bring many soldiers, Great Lord," said one of the camouflaged elves, the tarnished silver torque around his neck the only sign of rank.

"I hope so, Nalaryn."

Porthios pushed back his hood. Despite the warming temperature, he did not remove the mask. "The more force our young whip brings here, the better for my plan."

Nalaryn whistled, drawing more green phantoms from the woods. They set to cleaning the site, removing every item left by the Nerakans. In part, it was to preserve an air of mystery, to deny the enemy clues to their methods, but it also served to supplement their own stores. Every scrap of metal and leather was precious.

"How are the prisoners?" Porthios asked.

"Cowed, Great Lord."

Porthios followed the Kagonesti chief into the brush. Twenty yards off the north road, they came upon seven Nerakan soldiers, bound hand and foot, sitting in the undergrowth. All were blindfolded. The knight's fine horse was tied nearby, another green-camouflaged Kagonesti standing by its head.

"Who is senior here?" Porthios asked. One soldier grunted through his gag. At Porthios's nod, he was hauled to his feet and the gag and blindfold removed. Porthios asked his name and rank.

"Jeralund of Werim, sergeant of the garrison of Alderhelm."

"You should have stayed in Ergoth, Sergeant," Porthios said. "Your lives have been spared, but if any one of you offers the slightest resistance, all will be slain. Do you understand? If one of you errs, all will suffer."

The sergeant nodded. "What do you intend? None of us has rank enough to be ransomed."

"I'm not after ransom, but I do expect to turn a profit on you. We are going to Bianost, called by the scum who infest it 'Samustal.' "

"What's in Samustal?" Jeralund asked before his gag was restored.

"A great many evils, including, unfortunately for you, a slave market."

The captives were hauled to their feet and their blindfolds removed. Each man's bound wrists were joined to those of the man behind and before by vines, then the group was led out of the morning-bright clearing and into the shadowed forest. Their Kagonesti captors were each armed with a long, willowy spear, stone-headed maul, or light bow. Several had metal daggers gleaned from captured Nerakans. Most sported necklaces of goblin teeth. Some were female, although the distinction was difficult to make, what with the face paint, long hair, and lean physiques.

Since his fateful encounter in the forest, Porthios had begun putting into action the lessons the god had imparted. The most difficult part had been making contact with the elusive Wilder elves. They avoided Silvanesti and Qualinesti alike, regarding their city-dwelling cousins as arrogant, effete, and nearly as treacherous as humans.

Many Kagonesti had spurned him, calling him a soulless ghost who would lead them to ruin. Then he met Nalaryn. A former scout for the Qualinesti army, Nalaryn was more worldly than his fellows. When Porthios explained his purpose, Nalaryn readily agreed to join in. That had been the first step forward on Porthios's long journey.

Twenty-three of Nalaryn's clan, fourteen males and nine

females, had followed their chief. They made up Porthios's small army.

There were few greater horrors for elves than bondage. Samuval had declared all free elves in Qualinesti to be rebels, condemning them to slavery whenever and wherever they could be captured. Several slave markets had sprung up. One of the largest was in the town of Bianost, which the invaders called Samustal. The town was ruled by one of Samuval's most ruthless lieutenants, Olin Man-Daleth, who styled himself Lord Olin.

Porthios needed slaves to sell, to give him and his followers an excuse to enter the occupied town. Loud and clumsy as only humans could be, the prisoners were no prizes, even by the low standards of their race, but they were perfect for his plan. He was confident the Dark Knight would unwittingly do just as he wished. As the daughter of one of the Order's battle lords, she was bred to obedience. She would do her utmost to awaken her superiors to the menace facing Alderhelm. In the meantime, Porthios and his small band of Kagonesti would be heading in the opposite direction, herding their captives to the slave market of Samustal. With the Order's forces in Qualinesti marshaled to defend Alderhelm, the region around Samustal would be free of their troops. Porthios would have to contend only with Samuval's bandits.

And there was another reason Porthios was headed to Samustal. When Kagonesti met in the primeval forest, they always exchanged information about intruders or newcomers in their territory. Nalaryn had heard of a stranger who appeared quite suddenly by the Lake of Death. An elf, female and of quiet tread, Nalaryn was told. She smelled of blood, not her own, and even more of danger, so the Kagonesti avoided her.

Porthios was little impressed by Kagonesti gossip. He asked who the female was.

None of the Wilder elves knew. From the signs they'd found at a goblin camp, she had killed several before being taken by slavers, who were also traveling in the direction of Samustal.

"Soon enough all elves in Qualinesti will be free," Porthios said, regarding the lumbering humans.

Nalaryn nodded. He did not understand how selling humans into slavery would free elves, but the Great Lord had spoken and Nalaryn was pledged to obey.

4

Kerian awoke in pain. Her arms were tightly bound behind her, and she lay on her side in a noisome, rickety cart. The cart had barred sides and a wooden roof and was traveling along a heavily rutted road. Every bump caused her head to throb unmercifully.

Since her capture, she had been beaten and starved. The ogre-goblin gang she'd found in the forest had sold her to a large party of humans. The going rate for a female elf was twenty-five steel. The goblins sold her for only ten. Despite beatings from the ogre, she had managed to kill another goblin and assault all the rest. She had become a liability they were only too eager to be rid of.

The human slavers didn't question the low price; they assumed they were putting one over on the ignorant goblins. That feeling did not last. She was put in chains immediately. The instant one of the humans passed too close as the small group of slaves trudged along, Kerian cold-cocked him with a length of chain. Rather than beat her, the humans simply stopped feeding her. For three days she received no crust of bread, no drop of water. Nor would her fellow slaves share their meager rations. The penalty for helping a prisoner evade punishment was the loss of a finger, a toe, or an eye. The other captives were all Qualinesti. Floggings and starvation they could endure, but mutilation filled them with dread.

The human slavers sold her to a large band of mercenaries escorting several hundred captive elves to the slave market they called Samustal. During the exchange, she slipped her bonds and tried to run. Starvation and dehydration were her undoing. Recaptured, she was given over to the "trouble" cart. Its half-ogre driver beat her, tied her hand and foot, and flung her in a cage with other recalcitrant prisoners.

Hungry, thirsty, and in pain, she was in no way cowed.

"Someone's going to pay," she groaned as soon as she regained consciousness.

"Tell it to the driver," said a deep, gloomy voice. "*Orkosham* are such good listeners."

She hauled herself upright. Crowded into the wooden cage with her were three male elves and one dwarf. All were bound as she was. The dwarf had spoken.

"What did you call him?"

"*Orkosham.* Ogre-men. That's what the goblins call them. Mercenary captains like them because they're stronger than humans and work for less pay."

She rested her forehead on her knees, willing her abused skull not to split in two. Something touched her bare foot and she looked up. One of the elves had pushed a covered bucket to her. Using his teeth, he lifted the cover by its rope handle, set it aside, then took the curved end of the metal dipper in his mouth. As he held it steady, she drank tepid water from the cup on the other end.

When she was done, the elf covered the bucket again and pushed it to one side. Kerian thanked him. Grimly, he replied, "Don't be grateful. It's no mercy to live like this."

His sympathetic expression was reflected on the faces of the others. Even the dour dwarf was regarding her with pity.

"Who are you?" she said.

"We were free. Now we are slaves," the elf answered. He lifted his head and sniffed the air. "I can smell the slave market already."

She too could smell it. They were approaching from the east, and the wind carried the odors of wood smoke, open privies, and unwashed bodies. Kerian put her face to the wooden bars and peered ahead.

Like most Qualinesti towns, Bianost had been built to be, as much as possible, a natural part of the forest. With characteristic finesse, the elves shaped the living trees into homes and shops, and natural clearings were planted with the flowers and fruit trees for which the town became famous. Bianost apples and figs were renowned throughout Ansalon, and the honey collected from enormous hives on the perimeter of the orchards made the most potent mead in a thousand miles.

The floral glory of Bianost was gone. In its place squatted Samustal, a fetid settlement named for Captain Samuval and ruled by Lord Olin Man-Daleth.

Dusk had come, made darker still by the pall of smoke overhead. Fed by several large bonfires and thinner columns rising from innumerable cook fires and street torches, the wood smoke acted like a shield, holding in the odors of rotting garbage, open latrines, and hordes of unwashed inhabitants. The structures lovingly shaped from living trees by generations of Qualinesti were twisted and gnarled, bark black and peeling. A stockade of dressed timbers encircled the heart of the town. Outside that twelve-foot fence was a patchwork assortment of tents, huts, and lean-tos. The invaders had felled many trees to construct additional structures, but the new buildings showed signs of hasty workmanship: timbers poorly joined, walls leaning, roofs canted.

The cart was passing through the outer edges of the shanty town ringing Samustal. If she was going to do something, Kerian knew she must try it now, before they entered the stockade.

"We have to get out of here," she said in a low voice.

"Wonderful idea," the dwarf snorted. "We've fared so well thus far."

"If we all work together—"

"We'll all die together. Listen to me, woman. I tried to fight back. All I got for my troubles was a cracked skull, a broken rib, and a dead brother." His face twisted. "It's hopeless."

Pointedly, he turned his back on her. She looked to the three elves. They avoided her gaze.

"Listen to me! It's not hopeless!"

Kerian had been working at the ropes that bound her wrists and finally had succeeded in loosening them. Lying on her back, she drew her legs up and worked her wrists under her hips until they were in front of her. Her small success did not impress her fellow captives.

Fine. She would do it herself. Decades ago she had been forced into servitude by Qualinesti elves who thought they were improving the lot of a barbaric Kagonesti. No matter how benign the intentions or how kind the master, slavery was slavery, and the Lioness would not go quietly to such a fate.

She began to yell, kicking the wall of the cart behind the driver's seat with both feet. The cart abruptly halted. A goblin came to the side of the cage, yelling at the prisoners to be still. She heaped insults on him until the goblin foolishly shoved his spear through the bars at her. She took hold of the shaft with both hands and jerked. The goblin's face hit the wooden bars, and Kerian was on him instantly. She encircled his neck with her bound wrists, dropped to the floor, and planted her feet against his back. Pulling with her arms and pushing with her feet, she snapped his neck.

Kerian recovered the goblin's spear. The sharp head made quick work of the ropes tying the cage door closed. In seconds she was out the door and sprinting for the horse yoked to the cart. Despite their earlier lack of enthusiasm, her fellow captives scrambled out of the cage after her and took off in all directions.

Shouts rose, but Kerian wasted no time looking back. She cut the horse's tether with the spearhead and thumped heels against the animal's sides. It sprang forward—

—and immediately went down. She tried to jump free but her weakened body finally had had too much. She fell heavily on her side. The horse was struggling, neighing shrilly, and Kerian saw a fine cord wrapping its rear fetlocks. Each end of the cord was finished by a wooden ball larger than her fist.

Three goblins arrived and aimed their swords at her throat. Behind them came the half-ogre. It had thrown the odd weapon, which whipped around the horse's legs, bringing it down.

Turning its attentions to Kerian, the creature gave her a back-handed slap that split her cheek and blackened her eye. "No more trouble," the half-ogre commanded.

She was hauled to her feet, arms tied behind her back, this time at both wrists and elbows. Her ankles were hobbled with rawhide cord, allowing just enough movement so she could shuffle along. On the ground nearby lay the body of one elf, killed trying to escape; the other two had succeeded in getting away. The dwarf, slower than the Qualinesti, had been recaptured.

Two goblins carried Kerian back to the cage and tossed her inside. The door was secured, and soon they were rumbling on their way again. Panting and furious, Kerian cursed her failure, fully expecting her glum companion to join her. He did not. Instead, impressed by her deeds, the dwarf asked, "Who are you, woman?"

She glared at him through one good eye and one beginning to swell shut. "A free elf," she snapped. "And I will be no one's slave!"

She closed her eyes, rested her throbbing head on the filthy floor, and pondered her next move.

The dwarf regarded her in silence, a thoughtful expression on his face.

* * * * *

The captives were taken to a large cage outside the former town hall of Bianost. It was one of many similar cages sprawled in the city square, adjacent to the auction block. Before being tossed inside, Kerian and the dwarf were registered with the auction master, a rail-thin human with a hairless dome of a head and a pewter patch over his left eye. His displeasure at having his dinner delayed by the half-ogre's late arrival was lessened by the sight of Kerian. Young female elves were becoming harder and harder to find. Appreciation gleamed in his good eye.

True to her word, Kerian did not go tamely into captivity. She fought the goblins who carried her, kicking one in the stomach and the other in the face. The half-ogre did not intervene. The creature seemed pleased by her spirit, laughing uproariously with every hurt she inflicted on the frustrated goblins.

A dozen unfortunates were crowded into the holding cage, a low-ceilinged wooden box only fifteen feet on a side. The furious goblins didn't bother untying Kerian. She was simply dumped unceremoniously into the muck on the cage floor. The dwarf was shoved in after her and the door closed and barred.

"Why do you keep fighting them?" he asked. "What does it get you?"

"Satisfaction." She twitched her bound arms. "Can you get me out of these?"

He obliged, working patiently on the tough knots. She kept twisting and turning, studying their prison. "Hold still," the dwarf grumbled.

When she was free of the cords, she jumped up and prowled around the holding box, minutely examining the walls, ceiling, and floor.

"What are you looking for?" one of the other prisoners asked.

"A way out."

"There isn't any."

"There's always a way out. The trick is finding it."

The elf didn't bother responding, but the dwarf asked mildly, "Do you really believe that?"

She looked over one shoulder at him. "I do."

Kerian moved her arms, carefully working out the stiffness. "I've been captured before. All that's required for escape is persistence." A faint smile touched her bruised face. "And a little luck."

ALLIANCES

The elves scoffed at her bold words. They were local farmers, traders, and fishers, thoroughly intimidated by the slavers.

The dwarf related Kerian's escape attempt on the road into Samustal, how she had dispatched the goblin guard and allowed two of their fellow prisoners to get away. None of the elves commented, but his words affected them. When Kerian began to question them for useful information, they answered readily enough. They also shared the last of their bread and water.

The only guards they had seen were goblins and humans, who periodically brought additional captives or took some away. Kerian was pleased to hear the half-ogres didn't come there. Once a day the door opened and food and water was put inside by one guard while two others kept swords leveled at the captives. The next such delivery should occur within the hour, welcome news to Kerian's nearly empty stomach.

She put the time to good use. Without revealing her identity, she worked to energize the dispirited captives. Her resolve, her commitment to finding a way out, as well as the dwarf's own account of her previous success, began to rouse them from their passivity. By the time the guards returned, Kerian's plan was in place.

A thump on the door and a shouted command to move back heralded the guards' arrival.

The dwarf yelled, "I think she's dead! You killed the elf woman!"

A bearded human face appeared in the small window. Kerian lay on the floor just inside the door, her arms bound (very loosely) behind her.

"A trick," scoffed the human.

"I'm telling you, she's dead. She keeled over a few minutes ago. I don't think she's eaten in weeks."

The human was unconvinced but wavering. The dwarf added, "Fine. I don't care. But when Olin learns you let valuable property die. . . ." Thick shoulders rose in a shrug.

The human conferred with his compatriots outside. He still wasn't completely convinced, but a female elf, however bad-tempered, was the most saleable item of a sad lot. Lord Olin would be furious at the waste.

"The rest of you, get back from the door," he ordered.

The captives complied, shuffling as far back as the tight confines allowed. The door opened slowly. Two guards held swords leveled at the captives. The third advanced cautiously. He took hold of Kerian's arm and hauled her out the door. Eyes closed, head lolling, she allowed herself to be dragged like a sack across the rough planking. When she cleared the door, it slammed shut again.

The captives heard a muttered exchange, the tromp of booted feet on the cobblestones, then silence. They exchanged outraged looks.

"She lied to us!" hissed one. "She got herself out and left us here!"

In their preoccupation with the female prisoner, the guards had forgotten to leave food and water. The elves cursed the lack, cursed their own stupidity for believing the lies, and cursed the dwarf for making them believe.

"What are you waiting for?"

Thirteen pairs of eyes went wide at the sight of the Lioness's face in the small window. In moments the captives were out of the wooden box, staring in astonishment at two human guards lying unconscious (or dead?) in the shadowed lee of the cage. Kerian's face bore several new cuts, and a gash on one arm bled freely, but she held a bloody sword in one hand and a ring of keys in the other.

"How—?" the dwarf began.

She shoved the keys at him, saying, "Let's go!"

A dozen sets of keen ears allowed them to avoid detection as they wound their way around the crowded cages. Their greatest challenge was keeping excited prisoners quiet as they skulked by. Few guards were to be seen, which worried Kerian, but the lack was soon explained.

Several trestle tables had been set up near the center of the square, and the guards were enjoying a raucous meal. Fortunately, most had their backs to the row of cages. The prisoners were generally so docile, the guards had grown contemptuous and did not watch them closely.

Kerian, acting as lookout, signaled the others when it was clear for them to skirt the opening between the cage rows. Singly or in pairs, all twelve elves made their way across the naked gap, leaving Kerian and the dwarf to bring up the rear.

They found themselves in a back street littered with refuse. Still, the open air was a balm to those choked by the stench of too many goblins and humans in close proximity.

"Now what?" asked one of the elves, and the others looked to Kerian for an answer.

She itched to find an armory. But she had no idea where to go, and anyway, her band of fugitives was not made up of stalwart soldiers, so she shrugged. "We run. Quietly and carefully, we run."

To their left, the narrow street connected with a larger avenue, better lit and, hence, not appealing. To the right, the street dead-ended at a gate. Coming from that direction was the smell of horses. A mounted escape posed its own problems, but the added speed and mobility made up for those, Kerian decided.

With the sword-wielding Lioness in the lead, the little group made for the gate.

It wasn't long before she began to regret her decision. Two members of her little band, a pair of brothers who made their living fishing, confessed they could not ride. She told them to double up with others, but the brothers were afraid of horses, and none of the rest wanted a passenger anyway, not with Lord Olin's cavalry likely to be on their heels. The escapees fell to arguing in loud whispers.

They were hiding behind a pile of garbage just outside the corral. Every moment they delayed brought closer the time when their absence would be discovered and a search launched. Yet all Kerian's exhortations wouldn't move the elves one step closer to the corral. Furious, she told the brothers to make it out of town on foot.

The corral was unguarded but for a couple of stable boys. One had just returned with their supper and they had gone into the tack shed to eat.

Crouched low, the elves entered the corral. Kerian had told them what to do. They would mount quietly. Each rider would lie low on his horse's neck as Kerian opened the gate, then the animals would be whipped to a gallop. Riding in a body, they stood a good chance of making it to the stockade before anyone could stop them. At the stockade they'd have to trample anyone trying to bar the way. It wasn't much of a plan, but considering what she had to work with, Kerian knew it would have to do.

They'd barely begun to mount the horses when shouts rose from a nearby street. Kerian froze, listening, and it quickly became apparent they'd been missed at last.

"Go!" she hissed. She boosted the last elf atop a horse, and rushed to the gate.

The noise in the streets had drawn the stable boys from the shed. Both stood on the other side of the gate, beer tankards in hand, their backs to Kerian. Noiselessly, she lifted the latch then headed back to the rear. Drawing a deep breath, she shouted, at the same time slapping horses' flanks. The riders twined their fingers through the animals' manes, and the herd surged forward. Kerian grabbed a passing horse and swung herself aboard. The lead animals hit the unlatched gate. It sprang open. The stable boys dove clear, and they were away.

Lying low on her horse's neck, Kerian guided it left, away from the town square. Her mount was a young mare. It moved to the front of the herd, and the other animals followed. Responding to the pressure of Kerian's legs and feet, the mare veered farther left, into the street leading down the hill to the stockade gate.

Kerian heard a scream. One of the elves had lost his balance and fallen amid the pounding hooves. There was nothing to be done for him. The horses thundered on.

The escaping elves were poor riders, and riding bareback at a gallop took its toll. Three more fell off and were trampled.

By then mounted mercenaries had appeared from the side streets. They rode alongside the escapees, twirling loops of rope. Expertly thrown, the lines dropped around the necks of the galloping horses, pulling them up short. More and more ropes were thrown, and the whirl of horses dissolved into a neighing mass of confusion.

Kerian slid from the mare's back, landing in a crouch amid churning hooves. She spied the dwarf among the fallen riders and hauled him to his feet. If they could make it to the other side of the street, they might be able to vanish into the maze of dingy houses.

Something hit her leg, knocking her to the ground. She twisted around, but couldn't free herself. The dwarf had fallen across her leg. Two arrows protruded from his back. A third pierced his neck. He was dead and she didn't even know his name.

Hands dragged her roughly to her feet. The horses had been led away, clearing the street. Out of fourteen escaped prisoners, only Kerian and four other elves still lived. None of the others had made it to freedom. The five survivors were bound and hauled back to face Lord Olin.

* * * * *

The former residence of Bianost's mayor stood opposite the town hall. Bonfires blazed on its stone steps. The number of guards in evidence made it obvious Olin Man-Daleth had taken the mansion for his own. The sandstone facade was streaked with soot, and the elegantly tall windows were crudely bricked up, leaving only narrow openings through which archers could shoot. The ornamental bronze doors were nearly concealed behind a head-high breastwork of timbers and sandbags. The entrance was guarded by no fewer than fifteen armed bandits.

Lord Olin stood on the stone steps as the recaptured prisoners were brought before him. Tall, with iron-gray hair, Olin wore full armor and a heavy dark cape to disguise his thinness. Narrow, close-set eyes and a nose crooked from having been broken and inexpertly set gave him a sinister look. The news of the escape had interrupted his dinner, putting him in a foul mood. Despite his perpetual thinness, he had a hearty appetite, and food was one of the great pleasures of his life. Those responsible for disrupting his meal would know his wrath.

He glared at the bound elves kneeling at the bottom of the stairs. The female he ignored, concentrating his attention on the four males.

"How did you get out?" he demanded.

When no answers were forthcoming, a goblin struck one of the captives, knocking the elf onto his face. Olin repeated the question.

The elves exchanged frightened looks but still said nothing. The goblin lifted its sword, ready to take the head of a random prisoner, but Olin stayed its hand. His face was very red. He stomped down the steps, halting on the last one.

"Rebellion will not be allowed!" he shouted. "I will know who your ringleaders are and deal with them!"

He gestured at two of the elves. "Bring them to the tower. Return the rest to the cages." He swept up the stairs.

The captives were bullied and buffeted across the square toward the town hall. There they were separated, with Kerian and two elves returned to the holding cage, and the two elves chosen by Lord Olin forced into the long stairwell that led up the town hall tower.

Kerian asked her fellow captives what was in the tower. Neither would answer. They huddled in the far corner of the cage, their misery all the greater for their brief taste of freedom. Soon the three of them heard screams.

When the first echoed through the air, Kerian rushed to the door. Standing on tiptoe, she peered out the small window. Outside were three guards.

"What's happening, savages?" she demanded.

Two guards ignored her. The third, younger than the others, ambled over, regarding her with open interest.

Another scream ripped through the air, the sound of a soul in terrible torment. Kerian pounded a fist against the door.

The young guard smiled. "Lord Olin wants to know who to blame for the escape. In the tower questions are answered quickly or not at all."

"Leave them alone! Tell him it was me!"

"I'll be sure to do that." Laughing, the bandit moved away.

Nothing she said mattered. None of the guards believed her. Only the young one would even speak to her, and then only to make obscene suggestions. The distant screams continued intermittently.

Some time later, a sharp rap on the cell door jolted her awake. She didn't know how long she'd dozed, but the young guard's laughter brought her quickly to her feet.

"It appears you weren't lying. They both admitted you planned the whole thing." He shook his head, grinning appreciatively. "You're a firebrand."

"What has happened to them?"

"Oh, they're dead. Believe me, they're lucky. For you, it won't be so quick." She did not ask what he meant, but he volunteered the information anyway. "You're to be executed, as a warning to other would-be rebels. Day after tomorrow." He walked away.

Sick with guilt and helpless fury, Kerian slid to the floor.

5

The cemetery outside Gateway lay between two hills, hidden from the lights of town and the traffic on the coast road. The vale was low and boggy, so the graves were built aboveground. Bathed in starlight, they stood like ordered blocks of ice, white and polished. Most were unadorned stone boxes, but a few elaborate mausoleums bore the names of families long important in the province.

Like the nation itself, the cemetery had fallen on hard times. Weeds sprouted around the foundations of the monuments. Grass grew knee high and choked the pathways. Vines girded graves great and humble. Here and there, the stone boxes had collapsed from weather or the attentions of grave robbers. The broken graves were quickly claimed by weeds. Cemeteries were melancholy places in the best of times. The one outside Gateway was a somber testament to the tragedy of a nation.

Standing alone on one of the overgrown paths was a figure draped in a long linen duster. She stepped from the deep shade of an obelisk and starlight washed her pale features in cool radiance. Her face might have graced an elegant statue atop one of the finer monuments. Her astonishing beauty overlaid by deep pain, Alhana Starbreeze was the living embodiment of mourning.

The whir of a nightjar made her start. Then a figure, cloaked and hooded like herself, emerged from the grass-choked side path.

"What word?" she murmured.

The newcomer drew back his cowl, revealing a lean countenance, almond-shaped eyes, and a high, pale forehead. Like Alhana, Samar was a Silvanesti. There was a glint of iron at his throat, a warrior's gorget.

"Nothing to confirm the rumors, lady, but nothing to disprove them either."

The line of her jaw hardened. Every day she lingered in this land was dangerous and expensive. Danger she could bear, but there was little she could do to lessen the drain on her slender purse.

She asked no more questions, preferring to hear Samar's full report when they rejoined their party. They mounted their waiting horses and, with Alhana in the lead, left the deserted cemetery.

Samar followed three steps behind, as he felt was proper. Long acquaintance allowed him to recognize his lady's disappointment. Hope had buoyed her for a while, and she'd had precious little of it lately, but she was coming to realize the folly of the dream she chased.

Her only child, on whom she'd placed her hopes for the future of the elf nation, had been taken from her. No hero's death, nor even a worthy one, had been granted Silvanoshei. He had died a dupe, killed by the woman he loved, the false prophet of a dark deity. Porthios, the husband Alhana had married for duty but come to love, was gone as well, killed in the same war that had claimed their son. Blasted from the sky by a dragon's fiery breath, his had been a magnificent end for a warrior and a king. The crime, Samar thought, was that Alhana could not accept that her husband was dead. His griffon's incinerated body had been found, but its rider never was. From that slim hope, Alhana had built the fantasy that her husband might still live.

Their homeland was despoiled, their people scattered, but she would not give up the search. A resurrected husband might be too much of a miracle, but at the very least she intended to find his remains and see him properly interred. However, Alhana had not come to the long-unused cemetery to find Porthios's grave. Rumors had reached, even her in exile, of a mysterious leader who was forging the few remaining elves of Qualinesti into a rebellion. The old cemetery served as a private place to wait while Samar ventured into Gateway to gather what information he could about the budding revolt and its mastermind. Silent as a ghost, Alhana walked among the forgotten dead, waiting for word of her lost husband.

They'd been on the mainland just two days. Before that, Alhana and her small company of loyal followers had dwelt on the island of Schallsea, tolerated but not celebrated. She could have retreated to the forest of her own country. There were still hidden vales where a careful inhabitant could live with little risk of discovery. But with Silvanesti, Qualinesti, and Kagonesti slaughtered, enslaved in their own countries, or exiled to alien lands, Alhana would not seek sylvan peace for herself. For a long time, she wandered the lands of the New Sea until weariness and impending poverty brought her to a halt on Schallsea. From there she kept up her search, sending out agents to investigate hearsay and interviewing travelers who'd come from the former elf homelands.

It was more than rumors of a masked rebel that brought Alhana back to the mainland. Anyone could don a mask, for any number of reasons. But the Kagonesti who followed the rebel called him "Great Lord," a title usually reserved for the Speaker or his heir.

Samar argued that that was not enough reason for her to risk entering occupied Qualinesti. Kagonesti were truthful people but much given to mysticism and symbolism. Their Great Lord could be nearly anyone. Alhana's chamberlain, the venerable Chathendor, agreed with Samar. Alhana did not. She intended to go to Qualinesti. Whatever they felt about her quest, and despite her abdication of the throne, she would always be their queen. They and a few hundred Silvanesti warriors accompanied her across the sea.

The terrain east of Gateway was rolling grassland, long cleared of all but the smallest saplings and bushes. Alhana and Samar crested a low rise and reined up. The view showed nothing but a starlit meadow. In answer to Samar's low whistle, the hillsides seemed to come alive. From every low swale and scrap of cover rose elves, their green- and brown-clad forms shaded to black by the darkness.

One elf moved to greet the newcomers. Even among a long-lived race, Chathendor was very old, more than twice Alhana's age. Perhaps because he'd lived so long, he was the only truly fearless person Alhana knew. He'd once told her that at his age, death wasn't a terrifying abstraction to be avoided at all costs, but a patient visitor, awaiting its inevitable invitation. Bare of hood, his pale, curly hair was pearlescent in the starlight.

"What word?" he whispered, unknowingly echoing Alhana's question to Samar.

Both of them dismounted and Samar reported. "For weeks a band of Kagonesti, led by a masked elf, has been harrying the small Nerakan fort of Alderhelm, killing off mercenaries by twos and threes. Word reached Gateway that a Dark Knight sent to the fort to put an end to the troubles was herself attacked, and her entire command spirited away overnight."

"A kender's tale!" Chathendor scoffed.

"Evidently not. The knight dispatched a report to the Order's citadel in Frenost. The courier was kept occupied at an inn called The Saddle Horn, halfway between Frenost and Haven, while the contents of his bag were copied. The news reached Haven ahead of him and beat him to Gateway too."

"Was there a description, Samar?" Alhana asked, caring little how the news had come.

"Masked, covered head to toe by ragged robes, but well spoken, with the diction and vocabulary of a high-born Qualinesti."

"A Qualinesti," she echoed, her voice little more than a sigh. Perhaps her quest was not a fool's errand after all.

She controlled her emotions, reminding herself it was a slender thread. A "high-born" Qualinesti could be a courtier or a former officer of the royal army who had donned a hood to confound the bandits. And yet—something in her heart would not let that particular rumor go. She had suffered so many disappointments. For half a year she had stalked a supposed Porthios around the cities of Crusher's Bay, always one step behind, until finally catching up with him in a Walmish gaming house. The impostor passing himself off as her husband was no more than a quarter elf, a glib liar who'd managed to convince dozens of gullible folk he was the lost ruler of Qualinesti. It was merely a confidence game, a way for him to gull his way to an easy life. Caught, he confessed all. Alhana forgave him. Unbeknownst to her, Samar had not. When his sorrowing queen was out of sight, Samar made certain the impostor would ply his trade no longer, except as food for the fish of Crusher's Bay.

"We must go to Alderhelm," she announced.

Alhana's lieutenants protested. Bad enough she had come as far as she had, but entering occupied Qualinesti was unthinkably hazardous. Should Captain Samuval get his hands on the former queen of Silvanesti, she would surely die. There was no one left to ransom her.

Their arguments fell on deaf ears. Alhana silenced them with a sharp word. She had to know the truth for herself. She was tired of waiting in safety while others risked their lives to find out for her.

She thanked them both, telling Samar to prepare the troops and sending her chamberlain with him. She needed solitude, time to think.

She rode in the direction of the ruined cemetery but didn't go far. Samar would be frantic if she went out of sight. Reining up, she pushed back her hood and untied the scarf that concealed her upswept ears and bound up her hair. The night-black sheaf fell to the middle of her back. She looked up at the starry sky.

Was it truly possible Porthios lived, or was she endlessly deceiving herself? More than a mask and courtly diction were needed to bring her husband back to life, but his body had never been found. If anyone could survive dragonfire, it would be

Porthios. There was another, much harder question she did not like to contemplate: If he had survived, why had he left her to grieve his death and their son's death all alone?

Her solitude ended too soon. Samar and Chathendor rode up to report their people were ready to move. However much he might protest her course, Samar was the truest friend she'd ever had. Chathendor, with the bluntness granted by extreme age, was both wise and inventive. He saw angles others did not. More than once he'd saved her from ruin, just by his wits. Armed with her two champions, and her own resolve, Alhana was not afraid to enter Qualinesti.

* * * * *

Breetan Everride shivered. The sun was not yet up, but the sky, clear as a mountain lake, shaded from indigo in the west to azure in the east. A south wind carried the cold breath of Icewall, and she pulled her mantle close around her neck. She stood in a long, narrow courtyard hard by the outer wall of the Black Hall. The Hall was the seat of Lord Egil Liveskill, who was responsible for the peace and security in the Southward, as the Dark Knights designated the former elf kingdom of Qualinesti.

She had reached the Hall the evening before. Despite the lateness of the hour, she was escorted directly to Lord Liveskill's audience chamber. Liveskill sat at a great oval table, its obsidian surface covered with books, parchments, and sheaves of reports. The master of the Black Hall worked late nearly every night.

Liveskill's blond hair was still trimmed close, but since she'd last seen him he'd grown a short beard, confined to his square chin. He seemed paler than she remembered, but perhaps that was due to the combination of candlelight and the contrast of his dark blue tunic. Liveskill had once received a prophecy that he was in danger from fire, so no modern lamps were permitted within the Hall. How numerous racks of candles were safer than oil lamps, Breetan couldn't imagine, but they were certainly warmer. Breetan was sweating heavily in her armor.

"I hear strange tidings," he said before even looking at the document she held out to him. "You bring word of an insurrection in the Southward."

She wasn't surprised the news had preceded her; the Black Hall had spies in every town and village. Liveskill took her reports. Documents that had taken her a day and a half to write, he read through in moments, then sat back in his chair. His expression was unreadable.

"Why?" he finally said. "Why would this masked rebel leave you alive to send word of his deeds to the Order? Why deliberately attract our attention?"

Before she could reply, he answered his own question. "This is a diversion. He wants us to scour the Alderhelm forest for him while he strikes at his true target. Do you have any idea what that might be?"

His quick insight left her struggling to catch up. "My lord, I cannot believe he commands more than a few dozen foresters. It's one thing to harry a small outpost, quite another to think he could threaten the Order. The difficulties of counting the Kagonesti are well known, but our census estimates the total number in the Southward at three to four thousand. Even if he could command them all, that's hardly sufficient to bring down our fortresses."

He did not reply. Breetan sweated harder. Her failure against the masked rebel was galling, and the Order seldom forgave failure. She decided a bit of boldness was required.

"My lord, allow me to redeem myself. Give me a company and I will—"

"No."

His flat denial sent a shiver of doubt through her. Liveskill's distant gaze focused on her, and she steeled herself for whatever would come.

"The failure was yours alone. Alone you will redeem it."

Faint hope stirred. Perhaps her only choices were not disgrace or death.

Unfortunately he told her nothing more, only dismissed her, saying he would call for her at sunrise. His majordomo, Denius

Dukayne, escorted her to a sumptuous bedchamber, where a fine repast awaited. Was this a last meal for the condemned or simple courtesy for a fellow knight and member of the Black Hall?

She fortified herself with food, wine, and the uncommon luxury of a comfortable bed.

Sunrise was still half an hour away when Dukayne tapped at her door, but she was ready and waiting for him. He conducted her to the courtyard of the Black Hall, where Liveskill awaited her.

With him were two artisans in short tunics, baggy breeches, and ankle-high boots. Liveskill introduced them. The elder, with white hair and a wispy beard, was Gonthar, master bowyer. The other, nearer Breetan's age and clean shaven, was Gonthar's journeyman, Waymark.

As a chill wind swirled around inside the sheer black stone walls, Gonthar handed Breetan the velvet-wrapped package he held. It proved to be a large, elaborately made crossbow. Despite her uncertainty over her situation, she was intrigued. Liveskill knew the crossbow was her favored weapon.

Although large, it was remarkably light. The black ironwood stock had been inletted deeply along its length, hollowing it and making it far lighter than it appeared. There was no arrow trough. The bowstring was buried in the stock, not lying atop it. At the front of the stock was a square opening for inserting the bolt blunt end first. Odder still was the tube attached to the upper right edge of the stock. It was brass, carefully blackened except for the knurled rings at one end. In place of the customary trigger bar, a round hole had been bored midway through the wrist of the stock. Within was set an ivory trigger. The weapon was light enough for her to hold in one hand, her arm at full extension. No doubt it had been designed to be loosed that way, if need be.

At the far end of the courtyard, a hundred yards away, a very small white target was tacked to a pile of sandbags. The target was stark against the black wall.

Waymark lowered the front of the bow to the ground. He pressed a button and a plate opened. Breetan had been mistaken about the method of loading the weapon. The bolt was not loaded butt first into the front of the stock, but point first into the hidden opening. Waymark inserted three short bolts, then closed the hinged butt plate. Rather than a single shot, he would have three before needing to reload.

He cocked the bow by means of an iron lever, inlaid in the bottom front of the stock. The buried bowstring bent the steel limbs of the bow and locked over the trigger nut with an audible snap. With no more sound than the soft snap of the waxed bowstring over the trigger nut, the crossbow spat its black missile at the distant target.

Waymark handed the bow to Breetan and retrieved the target. The disk of paper was no wider than her palm, but the bolt's keen point had neatly pierced its center.

Lord Liveskill, who had been watching Breetan rather than the demonstration, said, "You try."

After cocking the bow, Breetan put the weapon to her shoulder. The dark tunnel of the sighting tube made the fresh white target stand out like a beacon. Her bolt hit low on the target, tearing the sandbags. Not bad for a first shot with an unfamiliar weapon.

Liveskill sent the craftsmen away. When they were gone, he told Breetan the crossbow was hers. She knew there was more to come. The master of the Black Hall did not bestow gifts.

"Go to the Southward, find the masked leader of the elves, and kill him," he said with uncharacteristic bluntness. "In the arsenal is a leather-bound case. It contains various bolts for the weapon. Each has a special use."

The kind she and Waymark had used was called a whisper bolt, which flew silently over its effective range of two hundred yards. There were also lightning bolts that could penetrate an inch of steel armor plate at a hundred yards. Fire bolts were loaded with an incendiary paste that ignited three seconds after being loosed. Dragon tooth bolts had gilded heads coated with poison.

"Use the dragon tooth bolts only when you have the rebel in sight. A scratch will cause certain death in a day. A deeper wound, and the victim may last an hour. Bury the bolt in his flesh, and he will be dead before his head hits the ground. You leave today."

"And my support?"

"None. Hire what porters or guides you need. Kill them when you're done with them. Understand?"

She did. Left unsaid but understood by both of them was that Breetan must succeed or die.

He departed, leaving Breetan alone in the vast courtyard. Wind swirled hair in her face. She'd been given a second chance. She would not fail. Her honor as an Everride was at stake, as much as her life.

Neither especially gifted as a fighter nor valiant in the accepted knightly sense, Breetan had long ago realized she would never come close to matching her famous father's deeds. She was determined to make her own mark, so she had chosen another path, away from battlefield glory. Lord Burnond had disapproved of his only daughter's decision to join Liveskill's order. Long retired to his estate near Lemish, he lived like any successful elder warlord, chasing bandits, banqueting on the anniversaries of his victories, hunting, and training men-at-arms. Concealed daggers and poisoned cups might sometimes be necessary, he said, but a true warrior did not seek them out. He likened the Black Hall to a tombstone, and branded it no fit home for honor. Breetan had braved his censure and taken her own path. If it lay in the shadow of a tombstone, so be it.

Beneath the lightening sky, she shouldered the new crossbow and put the third and last whisper bolt into the exact center of the target.

6

The journey to Samustal passed largely in silence. Naturally taciturn, the Kagonesti communicated among themselves with gestures and facial expressions. The captive Nerakans had little to say, and little breath left with which to say it. The elf in charge kept them moving, allowing only brief stops for food, water, or rest.

Among themselves the humans dubbed their masked captor the Scarecrow for his ragged appearance. It was obvious from his speech and manner he was an elf, and the men wondered why he kept himself so thoroughly covered. Near their destination, as they crossed a steeply banked creek, Sergeant Jeralund caught a glimpse of the elf beneath the rags.

In ages past, the Speaker of the Sun had maintained a forest patrol to inspect the bridges, roads, and tunnels in his realm and keep them in good repair. That necessary service had been neglected by the invaders who infested Qualinesti. As Jeralund, last in the line of prisoners, neared the end of the bridge over Claymore Creek, he felt the planks drop away from his feet. He cried out, expecting to be dashed to pieces on the boulders eighty feet below. Instead he was jerked to a halt, booted feet dangling in midair.

Gasping, he looked up. With one hand, the Scarecrow had clutched the vine connecting Jeralund's bound wrists to those of the man ahead. His other hand was clamped on the arm of the prisoner in front of Jeralund.

"Pull!" he commanded, teeth clenched with the effort of bearing the human's full weight.

The captives and Kagonesti fell to, hauling Jeralund up. The sergeant scrambled onto the bridge and crouched on hands and knees, breathing heavily and shaking with relief.

He looked up, eying the ragged figure standing over him. "You're stronger than you look."

Jeralund halted abruptly. The Scarecrow's robe had split across his stomach. The ragged gap revealed not pale skin or visible ribs, but vivid red flesh, bisected by angry scars.

The glimpse lasted only a moment. The Kagonesti jerked Jeralund to his feet, and the line of captives moved on. In the interim, the Scarecrow disappeared into the trees, leaving Jeralund to ponder the significance of what he had seen.

Their masked captor had been burned very badly. His flesh looked like the skin of a Karthay beach lizard. If the rest of him was anything like that, it was no wonder he covered himself from fingers to toes. As a soldier, Jeralund had known many disfigured men. The back streets of any garrison town were littered with men missing hands, feet, limbs, eyes. Such was to be expected among those who made their trade from fighting. The worst cases ended their days as beggars. But those were humans, not elves. Disfigured elves were a rarity for one simple reason: they usually took their own lives. Jeralund had known a Qualinesti officer who lost an arm in the battle that preceded the fall of the Dragon Overlord Beryl. The fellow had thrown himself from a high tower as soon as he had sufficient strength for the task. Obsessed with beauty and purity, elves could not bear disfigurement. Only the Kagonesti were different. With their body paint, tattoos, and ritual scarring, they seemed to revel in a tortured appearance.

The Scarecrow was city bred, Jeralund was certain of that, but there he was, dreadfully scarred and still alive. For a human, such an existence would be painful; for an elf, it was unthinkable. As he trudged along with his fellows, Jeralund wondered why the elf hadn't taken his own life.

Concealed behind an oak tree, Porthios felt as if his body had hardened into stone. He had thought himself beyond any sensation of shame, but when the barbarian looked upon his scarred flesh, he knew he'd been wrong. Humiliation surged through his veins like fresh fire. Strong as the raging river that had drowned Qualinost, it filled his throat with bile.

"Great Lord?" Nalaryn called out, unable to see his leader. "Great Lord, the band has moved on."

Porthios replied loudly, "Go. I will rejoin you."

The faithful Kagonesti departed. When Porthios was alone, he seated himself on a rock and took a small sewing kit from a pocket in his robe. Born to rule Qualinesti, he was no tailor, but of late he'd had a lot of practice sewing. His stitches were uneven but tight and strong. In minutes his shame was covered once more.

Night had fallen by the time they beheld Samustal. The dark seemed to hang all the heavier over the squalid town. An overcast sky pressed the smoky air down like a damp, choking mantle.

Porthios ordered Nalaryn to make camp at a nearby stream. He would enter the town alone to penetrate its defenses and find out what he could about any elves being held there. Unarmed as he was, he probably could have used the main gate with no more hindrance than a bribe to the guards, but that would mean submitting to a search—an intolerable notion—so he chose a stealthier course.

He circled away from the gate, moving carefully over the open killing ground beneath the walls while watching the parapet above. Lord Olin had built the stockade quickly. His men hadn't bothered leveling the ground first, so some places were closer to the top of the wall than others. Porthios found a spot where the sharpened points of the stockade were only eight feet above the ground. He backed until he came up against a line of bark-covered lean-tos then ran at the stockade wall.

He leaped and jammed his right foot onto the scant toehold offered by the stump of a branch sawed off the side of one of the stockade palings.

His muscles screamed, and his lips drew back in a grimace of pain. The hand-to-mouth existence in the woodlands and the ravages of his wounds had left him weakened. Tight, scarred skin pulled over his emaciated frame as he levered himself upward.

The pain was unbelievable, but just as fierce was Porthios's will. He flung his left hand at the wall of logs. His nails bit into the wood through his gloves. With his right hand, he reached higher, finding a chink between two timbers. When at last he grasped the rough-sawn peak of the stockade, he felt a warm wetness soaking through his gloves. His hands left dark stains on the wood. Still he moved with deliberate care, making certain no one had observed him. He finally dropped onto the battlement and lay still. He trembled all over and his gloves were stiff with drying blood, but he was inside.

This was the secret of Porthios's new life: dogged indifference to any level of pain and the willingness to go where others dared not. He'd lived long enough with his disfigurement to have given up luxuries such as fear or worry. What had he to fear? His own body was a horror worse than death.

The only sentinel in sight was a human seated in a plank sentry box twenty paces along the wall. A dented pot helmet rested over his eyes, and he snored with great dedication. At his feet a clay jug lay on its side. The sentry wasn't going to awaken any time soon.

Porthios sidled up to the sentry box. Pulling the torch from its bracket, he dropped it to the hard-packed ground outside the stockade. It went out. Keeping clear of the snoring sentinel, he squatted in the narrow sentry box and carefully peeled the bloody gloves from his hands. He rinsed his gloves in the filthy water of the guard's fire bucket. Lifting the discarded clay jug, he heard liquid sloshing within. He poured it over his hands.

Unfortunately it wasn't wine, but brandy, and it burned like vitriol on his insulted hands. Violent words bubbled in his throat, but he choked them down as he shook his stinging hands to dry them. Ablutions done, he tucked the damp gloves into his sash and slipped out of the sentry box. He descended the ladder to the ground.

By night Samustal was busy. The clang of smiths' hammers striking anvils mixed with incoherent shouts of revelry and the sound of glass shattering. Dogs barked and donkeys brayed. Porthios hoped he wouldn't encounter any animals. Human senses were feeble compared to those of elves, so wily raiders such as Samuval and his lieutenants kept packs of fierce hounds with them in Qualinesti. Dogs could see or scent elves where a human never would.

The elaborate arbors of Bianost had been hacked down and its famous gardens turned into pasturage for war-horses. Free fountains, found in every square of a Qualinesti town, were broken, and the basins were filled with garbage. Over everything hung the same ugly stench he had detected while still in the woods outside of town.

Evidence of looting and violence was everywhere. No glass remained in the street-level windows of any house, and the openings were boarded over. If any of the original inhabitants remained, they didn't dare show any sign of life to the marauding brigands outside. Some houses had been burned out, leaving only blackened shells, like the gaping mouth of a corpse. The smell of fire still clung to the ruins. Every gutter was clogged with broken stones, burned timbers, smashed crockery, and innumerable rats, living and dead.

Fortunately one landmark remained: the town hall tower. Porthios had learned the slave market was held in the town's central square. The town hall fronted the square. Using the tower as a landmark, and keeping to the darkest alleys and side streets, he worked his way toward the square.

A bonfire blazing in the middle of the intersection of two broad streets halted him. Illuminated by it was a quartet of armed bandits talking in loud voices.

"Goin' to the execution?" asked one.

"Can't," replied a second. "Got guard duty at the gate."

"Too bad. Should be something to see."

"Ah, it's not like she's a real woman, just an elf one."

Porthios stiffened.

"Should be a sight to see, though. Lord Olin ordered her flayed alive. He brought an ogre all the way from Broken to do the job proper!"

Harsh laughter sounded, and the third bandit said, "Olin knows how to send a message! She helped a dozen slaves escape the holding cage, and was riding off on Lord Olin's own horse when they caught her!"

More laughter erupted. Ugly remarks were exchanged, ignorant speculation about the anatomy of elves compared to that of humans. Porthios felt his initial anger swell to cold fury.

The first bandit gestured at a dark heap lying on the ground several yards away, just beyond the fire's glow.

"How's he doing?"

One of his comrades went and prodded the heap with a booted foot. Porthios realized the shapeless pile of rags was a person, lying facedown on the pavement.

The bandit returned, reporting, "Out cold, but still breathing."

They debated whether they should rouse their captive. Evidently the four had been questioning him rather vigorously and the poor wretch had passed out, unable to bear his suffering.

Porthios circled around the bonfire, keeping to the deep shadows. When he reached the prone figure, he knelt and rolled the fellow over.

The unfortunate captive was an elf of considerable age. He'd been badly beaten. Porthios lifted the lid of one eye to see if he still lived.

The blue iris fixed on him, eye going wide in fear. "Peace. I will not hurt you," Porthios whispered.

"Do not give me away," the elf gasped, speaking Qualinesti as Porthios had. "I need this respite."

PAUL B. THOMPSON & TONYA C. COOK

"Who are you?"

"Kasanth, once councilor to the lord mayor."

"Why do they torture you?"

"They seek the treasury." Kasanth swallowed with difficulty. "It was hidden before they came."

"Why not tell them what they want to know?" A town's treasury couldn't be worth so much suffering.

The aged elf's eyes gleamed with pride. "The Speaker himself charged me with its protection."

For a moment Porthios thought the poor fellow meant him, but of course Kasanth was referring to Gilthas. He admired the old councilor, enduring such agony for the sake of honor, but that it should be done on behalf of Gilthas disgusted Porthios. Gilthas might be the son of Porthios's sister, but that could not erase the taint he carried, the human ancestry of his father, Tanis Half-Elven.

In the seconds it took for those thoughts to pass through Porthios's mind, Kasanth's expression altered, and he seized Porthios's arm. With a surprising burst of strength, he pulled himself up until they were eye to eye.

"My lord! Is it you? You've returned!" he gasped, joy suffusing his bloodied face. "The treasure is in the sky!"

Porthios shushed him, but the damage had been done. As the old fellow collapsed, dead, the bandits turned to spot the intruder. They yelled at him, but he melted into the shadows, easily eluding their clumsy pursuit.

My lord! You've returned!

Had the old elf recognized Porthios, even through the mask? Or was it a last delusion? The dying sometimes were granted more than mortal vision. Either way, Kasanth's murder was added to the many outrages Porthios had witnessed in the town. Very soon there would be a reckoning.

It was nearly midnight when he reached the town square. Wooden cages ringed the plaza, holding pens for slaves waiting their turn on the block. The pens were empty. The auction block itself was a wooden platform on the east end of the square, facing the lord mayor's residence. Twenty feet long and ten feet wide, the stout platform held five equally stout posts spaced along its length. From each post hung thick iron manacles.

In the center of the square was a public fountain, a marble obelisk from which (in better times) four streams of water flowed. Only one still worked. The fountain basin, carved by dwarf masons from a single block of soapstone, was cracked in three places. Moss grew on the pavers. A prisoner, Porthios saw, was chained to the obelisk.

Was the prisoner the rebellious female, awaiting her terrible execution?

Porthios studied the scene a long time before leaving the shelter of the slave pens and approaching the fountain. Few people were about. None paid the tattered figure any heed. He halted by the seated prisoner's feet.

She had been abused, though not so thoroughly as Kasanth. One eye was ringed with a black bruise. Cuts and older bruises decorated her face, neck, and arms. Her hair was filthy, and stood up in stiff spikes all over her head.

He thought her asleep, but suddenly she sprang at him, only to be jerked up short by her heavy fetters.

"Want to see more?" she hissed. "Come closer."

"A charming invitation, which I shall decline," he said in Qualinesti.

She sank back on the soapstone basin. "Who are you?" she asked in the same tongue.

"Someone who can help you."

"Then do it!"

"In good time." Porthios was intrigued. Despite a slight accent, she did not speak as an uneducated peasant. "What is your name?"

She glared at him. He repeated the question. When still she remained silent he added, "Perhaps you think someone else will come along to help you? Flaying is a terrible way to die, I hear."

"Step forward so I may see you better." He eyed her shackled hands, and she snapped, "You've nothing to fear from me if you're telling the truth!"

He stepped forward. The light from the distant bonfires showed her his mask and robes and her eyes widened. "What is this, a masquerade?"

"It is. Give me your name."

She rose to her feet, standing proudly although weighed down by many chains. "I am Kerianseray, general of the armies of the united elven nations, wife and consort to Gilthas, Speaker of the Sun and Stars!"

He stared. Was she mad or merely lying? If Olin or his master, Samuval, knew they had the fabled Lioness of Qualinesti in their hands, they would shout it from the rooftops. Then they would sell her to the Knights of Neraka for a king's ransom. Despite the improbability, Porthios halfway believed her. He'd come looking for a diversion to start a revolt. Instead he'd found a weapon of great power.

"Can you prove what you say?"

"Get me out of here, and I'll prove anything you need!"

Porthios didn't hesitate. He wouldn't allow an elf of any caste to be executed by a filthy ogre.

"When are you scheduled to die?" he asked.

"The day after tomorrow. Two hours after dawn, before the slave auction begins. They want my carcass on display to frighten the rest."

He fingered her chains. There were many, but they were brass, not iron. A steel file would cut through them in no time.

He turned, and she hissed, "Where are you going?"

"Be patient. I'll be back tomorrow night."

"No!" She shook her chains, nearly shouting in her fury. "Get me out of here now!"

"Be patient," he repeated and was gone, vanishing among the slave cages.

*   *   *   *   *

The day of the execution dawned hot, with white haze rising to fill the sky early. Nalaryn and his Kagonesti knelt in the high weeds, bows resting in the crooks of their arms, and watched streams of travelers making their way into Samustal.

Porthios had returned from his reconnoiter the first night and shared what he'd learn about the doomed female prisoner, taking care to mention her name only to Nalaryn.

He was not with his band now. Conspicuous in his mask by daylight, he chose to make his own way inside.

When Nalaryn judged the crowd of travelers to be sufficiently numerous, he bade his warriors and the Nerakan prisoners rise. Crowded together, the humans muttered about making a break, looking to Jeralund for guidance. If they raised an outcry, nearby humans would surely help them against their elf captors.

The sergeant shook his head curtly. The travelers would be of no help to them. They were simple traders, local farmers, and craftsmen. The elves were armed, alert.

The sight of armed Kagonesti, many in full forest paint, sent the local folk scattering off the path. That the elves were escorting human captives excited much comment, but as Jeralund had expected, no one spoke out in the Nerakans' defense.

At the stockade gate, a tall human in russet leather demanded to know Nalaryn's business in Samustal.

"Same as everyone else," Nalaryn replied. He gestured with his chin at the Nerakans. "We have slaves to sell."

The guard was dumbstruck. He hastily consulted his fellows. There was no order forbidding trafficking by elves in human slaves. The opposite case occurred daily. Unable to find even a flimsy excuse to exclude the Kagonesti, the guard said he'd be happy to admit them as soon as they paid the entry tax. The amount he named was double that demanded of previous parties.

"I'll give you twenty steel pieces. That is enough."

The bandit took the threadbare velvet purse Nalaryn handed him, but did not move away. Grinning at his fellows, he demanded more steel.

The Kagonesti leader regarded him for a moment then said quietly, "I do have more steel."

"I'll take all the steel I can get!" The bandit stuck out his hand.

Nalaryn wore a dagger given to him by the commander of the Qualinesti Rangers for his service to the Throne of the Sun. In a swift, smooth motion, he drew the dagger and drove its steel blade through the outstretched palm. The bandit shouted hoarsely and dropped to his knees. His comrades reached for their weapons but found themselves facing nineteen Kagonesti bows at full draw.

Nalaryn sheathed his knife after wiping the blade with two fingers and flicking the blood to the dusty soil. He started through the gate. The guards hesitated then fell back, unwilling to challenge twenty Kagonesti. Once Nalaryn passed through the opening, he stood aside and waited for the line of elves and prisoners to pass.

None of the injured man's comrades came to his aid. They turned back to their duties, with a different bandit inspecting the next party waiting in line. Nalaryn fell in at the rear of his band. The human must have been using his position to line his own pockets, and not sharing with his comrades, else they probably would have been more willing to avenge him. He would be lucky if they didn't cut his throat and rob him of the steel he'd already squeezed out of the day's entries.

When Nalaryn was once more at the head of the line, Jeralund hailed him. "You played that well."

"I've met his type before."

"Human trash?"

Nalaryn shrugged. "I did not say so. It would be easier if all despicable folk were of one race, but they're not."

The crowds grew thicker as they drew near the main square. Aside from the obvious merchants and peddlers, there were many folk unencumbered by wares, dressed well, and discreetly armed with slender, courtly blades. They were called "buntings," nicknamed for the colorful migratory birds. They had come to Qualinesti after the fall of the elves, bought (or stole) land, bribed the new masters to favor them in business, and exploited the poor with low wages and predatory lending. Most were humans from regions less damaged by the war, but there were a few dark elves among them. If anyone in Qualinesti was hated more than Captain Samuval, it was the richly bedecked buntings who had followed in his wake.

The progress of the Kagonesti and their human captives through Samustal did not go unnoticed. Windows above street level opened, and hard-looking men leaned out of them. They were Lord Olin's men, still bare chested from having been roused from their beds. They followed the procession of armed elves with hostile eyes, but no one interfered with Nalaryn's band.

The pens in the square were filled with unfortunates waiting to be sold. Each cage held as many as a dozen captives; slave drivers armed with whips and clubs stood ready to quell any resistance.

The air of excitement was thick. Jeralund stretched to see over the crowd, looking for the doomed female elf at the heart of it all. An especially tall figure draped in black he took to be the ogre executioner hired by Lord Olin. A ring of bandits, swords drawn, stood shoulder to shoulder around the central fountain. The wall of bandits prevented Jeralund from getting more than a fleeting glimpse of the chained prisoner.

Nalaryn was unnerved by the crowd, which was especially boisterous, come not only to buy and sell slaves, but to see the bloody execution. His party was drawing a great deal of attention. Many people pushed in to get a closer look at the unlikely spectacle of elves with human captives.

He finally reached the head of the line at the auction master's table. "We have eight humans in prime condition," he announced.

The auction master squinted, his one-eyed gaze raking over the curious sight before him. "Soldiers don't usually sell well," he said, shaking his head. "Tend to be troublemakers."

"These aren't professionals, just hired blades. Someone could buy them for bodyguards."

The auction master thought a moment then nodded and pulled out a parchment slip. His assistant spilled a blob of molten red wax on the bottom, and the master pressed a heavy brass seal into the wax. He wrote a three-digit number on the slip with a few quick scratches of a quill.

"This is your seller's mark. When the lot sells, the buyer will get an identical sealed slip, with the same number. Don't lose it. You can't collect a copper without it."

The Nerakans were turned over to the slave drivers. As they were herded to the pens, they protested, insisting they were free men, soldiers of the Dark Order. Their complaints were ignored. Most of the slave drivers were goblins, indifferent to the most pathetic appeals for help. With cracking whips, they herded the Nerakans into a cage and secured the heavy wooden door with a brass lock the size of a smoked ham.

Thinking their last chance to break away had passed, the terrified soldiers fell on Jeralund, cursing him for his poor leadership. That earned them a dousing from buckets of filthy water thrown by the slave drivers outside.

"No fighting in the cage! Next one who throws a punch gets branded!"

Nose and upper lip bleeding, Jeralund hunkered down alone on the far side of the cage. Locked into a cage and awaiting the auction block, he still held onto hope. It wasn't too late. Not yet.

"You have faith, human."

Jeralund was smart enough not to whirl toward the voice. He hissed, "What are you up to, Scarecrow?"

Something hard pressed against his shoulder. Jeralund put a hand behind his back and his fingers closed on the hilt of a rag-draped sword. His eyes widened.

"I have four weapons. That's all I could conceal."

Jeralund pulled the swords around and tucked the pommels into his armpit. He called to his comrades. Three sullenly approached. When the sergeant passed each of them a sword, their gloom evaporated. They wanted to know how he had managed to get the weapons.

"Ask the Scarecrow," he said, gesturing with his chin over one shoulder.

There was no sign of him. Jeralund did see a rather thin slave driver walking away. The fellow wore the usual leather jerkin and floppy trews and carried a coiled whip in his gloved hand. He also wore a broad-brimmed hat pulled down low on his head. None of the other slave drivers were gloved or hatted. He was quickly swallowed by the churning crowd.

One of Jeralund's men railed at the strange development. Why drag them to Samustal as prisoners then give them arms to fight? The sergeant realized the truth. The Scarecrow wanted to get himself and his followers into Samustal. A party of armed elves would have been barred, but as slavers escorting prisoners, they would more likely be allowed in. With his need for captives at an end, the Scarecrow was giving them a fighting chance to escape.

That still didn't answer the question of why the Scarecrow needed to get inside Samustal. Jeralund didn't care at that moment. He had to concentrate on their escape.

He studied the cage. The oak bars were as thick as his wrist. Their swords would never chop through before the slave drivers noticed. The same was true of the massive brass lock; hacking through it would take time and draw the attention of the guards. What did that leave?

Hinges. The hinges of the cage door were thick leather straps. If their borrowed blades were sharp, one or two strokes would be enough to sever the hinges. Jeralund called his men together and quietly shared his plan.

Porthios continued to wend his way through the crowd. For once, he blessed the mask he wore. It covered the emotions he knew were showing plainly on his face. The proximity of so many nonelves and their revolting activities sickened him. This was what came of allowing inferior peoples too much latitude. How low the world had fallen into corruption and decadence!

Consider the ants, not the solitary cicada. Like the bloated, doomed cicada, the slave market was about to encounter Porthios and his ants.

A brace of tin horns blatted, and the crowd quieted a bit. A man wearing a feathered hat and gray velvet tunic stepped up onto the fountain platform and opened a parchment scroll. Apparently he had memorized his speech since he never glanced at the scroll.

"Pray heed and hear all! Hear all!" he shouted. The throng calmed a little more. "Know you that Olin Man-Daleth, Lord of Samustal, has passed judgment on this wretched, nameless slave. For treason against her rightful masters, for flight from bondage, and for general mayhem, Lord Olin has sentenced this worthless creature to death. So that her paltry end may stand as an example to all, she is to die by flaying, and her miserable remains will be exhibited here until the flies and crows claim her!"

He let the scroll curl shut. "Executioner, do your duty!"

The hooded ogre stomped onto the platform. Four slave drivers wrestled a wooden frame toward him. Comprising two lengths of timber, crossed in the center, with shackles on each end point, it was where the prisoner was to be chained during the awful procedure. The men struggled to shift the heavy timber frame into place. The ogre bellowed for them to hurry. As they set the frame into place and began pegging it down, the executioner approached Kerianseray, leering at her with mouth agape.

An arrow sprouted from his throat.

The arrow seemed to appear by magic. With a gargling roar, the ogre wrapped a hand around the shaft and jerked the arrow free. Blood welled from the wound. Many in the crowd cheered, thinking the festivities had begun.

When a second arrow buried itself in the ogre's right eye, he toppled backward like a felled tree. People closest to the fountain shouted in alarm. The screams increased as an entire volley of arrows rained down around the obelisk, taking out all the sword-wielding guards and several onlookers as well. Those in the crowd nearest the obelisk tried to get out of the way; others, farther away, surged forward, trying to see what was happening. Chaos bloomed. Pushing and shoving led to fistfights and dagger drawing. A second fall of arrows completed the transformation from execution to full-fledged riot.

When the sword-wielding guards went down, the Lioness stood up, cradling an armload of brass chains. She had been working on them for hours, sawing away with the file slipped to her by the masked stranger. She began breaking apart the weakened links. From a distance, it looked as though the elf woman had supernormal strength, tearing apart metal with her bare hands. New panic erupted in the crowd.

A slave driver, whip in hand, scrambled onto the stone platform. The Lioness planted a foot on his chest and shoved him back into the melee. The whir of approaching arrows drew her glance upward. With uncanny accuracy, the volley fell in a neat circle around her. People who had ventured too close to the obelisk retreated.

The Lioness stood over her fallen executioner. The ogre was still breathing. She drew one of the flensing blades from his belt and swiftly cut his throat. Too bad the beast didn't wear a sword.

From the corner of her eye, she saw a green-clad figure spring onto the fountain beside her. She turned, knife in hand, and found herself facing a Kagonesti armed with a forester's maul.

"I'm Nalaryn—a friend! The Masked One sent me!" he cried.

"Those are your people on the bows?" He nodded. "Good! Let's get out of here!"

This was not so easily done. A space three yards wide had opened around the fountain, but as soon as Nalaryn jumped down, ten bandits stormed forward, hacking down anyone who got in their way. The Lioness dragged her would-be rescuer back up.

With maul and knife, the two Kagonesti fended off the soldiers. A shower of arrows arrived to help, but the missiles were fewer than before. Nalaryn's archers were fighting their own battles. Above the heads of the boiling mob, Kerian could see mounted, lance-armed bandits boring in as well.

"Now what?" she shouted.

"Trust the Great Lord! This moment has been planned!"

Indeed it had. When the riot erupted, the Nerakan soldiers realized it was their time to escape. They slashed at the hinges of the cage door. Using the door like a battering ram, they bludgeoned their way clear.

Jeralund shouted to his men, "Open the other cages! Free all the prisoners!"

The unarmed Nerakans cared only for their own hides. Ignoring the sergeant, they promptly disappeared into the panicked mob. Jeralund cursed them as cowards and led his three armed comrades down the line of cages, cutting the hinges on each door. Slave drivers tried to drive them off, but with swords in hand, the soldiers could not be deterred. In quick succession they opened all the cages. Humans, elves, a gaggle of goblins, and a pair of dwarves poured out. Many of the liberated were in poor condition and could do little more than hobble away. Others put themselves at Jeralund's disposal. Unfortunately he had little to offer beyond encouraging words. It was every man for himself.

Lord Olin's lancers at last managed to cut through the mob, a dozen riders laying about indiscriminately with their weapons. Hard wooden shafts knocked friend and foe alike senseless. Breaking into the open by the slave cages, they rode hard at the escaping prisoners, impaling several before the rest swarmed over their horses and dragged them down.

A red-haired Qualinesti with a gash on his forehead appeared before Jeralund. He was leading one of the lancer's horses. The sergeant was taken aback when the fellow handed him the reins. He could have taken the animal for himself, but he presented it to the human who had set him free. Jeralund swung into the saddle and extended a hand to the elf.

The Qualinesti declined. "This is my city. I stay!" he cried and dashed into the mob.

From his higher vantage, Jeralund could see a fight still raging around the fountain. He hesitated but a moment before smacking his horse's flank with the flat of his sword. The animal sprang toward the distant fracas.

Nalaryn and the Lioness had their backs to the obelisk. Thus far they'd fended off every attempt to storm the platform. The lancers had been drawn off by the escaping slaves, but the Kagonesti archers had ceased firing too. A solid group of bandit foot soldiers had surrounded the fountain and showed no signs of giving up. They were inching closer. They well knew the penalties Lord Olin would exact if they allowed the Kagonesti female to escape.

After knocking out an especially persistent bandit, Kerian tossed a quick thank you to Nalaryn. "This is a much better death than I expected to have today, brother," she panted.

Nalaryn swung his maul, catching a bandit under the chin and sending him flying. "The Great Lord will come," he said. "Have faith!"

Kerian almost laughed. Faith? He sounded like Gilthas.

Jeralund was halfway to the fountain when he noticed the Scarecrow, standing alone and unmolested in the midst of the shrieking riot. The mysterious elf leader had shed his slaver guise, except for the hat pulled low on his forehead. People ran screaming all around him, some shouting for mercy, others for blood, but he stood silent and solid, like a tree amid a herd of stampeding cattle. Jeralund guided his horse toward the robed figure.

"Quite a storm you've raised," the sergeant called out.

The mask framed burning eyes. "It is only the first of many to come."

The tiny island of calm around them abruptly vanished. A swarm of people rushed eastward, away from the rampaging slaves. A tide of traders and buntings blundered west, trying to get out of the way of Lord Olin's enraged troops. They crashed together where the Scarecrow stood. It seemed inevitable he would be trampled to death. He disappeared beneath the crush. Jeralund lashed out with controlled fury, keeping the terrified people from toppling his horse. The mob parted for him, and the Scarecrow was gone.

Jeralund looked to the desperate fight at the fountain. Even as he watched, Nalaryn sustained a stunning blow to the back. The female elf prisoner, wielding nothing more than a knife, leaped forward and drove back his attacker, giving the Kagonesti chief time to struggle to his feet. Three more bandits bore down on them. She faced them, a broad grin on her dirty face.

"Pestilence!" Jeralund cursed, and drove his heels into his mount's flanks.

The Lioness saw the rider coming. She shifted the knife in her hand, ready to throw it. Nalaryn caught her wrist.

"No, wait!"

She stared at him as if he were mad, and the arriving horse bowled over three of Olin's men before skidding to a stop by the fountain.

"Need help, forester?" the rider bellowed.

"Every soul needs help sometime," said Nalaryn.

The human slid off the horse's right side. The two elves mounted from the left, and the Lioness took the reins.

Touching the sword hilt to his chin in mocking salute, the human said, "Good luck, forester! You and the Scarecrow will need it!" He jumped aside and melted into the surging press. They saw him no more.

Kerian urged the horse into a canter. Those who couldn't or wouldn't give way were knocked down as she made straight for the western gate. The stockade was undoubtedly locked up tight, but they stood a good chance of escaping under cover of the terrific confusion. Kerian's hand ached for a sword. She felt naked without one—worse than naked. Modesty she could live without, but a sword was an absolute necessity.

Outside the square, the mob was reduced to random folk running away and bandit patrols trying to catch slaves and restore order. Kerian and Nalaryn galloped by a company of twenty mercenaries who failed to recognize the Lioness as an escaping prisoner. Eventually the Kagonesti arrived at the approaches to the west gate. To their surprise, the timber portal was open.

They rode up slowly, wary of a trap. Dead bandits littered the street. The guards seemed to have been overwhelmed.

Nalaryn told her to stop. He dismounted and helped himself to a spear lying next to a slain guard. He retrieved a sword and handed it up to her.

Kerian turned the horse's head back to the gate. A single figure stood in the opening, silhouetted against the sun-drenched meadow beyond. Kerian rode forward slowly, the sword's wire-wrapped pommel heavy in her hand. Like the weapon, she felt hard and dangerous. The scum in this town owed her a great deal for the mistreatment she'd suffered and the deaths they'd caused.

Nalaryn, walking alongside her horse, raised the spear over his head and called, "Great Lord!"

The silhouetted figure waved in response. Kerian cursed silently. All set to have at somebody, instead she'd come upon her savior.

He gestured for her to stop. "Turn around," he said. "We're not done yet."

"What are you talking about?"

"Freeing you was only part of this day's work. The balance will be done when we liberate Bianost."

Gods protect us, he's mad, Kerian thought. She said, "Worthy goals, stranger. Exactly how do you plan to liberate the town? The garrison must number several thousand."

"Two thousand, by my estimate."

"Only two thousand! That makes it easy, then!"

"You have performed greater feats of arms than this, Kerianseray. "And you forget," the stranger added, "we aren't facing disciplined troops. If we storm the mayor's palace and slay Olin, the common bandits will flee."

She glanced at Nalaryn. He obviously was prepared to do whatever his Great Lord desired. She asked how many troops they had. Twenty, Nalaryn said, if all yet survived.

Her laugh was short and harsh. Twenty! Against Olin's household guard? "Even if we can do it, what's the point, here in the heart of occupied Qualinesti? Samuval will send an army to retake the town, and his revenge will be ferocious!"

The stranger came forward until he stood by her horse's nose. He patted the animal then tilted his head to look up at her. She frowned at the mask he wore, wondering what this odd creature was playing at. His accent told her he was Qualinesti, although it was possible that could be faked.

"All fires begin with a single spark," he said. "Besides, a rebellion must have steel as well as arms, and there's a treasure hidden in this town. Olin hasn't been able to find it. I can."

"What kind of treasure?"

He didn't answer but looked beyond her as new shouting welled from the center of town. The swell of noise rolled over them like a great wave. The riot in the slave market was spreading. If the town rose up, the bandits were doomed. Many in Samustal hated Lord Olin's rule.

"The town may be sacked before Samuval comes, Great Lord. If there is treasure, we'd better act swiftly," Nalaryn said. He went to stand at his leader's right shoulder. They waited in silence for Kerian's answer. It wasn't long in coming.

"I'll fight for you on two conditions." Her chin lifted. "*I* command your army, such as it is. I answer only to you."

Nalaryn raised an eyebrow but made no objection. The masked elf nodded solemnly.

"Second," Kerian said, "I must know your identity. If I'm to follow you and believe in your cause, I have to know who you are. After all, this could be some strange Nerakan plot to undermine resistance in Qualinesti."

For a long moment, he stood motionless, pondering, then spoke quietly to Nalaryn. The Kagonesti chief moved away to the gate and turned his back. When he was gone, the masked elf came to stand only inches from her horse's side.

Very softly he said, "On the scaffold, you revealed yourself to me, so I will do the same. But believe me when I tell you that if you betray this confidence to anyone, you will die."

Threats did not usually impress her, but something in his voice, and in the eyes that bored into her own, told her he was in deadly earnest. She nodded once. She would keep the secret of his identity.

He put a finger below the bottom edge of his mask. A heartbeat passed, and another, then he lifted the cloth up to his forehead.

Kerianseray, battle-hardened Lioness of legend, recoiled in horror. The mask came back down.

"I was once Porthios, Speaker of the Sun," he said. "Now my fate is yours, and yours is mine."

7

Fighting raged in the streets of Samustal all day and into the night. The small band of elves moved through the town, striking anywhere the bandits managed to rally. Despite the intense fighting, not a single Kagonesti was injured. Kerian received a few cuts and bruises—nothing compared to what she'd already been through—and Porthios, unarmed and unafraid, did not get a scratch. He walked through furious skirmishes like a shadow, seemingly impervious to harm.

Despite the elves' spectacular showing, the victory really belonged to the oppressed people of Bianost, who rose up when trouble erupted. Armed with sticks, tools, whatever came to hand, they threw themselves on their oppressors. Weapons weighed down by the bodies of courageous attackers, the bandits were overcome as waves of angry townsfolk flooded over them.

The cost to the elves was terrible, but they took on Olin's mercenary legion and destroyed it. The last bandits abandoned the town before dawn, piling into carts or riding any four-legged animal they could steal. As they fled, they were pelted with rotten fruit, stones, and the jeers of the townsfolk.

Porthios, the Lioness, and the Kagonesti band went to the mayor's palace. The bulk of Olin's troops were gone, slain in the rioting. His personal guard still stood watch at the mayor's residence, but they had abandoned the outer porticos to cluster together by the main door, trapped by the riot. Porthios led his band directly to the palace's front steps. The elves marched in close order, wearing mantles and helmets taken from fallen bandits. Arrows found vital organs, mauls cracked skulls, and the guards fell. Then the way was clear.

The Lioness dueled with a bandit officer until a helpful archer put an arrow through his throat. Porthios stood apart, watching her wade through the fracas.

When she rejoined him, bloody and panting, Porthios remarked, "You're not the fighter I expected, though you have the reputation of being quite a slayer."

"I wasn't born in a palace. I never had fencing lessons," she retorted, sheathing her captured blade. "I have killed many enemies. It isn't style that matters, only winning."

Porthios couldn't argue with that. One shouldn't expect style or finesse from a peasant, no matter how experienced.

He led the way inside. Ignoring his followers' objections, he threw open the mansion's double doors. Three crossbow bolts thudded into the panels next to his head. Unimpressed, he shouted, "Olin Man-Daleth! Come out and face justice!"

Kerian dragged him aside as more bolts whizzed down the hall. Behind her, Nalaryn had glimpsed the bowmen. With silent gestures, he dispatched four of his people down the side corridors to deal with them.

"You're too bold for your own good," Kerian told Porthios tartly. "This revolution will come to a sudden end if you stop an arrow."

"You're wrong. What has started cannot be stopped by a single arrow."

He entered, striding down the center of the ornate hall, calmly examining the bas-reliefs that depicted the rise of the Qualinesti nation. The hall had been defaced by Olin's men. Statues had heads and limbs hacked off, and the travertine floor showed deep scratches where hobnailed boots and spurs had scored the stone.

They investigated the entire palace, flushing out a few hidden bandits, who died fighting. When they reached the lord mayor's audience hall, they found a crowd of servants huddled behind the sky-blue and gold tapestries. Kerian drove them out from concealment at sword point. There were eleven, five women and six men. All wore Olin's livery, a dark green tabard with a triangle of silver daggers.

"Please, good lords, don't kill us!" one quavered. "We're humble folk pressed to duty against our will!"

Porthios would've dismissed them, but Kerian did not waver. Something didn't feel right, she said. The servants could have fled at any time, and why were they still wearing Olin's colors, unless they were supposed to be found so dressed?

She told the archers to keep them covered and grabbed the closest servant, a middle-aged woman with brindled hair. She turned the woman's hand palm up then sniffed her sleeve.

"Kitchen. Scrubwoman," she announced and pulled the tabard over the woman's head. "Go on, get out."

She repeated this performance for each human, announcing their place in the household by the marks on their hands and the smell of their clothes: baker, wine steward, scullery maid, keeper of hounds.

The sixth, a man, revealed a pair of callused palms with clean, well-trimmed nails. It didn't take a sensitive nose to notice he was wearing scent. She laid her sword on his shoulder.

"Who are you?"

"Theydrin. Lord Olin's valet."

"Where is Olin?" Porthios demanded.

The man glanced at his masked captor with curiosity. "I don't know, sir. May I go?"

In response, Kerian slashed hard across the man's chest. His green tabard fell away, showing them a close-fitting shirt of fine mail.

"It's Olin!" Kerian shouted, leaping back.

The fellow's reply was to take hold of the female servant closest to him and put a curved dagger to her throat. "I'll slit her gullet if you try to stop me!"

Porthios shrugged. "So? One less human will hardly distress me."

"Wait." Kerian spoke as much to the Kagonesti as to Olin. Nalaryn's band had nocked arrows and was preparing to draw.

"Kill them both," Porthios ordered.

Bows creaked back to full stretch. The implacable faces of the Wilder elves were too much for the bandit lord. He released his hostage. Kerian pulled her out of the way. Olin dropped his dagger and held out his hands.

"I have treasure! I'll pay a ransom! You'll all be rich!" he babbled.

"Treasure stolen from the people of Qualinesti."

So saying, Porthios lifted a hand, and two of the Kagonesti loosed. They aimed low, and their arrows took Olin from opposite sides. He shrieked in agony and slumped to the ground. Another Kagonesti finished Olin with a blow from his maul. Horrified, the last weeping servants fled.

Kerian returned her blade to its sheath. "Is this how it's to be?" she asked. "No quarter?"

"You would show mercy to the man who ordered you flayed alive?" Porthios stared up at the ornate ceiling. "Olin was a brutal killer. All murderers can expect the same. Does that trouble you?"

Kerian knelt by Olin and took his purse. It contained steel coins, several large gems rolled in a silk scarf, and a ring with a dozen iron keys. She shook the ring of keys.

"We should see what locks these open. Prison cells, or treasure rooms, as he said."

"Free the elf prisoners. I don't care what you do with the rest. Let the people of Bianost have his stolen hoard."

His continuing distracted study of the ceiling caused Kerian to look up. The arched ceiling of the audience hall was covered by a mural depicting Kith-Kanan flying on Arcuballis, his famous griffon. The pair soared across a blue sky dotted here and there with puffy white clouds. The painting was well rendered, but the scene was a common one in official Qualinesti buildings. Testily, she asked whether he was enjoying the artwork.

"Very much," he murmured. He told them of Kasanth, the councilor he'd found being tortured for not revealing the whereabouts of a royal trove.

"He said the treasure was in the sky. I think Olin was closer to it than he ever imagined," Porthios said, pointing upward. "We must get up there."

The way proved fiendishly difficult. The Bianost palace was old, with a convoluted layout comprising many rooms. Only by rapping on the walls and finding a hollow spot did the elves locate the concealed door. Behind it was a dark, very steep stairway.

Gifted with excellent vision in the dark, the elves needed no torches. Porthios immediately entered, and the others were close behind. Kerian commented that although the door had been well hidden, the wooden steps were clean of dust. Someone had passed that way not too long ago.

The stairs reversed direction, obviously angling out from the wall and following the rise of the arched ceiling. As the party climbed higher, the stuffy heat increased. The passage ended abruptly on a stone wall with no door, no hatch, nothing.

"No one builds a stair to nowhere," Kerian muttered. "There must be a hidden door."

Porthios told his followers not to bother with subtlety, so the Kagonesti battered the walls until something yielded. Low to the floor, a thin wooden panel, painted to resemble stone, shattered under their blows. Wincing with stiffness, Porthios knelt on one knee and peered in, but even his keen eyes could not pierce the profound darkness beyond.

One of the Kagonesti produced flint and steel. A wad of cloth was tied to an arrow shaft and set alight. Porthios thrust the fitfully burning torch inside.

Kerian fidgeted at his silence and even faithful Nalaryn couldn't bear the suspense. "What do you see, Great Lord?"

"Wonderful things!" Porthios said, hoarse voice filled with emotion. "I see the freedom of our race!"

* * * * *

ALLIANCES

Like a drop of oil spreading out on the surface of calm water, the bandits, buntings, and slavers expelled from Samustal raced in all directions, seeking other havens in Samuval's stolen realm. Some went no farther than Griffon's Ford, fifteen miles from Olin's fallen stronghold, where they found another of Samuval's lieutenants encamped.

Gathan Grayden was known as Gathan the Good, an ironic appellation earned by his carefully chosen appearance. Most bandit lords affected a fearsome exterior, with garish tattoos, gaudy armor, extravagant weapons, and a loud, blustering manner. Not Gathan. He dressed simply but in the finest style, spoke softly, and carried himself like a nobleman of impeccable lineage. In fact he was easily the most ruthless of Samuval's underlings. His fief, centered on the town of Frenost, northwest of Samustal, was the most pacified in all of Qualinesti.

Once a month he led most of his troops on a long, circuitous march through his territory. That kept his soldiers fit and reminded his subjects who was in charge. Gathan was returning from one of those marches when the first refugees from Samustal reached him at Griffon's Ford. In two days' time, several hundred bandits had gathered, swelling his total complement to two thousand soldiers. Behind the army, a mob of slavers, displaced buntings, and their lackeys gathered. They believed Gathan would restore order in no time, and they wanted to be close at hand when Samustal was recovered. Most had fled with no more than the clothes on their backs.

Gathan led his army south. As he advanced, he sent parties east and west to sweep the countryside for rebels. None were found. Scouts brought word the town still stood and was eerily calm. A few bold bandits entered the outskirts for a closer look. They reported no defenders in sight. Dead bodies there were in plenty but no rebels.

Sensing a trap, Gathan sent scouts to reconnoiter. The squalid squatters' camp ringing the old town had been burned, but the city proper appeared only lightly damaged, although in Samustal it was hard to know what was new damage and what was mere decrepitude.

The scouts entered through an unguarded gate, the clopping of their horses' hooves disturbing clouds of insects. The smell of death was familiar to all who took Samuval's coin, and it overpowered even the usual stench of Samustal. The bandits rode past the bodies of comrades, slavers, and elf townspeople. Flies and vultures were having a feast.

The captain of the scouts decided the rebels had indeed chosen the coward's course, fleeing Samustal after their coup. He summoned a rider to carry word back to Lord Gathan. The courier was just turning to canter away when an arrow took him in the side of the neck. Before he hit the ground, fifteen of his fellows likewise thudded to the dirt, arrows sprouting in necks, chests, and backs.

"Ambush! Withdraw!" the bandit captain shouted, wheeling his mount. A second volley arrived, and another ten men fell, and the captain finally caught sight of the archers. They were on the parapet of the stockade. The scouts had ridden right under them. The captain cursed the bandits who had reported the town empty of rebels.

Atop the timber wall, Kerian was doing some cursing of her own. The Kagonesti archers lined the parapet, while below several score townsfolk huddled out of sight, clutching captured arms. Since Olin's overthrow, many of the bolder residents had come and asked to serve Porthios. He allowed them that honor.

"You missed the commander," she snapped at Nalaryn, crouching near her.

"We hit where we aim. The first rider would've carried word back to their general."

"We ought to have taken them all," she said darkly. Any that survived could warn their comrades as well as the first one.

The late-afternoon sun threw long shadows across the streets below, and bandits could be seen riding up the side streets parallel to the stockade. Roofs and chimney pots shielded the enemy. The Kagonesti ceased their punishing rain. Porthios did not send out his newly formed militia; the townsfolk would be no match for the mounted bandits.

"They must have more troops nearby. We should never have delayed. We should've left this place immediately."

Kerian knew her grumbling was pointless. Liberating the secret cache from the attic of the mayor's palace had kept them in Bianost when they otherwise would have made straight for the safety of the woodland. Nobody had expected bandits to return so quickly or in such numbers.

"Do you fear the enemy?"

Kerian turned. Porthios was climbing the stairs to the battlement. His ragged robe flapped around his gaunt legs like the wings of the crows that infested the town. She glared at him.

"Of course I fear them! Twenty warriors and a mob of civilians against an unknown number of trained mercenaries?"

He looked away, seemingly unconcerned, and her anger grew. She yelled down to the townsfolk below, describing the red and yellow livery of the bandits the Kagonesti had stung. She was told those were the colors of Gathan Grayden.

Kerian recognized the name. She had learned a lot about conditions in Qualinesti during her brief but turbulent time as a slave. Porthios seemed unimpressed by her description of the bandit leader as the worst of Samuval's lieutenants. He stared out over the parapet, although there was little to see. Gathan wasn't foolish enough to parade his army for his enemies to count.

In fact, Porthios was deep in thought. The strain of taking the town, coupled with finding an unexpected bounty concealed in the mayor's palace, had set his mind racing. He'd half expected to die liberating Bianost from Lord Olin's yoke. The future, once confined to a narrow woodland path and a nameless death, appeared much wider. But he had to proceed carefully. He must continue to be bold, or his rebellion would be crushed by Samuval's superior might. Yet every move had to be considered with care. The entire responsibility lay on his shoulders. Kerianseray was a patriot and a good fighter but hadn't the finesse to guide the campaign Porthios imagined. His small force must be led with the right attitude.

A leader must ignore the petty troubles that plague lesser minds. Porthios's divine encounter in the woodland had taught him that. He could not allow himself to be distracted by tactical problems. He must concentrate on the grand strategy. The god had shown him that only by looking beyond the obvious and the commonplace could he free his people.

A shout from the Lioness drew his attention to the street below. The surviving bandits had made their way to other gates and were spurring for the north road. Before they reached the woods, more of their mounted comrades appeared among the trees, along with sizable companies of foot soldiers. A veritable hedge of pikes filled the road.

"Are they massing to attack?" Porthios asked.

Kerian slumped, turning to sit on the narrow parapet with her back against the stockade. "No," she said glumly. "They're encircling us. Grayden doesn't need to storm the town. He can't know how many we are, so attacking the wall would be a waste of soldiers. He's only got to trap us here till hunger and thirst force us to yield, or until he can overwhelm us."

"How do you know?"

"It's what I would do."

Grim silence reigned. Then Porthios drew a deep breath.

"We can't allow the cache to fall into bandit hands. I'd rather see it destroyed first," he said. "So we must fight."

He stood. Instantly, an arrow whizzed by his shoulder, ripping his sleeve as it passed. Kerian grabbed the front of his robe with both hands and dragged him down behind the sharpened logs.

"Take your hands off me."

She remembered the face under the mask and let go abruptly. With much affronted dignity, Porthios stood again and descended the steps to the street.

Kerian shook her head. She'd known other warriors like him. Bravest of the brave they often were, but frightening. Placing little value on their own lives, they often didn't value anyone else's either.

She and Nalaryn peered carefully over the barrier. Here and there, elf eyes could pick out bandit archers settling into position among the burned-out ruins of the squatters' camp.

Telling Nalaryn to hold his place, Kerian climbed down to the street and followed Porthios back toward the town square.

Once the setting of slave auctions, executions, and Olin's unsavory entertainments, the square was again a gathering place for the elves of Bianost. Kerian had thought most of the original inhabitants were long gone, driven out or sold away into slavery. But several hundred had gathered, eager to serve their liberator. The word had spread to gather in the square, and the sudden arrival of Gathan Grayden seemed only to whet their appetite for battle.

Porthios walked ahead of Kerian. As he entered the square, his pace slowed. The crowd of elves shifted toward him, determined to get a closer look at their benefactor.

The scene felt oddly familiar to Kerian, reminding her of Gilthas's progress through the tent city of the exiled elves in Khur. The Speaker of the Sun and Stars was regarded as the noblest being in the world, but while his grateful subjects were welcome to approach the kindly Gilthas, none tried to accost Porthios. Curiosity and gratitude brought them near, but his forbidding demeanor arrested their enthusiasm. Scores lined the way, but not one hand reached out for his ragged robe. Their expressions were different too.

She had nearly reached the fountain in the center of the square before she identified the difference. The Speaker of the Sun and Stars represented a lofty ideal. Porthios was a reflection of each of them, the rage and shame of every elf in the subjugated lands, personified in one gaunt, shabby frame.

The slave pens had been torn down by the mob. Since then, debris and garbage had been removed from the central fountain. Seeing that, Kerian wondered aloud about restoring the flow of water.

An elf standing on the stone platform by the obelisk said, "There is no water."

"What, none? None at all?"

He explained the feeder pipes were broken or choked with garbage. "Olin never bothered to keep them up. For months, all water has been carried in."

"In from where?" asked the Lioness, eyes narrowing.

"From the springs in the meadow south of town."

The squatters' camp had grown up when traders became tired of tramping in and out of the stockade for water. They moved outside to be closer to the springs.

Kerian gestured peremptorily for Porthios to accompany her. Conscious of being watched by hundreds, he followed. They ascended the steps of the mayor's palace.

Out of earshot of the crowd, she hissed, "Did you hear? The bandits have us cut off from our only water supply!"

"There are rain cisterns under the streets. We'll drink that."

Heatedly, she pointed out the cisterns were likely nearly dry after the long summer drought. Any water in them would be stagnant, an invitation to disease.

"Then we will fight and win before we get thirsty," Porthios said.

The Lioness's famous temper nearly broke. Porthios had achieved amazing things, but his bland indifference to their safety made her furious. All the old enmity between city lord and woodland elf welled up inside her for the first time since leaving Khur. This arrogant, mutilated noble was gambling with all their lives!

There was no telling what she might have done had not fate intervened in the person of one of Nalaryn's Kagonesti, a female called Sky. She jogged up the steps, calling for Kerian and the Great Lord. They were wanted back at the north wall.

Kerian clutched her filthy hair with both hands. "What now?" she groaned.

"The bandits are fighting," Sky said and took off.

Kerian took that to mean Nalaryn's band was in peril. She headed down the steps without even looking to see whether Porthios followed.

The crowd of elves in the square peppered her with anxious

questions. She fended them off but quickly realized that was a mistake.

"The bandits are coming back," she announced, not breaking stride. "If you value your liberty and love your race, follow me and bring a weapon. The battle is now!"

There were only a few cries of fear. In a body, the elves grabbed whatever makeshift weapons they could find and streamed after the Lioness.

Near the stockade, Kerian heard the telltale sounds of battle. Entering the last street inside the wall, she was surprised to see Nalaryn's Kagonesti crouched below the parapet. They did not appear to be engaged, so who was fighting?

She raced up the steps. Behind, the elves of Bianost gripped unfamiliar weapons, their strained faces turned upward.

"What's going on?" Kerian demanded.

One of the Kagonesti pointed wordlessly. Kerian put an eye to a chink between the logs and peeked out. She drew a breath in sharply.

Beyond the wasteland of squatters' shanties a considerable battle was indeed taking place. Gathan Grayden's soldiers, some on foot and some mounted, were milling around their leader's fluttering standard. No one on the stockade could identify his foe through rising clouds of ash and dirt, but Nalaryn offered a bleak and logical opinion. The rats who'd fled Olin's town had carried word of his downfall in all directions. The newcomers were probably troops of another bandit lord who sought to grab Olin's former territory.

"This may be a well-chewed bone, but they'll fight like rabid dogs to possess it," he said.

Kerian watched as lancers in bright breastplates charged through Grayden's disordered ranks. His attention had been focused entirely on the town. He had not expected an attack from elsewhere. The mercenaries formed squares to hold off the cavalry, but they were isolated from each other and unable to do anything but fight to stay alive.

Before the sun set, the battle was over. Grayden himself, surrounded by his best retainers, abandoned the field. His men he left to the mercies of the victor, and like Olin's mercenaries before them, the bandits broke and scattered. The last Kerian saw of Gathan Grayden was his standard, borne away by a warrior on a black horse.

The townsfolk, watching the melee through gaps in the logs at ground level, set up a cheer when Grayden's soldiers fled. Kerian silenced them with a thunderous command. The cure might prove worse than the disease.

A block of mounted warriors trotted toward the stockade. The Kagonesti nocked arrows and awaited the order to loose. The approaching column numbered perhaps three hundred.

It was either fight or surrender, and for her part, Kerian had no intention of allowing herself to be chained again. Better to die right here and now.

She gripped her captured sword tightly. Only a modest archer, she left that art to those far more capable. Soon there would be plenty of fighting to go around.

The mounted column halted at the edge of the burned-out section of shanties. A smaller contingent of two score riders came on.

Still peering through the gap between the timbers, Kerian muttered, "I wonder if the Scarecrow has a secret weapon."

"Only my mind, and my vision."

He was not two feet behind her, looking out over the notched parapet with customary nonchalance. One day he was going to stop an arrow. She said as much.

"But not today. Can you not see? Those are elves."

Had he showered the assembled defenders with steel, he could not have astonished them more. Kerian rose partway from her crouch, looking over the top of the timber bulwark. The riders' armor was commonplace half-plate; their helmets open-faced. Mercenaries from Beacon to Rymdar wore the same harness. Neither did their horses' trapping reveal any distinctive elven style. What did Porthios see?

The contingent halted just within bowshot. A cloud slid across the sinking sun, and when its shadow covered the field, Kerian finally saw the riders' insignia. Their bright breastplates bore a symbol inlaid in silver. In full light the contrast was too poor to see at a distance.

The symbol was a star, the eight-pointed star of Silvanesti.

At the forefront, the ranks parted, and three riders emerged, leaving the others behind. The riders on each end were male, one in a commander's helmet and mantle, the other a well-dressed noble. Riding between them, mounted on a white mare, was a female elf of great beauty. Her riding clothes were jasperine, a fine white cloth woven with gold and red highlights. She put back her hood, revealing black hair.

Kerian stared. The rider looked like . . . but it couldn't be. It was too unlikely.

The elderly noble accompanying her hailed them. Atop the log wall, no one breathed, much less answered.

"Great Lord, will you speak?" whispered Nalaryn.

There was no reply. For the first time, the unfailingly confident, supremely smug Porthios was speechless. When Kerian saw his state, she knew her guess about the woman's identity was correct. His eyes were wide. His bony shoulders trembled.

"I cannot!" Hoarse, agonized, the words fell from his lips like blood from a fresh wound. He made choking sounds. "I cannot!"

Everyone was staring, especially the local elves. What new threat could so unnerve the bold savior of Bianost?

Then, astonishingly, Porthios turned and scrambled down the ladder. He stumbled at the bottom, almost falling on his face, regained his balance, and whirled away, parting the amazed townsfolk like a plow turning fresh soil.

Outside the stockade, the noble called out again. Kerian sheathed her sword and headed for the ladder.

Nalaryn stayed her with a hand on her arm. "Are they friends?" he asked.

"They are gifts from the gods!"

She went to the sally port door cut into the stockade gate. Some of the Bianost elves, not understanding the situation, protested. She offered only brief reassurance before flinging open the door and stepping outside.

The white-clad elf woman guided her horse closer. Kerian gripped her sword hilt and stood stiffly at attention, aping the posture of a palace guard.

"Greetings," the rider said. Her voice was warm and honest. "I am glad we arrived in time. The bandits were spread thin trying to surround the town. We were fortunate to rout them."

Feeling very shabby and unkempt, Kerian passed a hand over her cropped hair and offered a bemused smile. Although the rider had spoken Qualinesti, Kerian answered in Silvanesti. She was not fluent, but more proficient than when last they'd met. "We are glad of it, too, Highness. I'd hardly expected to be rescued by family," she said.

The lovely face went blank for a handful of seconds, then: "Kerianseray?"

The name was a disbelieving whisper. Kerian's smile broadened into a grin.

Nalaryn emerged with his foresters. The Kagonesti chief asked who the noble lady was.

The mounted elf smiled at him. "I am Alhana Starbreeze, at your service."

8

Smoke drifted across Bianost's town square, fed by the still-smoldering ruins of houses all around it. Moving in and out of the swirling smoke, Kerian and Nalaryn led Alhana Star-breeze toward the mayor's palace. Alhana was accompanied by Samar, Chathendor, and a small honor guard. The bulk of her warriors remained behind to patrol outside the stockade and make certain Gathan Grayden and his bandits did not recover their nerve and return.

At the foot of the steps to the mayor's palace, Kerian turned to face the square and Alhana. The residents of Bianost looked on with great interest. The white-clad elf lady was certainly very beautiful, but few of them knew who she was or why their mysterious leader appeared so stricken by the sight of her.

And stricken Porthios was, more deeply affected than he had been in many a day. He had not expected to see his wife again this side of death. He stood at the top of the steps, staring. More than ever he resembled a scarecrow, and his silent immobility only enhanced the likeness. His robe hung around his emaciated frame in limp, loose folds. The rough sash that cinched its waist had loosened, and the garment's hem dragged on the stones.

Alhana and her two lieutenants reined up, and she called, "Who commands here?"

The townsfolk turned to look at Porthios. It required no great leap for Alhana to realize the ragged figure was the leader she sought. She waited for him to speak.

He did not. In a swirl of ragged cloth, he turned and disappeared into the mayor's mansion. Alhana blinked. She had expected at least a comradely greeting. The masked stranger's sudden departure left her speechless. Her escort was deeply affronted, and a worried murmur went up from the crowd.

Kerian could understand Porthios's shock. He had been saved from destruction by his own wife. He'd probably not seen her since his terrible disfigurement. Perhaps he'd allowed her to think him dead. But whether it was shame for his disfigurement or shame at having been saved by the wife he'd abandoned, Kerian was annoyed by his silent rudeness. Alhana and her soldiers deserved better.

Etiquette and diplomacy were not her strong points, but Kerian stepped into the breach. Her earlier reference to Alhana as family had been more in the nature of mild teasing. Gilthas was Porthios's nephew, but Kerian and Alhana had never been particularly close.

Still, raising her voice and lifting her sword high, Kerian proclaimed, "Greetings, Alhana Starbreeze. Welcome to Bianost! Your timely intervention saved us all!"

Alhana made a gracious reply then introduced Samar and Chathendor.

Samar stared at Kerian as though he could not credit the evidence of his eyes. "We thought you were in Khur, with the Speaker," he exclaimed. "How did you get here?"

"That is a long and tangled tale, which will keep." Kerian introduced Nalaryn. Samar knew him by name and reputation. Nalaryn had been a famous scout before the war.

To Alhana, Kerian said, "You'd better come inside. There is much to discuss."

Alhana glanced at the doorway through which the masked fellow had vanished. Much to discuss indeed, she thought.

She dismounted. In a body, the common folk of Bianost knelt. Although they were Qualinesti and she Silvanesti, they offered silent tribute. Lifting her hem, Alhana climbed the steps with solemn grace. Kerian followed.

At the top of the steps, Alhana paused. The moment of reverence had passed. Weary townsfolk resumed clearing away the broken and burned remains of the slave market.

The former queen sighed. "This used to be such a beautiful town," she said. "I remember the day this palace was dedicated. It was spring, and the scent of hyacinths was intoxicating. Hundreds and hundreds of the living flowers were brought into the square and arranged in a mosaic of colors."

Kerian could scarcely conceive it. Today there was only smoke, sweat, and the reek of blood. She looked beyond Alhana into the audience hall. Porthios wasn't in sight. She spoke privately to Nalaryn, telling him to find his leader and bring him here.

Nalaryn was not confident. "If the Great Lord chooses not to come, I cannot force him."

"Fair enough. But tell him I intend to show Alhana the treasure."

Nalaryn departed. Alhana's retainers, Chathendor and Samar, were discussing their rout of the bandits.

"They never could stand up to us in a fair fight," Samar said. "If the beast Beryl had not weakened us, if the Knights hadn't ridden in, those bandits would never have found a haven here!"

Yes, Kerian thought sourly, and if horses had horns, they'd be cows.

Shifting the subject, she asked Alhana how they came to be here.

"Word reached me of a rebellion, led by a masked figure with great skill in war. I summoned my old guard from around the lands of the New Sea and came at once to lend my support."

It sounded very simple but also rehearsed. Kerian had been among royalty long enough to recognize a diplomatic lie. Could word of Porthios's little victories have reached so far so soon? If so, the elves' enemies would know of them too.

The audience hall was a sight. Torches illuminated a makeshift scaffolding knocked together from fire-blackened timbers scavenged from the slave cages. The tower of planks and posts rose in the center of the hall to a gaping hole cut in the painted ceiling.

At Kerian's invitation, Samar scaled the scaffold. He stood with head and shoulders inside the attic and studied the space by torchlight. It did not display the usual airy delicacy that marked elven construction. Thick beams had been added to supplement the slender ceiling joists, and planks had been laid over the whole to make a floor. Heavy planks, he noted. Overhead, a beam still bore signs that a block and tackle had been attached. Whatever had been hidden there, it was very heavy. All that remained were snippets of rope and cloth sacking. He turned and climbed back down the scaffold.

In the hall below, Chathendor had made his own discovery: several sacks discarded in a heap. The linen sacks were too flimsy to have held bullion. Steel ingots would have torn right through. Samar caught a faint odor coming from the cloth. The smell was mineral oil, and something else. He thrust a hand into an empty sack and felt along the seams. His fingers came out covered in sticky yellow beeswax.

He uttered an oath. Chathendor chided him, reminding him of the presence of Alhana. "And of Lady Kerianseray, of course," the elderly retainer added, somewhat belatedly. Kerian snorted in amusement.

Samar knew the significance of the sacks. He gave her a keen look, demanding, "How did you find them?"

"Them?" asked Chathendor.

Kerian told of the dying councilor's cryptic clue regarding treasure in the sky.

Although her confusion was plain, Alhana was too well bred to insist on quick answers. Chathendor had no such compunctions. "What treasure?" he demanded. "What are you both talking about?"

Samar said, "A trove not of steel or jewels, but of weapons!"

Kerian confirmed his deduction. A parchment left with the cache in the attic had told the tale, she explained. In the waning days of Qualinesti, the great arsenal of Qualinost was stripped of weapons, part of a desperate plan to arm every elf of fighting age in the country. The royal arsenal was divided into three parts. One part was kept in the city and was lost when Beryl destroyed it. A second part was sent to the fortress at Pax Tharkas, but never arrived. A fast-moving band of Nerakan cavalry intercepted the caravan and stole the arms. The final third was intended for a new army being raised in the Forest of Wayreth. It, too, never reached its intended destination. Events overtook the caravan, and the weapons were hidden in the mayor's palace in Bianost. In the ensuing chaos, only the single councilor of Bianost who remained remembered where the arms had been concealed.

"Olin's men heard rumors of a secret cache and assumed it was treasure," said Kerian. "They tortured Kasanth, but he kept the secret. He passed on a single clue to"—she stumbled only slightly—"our leader, who deduced the cache's location."

Alhana gazed at the ruined ceiling. "Amazing. Where are the weapons now?"

"Divided into lots and hidden in buildings around town. We were collecting wagons and draft animals when Grayden's army showed up."

"Where did you plan to take it?" Samar asked.

"The forest. We'll raise the banner of Qualinesti and rally all able-bodied elves to our cause."

Samar and Chathendor didn't think much of that plan. A few thousand elves remained in the whole of Qualinesti, and that included males, females, children, and a large proportion of Kagonesti who cared little about repairing the Qualinesti state.

Kerian thought of the seasoned warriors she'd led in Khur. If only she had them with her. But they were in the desert, chasing Gilthas's foolish dream of a new homeland.

"I would speak with your leader."

Alhana's voice broke in on Kerian's grim thoughts. "I sent Nalaryn to find him. He's a very mysterious fellow. Comes and goes at all hours, and keeps no counsel but his own."

Alhana seated herself on the pedestal of a broken statue, once the proud image of a former Qualinesti leader and, thanks to Olin's despoilers, reduced to scattered lumps of stone.

"I shall wait."

Kerian nodded. It would be worth waiting for, she thought. Alhana deserved to hear the truth.

"I'll make every effort to send him to you," she said. "Until then, I must see about finding more carts and horses. We'll gain nothing if our enemies retake Bianost with the arsenal still here."

She departed and Samar followed, intending to see how the royal guards were faring in their patrol of the outer edges of the town.

* * * * *

The sun set, and the diffuse glow of twilight faded slowly. Chathendor moved around the ruined hall, commenting on the decorations and architecture. His lady returned no answers, only listened politely to his chatter. At last, exhausted by the day's events, he righted a large chair and seated himself. The first stars appeared in the hall's high windows. The sound of voices outside was a low, soothing murmur. Chathendor began to snore.

Alhana sat immobile, her face reflecting none of the uncertainty swirling in her heart. Could this masked rebel leader be her husband? She had barely glimpsed him before his abrupt departure. So she waited, with the considerable patience of a long-lived elf, a well-trained queen, and a wife fully intending not to stir one inch until she had the answers she sought.

The sound of footfalls caused her to flinch, revealing how thin was her veneer of calm. They came from the shadows at the far end of the hall, deliberate and steady, like the tread of a herald determined to be heard. Alhana clenched her hands, cold as ice, in her lap. A silhouette appeared twenty feet away, featureless in the weak starshine. Her heart beat faster. She drew a shaky breath.

"You have nothing to fear." His voice was low, hoarse, and completely unfamiliar.

Her back straightened. "I am not afraid."

"You are. Your heart hammers like a gong."

"I'm not accustomed to holding conversations in the dark." Without moving from her perch, she looked around. "Is there no candle or lamp?"

"Light one, and I will go."

It was her turn to offer reassurance. "You have nothing to fear from me. I am unarmed and"—Chathendor's snores increased in volume—"well, not completely alone."

He came a few steps closer, resolving into a shadowed form clad in a tattered, loosely fitting robe. Face and head were completely concealed by the robe's hood.

"Why did you come here?" he asked.

"To lend my support to this rebellion."

"You could have sent soldiers. Why did *you* come?"

With deliberate emphasis, she said, "To find you."

"And who am I?"

His voice had changed. The difference was subtle, but to Alhana it was clear as a beacon. The timbre and cadence, the very feel of it, was excruciatingly familiar. He was Porthios!

Relief so strong it made her head swim was followed immediately by a surge of adrenaline. Her heart began to pound again. She wanted to hurl herself at him, to hold him in her arms, to demand answers. Most of all she wanted to tear away the ragged mask that stood like a wall between them.

She wanted to, but she did not. Instead, terrified of frightening him away, she held herself utterly still, a living statue seated on the broken alabaster plinth. Her only movement was the shifting of her eyes as she studied him.

"You are—" She cleared her throat. Even so, it came out as the barest of whispers. "You are someone I love."

He withdrew suddenly, and Alhana feared he had gone,

but when he spoke again, his voice came from the darkness to her right.

"If that were true, you would have stayed away."

"Stayed away! How could I? As a queen, I lost my country. As a mother, I lost my child." Her voice broke. From the corner of one eye, she saw him take a step toward her then subside again into stillness. She drew a deep, shaking breath. "I don't live. I merely exist in the center of a great emptiness. It does not matter where I go or who I am with; the void is always with me. To answer the smallest part of 'why,' I would plunge to the bottom of Nalis Aren or climb the Icewall. Coming here was nothing!"

Giving voice to words carried so long unspoken calmed her. Not so Porthios.

"You want to know why?" he hissed. "Sometimes there is no why! Sometimes there is only what fate delivers. When the gods left us, they didn't take Fate with them. It stayed in the world, cruel, capricious, and callous. It took away my life, but would not allow me to die. So here I am, caught between the two. Alone."

She turned toward him. She sensed him shrink back but couldn't stop herself. "You need not be alone! Will you not take my hand?"

Her question and her outstretched hand hung in the air for a long moment. Finally, he whispered, "Go back to where you came from. Leave your warriors if you choose, but go. I will win this campaign, then I shall die. It's my reward for saving our people. If you stay, you'll die too, and I should not have to endure that. Everything else I will bear but that, Alhana."

The rustle of a ragged hem through the debris on the floor told her he was gone. Instead of loss, elation sang in Alhana's veins. During his speech, she'd felt a growing despair, until he'd said her name. He imbued the single word with such emotion, she knew at last that her quest had not been a hopeless one. He might be as cold and unreachable as the stars above, but Porthios was alive.

Voices announced the return of Samar and Kerian. The Lioness carried a flaming torch.

"Alhana?" Kerian called, surprised to find her still seated in the dark. "Are you all right?"

She flicked a hand over her cheeks. "I'm fine."

"Were you taking to someone?" asked Samar.

"Only Chathendor." Her aged retained was just now awakening, giving the lie to her words, but Samar would never contradict her.

Neither would Kerian since she knew the truth. Alhana had been talking with Porthios. Her tears alone were proof of that.

* * * * *

Two days went by without any sign of Porthios. At first Nalaryn and his Kagonesti were not worried by their leader's absence. He frequently went off on his own. But in their present situation, his continuing absence began to feel ominous.

The residents of Bianost were restless too. They had rallied to the mysterious masked leader and overthrown their oppressors, but their leader was missing, and no one knew what to do.

Kerian made sure military matters were attended to but wasn't concerned by Porthios's absence. It struck her as only right he should be overcome by the sight of the wife he had abandoned. In a way, she understood how he felt. If Gilthas had arrived at the gates of Bianost, she might want to run away, or clout him. Either was equally likely.

Samar was in charge of the royal guard, but he was disdainful of the Bianost militia and suspicious of Nalaryn's Kagonesti. He told Alhana none too diplomatically that at the first sign of trouble, the townsfolk would run away and the Kagonesti would vanish into the woods, leaving the rest of them to fend for themselves against whatever army Samuval sent against them.

Angered by his arrogance, Kerian reminded him the Kagonesti and the folk of Bianost had defeated Olin's entire company.

Samar waved a dismissive hand; Olin's cowardly mercenaries had crumbled even before their leader was dispatched. He implied Olin's death had been the result of dumb luck rather than any skill on the part of Kerian and the Kagonesti.

"A bold conclusion from one who wasn't even here!" Kerian retorted. "Do you always fight your battles with your mouth?"

Before even hotter words could be exchanged, Alhana and Chathendor diverted the headstrong warriors. Chathendor asked Kerian to take him around the town to review the caches of weapons from Qualinost. Alhana sent Samar out with sixty riders to sweep the countryside around Bianost for signs of bandits.

As the sun began to decline on the second day of Porthios's absence, Alhana realized she must meet with the townsfolk to help calm their growing fears. She sent Chathendor to invite the leaders of the Bianost volunteers to attend a council that evening after sundown.

The city square had been cleared of wreckage and bodies and a bonfire kindled. Alhana seated herself on a camp stool three steps above ground level before the mayor's palace. Standing below on Alhana's right were Chathendor and Samar. Kerian stood with Nalaryn on Alhana's left.

The Lioness was not happy with Samar's report from his reconnaissance of the area around Bianost. He had found nothing. Kerian was sure the town was being watched, and she didn't think much of Samar's skills that he failed to find any bandit scouts or spies.

The townsfolk of Bianost sent three representatives: Vanolin, a scrivener; Theryontas, a goldsmith; and Geranthas, a healer of animals. Alhana welcomed them graciously, praising their valiant actions in helping to save their town. The three were clearly awed to find themselves in her presence, but anxiety gave Theryontas, their spokesperson, the courage to speak his mind.

"Great Lady, the people of Bianost are alarmed by the disappearance of Orexas," he said.

"Who?" Alhana blurted, and Kerian suppressed a snort. The Qualinesti word meant merely "director" or "manager," but Kerian knew that in the eastern homeland it was applied to those who led orchestras or chorales. She found the implication of gentle artistry singularly amusing considering Porthios's cold, calculating leadership style.

Theryontas was explaining how the people of Bianost had bestowed the name on their masked deliverer, having no other name by which to call him. Kerian interrupted his long-winded speech.

"Whatever you call him, it won't change the fact he's missing," she said bluntly. She looked to Alhana, who had last spoken with Porthios before his disappearance. "Is he coming back?"

The wavering firelight deepened the lines of Alhana's face, and for a moment her alabaster beauty appeared an aged mask. It lasted only an instant, and might have been a trick of the wavering firelight, but Kerian, standing closest to her, felt she'd glimpsed the agony the elegant lady kept carefully concealed.

"I'm not certain," Alhana answered. "But until he does return, we must carry on."

Theryontas and the town delegation were plainly distressed. "What does this mean?" he asked. "We've begun a revolt. Is it over now because Orexas is gone?"

"No, it's not over!" Kerian said quickly. "We can carry on. Remember, we have weapons to equip a great army."

"What army?" Samar wanted to know. "Three hundred royal guards, twenty Wilder elves, and a few score townsfolk?"

Theryontas corrected him, deferential but precise, giving the total number of Bianost elves as three hundred forty-nine.

"Still not much of an army," Samar said.

"We took Bianost with far less and defended it too," Kerian said tartly.

"The bandits were surprised. When Samuval learns what happened here, he'll take the field himself. He has twenty thousand men and can call up at least that many more goblins. How will you trick a host of forty thousand warriors, lady?"

Kerian crossed her arms over her chest, hands gripping her upper arms tightly in anger. "It has been done. I fought the Knights to a standstill with much less."

"You had safe havens then. Where are your havens now? You had the clandestine support of the Speaker of the Sun and most of the population of Qualinesti. Where are they now?"

"Enough."

Silence descended at Alhana's command. Samar, his professional pride aroused, had taken a step toward the Lioness during their debate. He moved back.

"It is clear we have difficult choices to make," Alhana went on. "First and foremost, we must remove the cache of weapons and hide it safely elsewhere."

She was interrupted by the arrival of a rider. One of her guards came cantering across the square. His easy approach told them that whatever news he bore wasn't urgent. Samar went to receive the courier's message. After a brief exchange, Samar returned and reported to Alhana.

"Two strangers have been found. Elves. One is gravely injured. They have the look and manner of warriors, but their arms and clothing are most strange."

Samar waved the rider forward and asked him to explain further. "They are ragged," the elf said. "Obviously they have come a very long way. The injured one has a sword wound in the ribs, badly festered. He was on horseback. The other was leading the horse. Each was wearing an ankle-length, straight robe, once light in color, but now very dirty. Their helmets are conical, with a spike on top."

Shock tingled through Kerian's body. "And their swords?"

"Long curved sabers that seem to have lost their guards—"

Her whoop of excitement caused everyone to flinch.

"Those are Khurish swords!" she shouted. "Did they give you their names?"

"The one leading the horse did. He speaks like a rough trooper, but gave a noble name: Ambrodel."

"Hytanthas!"

With that, Kerian sprinted toward the rider, vaulted onto his horse's rump, and cried, "Take me to him! I know him!"

Samar protested that the council was still in session, but Kerian ignored him. She kicked the horse into motion, and they clattered away across the square. They left Bianost by the east road then turned to cut across the burned squatters' camp. Skirting an overgrown grove of apple trees, they galloped down a dirt path until they reached a knot of mounted guards.

"Where are the two strangers?" Kerian demanded.

The guards couldn't see her very clearly but knew she wasn't one of their officers. One asked her name.

"I'm Kerianseray, commander of the army of the Speaker of the Sun and Stars!"

It sounded most impressive, and every elf snapped to attention, not an easy task when mounted. They escorted her and the courier down a gully to a dry streambed choked with willow saplings. Sheltered from view by the high banks of the dry creek was a small campfire. Elves were gathered around it. Kerian slid off the horse and pushed through the elves until she reached the fireside.

Amid the polished ranks of royal guardsmen sat a particularly filthy elf. Matted hair fell across his gaunt face, but the blue eyes that looked up at Kerian were those of her young comrade.

"Hytanthas!"

He rose, too quickly, and staggered. The elves nearest bore him up.

"Commander? Lady?" He put out a thin hand as if to reassure himself he wasn't hallucinating. Grinning widely, Kerian stepped forward and embraced him. He felt like a child in her grasp, all bones and airy sinew.

"It *is* you," he murmured, amazed.

"What happened? How did you get here?"

"I might ask you the same thing, Commander," he joked wanly. "Mostly I walked, all the way from Khur."

He was swaying on his feet. Kerian helped him sit again and sat next to him. He gestured to his emaciated, fever-ravaged companion lying by the fire. "That's Camaranthas. We two are all that remain of the party the Speaker sent to find you."

As they turned to look, the elf tending Camaranthas shook his head. Hytanthas's last comrade had succumbed. Without a word, the surrounding warriors bowed their heads, clapped their hands together twice, paused, and clapped twice again, the ancient salute to the dead from House Protector.

"He never knew we made it." Hytanthas's face had the dull, vacant look of one who has mourned too much already.

Kerian sympathized with his loss, but time was pressing. "You must come with me. I must hear your tale. There are important people you must speak with." Belatedly, she added, "Have you eaten?"

He had. Alhana's guards had given him food and water. What he needed was sleep. Camaranthas had been wounded in a goblin ambush four days earlier. Hytanthas had sworn he would find a healer and had not dared to rest, lest his comrade perish.

Kerian promised he would sleep soon in the best accommodations to be found in Bianost, but he must hold out just a little longer.

As horses were brought for them, Hytanthas said, "Lady, I have dire news. The Speaker and all our people are in grave peril!"

She suppressed an impatient sigh. "As they were when I left. As they will always be in Khurinost."

"They're not in Khurinost any longer!"

He explained the Speaker had begun the great trek to Inath-Wakenti with the entire nation. Swarms of nomads dogged their heels. The last news Hytanthas had gleaned from other travelers was two weeks old. It said that the Speaker and the nation were near the northern mountains. Many had died from nomad attacks. The Speaker intended to make a stand, to hold off the growing threat from the desert tribesmen.

Kerian's impatience vanished, replaced by disbelief. Make a stand? They'd had a defensible position at Khuri-Khan, but Gilthas had abandoned it. Instead, he'd led their nation into the desert to die!

She took a deep breath, working hard to regain her composure. "Come," she said, taking his arm and gently propelling him toward his borrowed horse.

They mounted. On the way, she explained about the council being held in the newly freed town, of the presence of Alhana Starbreeze, her guards, and several hundred town elves ready to throw off the bandit occupation.

"They all must hear what you have told me," she finished.

"Then will we return to Khur? That was my mission, to bring you back to the Speaker."

She looked away, toward the torchlit town. "If what you heard is true, Hytanthas, there is no Speaker anymore. No elf nation, either."

9

Rising out of the vast expanse of Khur's northern desert were a series of rocky pinnacles. Before the First Cataclysm they were part of the Khalkist range to the north, connected to those mountains by long ridges that projected into the arid southern plain like great bony fingers. Time and catastrophe had eroded the fingers, leaving only the isolated pinnacles. There were six of them, known to the nomads as the Lion's Teeth. Individually, from northwest to southeast, they were called Pincer, Ripper, Great Fang, Chisel, Lesser Fang, and Broken Tooth. Great Fang was the tallest; Pincer, the smallest. Broken Tooth covered the largest area and sported a wide, flat top.

Distributed around the bases of these spires were thousands of elves, survivors of the exodus from Khurinost, their tent city under the walls of Khuri-Khan. In six months the ponderous column had progressed barely sixty miles. Apart from the massive logistical problems of moving so many people, their possessions, and their livestock across the inhospitable terrain, the elves had been dogged every step of the way by growing numbers of Khurish nomads.

The desert tribesmen had always resented the presence of outsiders in their sacred land, but they had largely ignored the elves until Adala, female chieftain of the Weya-Lu tribe, awakened to the special danger the elves posed. It was not their trespass (considered a grave sin among nomads), nor their trampling of Khurish traditions that provoked Adala to action. As long as the *laddad* remained in their squalid tent city, Adala could ignore them. The spur that finally caused her to raise her people against them was their Speaker's decision to lead his people away from the Khurish capital to settle in a valley on the northern border of Khur. The elves called it Inath-Wakenti, the Vale of Silence. City-dwelling Khurs knew it as the Valley of the Blue Sands and considered it little more than a fable.

Nomads knew better. To them, the valley was *Alya-Alash* (Breath of the Gods), the home of Those on High when They dwelt on the mortal plane. Strange forces lay quiescent in its cool, misty recesses. Disturbed by interlopers, the powers might leave their mountain haven and wreak havoc on the desert peoples. The world itself might come to an end if the sacred silence of Alya-Alash were broken.

Those on High had filled Adala with Their holy purpose. Her *maita*, her divine fate, was to unite the people of the desert against the intruders. *Maita* and the grace of Those on High would allow the nomads to overcome the subtle ways and superior warcraft of the *laddad*. Unfortunately, *maita* was no one's servant, to be commanded at will. Adala had gathered six of the seven tribes of Khur to her cause, and they had won several victories, but the final destruction of the elves eluded them. Protected by the khan's army, the *laddad* had escaped from Khurinost and begun their journey northward. With both Sahim-Khan's formidable troops and elf cavalry arrayed against them, the nomads could do little more than harass their enemy. As the miles increased, the khan's soldiers turned back home, and nomad attacks on the *laddad* grew stronger, more determined.

In the shadow of the Lion's Teeth, nomad horsemen struck the left side of the elves' formation while it moved slowly, steadily north-northwest. The hard-riding men of the Weya-Lu and Mikku tribes sliced a bloody swath through the terrified elves, driving warriors and civilians back upon the center of the column. Panic-stricken civilians hampered the warriors' efforts to re-form and counterattack. A rout seemed inevitable. The elves would be scattered across the sun-baked wasteland and slaughtered.

Traveling in the midst of his footsore nation was Gilthas Pathfinder, Speaker of the Sun and Stars. When the fighting reached him, he halted his horse amid the backwash of his terrified people. An iron ring of warriors formed around the Speaker, trying to hold off the nomad horde.

"Great Speaker, you must withdraw!" said General Hamaramis, commander of the Speaker's private guard. Blood streamed down his forehead.

Warriors and ordinary elves alike added their pleas to withdraw, but Gilthas would not remove himself to a place of safety. Even as nomad arrows flicked past him, he remained where he was.

"You've done your best, General. Now we must help you push back this attack," he said then turned in the saddle to address his people. "Elves of the two nations! We have been driven from our homelands, persecuted, robbed, and slaughtered. This may be our last trial. Let us go no further. Let us meet our fate as true descendents of Silvanos and Kith-Kanan, and never bow to the murderers' blades!"

The elves let out a roar, and Adala's fickle *maita* ebbed. Elves of every stripe—nobles, commoners, artisans, farmers, male and female—surged forward around the Speaker's horse. Armed with anything that came to hand, they fell upon the nomads. Astonished Khurs were dragged from their saddles or had their mounts pushed over. The enormous mass of elves pressed in on two sides, squeezing the Khurs between them. Many elves fell to nomad swords, but the momentum of the whole nation could not be stopped. Like a slow flood rising over a sandbar, they wore away the ranks of nomads and threatened to engulf them completely.

Some Khurs in the rearmost ranks gave way. More followed, and more still. Robbed of impetus, the nomads' deadly thrust collapsed. When at last their line broke, their spearhead—several hundred warriors of the Weya-Lu tribe—was surrounded by elves. Hamaramis called for the humans to surrender.

Their reply was blunt and rude. Regretful but unyielding, the general signaled his re-formed cavalry and left the nomads to their inescapable fate.

Gilthas had saved his people, but the cost was high. Hundreds were killed, hundreds more wounded, and irreplaceable supplies were lost in the mad rush to fend off the nomads. Carts were overturned, and oil, water, and other precious liquids soaked the pitiless sand. Foodstuffs carefully preserved and hoarded were trampled.

While the elves marveled at their survival, despite the high cost they had paid, the dispirited nomads returned to their hidden camps. For an entire month, they'd marshaled their forces, gathering together far-flung tribes and clans from every corner of Khur. That was to have been the decisive battle, the final defeat of the *laddad* pestilence, and it had failed. Their supreme effort had been repulsed.

Some of the clan chiefs and warmasters spoke openly of quitting. The valley to which the *laddad* were headed wasn't really part of Khur after all. No nomads lived there. No nomads even visited there. Why not let the *laddad* go to the valley and be cursed by the forces within it? Why sacrifice more Khurish lives to hasten the death that surely awaited the *laddad*?

The chiefs and warmasters gathered around their leader. Their sturdy desert-bred horses were shorter than the war-horses ridden by elves, but still towered over Adala's donkey.

Known as the Weyadan, Mother of the Weya-Lu, but more frequently called simply "Maita" by her followers, Adala sat on Little Thorn's back beneath a square of black damask supported by four tall poles. As always, her hands were busy. She was darning holes in the robe of one of her kinsmen. Months ago most of the Weya-Lu women and children had been slain in a night raid on an unprotected camp. The atrocity was blamed on the *laddad,* who had a warband in the vicinity. Since then Adala had taken on various domestic tasks for the surviving wifeless men. Chief of the Weya-Lu and anointed leader of the temporarily united desert tribes she might be, but she also sewed, mended, and cleaned as necessary to support her loyal warriors.

"What say you, Maita?" asked Danolai, warmaster of the Mikku. "Why waste our lives against a departing foe?"

"The blood of our people is still hot upon the sand," Adala replied evenly. "Who would not avenge his kinsmen, wrongly slain?"

The men looked away. Adala's youngest daughters, Chisi and Amalia, had been among those slain in the treacherous night raid. Adala had always been certain the *laddad* were behind the terrible crime. Her followers had been less sure until the tracks of shod horses were discovered nearby. Nomad ponies wore no shoes.

"They are too great for us, Maita."

It was obvious most of the men present agreed with Danolai. Adala looked at him, her eyes hard.

"Then go home," she said. "If you think the *laddad* are greater than you, then you are nothing. Take the other nothings and go, but leave your swords in the sand. You have no right to bear arms."

The men blanched. A nomad's sword, narrow bladed and bare of guard, was as vital a part of his identity as prowess on a horse or skill as a storyteller. He could experience no greater shame than to have his sword taken away and driven pointfirst into the sand. The gesture implied every degree of cowardice.

Adala's cousin Wapah, sitting a horse at her side, spoke. "Our great throw did not succeed. But while we live, we can fight again." His pale gray eyes were unusual among nomads, but common in Wapah's Leaping Spider Clan.

"Every fight weakens the *laddad*. This is not their land. This is not their climate. One day their foreign ways will fail them, and they will be ours."

Kindly folks called Wapah a philosopher. Those less charitable labeled him a garrulous gossip. But his was the only voice of reason between Adala's unyielding belief in her *maita* and the chiefs' despair. Old Kameen, the only clan chieftain

from the ruling Khur tribe to join Adala's cause, seconded
Wapah's words.

"We should be patient," he advised. "Keep a close watch on
the *laddad*. Gather the tribes again, and strike when the time
is right."

Adala finished her sewing and bit off the thread. "Kameen
speaks wisely," she said, folding the mended robe. "We will
hang on the heels of the *laddad* until my *maita* shows us when
to attack again."

No one had a better idea to offer, and no one showed any
sign of abandoning the fight. Fear of shame and a ferocious
commitment to honor ran deep among the Khurs.

Several miles away, the elves were facing a crisis of their
own. The damage to their dwindling supplies proved worse
than first thought. One-fifth of their available water and a sixth
of their edible oil had been lost in the attack. The great number
of wounded meant the column could not maintain even the
slow pace it had been making. Their time in the desert would
be prolonged, and they did not have the supplies to meet the
needs of everyone.

Planchet, Gilthas's valet and bodyguard, arrived with
General Taranath and other officers of the army. Planchet had
been leading the right wing of the elves' column. Surveying the
destruction, his sunburned face paled a little. The carnage of
men, elves, and horses traveled in a direct line to the Speaker.
Planchet knew his sovereign well enough to realize he hadn't
retreated an inch.

Standing next to his horse, Gilthas was a thin figure clad in
Khurish attire. Most elves had adopted the practical desert dress.
Some, like Hamaramis and Planchet, added Qualinesti-style leg-
gings, feeling uncomfortable on horseback without them. The
Silvanesti among the Speaker's councilors clung stubbornly
to their silk robes, no matter how frayed and threadbare.

Planchet hailed his liege with great relief. "Sire, what is
your will?" he said, dismounting.

"To lie in the cool shade of a birch forest with my feet soaking in a crystal stream." Gilthas smiled wanly at the elf who

was his valet, bodyguard, sometime general, and close friend. "What do you want, good Planchet?"

Amused, Planchet nevertheless answered seriously, pointing to the distant spires of the Lion's Teeth. "Scouts tell us those peaks are easily defensible. I think we should make for them without delay."

"Do you propose our people climb mountains?" asked Hamaramis.

"I do. We're too vulnerable in the open desert. Another attack like today's, and none of us will live to see Inath-Wakenti."

The old general scowled. "We'll be locking ourselves in a dungeon cell. The Khurs will never let us out again."

All the officers had dismounted. Gilthas parted their ranks with a wave and walked a few yards beyond, where thousands of elves stood, knelt, or squatted on the sand, waiting to hear what he would ask of them next. Weary and frightened they were, but each and every face wore the same trusting expression. They believed Gilthas would lead them out of the fiery crucible of the desert just as he had led them from their shattered homelands when minotaurs, bandits, and goblins invaded. They had proclaimed him Gilthas Pathfinder. Such trust was an enormous source of strength for the Speaker of the Sun and Stars. It was also an enormous burden.

Gilthas inhaled deeply the dry, overheated air. His sandaled toe nudged a broken amphora. The golden olive oil inside was gone, lost to the insatiable sand.

"How far to the nearest of those peaks?"

"Broken Tooth is nine miles away, Great Speaker," replied Planchet.

"And how far is the last peak from Inath-Wakenti?"

No one knew. As Gilthas returned to his officers, there was a flurry of activity as maps were produced and consulted. Planchet reported, "From the westernmost peak, Pincer, the mouth of Inath-Wakenti appears to be twenty-five to thirty miles away."

"That's a broad range." In the desert, five miles could easily mean the difference between survival and destruction.

Planchet assured him they would refine the calculations. Gilthas studied the map Planchet held for him then announced his decision.

"We will go to the first pinnacle. We will occupy each spire in turn, using it as a fortress against the desert tribes."

The sun was sinking in the west. Gilthas returned to his horse, and Planchet went with him. Watching them ride away, one of Hamaramis's younger officers made a disparaging remark about the Speaker's wits. The old general whirled and struck the offender with his gauntleted hand. The elf hit the ground, blood trickling from his lip.

"How dare you!" Hamaramis rasped. Heat and the shouting of commands had taken a toll on his voice, but fury was clear in every hoarse word. "The heir of Silvanos is not to be insulted!"

The young officer, a Silvanesti protégé of the late Lord Morillon, arose with much wounded pride. "I ask forgiveness," he said stiffly. "But you yourself said going there would be like jumping into prison."

"So it may be. And if the Speaker commands it, jump we will!"

The chastened captains dispersed to their waiting troops. General Taranath remained with Hamaramis. "You fear this development?" Taranath asked, his gaze following the insolent Silvanesti.

Hamaramis shrugged, wincing at the pain in his shoulders. "It's difficult to know the future. I am no seer," he rasped.

"I said that once to Hytanthas Ambrodel. His reply was, 'The future always arrives, whether we want it or not.'"

"I miss young Hytanthas. One of many fine officers we've lost."

Taranath did not correct the old general. Hytanthas had been sent by the Speaker to find his missing wife. No word had come from him in months, but as far as anyone knew, Hytanthas was not dead.

A ragged blare of trumpets brought the mass of exhausted elves to their feet. They prepared to resume their trek.

Hamaramis and Taranath solemnly clasped hands. This close to destruction, each parting felt like the final one.

* * * * *

They succeeded in achieving the heights. As Planchet's scouts had reported, the Lion's Teeth were scalable, especially for those as motivated and agile as the elves. For days they had been clinging to the windy fortresses. Days of scalding sun, chill nights, and an ever-shrinking water supply. Two-thirds of the elves, including the Speaker and Planchet, camped on Broken Tooth. A much smaller band was dug in on the much steeper neighboring peak, Lesser Fang. Beyond them, the remaining elves had taken refuge on Chisel. By means of signal mirrors, those on Chisel notified the Speaker they had found a small spring bubbling in a cleft on the pinnacle's side. It was difficult to reach in the best of conditions and nearly impossible under the constant sniping of nomad archers, but Taranath, in command of the elves on Chisel, rigged a chain of leather buckets to haul water from the spring under cover of darkness. Those on Chisel would not go thirsty but had no way of sharing their life-giving find.

Daily the desert floor around the pinnacles echoed with the sounds of battle. General Hamaramis and the remaining cavalry fought to keep clear the gaps between the steep mountains. The nomads no longer sought or accepted pitched battle. Instead they tried to ambush small parties of elf warriors, sniped at the peaks with arrows, then vanished into the blazing desert when Hamaramis brought the weight of his army to bear. The Speaker ordered bonfires burned atop the peaks every night. The bonfires served a dual purpose: not only dissuading the nomads from sneak attacks, but signaling to the elves on the adjacent peaks that their comrades were holding out.

One night, just before midnight, the beacon atop Lesser Fang went out. Word was sent to the Speaker, and he convened a hasty council. It was held atop the cairn they had constructed on Broken Tooth. The cairn afforded them an unobstructed view of the black outlines of Lesser Fang, Chisel, and Great

Fang. Great Fang, highest of the pinnacles, blocked any view of Ripper and Pincer beyond.

"Perhaps they ran out of fodder for the flames," said a Silvanesti councilor. Oil was more precious than steel at that moment, and little wood could be had for fires. Dried dung was the usual fuel in the desert.

"We cannot assume that," Planchet said. The warriors around him murmured in solemn agreement.

"You've heard nothing?" Gilthas asked.

"Nothing at all, sire."

The human blood in his ancestry meant Gilthas's senses were not quite as acute as those of a full-blooded elf. If Planchet and the others did not hear anything from Lesser Fang, then there was nothing to be heard. Despite that, Gilthas leaned forward over the rickety wooden railing atop the cairn platform and peered into the blackness toward Lesser Fang. He strained to see until tears came to his eyes, but neither sight nor sounds reached him.

"We must know!" he said, driving a fist into his palm. Not for the first time, he wished for the presence of a mage or seer. Since the elves' exile, these had been in short supply, targeted by both the minotaurs and the Knights of Neraka to blind the elves' resistance and spread fear and despair.

Two young warriors volunteered to go to Lesser Fang, to find out what had happened. The peak was only a quarter of a mile away, but the two would have to descend Broken Tooth, cross open desert, then climb the steep side of the neighboring peak, all in darkness while evading vigilant nomads.

Gilthas saw no other option. He warned the ardent young elves not to waste their lives. "If the enemy has taken the mountain, come back at once. Don't attempt a rescue. Come back and report what you find to me."

They saluted and hurried away. The ever-present wind atop the peak freshened, swirling around the cairn. Gilthas coughed. The spasm didn't stop, but grew stronger. Faithful Planchet laid a hand on his shoulder.

"You are ill, sire."

Gilthas shook his head, drawing a shaky breath. "It's only the chill night air. It dries my throat."

The valet didn't believe that for a moment, but it did give him a reason to urge the Speaker to leave the exposed sentinel post. The two of them descended, but Gilthas would not return to camp.

"I will remain here, in the lee of the cairn," he said.

His tone told Planchet that the valet's mothering would be tolerated so far but no further. Planchet gave in with good grace.

"An excellent idea. We will call you if there are any developments." He climbed back up the stone pile.

Gilthas pulled his *affre* close about his throat. The coughing was becoming more and more difficult to stop once it began. Sometimes he coughed up flecks of blood.

He knew what ailed him. Consumption wasted the body and rotted the lungs. Legend held a consumptive grew more beautiful as death drew near. The glimpses he'd caught of his reflection told him he was not beautiful. He was a good fifteen pounds lighter than when he had dwelt in Khurinost. His eyes were heavily shadowed, yet red rimmed, and despite the sunburn on nose and cheeks, his pallor had grown markedly. No, certainly not beautiful, so he must still be full of life. But his cough was becoming more frequent, and his eyes were more sensitive to the brilliant light of the Khurish sun than they had been. Deep in his chest, there was a hollowness, a sort of dead emptiness, as if a block of wood rested there.

Sweat suddenly broke out, and he loosened the neck of his robe. He knew the unnatural heat would pass quickly, leaving him even more chilled than before, but while it lasted, his body burned as though roasted over a fire.

Leaning against the cool stones of the cairn, alone for the first time in days, Gilthas allowed his thoughts to drift to other times and places. He imagined Kerian's reaction to his illness. You're not sick, she would declare, her strong features softening as she looked at him. You just need rest, good food, and lots of hot baths.

ALLIANCES

His wife was a great believer in the nearly miraculous powers of hot water and soap, probably because she'd been an adult before having easy access to either. Limitless hot water, a well-constructed tub, and rose petal soap represented the height of civilization to the Lioness, among the very few things worth leaving her beloved forest for.

A bead of sweat ran down Gilthas's forehead. He wiped it away. His skin was hot to his own touch. Wind swirled around the makeshift tower at his back, setting the hem of his *geb* flapping and raising gooseflesh on his arms. He shivered, although the sweat still trickled down his face. This was a particularly intense episode of the fever.

A rustling noise drew his attention away from his bodily ills. Leaves tumbled over the stony ground at his feet. He blinked, wondering if he could be hallucinating. Nothing grew on Broken Tooth, not even weeds. He picked up a leaf. It was an ash leaf, green and supple. Where could they be coming from?

Another sound interrupted his musings. His councilors on the lookout post above were exclaiming in surprise. Stepping away from the cairn, Gilthas looked up. A cloud of bats was whirling overhead. Some of the elves were swiping at the darting creatures, trying to shoo them away.

Gilthas told them to stop. Bats and leaves appearing from nowhere in the lifeless desert? These had to be omens. Whether good or bad, he didn't know, but they should take care not to antagonize whatever forces were at work. Perhaps the elves were near enough to Inath-Wakenti that the power there was affecting their surroundings.

Gilthas choked suddenly. The wind had hurled a leaf directly into his open mouth. Instinctively he spat it out then abruptly bent, picked up another, and placed it on his tongue. His eyes widened. He hadn't imagined it; the ash leaf tasted very good, like asparagus, his favorite vegetable.

The councilors descended to find their king crouched on the ground, stuffing green leaves into his mouth. Before Planchet could protest, Gilthas thrust a handful of leaves at him.

"Try them! They're good!"

With the air of an elf humoring an insane request, Planchet bit the tip of one leaf. He could hardly credit the sensations in his mouth. The taste was bright and crisp, like a fresh radish. Planchet loved radishes, especially those grown in the meadows surrounding Bianost, from whence he hailed.

"Gather them up!" Gilthas commanded. "We have fresh food!"

Even the haughty Silvanesti councilors went to work with a will, gathering the leaves still falling from the sky.

Word of the unexpected bounty flashed across the mesa. Elves sleeping fitfully on cold stone awoke. Confusion changed to laughing astonishment as each of them tasted the leaves. The more alert rigged blankets and tarps to catch a greater harvest.

For an hour, the wind blew ash leaves over the crowded mountaintop. The elves gathered all they could until the wind died out and no more leaves fell.

Gilthas surveyed the scene with quiet delight. "What do you make of this, Planchet?"

"A miracle from the gods, sire." Planchet ate another leaf. He and the Speaker had compared their experiences, but no matter how many leaves they tried, each tasted like asparagus to the Speaker and like radishes to his valet.

Into the celebratory scene came the two scouts returning from Lesser Fang. They arrived, gasping for breath from having run all the way back.

Their ashen faces told Planchet their report would be better given to the Speaker in private. Before he could suggest that, the scouts blurted out their news.

"They're gone, Great Speaker! All of them!" said one.

The other added, "There is no one on Lesser Fang!"

Gilthas took a step back, visibly shaken. Thousands dead? It wasn't possible. Not since the elves' arrival in Khur had the nomads achieved such a victory.

"Did you find evidence of a fight?" Planchet said sharply.

Some, they said. The rocky path up the north face of the pinnacle held the bodies of eight slain nomads. At the top, threescore elves had fallen defending the plateau. Gilthas questioned that figure, wondering where the rest had gone. One scout suggested that the bulk of elves, fearful of being overrun, had evacuated to Chisel. That did not seem likely. The beacon on Chisel was burning as before. If something grave had happened, the Speaker was certain Taranath would have signaled him, perhaps by lighting a second bonfire. No such sign had come from Chisel.

Still, that possibility had to be investigated. Fresh scouts were dispatched to make the dangerous trek to Chisel. The Speaker also ordered the army be recalled. Hamaramis kept it hidden unless it was engaged. This night the army was lying among the high dunes southwest of the Lion's Teeth, a half-hour's walk from the base of Broken Tooth. One of the few horses on Broken Tooth was saddled and a rider sent to fetch the army.

"This is impossible," Planchet insisted. "Sire, we would have heard something! If they all were massacred, we would have heard it!"

Gilthas laid a hand on his distraught valet's shoulder. He agreed with Planchet, but there was little more that could be done until daybreak. With Planchet at his side, he walked among his anxious subjects, reminding them of the miracle of the ash leaves and reassuring them about their missing brethren. The elves on Lesser Fang likely had been surprised by the nomads and decided to escape to Chisel or hide in the desert, but they would be found.

The Speaker's reassurances and his presence comforted his subjects. With lightened hearts, the elves finished storing away the bounty of leaves then settled down to sleep for what remained of the night.

Despite the confident face he showed his people, Gilthas was deeply worried about his missing subjects. He didn't suspect the Khurs, but a more mysterious cause. Only with Planchet had he shared Kerian's report of the disappearance of many of her warriors in Inath-Wakenti. Perhaps the elves on Lesser Fang had been spirited away by a similar unknown force.

Kerian herself had vanished near Khurinost, after riding to face certain death at the hands of the nomads. None of the desert-dwellers they'd captured and questioned had been able to give them any information about her. Privately Gilthas thought that a good sign. If the Khurs had captured or killed the fabled Lioness, they'd have boasted to the heavens about it.

No word at all had been received from Hytanthas and the five experienced trackers Gilthas had sent to look for Kerian. For all Gilthas knew, the six searchers were lost too.

The starlit pinnacle was quiet. A breeze, weaker than the leaf-bearing wind but colder, had everyone reaching for blankets, rugs, spare *gebs* and *affres,* anything to ward off the chill.

Planchet had spread Gilthas's bedroll under a canvas lean-to. The shelter was barely larger than the bedroll it covered, but it kept the constant wind at bay. As Gilthas lay down on his lonely bed, he knew in his heart that his wife was alive. The day she died, the colors of life would fade, the tumult of the living world would still, and wherever Gilthas Pathfinder was, he would know she no longer drew breath.

Oddly comforted, he lay down amid bales of ash leaves and was soon asleep.

10

The dining room of the mayor's palace in Bianost once more hosted a gathering of elf notables. Unlike meals of decades past, this was no rich repast, carefully planned by kitchen artists. Kerian, Alhana, Chathendor, and Samar were seated at one end of a table meant to hold many times their number. The fare was simple, and the diners served themselves—all except Alhana. Chathendor performed that duty for her. Long experience had taught her that protesting was pointless. By the amber glow of candles and oil lamps, the diners discussed their options.

Since the arrival of Hytanthas Ambrodel, tensions had only increased among the liberators of Bianost. Hytanthas was ensconced among the wounded, tended by healers and slowly regaining his strength, but Porthios remained missing. In his absence the townsfolk had turned to Alhana for guidance. She pointed out that Kerian, as wife to the Speaker of the Sun and Stars, should rightly hold that place. Blunt as always, the Lioness told her not to worry about such niceties: "None of us is king or queen here. If it comforts the townsfolk to look to you, that's fine—as long as it's understood I take the lead in military matters."

This was said with a pointed look at Samar, who bristled just as Kerian must have known he would. Alhana stepped in to forestall the disagreement that always seemed to hover in any encounter between her trusted commander and the Lioness. With an apologetic glance at Samar, Alhana agreed.

Alhana said they should follow Porthios's original plan: abandon Bianost as soon as possible and take the huge cache of weapons into the forest for safekeeping. She and the Lioness were in accord on that point. For once, however, Samar did not side with his queen. He favored seizing another bandit-held town deeper in the forest, such as Frenost. Another coup like Bianost, he insisted, would rally every elf in the nation and seriously demoralize the bandits.

Kerian shook her head. "It won't work," she said.

Pushing away her empty dinner plate, she leaned down and lifted a heavy roll of vellum from the floor next to her chair. Unrolled, it proved to be a fine map of Qualinesti, painted in four colors and showing details as fine as individual wells, houses, and footpaths. She had found it in a heap of documents the bandits had been using as tinder to start cook fires in the kitchen. More startling than that casual disregard for so fine a document was the notation on the back of the map: "Copied by Favaronas, royal archivist, Qualinost. Year VI," meaning the sixth year of Gilthas's reign.

The sight of Favaronas's name had been a jolt, reminding Kerian of Inath-Wakenti, and Khur in general. What had happened to the timid librarian and the good warriors who'd accompanied her to the Vale of Silence? She'd been too busy lately to spend time contemplating their fate. Standing in the kitchen of the mayor's palace, clutching the heavy map, she summoned their faces, but the panoply was quickly overwhelmed by her husband's face, smiling in his exhausted, gentle, yet unyielding way. She had banished it by kicking over the pile of manuscripts and books.

"The capture of Bianost was due to surprise and the woeful unpreparedness of Olin and his troops," she declared, speaking to Alhana at the table's head. "The bandits are aroused now, and their defenses will be strengthened everywhere. We don't have the numbers or experience to storm a fortified town, much less besiege it."

"What do you think we should do?" Alhana asked.

"Disperse." Kerian waved a hand across the surface of the map. "Form a hundred small bands, each with arms to equip a thousand, and spread to every corner of Qualinesti and beyond, into Abanasinia, Kharolis, and Tarsis. Like termites, we'll work from within, weakening Samuval everywhere while exposing a minimum of our people to danger. Before long the whole rotten structure of Samuval's realm will collapse."

Samar disagreed, the gist of his argument being that Alhana's royal guards could certainly do what Porthios, Kerian, and a handful of Kagonesti had done. The victory in Bianost should not be squandered. They should strike again.

Chathendor set aside his silver knife and fork, which bore the arms of the lord mayor of Bianost, and spoke. "Lady Kerianseray's plan seems an admirable one—for the future, but what of the present, the next several days even? The town volunteers, although enthusiastic, I am sure, are new to fighting. Won't they need training before going up against bandit mercenaries?"

Diplomatic as always, the old chamberlain had asked a question to which he knew the answer as well as they. Rising up on the spur of the moment to strike one's oppressors was one thing. To live wild and plan and execute attacks against a seasoned and ruthless foe were quite another. The militia would be no match for the bandits.

"I'll not forsake them," Alhana said firmly. "They risked all to regain their freedom. I'll not abandon them to the mercy of Samuval's barbarians."

"A noble sentiment."

The voice echoed from the eastern end of the hall. Out of the deep shadows Porthios emerged.

Kerian glared at him with unconcealed annoyance. "Where have you been?"

"A better question: Why are you still here?"

"We've been readying the cache of weapons for travel. There still aren't enough draft animals—"

"Gathan Grayden is twenty miles away with an army of several thousand."

All were on their feet instantly. Alhana gasped, and Samar muttered a curse. Kerian stabbed a hand at the map on the table. "Where, exactly?"

He did not approach. "Under the walls of Mereklar."

Mereklar was a city southeast of Bianost, in the foothills of the Redstone Bluffs. According to Favaronas's map, it was just less than twenty miles away.

"Is he coming this way?" asked Chathendor.

"He will break camp within a day or two. His line of march is the High Road." This was the paved way that connected Mereklar to Bianost and continued northwest to Frenost.

"How do you know all this?"

The masked head turned toward Kerian. "I know. We must leave tonight."

Alhana sent Samar to see to the guards' preparation. Kerian reminded her that the Bianost militia needed to be mustered first. Untrained and on foot, they would require longer to get under way. Also, what of the shortage of draft animals to pull the wagons loaded with the weapons cache?

"What can't be moved must be hidden or destroyed," Alhana said. "You will see to it?"

Kerian nodded. She and Samar departed in haste. For as long as their voices could be heard, they argued loudly about whether to hide or destroy the surplus weapons.

Chathendor, rushing away to see to their belongings, paused and glanced at Porthios, whom he did not recognize. "Lady," he whispered, "perhaps you should not be alone with this person?"

She clasped his hand and gave him a reassuring smile. "It's all right, my friend. I am perfectly safe. Now go. We must be ready to depart without delay."

When the chamberlain had reluctantly withdrawn, Alhana filled two pewter goblets from a slender silver ewer. Lifting one, she gestured at the other. "Refresh yourself. It's a long way to Mereklar and back on foot."

Porthios entered the warm light of candles and oil lamps. Despite his ragged, too-long robe, he moved with exceptional silence, even for an elf. Watching him take the cup, Alhana was struck by the familiarity of the gesture. Whatever metamorphosis he'd undergone, masked and gloved or not, she would have known him anywhere just by the way he cradled his goblet. The stem nestled between his thumb and middle finger; his other fingers did not touch the cup.

"What are you watching so intently?" Porthios asked.

She told him. He glanced at his hand. "Habits are hard to change," he muttered. He wondered if others could recognize him by such telltale trifles or if that was a skill possessed only by his observant wife.

Former wife. Part of the life that had been ripped away in fire and pain and blood. But if that were true, then why did he still feel bound to her? Despite his firm intention to remain apart from her, he found himself unable to leave the room. The untouchable nearness of her was agony, but he drew it out a moment more.

"Where will you go now?"

Surprise widened her violet eyes. "My habits have not changed either. I go with Kerianseray and the others."

"Even if it costs your life?"

She extended her goblet, tapping it gently against his own. "We all must die, Porthios."

His name on her lips was like a thunderclap. Dropping his eyes, he sipped wine. The fine Qualinesti vintage burned his tongue yet had no taste at all. Since the fire, no food or drink smelled or tasted right. The only exception had been the honey-dew wafers given him by the god in the forest. The wine did warm his belly, so he emptied the goblet and held it out to be refilled. She poured, and before he could withdraw the cup, she covered his hand with her own.

Porthios flinched, but to Alhana's joy, he did not draw back. Through the gloves all she could feel was bone. It was like grasping the hand of a skeleton. But this skeleton still lived. Without warning, he released the pewter goblet and took hold of her hand, gripping it tightly with both of his own as spilled wine spattered her feet.

*   *   *   *   *

Well after midnight, the elves abandoned Bianost.

Kerian advocated burning the town to obscure any evidence of what had been found there, but the local militia objected. Despite the pitiful state to which Olin had reduced it, Bianost was their home, and they could not bear the thought of its wholesale destruction. Kerian was not unmoved by their pleas but likely would have overruled them except for Alhana. The former queen also advocated letting the town stand, although for a different reason. If they were to win the hearts of the ordinary folk in Qualinesti, whether elf, human, or other, they had to demonstrate their superiority to the enemy. Torching the empty town was exactly what Samuval's bandits would do.

Kerian accepted that logic. With a grin, she said that leaving the town intact would probably delay their pursuers, who would have to work their way through the scabrous dwellings, searching for rebels.

With wagons laden with much of the arms cache, the elves departed. Hytanthas rode in a wagon with the cargo because he was still too weak to sit a horse. He had come down with a fever soon after being found. One of Nalaryn's Kagonesti called it a fever of exhaustion, brought on by weeks of little or no food, water, or rest. They made him as comfortable as possible but he knew nothing of the lambswool blankets and soft pillows that had been found for him. He fought phantom nomads and monsters while his fever raged. In his lucid moments, he tried to convince the Lioness to return with him to Khur, to aid the beleaguered Speaker. She rebuffed every attempt. She had been cast aside, she said. Gilthas hadn't even heard her out. He didn't need her, didn't want her help. For all they knew, the elf host had been decimated and Gilthas captured. What was the point in returning to Khur if the war there was over? The future of their race lay in Qualinesti, in the ancient homeland. Strange magic had delivered her here even as Orexas had begun his promising rebellion.

After consultation with Alhana and Porthios, Kerian led the elves due east out of Bianost. Twenty-five miles down the wide, royal road (its pavement broken, the cracks thick with weeds) lay the former site of Qualinost, where there was only the Lake of Death. The bandit host was bearing down on Bianost from the south. They would expect the elves to make for their home forest, west of town. Kerian hoped an eastward track would confound the bandits and allow her to put more distance between the fleeing elves and Gathan Grayden's vengeful host before she turned the column north into the forest.

They moved by night, resting under the overhanging trees by day. Spies and informers were everywhere in the dark heart of the ruined elf kingdom. Daily Alhana's vanguard flushed goblins out of the woods, slaying them without mercy. Surprise was one of their few assets. They couldn't afford to have their position betrayed too soon.

Caution, as well as the laden wagons and the many civilians on foot, kept their pace slow. Samar chafed at the delays.

"What a miserable crawl! Oh, for the days when royal elves flew into battle on the backs of griffons! No foe could stand before them!"

"As I recall, the imperial hordes of Ergoth managed," Chathendor said dryly.

That launched the two on an involved discussion of the tactics and strategy of the long-ago Kinslayer War. They proved well matched. Samar was a student of history, and Chathendor had once been a warrior of considerable prowess.

They rode in company with Alhana and Kerian. Nalaryn remained with his clan, which kept to the fringes of the woods on each side of the road. Porthios, as was his wont, came and went without a word, disappearing and rejoining the march at will.

Alhana rode slower and slower. So caught up in their argument were Samar and Chathendor, they never noticed her falling behind. Kerian circled back to collect her.

"Alhana, you must keep up," the Lioness chided.

"If we had griffons, it would redress many imbalances," Alhana mused.

It would indeed. Kerian mentioned her own griffon, Eagle Eye, who had seen her through many tight spots.

"But he's far away, with—in Khur," Kerian finished awkwardly. She reached for the bridle of Alhana's white mare. "Highness, we should catch up to the column."

Alhana shook off her reverie. She regarded Kerian for a thoughtful moment. "Would you call me 'aunt'?" she asked. "We are family, are we not, Kerianseray? And I have so little family left."

Surprised by the request, Kerian consented readily enough. She was even more surprised when Alhana leaned sideways and rested a hand on her shorn head. "Your beautiful hair," Alhana said mournfully. "I know it was hardly the worst that might have happened, but it was a vicious, hurtful thing for them to have done."

Kerian realized her mistake. "Oh, it wasn't Olin's trash who cut it. I did it myself, before they caught me. Seemed a good idea to conceal my identity."

Alhana blinked at her for a heartbeat then exclaimed, "What an indomitable spirit you have, niece!"

Kerian flashed her a grin, and they urged their horses into a trot, catching up with Samar and Chathendor then passing them.

The column was still more than eight miles from the Lake of Death when signs of the devastation appeared. Broken treetops, toppled markers, and blasted hedges spoke of a huge explosion. The shattered treetops sprouted new leaves, but the effects of Beryl's fall were unmistakable.

The Kagonesti grew restless. Normally the most uncomplaining of elves, they dragged their feet. None wanted to penetrate farther into the blighted site of Qualinost. Theryontas and the volunteers from Bianost, who had been at the rear of the line, passed the balking foresters. Kerian had to double back to speak to the laggards.

"This land is cursed!" one insisted, and another said, "All who enter will be tainted by evil!"

"I fell in the lake when I first arrived, and I survived," she told them. Of course, soon thereafter she was captured by slavers, beaten, starved, and nearly flayed alive. Perhaps there was something to their fears after all.

The end of the caravan rounded a bend, leaving Kerian and the Kagonesti behind.

"I can't force you to come," she said. "But what would the Great Lord have you do?"

"We will ask him," said Nalaryn, pointing behind her.

She whipped around in the saddle and saw Porthios limping along the edge of the road. She rode to him, asking where he'd been.

"Here and there. I had tasks to perform."

"I saved a horse for you. You could ride with Alhana."

Even shadowed by the mask, Kerian knew his eyes were glaring at her. "Keep your mind on your own affairs," he snapped.

We are family, are we not?

Kerian knew no feeling of kinship with the short-tempered, arrogant elf before her, but with Alhana's plaintive question echoing in her mind, she inclined her head with unusual diplomacy to the former Speaker of the Sun and explained the Kagonesti's reluctance to proceed.

"They are wise. This land is poisoned." His mood shifting abruptly, he suddenly added, "Of course! It's perfect for our purpose! Even brutish humans cannot but be sickened by its miasma. The lake will cover our line of march!"

"What do you mean?" Kerian asked.

He told her. They would continue on their current path and not turn north, as Kerian had planned. Instead, they would circumnavigate the Lake of Death: skirt the north shore, turn south to pass around the eastern end, and at last return along the southern shore.

"To what purpose?" Kerian demanded.

"We will strike Mereklar."

Her jaw dropped. Was he insane? Attack a large, well-defended city?

Before she could say more, one of the Kagonesti announced Alhana's return, and Porthios vanished into the trees. "Come back here!" she hissed. "I'm not through with you!"

"Kerianseray!"

Left with no choice, she turned her horse to meet Alhana. The former queen was cantering down the road, escorted by Samar and three warriors. "I have an important idea!" Alhana cried. "Griffons!"

Her face was alight with excitement, and her thick black hair, for once not confined in its usual scarf, streamed behind her. Nature is not fair, Kerian grumbled silently. She'd washed away the worst of the filth in Bianost and wore clean buckskins borrowed from one of Nalaryn's clan, but next to Alhana she still resembled a Khuri-Khan goat herder. Alhana was several times Kerian's age, yet no one would know it to look at her. When Kerian reached that age (if she lived so long), she would probably look like an old boot.

Kerian repeated politely, "Griffons, aunt?"

"Yes. If memory serves—and it has been many, many years—there was a haven of griffons on the south face of the Redstone Bluffs. Trainers from Silvanost made pilgrimages there to take griffonlets to raise as war steeds. Perhaps some still remain!"

It was a captivating notion. Even a handful of griffons would greatly augment their strength. With just Eagle Eye, Kerian had foiled minotaur ambushes and fended off serious nomad attacks.

"The Kagonesti refuse to go any closer to Nalis Aren anyway," Kerian said. "We could send them to Redstone to check."

The Kagonesti chief was intrigued. He'd never seen a griffon in the flesh. His clan weren't mountaineers, but the new task was eminently preferable to going any closer to Qualinost's tomb.

"We will do as Broom says," Nalaryn announced.

Kerian grimaced. The Kagonesti had bestowed the new sobriquet on her in Bianost. Hardly as fierce or romantic as "the Lioness," it unfortunately described her mangled haircut all too well. They knew she disliked it, but she knew it would do no good to complain. Her people loved nicknames. Each Kagonesti might be called by two or three different ones at the same time. Among Nalaryn's clan were elves called Sky, Runner, Three-Fingers, and Breakbow.

"If you can call up Orexas, tell him of the lady's plan," she said.

Nalaryn shrugged. "He will know. The Great Lord has ears upon the wind."

The small band quickly vanished into the trees on the south side of the road. Kerian felt oddly at a loss without them. Through all the struggle for Bianost, not a single Kagonesti had been hurt or killed. They were like warriors of smoke, creatures whom bandit blades could not touch.

She told Alhana of Porthios's freshly minted notion to drag them around Nalis Aren and attack Mereklar. She expected outrage to match her own, but Alhana, after brief surprise, supported Porthios's plan.

"He was always a bold strategist," she murmured.

It was as close as she had yet come to acknowledging the identity of their leader, but all Kerian could think was that Porthios's wife was as insane as Porthios himself.

The slow-moving column trudged on. The landscape began to look familiar and nightmarishly different at the same time. Shattered stones appeared along the road. Some were the ruins of local buildings; others were debris thrown out of Qualinost when Beryl hit. Vines with blue-black leaves held the broken stones in a vicious grip. Lofty spires lay like colossal fallen trees, stark white against the twisted foliage. Just a few feet from the road's edge, the south shoulder sloped away more steeply, adding to the uncertain footing. The weird, toxic atmosphere affected all of them. Conversation faded. Draft animals became sluggish.

With dawn only two hours away, the column was strung out along the road. A mist was rising, a grayish fog that smelled faintly of rotten flesh. The odor was too much for many of the Bianost elves. Sickened, they fell out of step to find relief by the roadside.

Even a seasoned campaigner like Samar found the stench hard to bear. Ashen faced, he asked, "Are we doing the right thing? If the air gets much worse, we may not be able to continue!"

"It certainly will discourage the bandits from following us," Alhana replied, swallowing hard.

Samar was silent for a moment, debating how best to bring up the topic that had consumed his thoughts for days: he knew the identity of the masked elf.

For as long as he could remember, Samar had been in love with Alhana. She did not know, and he intended she never would. Even after her husband's presumed death, Samar had not allowed his feelings to intrude on her peace. But what would happen to that peace now? Samar feared there could be only one logical reason for Porthios's masquerade. The fire that had not killed him had maimed him so horribly he could not be seen without his mask. If so, what kind of future could Alhana hope for with him?

So disturbed was he by his concerns, when he spoke at last his words were far sharper than he'd intended. "I see our masked leader is nowhere to be found. I imagine he chose a more salubrious route for himself."

Immediately, he regretted his harsh words, but Alhana reined up and turned on him before he could temper them.

"You know nothing about him! How dare you presume to judge?"

In the stillness, her voice was very loud. Samar bowed his head. Flushed with anger, Alhana touched heels to her horse's sides and cantered past Kerian and Chathendor, who were riding ahead.

"My lady," the old chamberlain called. "This place is not safe! Stay with us, please!" He urged his balky mount after her.

Kerian glanced back at Samar. For a moment, the Silvanesti's perpetually hard face showed one overriding emotion: fear. She realized it was not personal fear of the dangerous journey, but concern for Alhana.

It was then Kerian realized something else: Porthios and Alhana had come to some sort of an understanding. Whatever it was, it had eased the anxiety that shadowed Alhana's face. Good for her, Kerian thought; no one should be that lonely and alone.

As for Porthios, wherever he was Kerian wished him bathed in twice the stink that was clogging her nose.

* * * * *

Dawn was beginning to lighten the sky when the wagon carrying the feverish Hytanthas passed under a low-hanging tree limb. A figure dropped from the branch and landed silently in the open cargo box. Hytanthas stirred.

"Who's there?" he murmured.

"A friend."

Bare fingers touched Hytanthas's forehead then withdrew. A twig was placed against his lips.

"Chew this, but don't swallow."

"Are you a healer?"

"Don't ask questions. Chew."

Hytanthas chewed until the voice told him to spit out the bitter-tasting twig. In minutes, he rested easier, the ache in his limbs subsiding for the first time in days. With a sigh, he relaxed, his head lolling against the lambswool blanket that softened his bed atop bundles of Qualinesti weapons.

"What news have you of Gilthas?"

Halfway lost to slumber, Hytanthas mumbled an answer. Under the stranger's gentle but insistent questioning, Hytanthas told of the elves' predicament in Khur and of the Lioness's reluctance to return. He withheld nothing, not of what he knew or his opinions. The questions finally ceased, and the medicine bark that soothed his fever and loosened his tongue lowered Hytanthas into a deep sleep.

Porthios sat back against the wagon's side. For a long time, he stayed there, staring at nothing, lost in thought.

11

Breetan Everride had been in conquered Qualinesti less than two months, but the changes wrought in that time were profound. When she traveled to Alderhelm to investigate the disappearance of Nerakan mercenaries, she rode through a land at peace—the peace of those broken in spirit. However, riding from Frenost to Samustal, she passed through a countryside tingling with alarm, the roads choked with people fleeing north or west. Most were buntings heading to the coast, to take ship back to wherever they'd come from. Mixed in with them were the camp followers and sutlers who always trailed mercenary armies.

A few questions, accompanied by a few coins, posed to refugees elicited surprising news. All over northern Qualinesti, natives were rising up against their oppressors. With Beryl gone, and the Knights of Neraka quiescent in the south, the local folk had only Samuval's bandit army to contend with. The success of the masked rebel in Samustal had shown them victory was possible. In a hundred locations, bandit detachments had been ambushed. Some of these were carefully planned traps; others, spontaneous uprisings. The bandits seemed incapable of regaining control. Whenever they moved to crush one outbreak, two more would erupt behind them. Slowly but surely, Samuval's men and their allies were abandoning the open countryside and holing up in fortified towns.

Although she wore the full panoply of her Order and carried her new crossbow openly, no one molested Breetan. Rebels kept well clear of the Dark Knight. Bandit officers, conscious of their failings, remained aloof lest their weakness inspire her to intervene against them. Only refugees approached, begging for help and steel. Breetan paid for useful information, but refused otherwise to aid the greedy, defeated leeches.

She reached Samustal as dusk was falling. Her target, the rebel leader known as the Scarecrow, was unlikely to be so near the scene of his first victory, but she might glean valuable information there. Besides, she wanted dinner, drink, and a place to rest for the night.

A pall of smoke hung over the center of town. Gossip was divided as to who was responsible for the town's torching: bandits or elf rebels. The old core of the city, which Lord Olin had surrounded with a stockade, was a smoldering ruin. With night fast approaching, traffic was hurrying to the town's south side, where Lord Gathan had erected a palisade around an earthen mound. Breetan headed for that.

There was no gate, just a baffle of timbers to guard the single entrance. The palisade had been erected in obvious haste. The timbers still carried their bark and hadn't been squared; gaps existed between nearly every one and its neighbors. Some of the gaps were wide enough to admit longbow arrows. Breetan saw no guard towers, just a few open platforms atop the wall. She shook her head. Grayden was garrisoning a deathtrap.

Three foot soldiers barred her way at the baffle. "Who're you?" growled one.

"A traveler in search of a meal and a bed."

He laughed harshly. "This isn't Palanthas. They're sleeping on mud in there!"

"Mud protected by a wall," she said mildly.

He stood aside, and she rode through. The enclosed space within the log wall was only two hundred yards across. In the tight confines, tents and shanties had been thrown up in complete confusion, leaving no clear lanes for defenders to reach the wall if there were a general attack. Breetan was disgusted anew. One determined assault and the place would fall like a rotten apple in an autumn breeze.

Ahead, a long tent bore a hand-painted sign proclaiming that Wine, Meat, and Bread (the last two misspelled) could be had within. She dismounted and tied her animal to the picket line. Crossbow in hand, she ducked under the low canvas roof.

Along the far wall was a bar comprising planks laid atop barrels. A muscular man, his head completely shaved, was pouring drinks with both hands. His apron was shockingly white amid the general squalor.

"Step up and state your pleasure!" he boomed.

She called for wine and—after a brief discussion with the proprietor—beef, bread, and whatever came with it. He bellowed the order toward a flap in the back of the tent. She glimpsed flames and saw a large calf turning on a spit.

The wine was a surprisingly good vintage, a Coastlund red. Before her first cup was gone, a trencher of food was placed before her. A generous slab of beef, still red in the center, was surrounded by boiled potatoes, onions, and carrots. Half a round loaf of bread lay atop the meat.

"No food shortage here," she remarked.

He laughed. "Not for them that can pay!"

She ate standing at the bar, for there were no chairs in the place. At the waist-high tables scattered throughout the room, various folk worked the crowd of bandits and refugees, offering gambling, soothsaying, and love for hire. A few feet down the bar, a blind man played a flute for alms. His cap contained a great many broken seashells and very few coins.

While she ate, Breetan questioned the bartender. He'd been there less than a week and considered ruined Samustal a "ripe opportunity." He certainly looked able to take care of himself. Replace his wine urn with a sword, and he'd make a formidable fighter.

He wasn't stupid, either. Eyeing her as he refilled her cup, he asked, "Looking for rebels, Lady?"

"I'm having a look around," she replied carefully.

"The Knights might need to come in, if Samuval can't restore order. Roads are so clogged with fools hightailing it out of the area, he can't get his men where they're needed. I reckon he'll lose the province by autumn."

Breetan swallowed a bite of rare beef. "Are these rebels really so dangerous?"

"They're fighting for their homeland. Makes them dangerous enough."

He was called to the far end of the bar to fill tankards. When he returned, Breetan laid several steel pieces on the bar, making sure her trencher concealed them from the room at large.

"I can see you're a man of wit. Are you also a man of discretion?" she asked. He put his rag over the steel and smoothly drew the coins off the bar. That was answer enough. "What do you hear about the leader of the revolt?"

For the first time, he lost his jovial, assured air and dropped his gaze. He pretended to mop the plank around Breetan's trencher with his rag. She kept quiet, allowing him to think it over, and he finally answered.

"He's a wizard, they say. An elf wizard. And he always wears a mask!"

Breetan covered her excitement by chewing and swallowing another bite of food. Striving to keep a casual tone, she asked, "Any word where he is now?"

He looked uncomfortable and edged away slightly. She put more steel under his rag. He took it as before.

"Lord Gathan is said to be pursuing a band of elves led by the masked rebel. Talk is, they're fleeing to the Lake of Death."

That was a strange place for elves to hide. If she could confirm that lead, she would go to the Lake of Death, regardless of the danger.

She learned nothing more from the bartender. Spooked by her questions, he retired to the opposite end of the long plank bar and turned his back on her.

She drained her cup and was about to call for another refill when a heavy hand landed on her shoulder. Her crossbow was on the floor, its stock leaning against her leg. She eased a hand down to grip the weapon.

"Don't shoot, Lady. It's Jeralund."

The sergeant moved forward and leaned against the bar next to her. He was unshaven and had a black eye and an ugly cut beneath his chin.

"You look hale," she said dryly.

"I'm pleased to see you, too. Another day and I would've joined the bandit army."

He related his adventures with the Kagonesti, his entry into Samustal, the riot, and his subsequent survival on the run in the fields and farms around the city. When Gathan Grayden's army showed up, Jeralund returned, claiming to be one of Olin's hirelings who'd lost his company. For a lifelong soldier, service to Samuval was better than any other work he could find.

As he finished his story, Jeralund licked his lips and cast a look at the remains of Breetan's meal. She pushed the trencher to him and called for wine. The proprietor set another cup in front of the sergeant. Before he could make a hasty retreat, Breetan told him to leave the wine jug. She dropped several coins on the bar, although she'd more than paid for her meal and the half-empty wine jug with surreptitious steel.

The sergeant wolfed down the last of the potatoes, meat, and gravy then drained his cup and poured himself another measure.

"Thank you, Lady. I may live!" he exclaimed.

Hunger and thirst appeased, he asked if he could be of use to her on whatever mission she had undertaken. She pondered only a moment then nodded. It would be good to have a man she could trust at her back, and she was gladder than she'd expected to find him safe and mostly sound.

Stars were shining weakly through the smoky haze when the two of them emerged from the tent. The meal lay heavy on Breetan's stomach, and she pronounced herself ready for bed. Jeralund eyed her skeptically, rubbing his bearded jaw.

"Lady, there's nowhere in this hole I'd feel safe to sleep!"

"So we'll take turns standing watch."

They found cribs at an establishment nearby that called itself an inn, although it was nothing more than a three-sided log structure with a canvas roof. Each crib comprised planks laid side by side, with narrower side slats to keep the sleeper from rolling off. It was the best they could do, and wasn't cheap, but at least they would be out of the mud.

Jeralund sat up in his crib, unsheathed sword across his knees. Breetan unrolled her blanket and lay down next to her crossbow. Sleep was a long time coming. The denizens of the fort all spoke at the tops of their lungs, and every action seemed to involve clanging, clattering, or crashing. Torches burned all night as sentinels watched nervously for rebels prowling the ruins. There were three alarms, all false. Breetan had been dozing less than an hour when Jeralund's watch ended. She took her turn without complaint, but watching the veteran soldier curl up on his bedroll and promptly fall asleep did cause her a great deal of envy.

Hollow-eyed, she stared into the darkness, flinching at every sound, until the brightening eastern sky finally brought the noisy, anxious night to an end.

* * * * *

Flushed with their first victory in many days, the Khurish nomads gave thanks to Torghan, desert god of vengeance. Each family sacrificed a goat or sheep. When the ceremonies were done, the camp reeked of blood and resembled a battlefield.

Adala sat under the shade flap of her small black tent, wrapping yarn around a spindle in preparation for weaving. Wapah approached, out of deference not speaking until his shadow fell across his cousin's lap.

"Maita," he said, "I've chosen a fine white goat for the sacrifice. As head of the family, you should offer it."

She continued to concentrate on her work, wrapping the yarn in smooth, straight loops. Tension was critical in getting a tight weave. Only if the yarn was uniformly wrapped on the spindle would the tension be constant. Wapah waited in silence, knowing she would answer him in her own time.

"Spare the animal," she finally said.

"Shall I do it for you? If you're busy. . . ."

She paused, holding the yarn out taut from the nearly full spindle and looking up at him. "Cousin, if you spoil my work with your prattle, I will be very displeased!"

He bowed deeply, face to the ground. She gave a disgusted snort. "Oh, get up! Am I a khan that you abase yourself before me?"

He squatted on the warm sand and watched her resume her work, wrapping the yarn slowly at first, to get back the rhythm she'd lost. The yarn was a deep, golden yellow, a shade long associated with Weya-Lu weavers. The color was derived from a combination of flowers, including the common dandelion and the rare white desert rose. Other tribes had tried to duplicate it, but no other approached the richness and colorfast durability of Weya-Lu gold.

When Wapah spoke again, he kept his voice low, so as not to throw off Adala's concentration.

"All the families have offered sacrifices to the Desert Master." It was considered bad luck to speak Torghan's name, even among his children. "Will we not do likewise?"

"Not today. My *maita* spoke to me. It said, 'Keep your hands clean, and victory will be yours.' I take this to mean I am not to shed blood, even to honor the gods."

Wapah had to agree. After many deadly, frustrating encounters with the *laddad,* the children of Torghan at last had them at bay. The *laddad* khan had taken shelter on the Lion's Teeth. This was a grave mistake. It was easier for the *laddad* to defend themselves atop the Teeth, but it also was easier for the nomads to contain them. Time was the foreigners' enemy. Their food and water would dwindle, the sun and wind would steal their strength, and in the end they would be helpless before the tribesmen.

Already the downfall of the invaders was at hand. The *laddad* were isolated on two crags. The peak in between had fallen to the nomads in a surprise attack led by the Mayakhur. Southernmost and smallest of the seven tribes, the Mayakhur were renowned for their tracking skills and the acuity of their night vision. In a grand display of stealth, five hundred Mayakhur warriors, wrapped in black cloaks and barefoot for silence, scaled Lesser Fang. They took the *laddad* completely by surprise, and those on the neighboring peaks never knew. Several thousand *laddad* languished in a great pen that normally contained herd animals. Bound at wrists and ankles, the captives awaited Adala's judgment.

Wapah asked what was to be done with them.

Adala shrugged one shoulder. "I don't know yet. I await a sign."

None could say how Those on High would make Their will manifest. But make it known They would, Wapah knew, in Their own time.

When Adala had the spindle loaded, she called for the lap loom. It was brought out of the tent by Zayna, her twelve-year-old niece. The child had come to live with her aunt after the deaths of Adala's two youngest daughters in the *laddad* massacre. The lap loom was old, made of precious wood, and lovingly cared for by generations of Weya-Lu. The frame was worn smooth, its pale hardwood darkened by the countless fingers that had gripped it. Adala began threading golden yarn across the frame.

Wind stirred through the campsite, peppering Adala with stinging sand. She told Wapah to sit on her other side, to shield her work from the wind. He did not answer, only remained squatting on his haunches, forearms resting on his knees, his head down. His wide-brimmed hat protected his face from wind and sand.

Fool, Adala thought indulgently. Too many late night rides and starlight raids. Wapah was not a young man anymore.

Streaks of white cloud rose from the mountains and stretched across the sky, shrouding the afternoon sun and causing the temperature to drop. Adala closed the black scarf around her neck. When her fingers grew cold enough to make them clumsy, she told Wapah to start a fire.

Without raising his head, Wapah replied, "My breath

cannot be warded off by fire. You are cold, woman, because I will it."

That was not Wapah's voice. "Who are you?" she asked, setting aside her loom. "Who dares possess the Maita's cousin?"

Wapah's head lifted, and she flinched in surprise. His gray eyes were leaf green.

"I am the Oracle of the Tree."

"The Oracle was a man. He died many generations past!"

"I am he. Time and place mean nothing to me. I can converse with you now even as I walk the face of Krynn five hundred years in the past." Wapah's slack lips barely moved, but the voice coming from his throat was strong and deep.

Understanding dawned on Adala's face. "Are you the sign I was expecting?"

"You must release the *laddad* you have captured. Take your people from this place. Abandon your campaign against the foreigners."

She recoiled in shock. "But they are murderers!"

The memory of her dead daughters was a wound that would never heal: Chisi lying with one arm thrown across Amalia, as if to shield her gentle, older sister from the death that had ripped their bodies apart. No matter what, Adala had sworn never to rest until their killers were destroyed.

A fresh gust of wind, colder than before, flooded the Weya-Lu tents. They flapped as if trying to take wing. Adala covered the lower half of her face with her scarf and squinted against the rushing air.

"The *laddad* must be freed to continue on their way!" the voice boomed. "The balance of the world depends on it!"

"Vengeance *is* balance!" she retorted, as angry as she was astonished. "Keep your world! I know only the sands of Khur, and here, the *laddad* are a curse and will be dealt with!"

Leaders of the tribes had come seeking Adala's counsel regarding the strange frigid wind. A few arrived in time to hear the voice's last pronouncement. All saw Adala rise to her feet and shout at her cousin. Wapah's talkativeness annoyed them all, but no one had ever seen Adala lose her temper with him.

"I will see the *laddad* out of Khur one way or another!" she raged at her cousin. "This is my *maita!* Those on High have shown it to me! Do you dare stand against Them, ancient seer?"

Thunder crashed. There were no thunderheads in sight, just high streamers of white cloud. As one, the nomad chiefs threw themselves to the sand. Those who had not witnessed it for themselves had heard how Adala's *maita* brought down lightning from a clear sky and obliterated a Mikku warmaster who dared oppose her.

Adala raised her hands to the sky. "Do you hear that, false oracle? Your lies have aroused my *maita!* Begone before Those on High blast you down!"

"It is you who are in danger, woman. You have my warning," hissed the strange voice. Wapah's right arm lifted, fingers pointing limply toward the deep desert south of the camp. "Give up your aggression now, or you will find a *maita* you do not want: the fate that awaits all who hate."

Suddenly Wapah collapsed in a heap. Thunder pealed once more, and the icy wind ceased. Slowly the chiefs and warmasters got to their feet. Wapah seemed none the worse for his possession. In fact, he was sleeping soundly until two men shook him awake.

"Eh?" he said blearily. "I dreamt a storm was coming—"

He was interrupted by the cry from the nomad camp. Adala's tent was pitched on the east side of a low dune, sited to catch the first rays of the sun. She hurried over the rise, with her chiefs and Wapah trailing behind.

In camp, men and women stood outside their tents, staring southwest at a point where the sharp line between pale sand and blue sky was blurred. The hazy spot grew rapidly in size until all could see the tall column of dust that was rising above it, like a dagger pointing from sky to ground.

"Whirlwind!"

Dozens of voices screamed the dreaded word, and the warriors around Adala took up the cry. Those in camp dashed for their tents. The warriors with Adala vaulted onto their horses and rode hard for their threatened families. Only Adala did not panic. She stood calmly, alone until Wapah joined her.

"What a vivid dream I had!" he said, scrubbing his eyes with both hands. When he took his hands away, he saw the danger bearing down on them, and his mouth dropped open. "Maita, we must flee!" he cried.

Every nomad feared whirlwinds. They weren't frequent, but their terrible power was the stuff of campfire legend. The greatest hero of the desert tribes, the war chief Hadar, was said to have been carried off by a monster whirlwind, which flung him to the Dark Moon. Hadar battled the god of the dark moon for centuries. When Hadar finally defeated him, the god fled, convincing his brother on the White Moon and their sister on the Red to go as well, lest the stalwart war chief attack them too. That was when the sky had changed and the moons vanished, what foreigners called the Second Cataclysm.

Adala had Wapah's wrist in an iron grip. He strained against it, pleading with her to get to safety. She would not be moved.

"My *maita* will not allow this!" she said, eyes squinted against the rising sand. "My *maita* is stronger than any false oracle!"

And so she stood, one hand clamped on Wapah's wrist, the other drawing the scarf over her nose and mouth. Around her, men and women fled or dug holes in the lee of the dune, seeking cover from the killer windstorm. Adala closed her eyes. Terrified, Wapah did likewise.

The wind roared like the howls of ten thousand wolves. The sand beneath their feet was sucked away, and Wapah went down on his knees. Adala sank up to her ankles but remained proudly upright. She was shouting into the teeth of the storm. Wapah couldn't hear her words. He bent so his face touched his thighs. The wind pushed him backward slowly, until his arm, still held by Adala, was stretched in front of him.

He looked up. The column of wind writhed like a living thing, shredding tents and flinging their contents in all directions. A bronze pan, used to cook a family's communal meal, spun through the air and landed next to Wapah. The flat, three-foot span of metal buried a third of its width into the sand. Had it struck him, he would've been sliced in half.

He reached for the pan, stretching himself as far as he could since Adala stubbornly refused to move. He managed to wrap his fingers around the handle and dragged the pan close. With it in front of him like a screen, he began to inch forward on his knees. When he was directly beside Adala again, he banged his fist against her leg until he got her attention. He stood, and they held the broad pan before them. Sand sang off its bottom. Now and then a larger object torn from the camp caromed off the makeshift shield.

The center of the whirlwind passed directly over them. The bronze pan was torn from their hands. Adala released his arm, and Wapah fell to his knees. Adala's feet lifted six inches above the ground.

He threw his arms around her ankles. The force of the wind lifted him until only the toes of his sandals still touched the sand. Face buried in his cousin's robe, sand clogging the air, Wapah couldn't breathe and couldn't see. He felt Adala being pulled from his grip.

All at once, like a string breaking, the force holding them aloft suddenly was gone. They dropped onto a drift of sand. Wapah rolled away from Adala and began brushing sand from her sleeves and gown, all the while asking if she was all right, if she had been injured. She pushed herself up on her hands. He saw she was trembling, but one look at her face told him it wasn't fear that moved her.

"I have taken his measure!" she declared, eyes blazing with triumph. "The false seer thought he could forestall my *maita*. No one can do that! Those on High are with me!"

He helped her stand. Sand cascaded from their robes. As Wapah brushed himself off, Adala stared at the dissipating whirlwind. It tracked northeast, rapidly losing cohesion. Soon it was only a rolling cloud of dust, tumbling over the dunes toward the Lion's Teeth. She hoped it would hold together long enough to drop a load of sand upon the *laddad*.

Wapah's attention was fixed in the opposite direction. Their camp was completely wrecked. Not a single tent still stood. The ground in all directions was littered with debris. Here and there frantic men and women tore at mounds of sand, digging out those buried beneath. Adala's face wore a fierce grin, but Wapah saw precious little to be happy about. He was immensely relieved to see Adala's niece. Zayna was pulling the lap loom from the flattened remains of her aunt's tent. She began cleaning the mechanism with careful fingers.

Riders arrived from the camps of the other tribes. None but the Weya-Lu had been hit by the whirlwind. Even the Mikku camp, in direct line with the storm, had escaped damage. The storm had twisted wide around their tents, causing only minor problems.

It seemed a message directed at Adala and her tribe. Those few chiefs who had heard the voice tell Adala the *laddad* must continue passed that information on to their fellows. Many wondered aloud whether it might not be best to release the captives, so as to appease the wrath of the ancient oracle.

"In one more day," Adala announced, "the *laddad* khan will have his people back. Their numbers will swell the ranks of the hungry and thirsty on Broken Tooth and Chisel, and their khan will know his doom is at hand."

The chiefs were relieved. She had heeded the oracle's warning.

She seated herself in the shade of her tent, which Zayna had erected with Wapah's help, and picked up the lap loom. Since she obviously intended to return to her weaving, Wapah and the nomad chiefs began to drift away.

"One thing more," Adala called out, cleaning the last of the grit from the loom. "Let every male among the captive *laddad* be branded on the back of the left hand. Use the herd mark of the Weya-Lu."

Wapah stared at her in shock. He took a step toward her, hands held out as if in supplication. "But why, Maita? What purpose can such terrible cruelty serve, except to anger the *laddad* khan?"

"It will tell him, and everyone who sees the mark, that his people were freed by *our* will, not by the hand of Sahim-Khan, not by the efforts of the *laddad* khan, and not by the meddlesome false seer who calls himself the Oracle. The mark will stand as a sign of their failure and our *maita*."

The chiefs were not happy with the order. They were men of honor. Only slaves and herd animals were branded. To put such a mark on a captured enemy was a gross insult. But all had seen Adala stand before a whirlwind and emerge unscathed. Such courage demonstrated great power of the soul. Her survival underscored the awesome strength of the Fate that worked within her. They could not disobey her command.

As Wapah watched the chiefs and warmasters ride away, he felt something shift within himself. Perhaps it was the eyes of his soul opening wide at last, perhaps it was only the breaking of his heart, but in that moment, he knew Adala was wrong. Powerful forces were undeniably at work in his cousin, but he no longer believed that *maita* and the will of Those on High guided her actions. If he hadn't held onto her when the whirlwind had passed over, she would have been torn from the sand and flung heavenward like Hadar, never to return. He had felt the terrible pull of that wind, and it was he who had saved her, not divine fate. That and the pointless cruelty of the order she had just given were proof he could not ignore. Adala was on the wrong path. Hatred and pain had blinded her.

He found his horse, thankfully spared by the storm. Taking a skin of water, he rode out of the ruined camp. His mission—his *maita*—was clear.

12

Like a vast black mirror, the Lake of Death covered what had once been the great city of Qualinost. By day, the water was a deep jade color, but at dawn, before the sun first broke over the eastern rim of the sky, the water resembled the darkest ink imaginable. Despite the summer season, the air was chilly, and perpetual fog drifted over the lake. Beryl's impact had created so mighty a crater, the ground around the lake sloped down to its forbidding shore. Here and there, bits of masonry stood out dull gray against blasted trees that reached into the lightening sky like blackened, fleshless arms. Everything dripped gray moss and smelled worse than a hundred cesspits.

"You fell into that?" Samar exclaimed. "Somewhere there's a sorcerer who does not like you."

Kerian did not agree. Whoever had plucked her from Khur and dropped her here was watching out for her, not trying to harm her. A malign magician could have left her where she was, facing death among the nomads, or could have let her plummet unchecked into Nalis Aren. She had been saved for a reason. To fight in Porthios's rebellion? Perhaps. There were many questions. Being here again, beholding the awful lake, invited questions.

The column of elves paused briefly to rest just after dawn. No one wanted to leave the road and pitch a tent or unroll a blanket in the murky domain surrounding the lake, so they slept in or under their carts or didn't sleep at all.

The lake and its immediate environs were cloaked in a perpetual twilight. Only the elves' own innate sense of time told them when an hour had passed. Alhana rode the length of the caravan, rousing the Bianost militia and wishing them good morning. Weary shoulders straightened, and the townsfolk bowed their heads respectfully as she rode by. She was very different from Orexas, who appeared seldom, spoke rarely, and commanded by mystery. With a kind smile and warm words, Alhana revived their spirits as she progressed along the line.

At the tail of the caravan she asked Samar, who rode with her, to send a few riders back down their path to look for signs of pursuit. The heavy atmosphere around the lake blunted vision and smell to an alarming degree. They did not want to be surprised by bandits.

Back at the head of the column, Alhana found Kerian and Chathendor studying the map Kerian had found in Bianost. It didn't show the lake, of course, having been drawn well before the fall of Beryl, and they were trying to reconcile the current topography to that shown on the map.

"This must be the road we are on," Kerian said, tapping the map with a blunt nail. "Silveran's Way."

"I recall it," Chathendor said, eyes closed, drawing on his memories. "It wended gently across the land north of the city." Opening his eyes, he returned to reality with a jolt. "It does not seem possible."

Alhana asked if they'd seen Orexas. Kerian had. She'd been dozing on the ground when he ghosted by her, heading straight down the road.

It was time to follow him. No heralds cried; no silvery trumpets trilled. Alhana gave the word and it was passed through the royal guards to the Bianost militia. She led them forward. Kerian and Chathendor followed half a horse length behind, and Samar rode a few yards back, at the head of the royal guards.

A walking pace was the best they could manage, given the state of the road. The once smooth, well-tended way was cut by fissures. Mud, stones, and boulders from higher up the steep hillside had washed down onto the road. The town elves were not experienced drovers, and many of their beasts were not suited as draft animals. Frequently, elves had to jump down and push the wheels by hand to help the laden wagons over rough or muddy spots. Progress was so glacial, the lead riders were forced to stop and wait for the caravan of wagons to catch up.

"At this rate Samuval will die of old age before our revolt gets under way," Kerian observed.

The encouraging words Alhana meant to say died on her lips. Instead, she gasped, "Merciful E'li. Look!"

Above this end of the lake a sizable cloud of vapor had collected. It writhed as if stirred by contrary winds, yet the air was perfectly still.

"Do you see it?" Alhana cried.

"The fog, lady?" asked Chathendor, confused.

"Yes! It looks like a dragon!"

Kerian squinted, staring hard. "It does?"

"Its jaws are opening!"

The cloud dissolved, ribbons of mist snaking apart. Alhana turned sharply to her companions, but they reported seeing only an amorphous bank of fog. Chathendor murmured, "You are very tired, lady. You haven't rested properly since leaving Bianost."

Kerian was not so dismissive. "It may have been a vision, an omen meant for your eyes only."

"An omen of what?"

Kerian could not guess, but once the mist had thinned, she saw an odd yellow gleam over the lake. Alhana saw it as well, but neither of them could say what it was. Only Chathendor, whose aged eyes were too weak to pick it out, realized what it was.

"The Tower of the Sun," he whispered.

Formerly the seat of the Speaker of the Sun and the center of every Qualinesti's life and heart, the great monument was awash in the foul waters of Nalis Aren, the sunburst glory of its golden peak reduced to a faint ocher smudge.

Trying to dispel the murk before their eyes and in their hearts, Alhana called for torches. Branches were hacked from the skeletal trees. Kerian feared they would prove rotten, but it was not so. The wood was dry and very hard, almost petrified. It burned readily, with a flame so pale it was nearly white, and gave off little smoke.

Two riders went ahead, carrying torches. Almost immediately their light fell on Porthios, standing in the middle of the road. All of them flinched in surprise, and Kerian looked as though she had a choice obscenity for him, but she glanced at Alhana and stifled it.

"We cannot continue on this road," he told them. "The bridge that once spanned the White-Rage is destroyed."

The White-Rage River flowed north out of Nalis Aren. They could not continue their course unless they could cross it. Locating a ford suitable for the wagons would require a long journey north.

In the bleak silence, Porthios said, "Another bridge still stands."

Kerian slapped her thigh with one hand. "Why didn't you just say so? How much farther north?"

"Not far, but the only way to get there is. . . ." His ragged robe swung like a tattered banner as he pointed up the hillside. The way was not only steep, but the ground was torn up and strewn with boulders, making for a difficult climb.

Once more the map was called for. Studying it, they determined that the bridge Porthios had found was reached by Birch Trail, a narrow track that more or less paralleled Silveran's Way.

Hardly had they decided to ascend to Birch Trail when a rider came galloping recklessly down the broken road. He clattered to halt before Samar.

"My lord! The enemy is behind us!" he cried. "Less than an hour away!"

"In what strength?" Kerian demanded.

ALLIANCES

The Silvanesti guard didn't like answering a question from a Kagonesti, but Samar impatiently told him to get on with it.

"Five hundred horse and a thousand infantry."

Alhana quickly sent Samar off to organize their defenses. He and Kerian galloped away together, trading rapid-fire thoughts on how best to meet the threat. The two of them recently had discovered common ground: neither approved Porthios's plan to attack Mereklar.

Once the two warriors were out of sight, Alhana realized Porthios had come to stand by her left stirrup.

"We must protect the weapons cache," she said.

"*You* must keep out of the way. Let the warriors defend the arms."

Lifting her chin, she replied, "I choose my place, and my place is with my people."

Urging her mount forward, she moved into the whirlwind of activity filling the road. Kerian had gotten all the townsfolk who weren't actually driving wagons to clear off the conveyances and arm themselves. The first cart was beginning the climb up the hillside. Its driver stood on the box, reins in hand, and whistled and shouted to his horses. They started up gamely, but within a few yards, slipped on the thick, loose surface. The cart skidded sideways and overturned. Wrapped bundles of spears and swords spilled out.

Porthios directed the reloading of the cart. Once it was done, he told the driver to cut loose his team.

"What?" the driver and Kerian demanded together.

"With this uncertain surface, elves will fare better than horses. The carts must be dragged up by hand."

"That's madness!" exclaimed Kerian.

"Yes. Proceed."

The elves proceeded. Once the horses were cut loose, two elves grabbed the traces and two more got behind to push. Straining, they hauled the cart up eight feet. The wheels sank into the loose ground, but by heaving and rocking, the elves advanced the cart to a level spot above Silveran's Way.

Those watching cheered until Porthios snapped, "Why are you standing? There's work to do!"

Kerian watched in amazement as elves seized wagons and carts and started up the sharp grade. The first cart was dragged a further twenty yards. Its elves announced the discovery of another road, narrower than Silveran's Way but in better condition. They had found Birch Trail.

The caravan comprised thirty-one carts and thirty-five wagons. There weren't enough elves in the militia to haul all of them up at once, so as teams reached Birch Trail, they had to slide back down the hill and take another turn.

Kerian left them to it and headed down the road to find Samar and the guards, preparing to defend against five times their number of bandits.

"Orexas has them hauling the wagons up by hand," she reported. "The horses can't make it."

Samar glanced at his own mount. "How do we get up there?"

"We don't." Kerian drew her sword and rested the flat of the blade against her shoulder. Another rider joined them. Her eyes widened. "You're in no shape to fight!"

Hytanthas Ambrodel, pale and wan but sitting straight in the saddle, shifted the sword he carried. "I'll not be carried up a hill like freight," he replied testily. She could not argue with that.

Soon enough the tramp of many booted feet reached their ears, loud even in the deadened air of Nalis Aren. Another sound played counterpoint: the high crack of whips. Kerian knew the meaning of that.

"Goblin infantry! Stand by to receive an infantry attack!"

By sections, the warriors wheeled about and rode back sixty yards, halting near the end of the caravan. Coming toward them was a phalanx of goblins in black-painted armor. Behind each of the four companies, a human officer rode on horseback. On foot in front of him were half a dozen sergeants, driving the goblins forward with whips.

ALLIANCES

When the goblins spied the mounted elves, the foremost company halted and their ten-foot pikes dropped briefly. Then, with a concerted shout, they lurched forward again.

"Any tactical suggestions?" Samar asked, seating a helmet on his head.

"Kill them."

Smiling grimly, Samar raised his sword and shouted, "Elves! By section, charge!"

It was hard for the goblins to gather much momentum while marching uphill, but the downhill slope gave the elves extra impetus. The sight of the Silvanesti hurtling toward them caused the front ranks of goblins to miss a step, despite the whips driving them onward.

The two forces collided. The elves beat aside the goblins' pikes so they passed harmlessly overhead. The first two ranks of goblins fell beneath the weight of the horses. Kerian stood in her stirrups and laid about on both sides. The result was simple slaughter. The goblins' shields were slung on their backs, in marching order. Without protection, the creatures were defenseless once their pikes were deflected.

Despite the redoubled efforts of the sergeants and their whips, the rear ranks backed away. Goblins along the edges of the formation were shoved off balance and went tumbling down the hill, smashing into stones and tree trunks. The entire first company broke, retreating into the ranks of the second.

Samar gave the command to withdraw. Bloody but intact, the elves rode back to where they had started.

Wiping sweat from her eyes, despite the unnatural chill around the lake, Kerian saw a flock of dark birds take flight from trees higher up the hillside. They were carrion birds, the kind that collected at every battlefield, but something had frightened them into flight.

"Ambush!" she cried.

Her warning came a fatal second too late. A swarm of arrows plunged down among the guards. Some found their marks, and elves fell. The remaining guards scattered, with some trying to ride up the hillside at the concealed archers.

Their mounts met with no more success than had the cart horses. A second volley whistled down, and many of the riders struggling up the slope dropped from their saddles.

Something bumped Kerian's horse, and she heard a gasp. Samar swayed in the saddle, an arrow lodged under his left arm. He'd thrown himself in front of her and taken a missile that would have hit her. He slumped over and she yelled at him to hang on. At her command, Hytanthas grabbed the reins of Samar's horse and led the wounded elf away.

Surrounded by dead and wounded, Kerian turned her back on the bandit army. She lifted her buckler aloft to ward off plunging arrows and shouted, "Elves of Bianost, rally to me! Fight for yourselves! Fight for your people!"

In twos and threes, volunteers crawled out from under the remaining wagons. They were terrified, faces pale as snow, but Kerian was proud of them. They were none of them warriors, yet they came.

"Yes! Well done!" she cried. "We won't let them sting us like this! Rally to me! Let's flush out those hornets!"

Theryontas and a dozen elves armed with a mixture of weapons formed up behind her. Another volley of arrows rained down. Heeding the Lioness's warning, shields came up and the elves warded off the arrows—all but one. One elf found the thrum of missiles in flight too much for his curiosity. He peered over the rim of his shield and took a shaft in the face.

"Keep your shields up!" Kerian dismounted and ran to the uphill side of the road. "Stay together! Let's go!"

With the remaining guards holding off the scattered goblins, Kerian led her small band up the slope toward the hidden archers. More elves were cowering behind boulders and bushes. The Lioness told them to follow. By the time she reached the thin line of trees along Birch Trail, Kerian had close to sixty followers. A few were armed with bows. She set them to sniping at the archers half hidden down the trail.

While the groups traded arrows, she led a band of twenty higher up the hillside under cover of boulders, broken masonry, and twisted trees. At the first level spot, she directed them to crouch and follow her as she worked her way toward the bandit archers.

Unfortunately, one member of her band was too eager. Impatient with the Lioness's careful approach, Theryontas went rushing down the slope. He'd taken no more than three steps before an archer put a black-fletched arrow in his chest. The two elves who followed him also were struck down. Kerian gave the order, and the Bianost elves attacked the archers—seventeen humans in dark red brigandines. Most of the humans were still sniping at the elves below and didn't react in time. They quickly fell to the furious elves.

The enraged town elves would have killed every one, but Kerian halted them. She wanted to question the two remaining archers.

One, with a heavy dark beard, had a slash on his neck and could not speak. The other, a clean-shaven, teenaged boy, was so terrified Kerian had to ask his name twice before he stammered out the answer. He was Wycul, part of the Frenost Free Company, a mercenary band loosely affiliated with Gathan Grayden's host. The main body of the army had marched to Mereklar after receiving reports of uprisings in that town. The Free Company and the goblin infantry had been ordered to follow the outlaw elves wherever they went. The goblins weren't happy about entering the environs of the Lake of Death. There were things there that *ate* goblins, they said.

A horn blared from below. Several of Alhana's guards were waving to catch Kerian's attention. She ordered her little company back down to Silveran's Way. They helped themselves to the dead men's weapons. Bearing the bodies of Theryontas and their other fallen, and with Wycul supporting his wounded comrade, they descended.

With the defeat of the archer trap, the goblin infantry had fallen back out of sight, leaving the ruined road strewn with dead. Horses trotted back and forth, looking for their fallen riders.

Two of Alhana's royal guard met Kerian at the edge of the road. "Lady! A catastrophe!" exclaimed one. "Our royal mistress—!"

Fearing the worst, Kerian was already sprinting for the trees. She left the two human captives with the riders.

Alhana was not dead. She lay unconscious on the ground, her head cradled in Chathendor's lap. They were surrounded by anxious elves, but the rise and fall of Alhana's chest brought a relief so strong Kerian's knees felt weak. Samar lay unconscious beside Alhana. The wound under his left arm was tightly bound. He'd lost much blood, and his face was waxen, but he breathed. Kerian could see no visible wound on Alhana.

"What happened?" she demanded.

Chathendor said, "An arrow struck her horse. It bolted and she was thrown."

Carefully, Kerian touched the back of Alhana's neck. She thanked the gods Alhana's neck wasn't broken, but when her questing fingers found a wet spot above and behind her left ear, Kerian grimaced. A heavy blow could cause bleeding inside the skull, resulting in slow death. Alhana couldn't be moved for fear of worsening her condition. Yet the elves were in a terribly exposed position, athwart the road, with active mercenary bands at their heels.

With Alhana and Samar down, and Theryontas dead, the Bianost elves looked to the Lioness for leadership. She acted quickly.

"Everyone will ascend to Birch Trail. The rest of the carts and wagons will be left here, their loads divided and carried up the hill. Scavenge wood from the empty wagons to make litters for the wounded."

Elves hurried to carry out her orders. Chathendor's tear-filled eyes lifted from his mistress's still face. "What do we do, lady?" he whispered to Kerian. "Will she live?"

"She will. I won't allow her to die."

Porthios approached. For once, Kerian was extremely glad to see him.

He commanded the royal guards to block the road, to protect Alhana, who must remain where she was. His voice and bearing were such that the warriors obeyed without demur.

He had less success with Chathendor. The old chamberlain would not be sent away with the wounded.

"I do not leave my lady," he said flatly, and Porthios was forced to acquiesce. It was that or have the old elf lifted bodily.

The unconscious Samar was borne away, and Kerian prepared to go as well, knowing she could be of no use here. Before she departed, she cast one last worried glance at Alhana and said quietly to Porthios, "You're a healer? It will take one of uncommon skill to save her."

"I healed myself when I was nothing but blood and shattered bones. I will heal her too."

Porthios's voice rang with conviction. Kerian nodded, but in her heart, she was certain Alhana Starbreeze would not survive the coming night.

13

Gilthas stood on the extreme edge of the plateau, inches from a thousand-foot drop. Warm air rose from the desert, stirring his hair. The wind of the previous day had raised a mighty cloud of dust into the sky. The sun, shining through the haze, was a dully glowing scarlet orb, like an iron left in a forge fire.

A branding iron, he thought, gazing at the morose sky.

Spread on the plateau behind him were hundreds of his kith, captured by the nomads then released. They had been returned without the water, food, weapons, and tools that had been with them on Lesser Fang. Already supplies were reaching critical levels, and this added burden made the situation all the more difficult. There wasn't even the compensation of a renewal of their fighting strength. The nomads had maimed every male elf.

Just when Gilthas thought he had plumbed the lowest depths of injustice and suffering, the bottom of the abyss was lowered again. So many elves purposefully maimed. Not even the Knights of Neraka had stooped to such tactics. It was a blow worthy of a dragonlord, only none had ever thought of it.

Was the choice of the left hand intentional? Did the nomads know that most elves, unlike the majority of humans, were left-handed? Or had they considered themselves merciful, branding the lesser-used hand?

Gilthas nearly choked on the thought. In the end, it didn't matter. The horror of the deed made such fine distinctions irrelevant.

The nomads who escorted the freed elves to the foot of Broken Tooth kept assuring the elves that they were not responsible for the branding.

"You bear the mark of the Weya-Lu," they said. "We of the Mikku and the other tribes did not do this."

So all was not harmonious among the various tribes. That might be useful later.

Hamaramis arrived at Gilthas's vertiginous perch. The old general was followed by a group of young warriors. All were dusty and burned by sun and wind, and all burned just as fiercely with a desire for revenge. The expressions on their faces prompted Gilthas to cut Hamaramis off before he even started speaking.

"I will not hear plans for revenge, General. If you have other military matters to discuss, I will listen."

Hamaramis's face worked for a moment, then he burst out, "Sire, something must be done! Every elf on this summit knows what happened, and every one expects us to strike a blow for justice and for honor!"

He sounded like Kerian. Gilthas felt a great weariness drag at his limbs. With as much patience as he could muster, he said, "All that would accomplish is more death. Find another option."

Hamaramis's lieutenants openly seethed with resentment but did not speak.

"Our situation grows ever more dire, Great Speaker. If we don't fight our way off this peak, we'll never leave here alive."

That was only too true. They were fundamentally weaker than when they'd first scaled Broken Tooth and could not remain much longer in idle safety. The nomads were displaying unusual staying power, keeping out of reach yet remaining close enough to menace any force that dared descend to the desert. The capture of Lesser Fang had infused the Khurs with new confidence and weakened the resolve of many elves.

It would be all too easy for Gilthas to lead his warriors off the peak, crying, "Let us die fighting!" And that is exactly what would happen: the soldiers would die in battle and the civilians left behind would perish of heat and thirst. Thus would end the most ancient race in all the world. The flame of Kith-Kanan, of Silvanos, would go out.

As he stared at the hazed vastness of the Khurish desert, Gilthas's hands clenched into fists. His face stiffened with anger, and his sun-bleached brows lowered in a ferocious frown. He would not allow it to happen! His people would not die here, not while there was breath in his body.

He turned away from the precipice. "There is always another way, General," he said harshly. "To die starving or die fighting are not the only answers. Find me another!"

His injunction met only blank stares. His chin lifted. Despite the threadbare garb and matted, unwashed hair, Gilthas Pathfinder suddenly was every inch the Speaker.

"Let the word go forth," he said, using the terminology of a royal decree. "The Speaker of the Sun and Stars will go amongst his people and ask one question: How shall our nation be delivered off this rock?"

The warriors were skeptical, but they saluted their sovereign and hurried to carry out his command.

As sunset washed its usual scarlet and gold brilliance over the cloudless sky, Gilthas put on his best remaining robe—not a Khurish *geb*, but a gown of forest green silk with narrow bands of yellow at neck and wrists—and made himself as presentable as a comb and dry cloth allowed. With his councilors and highest-ranking warriors in tow, he set out to talk to his people. Stopping at every tent and bedroll on Broken Tooth was not practicable. Instead, he would visit the shared campfires that dotted the plateau.

The sentiment for peace, he quickly learned, was widespread. Even the elves who'd been brutally branded by the Weya-Lu voiced a great longing for peace.

"We'll find it," Gilthas vowed, "in the Inath-Wakenti. The problem is how to survive to get there."

Ordinary elves had only vague notions about their enemy. They saw the nomads as marauders, thundering on horseback across the blazing sands, with swords upraised. The politics of Khur, the religion of the desert tribes, and the meddling of the rogue mage Faeterus were not common knowledge. Many elves, when asked by their king how best to save the nation, said, "Could we not talk to the humans, Great Speaker?" The Khan of Khur had allowed the elves to dwell outside his capital for five years, in exchange for steel and trade goods. Surely the world-renowned eloquence of elf diplomats could negotiate passage to the valley.

It was a notion Gilthas promised to consider. No one had tried to parley with the nomads since the departure from Khurinost. The Khurs' rage was so extreme and so unfathomable, no one on the elves' side had considered talking to them. Perhaps the time was coming for that to change.

Some elves had no interest in negotiations. They wanted to defeat the Khurs in battle. Otherwise, they said, the sacrifice of all those who had died thus far would have been in vain. The nomads had shown themselves to be treacherous, irrational, and unbelievably cruel. No one could talk to an enemy like that.

Around midnight, when many of his entourage had given up from exhaustion, Gilthas was still moving from campfire to campfire, still listening. As he passed the tent of a well-born Silvanesti named Yesillanath, he was seized by a fit of coughing. Yesillanath and his wife, Kerimar, invited him inside. The coughing did not abate, and when blood began to trickle from the Speaker's lips, the two Silvanesti shouted for his escort.

Planchet burst in and found the Speaker sinking to the ground, his slender frame wracked by spasms of coughing, his face deathly pale. Planchet knelt, supporting his king against one knee. General Hamaramis arrived as Kerimar was offering the little wine they had left. The general asked for something stronger. Yesillanath handed him a vial of clear liquid. Hamaramis's eyes widened as he read its label, but he opened it and passed it to Planchet.

"Drink, sire!" Planchet urged.

Gilthas did, and it was his turn to look surprised. The vial contained Dragon Sweat, a distilled liquor mainly used in medicines. It was so potent Gilthas lost his breath completely for an instant, long enough to break the cycle of coughing. Planchet would have lowered him to the rugs spread out over the rocky ground, but Gilthas said no. It was easier to breathe where he was, sitting up against his friend's knee.

"You are ill," Planchet said reproachfully.

"Merely a cough."

The blood speckling the front of his robe belied that comment, as did Kerimar's bloodied linen kerchief, which Gilthas still clutched in one hand.

"This is no simple cough, sire!" said Hamaramis. "Tell me, is it consumption?"

Gilthas nodded, but insisted he had the problem in hand. Hamaramis listened to him with all deference then asked for a healer to tend the Speaker. Yesillanath said Truthanar, a Silvanesti, was the most skilled healer available. The general went out to dispatch warriors to find Truthanar.

Planchet carefully wiped the blood from his sovereign's lips. "Planchet, I must continue," Gilthas whispered.

"No, sire."

His tone and firm grip on Gilthas's shoulder brooked no argument. Gilthas smiled weakly. "Mutiny."

"Yes, sire."

A chill seized Gilthas. His teeth chattered and cold sweat beaded his forehead. Planchet laid him on the ancient rugs that covered the floor of the small tent and pulled a thinner rug over his shivering body. The carpets once had graced the halls of Yesillanath's mansion in Silvanost. Four hundred years old, they were the work of a master and worth a fortune. Gilthas commented on that, and Yesillanath shrugged.

"Out here, a rug is a rug, sire," he said. "And it is better to sleep on a rug than a rock."

Gilthas became delirious soon after, drifting in and out of consciousness. He mumbled, spoke nonsense to Planchet, conversed with friends long dead, and more than once said his wife's name, his tone hopeless and sad.

Planchet chafed at the delay, asking Hamaramis why it was taking so long to find the healer. Broken Tooth wasn't that large an area to search.

As if in answer, the rush of footfalls sounded outside the tent, but the relief of those within was short-lived. Hamaramis's warriors had returned alone.

"General, we bring strange news," panted one. "A nomad claiming to be related to the leader of all the tribes has surrendered himself to us!"

Not wanting to disturb the Speaker's troubled rest, Hamaramis kept his voice low, but fury throbbed in every syllable. "Where is the healer, fools? He'd better be on your heels, or by Chaos, I'll throw the lot of you off this cursed mountain myself!"

The second soldier assured him their comrades were bringing the healer. "But this human, my lord, he insists he can lead us off the peak and away from the nomads!"

Silence descended in the small tent. Gilthas plucked at Planchet's arm, and the valet helped him sit up. "What is this human's name?" he rasped.

"Wapah, Great Speaker."

"It's a trick, sire. They seek to tease us off our summit."

"The nomads are not so sly, General. I will speak with this nomad."

Two more soldiers arrived, bringing the Silvanesti healer, Truthanar. "Who sends soldiers to fetch me? I was treating branding victims!" the aged Silvanesti grumbled.

Gilthas cleared his throat. "I apologize, good healer. It was not my order, although I am the patient you have been brought to see."

Truthanar bowed and commenced his examination immediately. He peered in the Speaker's eyes and mouth, listened to his chest, and applied oiled mitrum leaves to Gilthas's forehead. By calculating the time it took for the leaves to dry and fall off, Truthanar could determine his patient's temperature. The diagnosis did not take long.

"Consumption, without a doubt. Aggravated by exhaustion, privation, and I dare say heartache. Your fever is high, sire, but as yet your lungs are not too greatly affected. A month from now, unless things change, it will be much worse."

"Don't worry, Master Truthanar. A month from now we shall all be in a better place."

Hamaramis feared the Speaker meant they'd all be dead, but Planchet knew his liege better. He wasn't surprised when Gilthas added, "Bring me the human Wapah. His help may be the difference between life and extinction for our entire nation."

* * * * *

Favaronas squatted on the west bank of the wide, shallow stream he knew as Lioness Creek and dipped a hand in the water. In his other hand, he held a bunch of wild watercress. The greens were bitter, but starvation was worse. If he was going to cross the haunted valley, he would need all the strength he could get.

A librarian by training, Favaronas had accompanied the Lioness's survey expedition to the mysterious Valley of the Blue Sands, hoping to find a new home for the elf nation. Although the valley was indeed a mild clime and green, they quickly discovered all was not well. The place known in Elvish chronicles as Inath-Wakenti, the Vale of Silence, contained no animal life at all, not even insects. Its only occupants were massive stone ruins and strange globes of light that roamed the valley by night and whose touch caused warriors to vanish. Beneath the ruins they found a network of fantastically painted tunnels and chambers.

After the Lioness had a vision of danger stalking her husband, she departed for Khurinost on her griffon, leaving the remaining soldiers to follow on horseback. Before leaving the valley, Favaronas had made an astounding discovery: the odd stone cylinders he'd found in a tunnel beneath the valley were actually scrolls. A brief glimpse of the knowledge they contained convinced him that tremendous power lay untapped within the valley, power unknown in the world since the Age of Light. If he could learn to use it, he could save his people and vanquish those who had invaded their homelands. At the first opportunity, he sneaked away from the warriors and returned to Inath-Wakenti.

For many fruitless months, he had dwelt in the valley, learning frustratingly little. The phantom lights, so numerous while Lady Kerianseray and her warriors were present, suddenly were nowhere to be seen. The entrance to the underground chambers was lost. Favaronas was certain of its location, at the base of an overturned sarsen, but although the huge stone remained, nothing marked the hole but a shallow pit. He dug down a ways but found only the blue-tinted soil for which the valley was named.

His efforts to map the extensive stone ruins likewise had been fruitless. The ruins were maddeningly irregular. Up close, the progression of wall, column, and monolith made superficial sense but, considered as a whole, added up to nothing. There were no traces of lesser structures between the cyclopean stones. If they were the remains of a city, then the city had no plan he could discern. It was as if an enormous ceremonial site had been begun and never finished.

Just the night before, when Favaronas had begun to fear he'd traded his old life for an unobtainable dream, he had a revelation. As he idled by the creek, using small pebbles to model some of the stone ruins he'd mapped that day, he suddenly realized the ruins were not ruins at all. The monoliths weren't the remains of larger structures. They were, taken all together, some sort of code or symbol. The problem wasn't recognizing what they had been, but what they were supposed to represent. The only way to do that was to see the whole, rather than the scattered parts. He needed an eagle's eye view of the field of stones.

The eastern mountains were the only accessible high point. To the west, the peaks rose sheer from the valley floor, like the walls of a forbidden fortress. The slopes of the eastern mountains were more gradual. Getting there posed a severe problem, though. He would have to leave the relative safety of Lioness Creek. The nightly apparitions and will-o'-the-wisps never came beyond the creek, so Favaronas made certain he returned each evening to its western shore. To reach the eastern mountains, he would have to travel several days on foot across the widest part of the valley.

With much trepidation, he resolved to do it. He had little choice. His habit of remaining within a day's walk of the creek meant he was stripping the land thereabouts of its meager provender. If he was going to discover the secret of Inath-Wakenti before he starved, he had to forsake safety and go to the eastern mountains.

He ate raw watercress and pondered how to carry the water he would need for his journey. It was a cool day, with a bright blue sky quartered by white cloudbanks. As he watched the clouds sail in stately fashion from east to west, he became aware of movement nearby. He'd spent so much time alone, he was very sensitive to the slightest motion. Lowering his eyes, he saw someone standing on the eastern shore of the stream. Favaronas recoiled so hard he fell backward.

The morning sun was brilliant behind a figure wrapped head to toe in layers of dusty dark cloth. The robes were so bulky, the stranger hidden so completely by them, he could be elf, human, or draconian.

"Who are you?" Favaronas called out.

He hadn't spoken in so long, his own voice sounded strange to him. When he'd first come to the valley, he'd talked to himself, as much for company as anything, but he'd soon stopped. Somehow it seemed wrong to disturb the silence.

The robed stranger did not reply. Instead, he began to move, gliding across the water. His sandaled feet touched the surface of the creek but didn't break through. Favaronas yelled. Before he could gain his feet and run, the stranger was in front of him.

"Rise and face me, Favaronas." The stranger's voice was low, its cadence deliberate.

"Who are you?"

ALLIANCES

"A seeker of knowledge, like you. Serve me, and I will protect you. I need someone who knows these ruins."

Honesty compelled Favaronas to disclaim such expertise since he hadn't dared venture more than a day's walk from the creek.

The robed figure asked what he feared. That was all the prompting the desperately lonely scholar needed. He told of the ghost he'd seen in a tunnel beneath the monoliths, the colored lights whose touch caused elves to vanish, and most bizarre of all, his encounter just outside the valley entrance with four half elf, half animal females.

The stranger cried, "This is just the knowledge I need!" He withdrew his hands from where they'd been hidden within his wide sleeves and gestured excitedly. "I am a mage, Favaronas. With my protection, you can venture away from the shelter of this stream. I will defend us both."

Judging by the shape and size of those pale hands, Favaronas felt sure he was in the presence of an elf. Somewhat emboldened, he asked the stranger's name.

"Faeterus."

The name was familiar. Favaronas felt certain he'd heard it in Khurinost. "Did the Speaker send you?" he asked.

A humorless chuckle sounded inside the deep hood. "I am here at no one's behest but my own."

Favaronas was torn. The strange elf's confidence was reassuring, but there was something unsavory about him, something more than his bulky, uncomfortable-looking robes. It was disquieting to know he'd heard of the mage in Khurinost, yet the fellow wasn't one of the Speaker's advisors. Skilled mages were in very short supply, and the elf nation needed every source of power it could obtain. The Speaker's edicts wouldn't allow a rogue mage to practice his art openly. There were some elves in the world who did not acknowledge the Speaker's authority. What kind of person was Faeterus?

"Follow me, Favaronas! You will learn the answers to all the questions crowding your mind."

"And if I choose not to?"

"Then I leave you to your fate. The mysteries of this valley will claim you, and you will never know why!"

Favaronas considered a moment more, but really, what choice did he have? He would be safer with a companion than alone. "I will go with you. Not as your servant or subject, but as a colleague."

His bold statement fell rather flat. Faeterus's attention had been diverted by movement in the bushes farther down the creek's western shore. Although faint, the noise was impossible to mistake. Inath-Wakenti was devoid of singing birds, chattering squirrels, or buzzing insects, but something was moving.

Whatever it was, it seemed to upset the mage, perhaps even frighten him. His lordly manner vanished, replaced by haste.

"Yes, yes. Colleagues. Now let us depart!"

Favaronas wouldn't be rushed. He didn't have many possessions but wouldn't leave behind those few he owned, especially the stone scrolls.

"Very well," Faeterus said. "Gather your things. Make for the eastern mountains. I will join you later."

"Later? But I don't—"

The rustling in the bushes grew louder, and the mage gave up all pretence of calm. "Remember our agreement!" he commanded then vanished. One moment he was there, ragged and bulky, the next, he was not. As Favaronas stared, even the impressions left by the mage's feet on the bluish soil rose up and smoothed away.

The disturbance in the bushes did not worry Favaronas. The valley's ghosts came out only at night, and they never crossed to his side of the creek. Nomads never entered the valley at all, for it was taboo in their religion. If someone was here, it could only mean the Speaker had sent another expedition, perhaps to find his favorite librarian?

He turned to retrace the route to his campsite and shrieked in surprise.

An elf stood by the bushes a few yards away.

"Who are you?" Favaronas was frightened but he was also angry. Weeks of utter solitude and two strangers appeared within moments of each other!

The fellow was no member of the royal guard. He was a Kagonesti but dressed more like a human. Eschewing the usual fringed buckskins and turquoise jewelry, he wore a leather jerkin, suede trews, and ankle-high canvas boots. Beneath a brown leather hunter's cap, short hair framed a face bare of paint or tattoos. On his nose were perched wire-framed spectacles with bright yellow lenses.

"Peace," he said. "My name is Robien. I mean you no harm."

"Why are you here?"

"I'm a hunter."

Favaronas frowned. "There's no game in this valley."

Robien removed his odd spectacles and tucked them carefully into a pocket in his jerkin. "Oh, yes there is," he said quite pleasantly. "You were just speaking to him."

14

Porthios sat by Alhana, his eyes never leaving her face. She lay on her back, hands folded at her waist, her head turned slightly to the right, toward him. A small droplet of blood appeared from one nostril, standing out against her pearl skin like ink on snow. He gently blotted it away with the tip of a gloved finger.

The two of them were alone, or as close as made no difference. After an hour sitting stiffly upright with Alhana, Chathendor had at last ceded his place and crawled a few yards away to sleep. The rest of the column had moved into concealment in the woods. No sounds or firelight betrayed their position, but a part of Porthios's mind knew they were there. The larger portion knew only Alhana, and anger.

Alhana did not deserve this fate. During the blackest days of his recovery, Porthios had built a picture of his wife's last moments. That dream allowed him to cling to the shreds of his sanity as his body healed. It did not entail their reunion. No thought of that ever entered his mind once he knew the extent of his injuries. He could never impose his hideous existence on one so beautiful, so refined and good. Instead, his dream was of a day, many decades distant, when Alhana was on her deathbed. A small golden box would be delivered to her. It would contain his ring and a short scroll detailing his reasons for staying away. She would read the scroll and finally know the depth of his love. She would shed a tear for his unshakable honor and perfect devotion, then, gently and painlessly, life would leave Alhana Starbreeze.

A death like this, bathed in the stench of Nalis Aren, with an aged retainer snoring nearby, was not to be imagined. Porthios had endured much. Knowing Alhana lived, although parted from him forever, gave him the strength to tolerate. But if he must watch her die—

She would not die. Dreams and romance aside, she simply had too much more to do. There was too much at stake, and far too much left unsaid.

He took her hand. "How can I save you?" he whispered. Her fingers were slack in his grip.

Pain had saved him from dying. The agony of burns and broken bones had raged so hard within him, he couldn't hear death's soft summons. He still battled pain during every waking moment. The endless war made him strong.

He realized he was squeezing her hand very hard. Rather than ease his grip, he increased it, crushing her fingers between his own. Had she merely been sleeping, she would have awakened and cried out. Abruptly, he lifted his free hand and struck her across the face. Her head lolled away from him.

"Don't you feel that?" he said, voice rising.

Despite the situation, shame twisted his stomach. In all their long lives together, he'd never lifted his hand to her. He felt bile rise in the back of his throat, but he struck her again. There was no response.

His eyes burned. Since his injury, he had been unable to weep proper tears. Grief sweated from his eyes.

The sound of footsteps brought his head up. Chathendor still slept, and he first thought Kerian was intruding, but the footfalls were coming from the road, not the woods. He did not bother to rise. Blinking moisture from his eyes, he merely waited.

Night at the Lake of Death was not much different from day. It was darker, though not much, and perhaps the stink was less. The mist clung to the lake's edges, creating the illusion the black cauldron was rimmed with snow.

A figure emerged into feeble starlight. He was human, a stout old man with short white hair standing out from his head in all directions. He leaned on a blackthorn staff and wore threadbare priestly robes. Porthios immediately recognized his mentor from the forest.

The old priest called, "Greetings, my faceless friend."

Porthios did not answer. The old man shuffled closer. "You grieve. I felt your sorrow far down the road."

"What do you want?" Porthios's voice was choked and dry.

"What I've always wanted, to lend my support."

Alhana's breathing faltered for an instant, and Porthios felt his heart skip a beat. "Support? If you really wanted to support my people, you would right the wrongs done to them."

The priest came forward. He halted a few steps from Alhana's feet. "This one I've known a long time. So many great mortals she knew, without ever quite achieving greatness herself." Porthios glared at him, but the old man went on, oblivious. "Direct intervention seldom works out well. Trust what I tell you, my wounded friend. It has been tried before, and the consequences inevitably are worse than the original problem."

"Damn your consequences! Help her!"

"You love her, yet you let her believe you were dead all these years." The old priest shook his head. "Strange pride you have."

"I've done what you asked," Porthios rasped. "I started a rebellion with a handful of followers against an enemy who commands thousands. We've achieved remarkable things. Must Alhana now die for the revolt to continue?"

The eyes in the friendly, jowly face sparkled with a strange inner light. "If I say yes?"

"Then I will die with her."

"You must save your people."

"Kerianseray can lead the rebellion, or Samar, or Nalaryn."

"No one but you can do it."

"Then heal her!" Porthios hissed, standing quickly. "You're a god, aren't you? It is within your power. Heal her, or I swear to you I will die with her this night!"

The priest's body wavered and evaporated like smoke. One instant he was there; the next, he was not. Porthios stalked to where the old man had been. He opened his mouth, ready to shout denunciations and accusations to the sky, but the priest's voice stopped him.

"Mind what you say, my proud friend." He was back, standing near Alhana's head, exactly where Porthios had been. "More ears than ours are listening, and some disapprove of my meddling." Porthios managed a sharp, sarcastic laugh, and the old fellow added, "Yes, as you deduce, no one approves. Hence the guises and trappings I'm forced to hide behind."

"I meant what I said. The choice is yours."

"You would sacrifice your entire race for this one female?" Porthios folded his arms across his thin chest. The old human sighed. "Very well. But after tonight, you'll not see me again for a time. I have too many irons in the fire." The priest shifted his blackthorn staff from one hand to the other.

"Try to appreciate my subtlety, will you?" he said rather plaintively. "Even when you can't understand it."

He turned and walked back to the road.

"Is that all?" Porthios cried, incredulous.

The old priest looked back, the odd light glimmering again in his eyes. "What more did you wish?"

He vanished.

Alhana moaned. Porthios dropped to his knees. "Alhana! Alhana, can you hear me?" he shouted.

"They can hear you in Schallsea," she muttered, both hands coming up to cover her ears.

Porthios smiled. None could see it, and the unaccustomed movement hurt the ravaged skin of his face, but he smiled nonetheless. He had no idea what price the god might exact for Alhana's life. At that moment he did not care.

The Lioness and a dozen guards crashed through the underbrush. A limping Samar followed close behind.

"What is it?" Kerian cried, brandishing a sword. "We heard you shouting!"

Porthios regarded her blandly. "I was merely speaking to the Great Lady."

They looked at him as if he'd gone mad. Alhana sat up. Voices exclaimed in amazement and Kerian cried, "Alhana, can you hear me?"

"Why does everyone keep saying that?" she replied crossly. "My head feels as though it may split down the center, but there's nothing wrong with my ears."

"Do you remember what happened?" Kerian asked.

"An arrow hit my horse. I fell?"

"You were dying, aunt!"

"Evidently her head is harder than we realized," said Porthios.

Kerian knelt and gently probed the back of Alhana's head. She found no blood, but Alhana winced sharply as Kerian touched the site of the wound. No longer life-threatening, it was still extremely tender. From the way Alhana held her left arm, it was obvious she had a variety of other bruises from her fall.

Everyone stared at Porthios, wondering what to make of the amazing development. Alhana opened her mouth to question him but realized it wasn't the time or place. Instead, she allowed Samar to help her stand, and the two injured elves leaned on each other.

"We've lingered long enough here," Porthios said. "The bandits will be back, and with reliable troops this time. We must get everything up to Birch Trail before morning."

Kerian scratched through her cropped hair. She was exhausted, having lain awake waiting for word that Alhana had succumbed to her injury. Instead, Alhana was alert and standing, albeit shakily. How had Porthios accomplished such a miracle? Certainly he was clever and fearless. Did he have magical skill as well?

"What are you waiting for?" Porthios asked testily.

"Inspiration," was her equally grumpy reply.

She left to rouse the Bianost volunteers and the Kagonesti. Samar and Alhana, still leaning on each other, went to marshal the guards. The mounted Silvanesti were withdrawn to the stalled caravan, leaving only a half dozen riders behind to keep watch on the climbing elves. Far down the road was a faint, ruddy glow, as of massed campfires.

The two human captives were a burden the elves could ill afford during the coming climb. Wycul and his injured comrade were bound and gagged, taken to a point several hundred yards away, and tied securely to two different trees.

In accordance with Kerian's earlier command, the wagons remaining on the road had been unloaded. Their wood was cannibalized for makeshift litters and the remaining detritus hurled down the hillside to conceal it as much as possible. Their loads were divided into lots and bundled onto the backs of elves. Everyone carried a portion, even the elderly Chathendor. Only Porthios and the wounded in their litters went unburdened. Torches were forbidden. The elves had to rely on their fabled night vision to complete their tasks and make the ascent. In the murky night of Nalis Aren, more than a few wished their eyesight were as preternatural as other races believed.

Worse was the lot of Alhana's mounted guards. Their horses simply could not make the ascent. After several falls, Porthios yielded to Alhana's calm insistence that the warhorses were too useful to be left behind with the draft animals. He ordered a small band of riders to lead the horses away and find a safer way up. The remaining dismounted fighters would stay by Alhana.

Alhana made the ascent in a litter of spear poles and blankets carried up the hillside by four strong warriors. She was none too steady on her feet and was forced to admit she would only slow them down should she try to climb on her own.

Porthios led the way. All through the night, the elves climbed, narrow lines of straining bodies snaking up the hillside. Laden with the bundles of arms, and bearing the litters of wounded elves, their progress was slow. By the time dawn cast its pitiful light on the hillside, the bottommost climbers were only yards above Silveran's Way.

Kerian was taking a breather against a boulder when word came up from the lowest level. Movement had been seen eastward on the road. With Nalaryn gripping her hand and acting as counterbalance, she leaned far out from the hillside and looked. The sun wasn't yet up, but there was light enough to show her a dark mass moving along Silveran's Way. She had no trouble identifying packed ranks of human soldiers, clad in burnished armor. The bandit horde was coming. Of the few warriors Samar had left to guard the road, there was no sign. They must have been overwhelmed.

She nodded, and Nalaryn pulled her back from the drop. "Pick up the pace! The bandits are coming!" she called up and down the hillside.

The two of them resumed their own ascent and reached Birch Trail in time to see the sun break through the fence of dead trees rimming the broad crater. About a third of the elves were there, including Alhana, Samar, and Chathendor. The rest were scattered across the face of the high hillside, in plain view of the enemy. Kerian asked where Orexas was.

"No one knows," Alhana grumbled. She sat on the ground, looking wan and small. The black cloud of her hair emphasized her pallor, and the linen bandage that cushioned her head wound kept slipping over her left eye, lending her a distinctly piratical air.

"Do your guards have bows?" Kerian asked.

"Of course," replied Samar. He understood what she wanted. Stiff from his wound, he moved among his guards, ordering them to string bows and take their places overlooking Silveran's Way. Just under a hundred lined up shoulder to shoulder, arrows nocked.

The broad column of bandit soldiers drew closer and closer until the very ground vibrated with the thud of their boot heels. They filled the road from side to side, two or three thousand in number. Each wore a hammered breastplate and polished pot helmet with a vertical comb, carried a shield, and bore a long pike ported over his shoulder. Beards curled under their helmet straps like exotic foliage. Kerian never could understand how human males could bear all that hair on their faces.

She lay on her belly and studied the enemy. At the head of the column rode a quartet of officers. Captains and subalterns plodded along the flanks. Kerian didn't recognize the green banner drooping above them. Gathan Grayden must not be leading the troop. As yet, none of the bandits had noticed the elves frozen in place on the hillside.

"Steady. Perhaps they'll pass on," she said to the archers, although she didn't really believe it.

The elves had tried to clear away all signs of their presence below. Unfortunately, there simply hadn't been enough time to remove every piece of ruined carts and broken traces. The lead horseman saw enough to cause him to halt the column. Kerian cursed softly but thoroughly in Kagonesti.

A voice shouted an indistinct command, and the leading company went clattering down the road to investigate. Pikes leveled, the soldiers advanced, their attention focused on the far side of the road, on the slope descending toward the lake.

Kerian nearly laughed in relief. They were looking in the wrong place!

With the bandit force seemingly distracted, some of the elves on the hillside unwisely resumed climbing. It didn't take long for a bundle of swords, awkwardly slung over someone's back, to clang against a rock outcropping. The mounted officers turned to look. Shouts went up. The elves had been seen.

"Prepare," Kerian said, rising to her knees.

The four remaining companies on the road swung around to their left and advanced. Kerian let them come. The pikemen clattered against each other as they began the difficult climb. Seeing them flounder, Kerian gave the command: "Now! Loose!"

Arrows dropped onto the closely packed bandits. In a harsh reversal of the ambush the elves had stumbled into, they commanded the heights and the mercenary soldiers suffered. A few, goaded by their officers, broke ranks and tried to get free of the confusion so they could climb, but the hail of death from above was too much. Despite the furious bellows of their commanders, the bandits fell back. Lowering their pikes, they interlocked shields to ward off the missiles.

Kerian hoped they might withdraw completely, but their officers stubbornly held to the road. Commands were shouted and the ranks parted. A lightly armed company of bowmen jogged forward. Judging by their long hair and dark faces, they'd been hired from one of the Blood Sea Isles, probably Saifhum.

"Aim for the archers," Kerian said, but the Silvanesti around her were already shifting to hit the new target.

With six-foot yew staves, the longbowmen could loft arrows to Birch Trail, but most of it was out of their view, screened by boulders, twisted bushes, or scraggly trees. The elves still climbing were not so fortunate. Long shafts hummed through the air, and elves began to fall. The bundles they carried burst on impact, scattering swords, daggers, and pieces of armor along Silveran's Way. The human soldiers cheered each time an elf toppled.

The Silvanesti archers gave as good as they got. With the advantage of height, their short bows could put a broadhead lengthwise through a man on the ground.

"Keep moving! Get up! Come on!" Kerian shouted, waving the climbers on. She clenched her fists, furious at her inability to help as elf after elf was hit and tumbled down the hill. Porthios's sudden, silent appearance at her side brought a flinch of surprise.

He regarded the fight with his usual detachment then announced, "We need a greater weight on our side."

"A brilliant observation. If you have extra archers concealed somewhere, I'd be happy to make use of them!"

"No, not arrows. Something bigger."

He studied the area. All around were bits blasted out of Qualinost to rain back down upon the ground. A particularly huge, wedge-shaped slab of stone stood on the edge of Birch Trail. Porthios pointed at it.

"That one. Over the side with it."

Kerian was aghast. The slab probably weighed three or four tons. No doubt, in days gone by, elf mages could have shifted it in the blink of an eye. Unfortunately, there were no mages in sight. Ignoring her sarcastic comment, Porthios walked away and called for all available elves to gather at the stone.

Spears and pike shafts were thrust under it as levers, but most of the elves simply took hold of the slab with bare hands. Samar joined in, despite his wound. So did Hytanthas. The archers continued to loose at the longbowmen below, but their supply of arrows was running low. As each one ran out, he joined the effort. The only ones not engaged were Alhana, sitting in her litter, Porthios, arranging bodies around the slab, and Kerian, who thought it a stupid waste of effort. When Alhana rose, straightened her bandage, and made her way to the slab, Porthios gave the Lioness a sardonic look.

She slammed her sword into its scabbard. "I will if you will!"

The slab rocked, encouraging them to new efforts. The elves redistributed themselves. Porthios counted to synchronize their efforts, and they heaved with all their might. Teeth clenched, sinews cracked. The slab came free of the grasping loam and rumbled down the slope.

"Get clear! Get clear!" Kerian cried.

The archers still in action darted aside. The slab toppled forward. As the narrower top hit the ground, the slab cracked in half. The front portion dropped down the steep hillside, followed immediately by the weightier rear.

Climbing elves in the path flung themselves aside, and a shout went up as the mass hurtled past. The first piece hit the ground in front of the bandits and shattered into a thousand fragments. The wave of stone shrapnel tore through the ranks, mowing men down in bloody heaps. Then the second, and greater, portion of the stone arrived.

The dense block survived the impact intact. It bounced, rising twenty feet into the air and tumbling end over end. Bandits scattered, climbing over their own comrades in their panic to escape. Down came the slab on the road, landing not with a crash, but with a solid, sickening crunch.

Kerian rolled to her feet. The bandits were deserting en masse, mowing down any officer who got in the way. The Saifhumi longbowmen had vanished. Most were crushed under the second boulder.

"Stop gawking!" Porthios said. "The enemy is still below. Loose arrows!"

He was striding among Alhana's royal guard, all of whom were standing and staring in dumb shock, their bows at their sides.

"They're running. Let them go," Kerian objected.

"Do as I command!" he shouted.

Reluctantly, they obeyed, sending a fresh cascade of death into the crazed mob beneath them. Porthios had them continue the bombardment until the last climbing elf gained Birch Trail. Finally, he gave the order to cease.

The Lioness was hardly the gentlest of fighters, but even she couldn't bear the carnage. "So you've finally killed enough?" she snapped.

"Not nearly enough. But for now, it will have to do."

Many elves had cuts, broken bones, and arrow wounds. Samar could not stand; his wound had opened as he strained to shift the slab. Hytanthas was on hands and knees, coughing uncontrollably. Porthios commanded all get up and follow him. Much to Kerian's surprise, they did. Those more able assisted the others, and water was quickly brought to the few in greatest need, but in minutes every elf was on his or her feet, burden shouldered, following their ragged, hard-eyed leader east on the new trail. Without draft animals, the carts and wagons were drawn by hand. Not to be outdone by the Bianost townsfolk, Alhana's guards, horseless, organized themselves to help carry the bundles of arms and armor. Kerian delayed her own departure to make sure no one was left behind.

Alhana was back in her litter. Helping to shift the stone had left her with barely enough strength to hold up her head, but her eyes were alight with triumph as she was borne past Kerian.

"We are saved! Our cause continues!" she said.

True enough, but the cost was high. Nearly two score dead since they'd arrived at Nalis Aren, and thrice that many more hurt. Porthios no longer evinced a deft touch. His tactics had become blunt and brutal, and the Lioness said so.

"You cannot judge him."

Kerian fell in step alongside the litter. "Why? Because he once wore a crown?"

"Because he suffers more than we do."

Alhana could never be less than beautiful, but grime and bruises had certainly taken their toll on her ethereal perfection. It was readily apparent that she, and the rest of them, had suffered, but how had Porthios been harmed?

"Did you notice how he held his right arm close to his chest?" asked Alhana. Kerian had not. "In shifting the sandstone slab, he broke his wrist."

"How do you know?"

"I toiled beside him. I heard the snap of the bone."

Despite herself, Kerian marveled at his fortitude. "But he never said a word!"

"No. He never did."

Unbelievable, Kerian thought. But was it really so strange? She could easily imagine Gilthas doing the very same thing, enduring agony in the service of his people. He'd never complain either.

She wondered where Gilthas was and how he was faring. The news brought by Hytanthas was at best thirdhand, but if true, then the elf nation was facing the gravest peril it had yet encountered in Khur. And here she was, hundreds of miles from the scorching desert, following a masked lunatic, in company with a former queen who called her "niece" and a band of town-dwelling elves and royal warriors.

A twisted shape caught her eye. Lying on the hillside below her were the remains of a tower, one of four that had supported the arched bridges encircling Gilthas's city. *This* is elf land, she thought with a stab of pride, nurtured and cherished by our race. The lifeless sand of Khur is not. It belongs to the nomads. Let them keep it. Much better to fight for the true elf heartland, here, and not for some alien desert.

She thought of Nalaryn's clan, seeking griffons. How she missed the freedom and power of flight on Eagle Eye! Give her a hundred such creatures, and she would sweep the bandit horde out of existence! The image was an intoxicating one, especially after the day's grim fight. If they could find griffons, as Alhana had suggested, then everything would change.

15

Another night, another ocean of stars shining down on the embattled elf nation. In a tight column three persons wide, the elves hurried across sand still hot from the sun. Behind them, bulking large against the night sky, Broken Tooth was alive with firelight.

Gilthas led the column. Like all his people, he was barefoot and bereft of even the smallest scrap of metal. Every bit had been removed and put away lest the slightest glint, the softest clanking, betray the clandestine departure. With Gilthas was the nomad Wapah, who made his way across the ocean of sand with all the confidence of a child of the desert.

Despite Gilthas's intention to speak with Wapah immediately, Planchet, ably seconded by the healer Truthanar, had convinced him to wait until the next morning. He returned to his small shelter, swallowed the mild sleeping draught Truthanar prescribed, and slept nearly twelve hours. Wakening at midday, he felt better than he had in months. At least he wouldn't disgrace himself with another collapse.

From the first, Gilthas believed Wapah's offer of help to be sincere. His councilors required convincing. He convened the group at the base of the stone cairn, fully intending to signal Taranath on Chisel once a plan for the elves' departure was reached. Planchet, particularly skeptical, repeatedly asked Wapah about his change of allegiance.

Wapah explained in his inimitable way: "A sick man craves medicine. A well man does not. Give a well man a specific medicine, and you might kill him. Withhold medicine from a sick man, and he may die."

"Which means what?"

"I do not love the foreigners who dwell in my country." Wapah's pale eyes flickered over the group. "But even less do I like what their presence has done to my people. The sooner you are all gone, the happier we shall be."

"A lesson you should have preached to your chiefs."

Wapah was unfazed by Planchet's coldness. He shrugged. "Alas, the Weyadan is beyond lessons. She has fallen from balance and no longer sees the hard edges of truth, only a single vista of vengeance. But peace and purity cannot be bought with blood. The former exists in each of us and is not a chattel to be coveted. And blood, once spilled, only calls forth more blood, until no more remains."

Gilthas allowed the discussion to continue for only a few minutes more. By means of mirrors, they signaled Taranath that they were coming. Taranath's reply came soon thereafter. He had gathered and saved every drop of water he could store for just such an event. His people would be ready when the Speaker arrived to lead them away.

One grave matter remained. The nomads were always watching the elves. Their view of the summit of Broken Tooth wasn't perfect, but they could not fail to detect the exodus of so many. It was Planchet who suggested a solution. Someone must stay behind to stoke campfires, make noise, and let themselves be observed atop the plateau.

Hamaramis and the Speaker agreed but wondered who would volunteer for such a task. Those remaining behind stood a good chance of falling into the hands of the nomads.

"I have a band more than willing." Planchet tapped the back of his left hand with one finger, a gesture instantly understood by all: he meant the male elves who had been branded by the nomads.

"How many volunteered?" asked Hamaramis.

"All of them."

Gilthas shivered. It wasn't illness that caused his reaction. Hundreds of elves had been cruelly maimed, their left hands rendered nearly useless. When an opportunity presented itself for them to aid their people, every one stepped forward.

"They needn't all stay," Hamaramis said. "The diversion can be accomplished with two hundred."

"And me," Planchet said.

Gilthas shook his head. "No. You're too valuable to me, and to the nation."

"More valuable than any of the others who would stay behind?"

Yes! Gilthas wanted to shout, but he did not. Hamaramis and Planchet argued briefly. The old general agreed that a leader was required but said any junior officer would fit the bill. Planchet stubbornly insisted there was no need to command a young warrior to take on a task for which he himself had volunteered. Hamaramis finally gave up and stomped away, radiating annoyance. Planchet turned to his king.

"Great Speaker, grant me this boon."

Planchet had been with Gilthas since his days as the so-called Puppet King in Qualinost. The valet-cum-bodyguard had been handpicked by Gilthas's mother, Lauralanthalasa, to serve her son. His background included service to the dark elf Porthios. Throughout occupation, exile, and battles beyond counting, Planchet had always been there, the solid center in Gilthas's turbulent life. Even before the estrangement from Kerianseray, the young king had relied on Planchet's sage council, his unwavering support. How could Gilthas let him sacrifice himself? How could he refuse?

With a heavy heart, Gilthas granted his wish but said severely, "Swear on your ancestors' house you will escape and find your way back to us. Swear it, Planchet!"

Unexpectedly, Planchet went down on one knee. He swore the oath. Gilthas rested a hand briefly on his friend's bent head, a lump rising in his throat.

During the afternoon and evening the elves prepared for their departure, and Planchet prepared to remain. He purposely chose the two hundred most disfigured, crippled, and handicapped out of the many volunteers. In addition to their maimed hands, most had wounds from sword, spear, or arrow. They would be most likely to slow the rest of the column down during the escape.

An hour before midnight, Planchet gathered his band at the northeast corner of Broken Tooth for the Speaker's review. Every elf stood as straight as he was able. Two hundred right hands rose as one, the salute of the Branded. Planchet lifted his right hand too.

"The Band of Deceivers stands ready to carry out our mission, Great Speaker," he declared.

"No, you are not deceivers." Gilthas thought for a moment. "You are the Sacred Band, heroes of our nation!"

No rousing cheer greeted his declaration. All were conscious of the need not to draw nomad attention to their activities. Planchet would have left it at that, but Gilthas could not. He stepped forward and embraced his friend. For a handful of seconds, he allowed himself to lean into Planchet's solid strength, then he stepped back.

Planchet saluted, lifting his sword to his face. "Farewell, sire. Preserve the line of Silvanos and Kith-Kanan at all costs."

What cost was left to pay? Gilthas didn't allow his bitter thought to show on his face as he walked slowly down the line of volunteers, meeting the eyes of each, saying thank you. When he was done, he addressed the group one last time.

"May E'li bless you all. We shall meet again!"

Taking his place at the head of the column, he followed Wapah down the steep trail to the desert floor. Their first destination was Chisel, to collect those holed up with Taranath and replenish their water supply. Very little food remained, but they could do without food far longer than they could go without water.

Yet it was not the peak before him, but the one behind that drew Gilthas's eyes over and over. On Broken Tooth, campfires glowed and cooking pots clattered. Small groups of figures were periodically silhouetted against the starry sky. If he hadn't known there were tens of thousands of elves behind him, he would have believed they all were still on the summit.

After the constant wind atop Broken Tooth, the desert seemed still as a tomb. The air cooled rapidly with the sunset, but sharp rocks and the heat stored in the sand, made the elves' barefoot progress painful. The few horses and other animals they possessed were muzzled with strips of cloth, shod hooves likewise wrapped. All their carts they'd left on the plateau. The elves could descend more rapidly without them, and creaking cartwheels were very noisy. Most of the heavy impedimenta they had carried since leaving Silvanesti and Qualinesti lay abandoned on Broken Tooth. The remaining burdens were carried on backs, in litters, or in simple travois. Like the elves, Wapah led his horse.

They passed north of Lesser Fang in utter silence. Wapah thought it likely his people would station lookouts there, although he had no way of knowing exactly where they might be. Dawn was only four hours away when they reached Chisel. Wapah held up his hand. The command to stop was relayed silently down the column. Every elf knelt and waited.

Hamaramis came forward to the Speaker. "Taranath's signal?"

"Not yet."

Gilthas's column could not make a sound or show any light, lest the nomads nearby discover them. It was entirely up to Taranath to time the meeting correctly and signal them.

Wapah calmed their fear of discovery by reminding them the nomad camps were all south of the Lion's Teeth. Mounted patrols would be abroad, but by dawn the elves would be shielded by Great Fang, largest of the peaks, which lay northwest of Chisel. By day, they could take cover in the caves that riddled Great Fang. Each night they would move farther north and west. The last of the Lion's Teeth, Pincer, was thirty miles from the mouth of Inath-Wakenti. When they left Pincer's cover, they would face their greatest danger.

Many interminable moments passed before a smoky red light flared on the side of Chisel. The light bobbed up and down a few times then plunged. Striking the rocks below, it burst into a shower of sparks.

The Speaker signed for everyone to stand. Limbs weakened by age, deprivation, and wounds had stiffened in the cold night air. From all along the line of refugees came muffled groans and gasps. Hamaramis frowned, but Gilthas could only shake his head ruefully. They were not the race of bygone years, whose grace and elegance had set the standard for the world. One day they would be again, he vowed. Within the shelter of Inath-Wakenti, they would grow strong. Elf civilization would rebound, becoming greater than ever. He believed it. He had to.

A double line of riderless horses emerged from the darkness. Each pair was led by a closely cowled elf warrior. The animals were laden with waterskins. The lead elf halted before Gilthas and whispered a greeting. Lord Taranath, he said, had sent water for the Speaker's company.

With hushed words and hand signals, the water caravan was brought forward. Soon, spring water was being doled out to elves who hadn't tasted fresh water in many days.

Wapah circled back. "This delay is not wise," he insisted. "We should move on."

"My people have suffered much. Let them drink," Gilthas said.

Taranath rode out of Chisel's shadow into the starlight. With him was the balance of the remaining cavalry.

"Great Speaker!" he said. "I rejoice to see you!"

"Rejoice more quietly, if you please," Gilthas warned, although he was smiling. He clasped Taranath's hand.

The cavalry went ahead to screen the slow-moving column from surprise attacks, and Gilthas led the rest forward. They would be well hidden by the peak of Great Fang by the time dawn began to lighten the sky. The next obstacle would be to cross the mile-wide gap between Great Fang and Ripper. Hamaramis counseled waiting for night to cross the open desert, but Gilthas considered delay risky. The nomads might discover them at any time.

Wapah also advised they keep moving. The deception on Broken Tooth wouldn't fool the Weyadan for long, and she would come looking for her hated foes. He said there was a wadi north of Great Fang. It ran northwest and would conceal them from riders on the desert plain above. However, using it would take the elves away from the shelter of the Lion's Teeth.

"We must quit the peaks sooner or later," Gilthas said. "We will follow where you lead, Wapah."

"It is a wise man who travels the lighted path."

"And wiser still is he who keeps his sword in his hand," countered Hamaramis.

The elves set out again. If all went well, they would reach the pass into Inath-Wakenti in three days.

* * * * *

Breetan Everride and Sergeant Jeralund entered the city of Mereklar at the end of a mile-long procession of foot soldiers. Virtually the entire army of Gathan Grayden was marshaled in the city. Jeralund cast a practiced eye over the assemblage of men, goblins, even a battalion of ogres hired out of Kern, and estimated the total strength at forty thousand. It might not be a cohesive force, but it was a formidable one.

The great concentration of might had been prompted by the debacle at the Lake of Death, where forces commanded by Lord Haym, bandit governor of Mereklar, had been bloodily repulsed. The time for economy was over. Lord Gathan intended to crush the elf rebellion once and for all, even if it meant using every able-bodied warrior in the region. Aside from a few small garrisons remaining in towns such as Shrivost, he had stripped his realm of every soldier he could find. The Knights of Neraka could seize western Qualinesti with no more than a palace guard if they chose. Breetan intended to use the Order's Mereklar envoy, Tagath Ellimer, to send a message saying just that.

Ostensibly a "commercial advisor," one who saw to it Nerakan traders were treated fairly by local merchants, Ellimer's actual job was to acquire information that might be of interest to the Order.

Mereklar was larger than Samustal but couldn't begin to hold forty thousand soldiers. Most were camped in a sprawling crescent of tents on the high ground south of the city. The smoke, smells, and noise that rose from the sea of canvas almost blotted out those from the city below it. Grayden would have to move soon. He didn't have the resources to support so large an army for long unless it could forage (that is, plunder) the countryside as it marched. Unfortunately, his goal was Breetan's too, and she had no desire to contend with him for her prize.

Rumors were flying thick and fast about where the elves were heading. Current betting heavily favored New Ports and the sea. One outlandish rumor Breetan had heard was that a fleet of elf ships was sailing down from the north to reinforce the rebellion.

At Tagath Ellimer's pleasant home, she and Jeralund were fed well and plied with excellent wine. Ellimer was a portly, merry-eyed fellow who laughed a lot and wore an extravagant mustache. Behind his jolly veneer, he was shrewd and ruthless. According to Jeralund, he once had been considered the greatest duelist in Neraka.

"The town's aboil," Ellimer said, pouring rose-colored wine into Breetan's goblet. "Haven't seen so much excitement since the demise of Beryl."

"Does Gathan know where the rebels are?"

The envoy laughed heartily. "If he knew that, Lady, the army would be there, not here!"

"Do you think he'll catch the elves, my lord?" Jeralund asked.

Ellimer sat back, paunch hanging between his knees. Draped in dark blue serge, with a massive gold chain hanging low from his thick neck, he looked like an ancient potentate posed on his throne.

ALLIANCES

"Lord Gathan will kill many. His army will sweep in and flush out every living soul but the rebels he seeks. That's assuming the evil in the Lake of Death doesn't rise up and claim his host first."

That was what Breetan had hoped to hear. She would not besmirch the Everride name with another failure. The Scarecrow was her trophy and no one else's.

"If you ask me," Ellimer said, although no one had, "the rebels aren't heading east to New Ports. I believe they will complete their circuit of the lake."

"To what end?" Breetan asked.

"To seize Mereklar and bring all the little revolts together into one conflagration."

The envoy certainly had a lively imagination. Breetan asked for his estimate of the rebels' strength.

"My colleague in Frenost says between five and six thousand, mostly woodland elves, with a few former royal army warriors to lead them." Ellimer chuckled. "He's insane, of course, quite insane. I believe there to be no more than a few hundred. Not even Kagonesti could hide an army of five thousand so effectively. Gathan's people are badly rattled. They see rebels under every leaf and stone."

He changed the subject, gossiping about politics within the Order. Breetan listened with impatient politeness until she could return the conversation to the topic that interested her.

"My mission is to find the rebels' leader," she said. "I can't follow in Gathan's wake. No elf in his right mind will be found within twenty miles of that mob!"

Ellimer agreed. He rang a silver bell, and a servant appeared. To Breetan's astonishment, the lackey was a Qualinesti elf, neatly liveried in blue velvet. The envoy sent him to fetch a map case.

"You're surprised by Azar, Lady?" Ellimer said to her. "Don't be. He's been my body servant for more years than you've lived. I beat him in fair combat thirty years ago, and he's been my faithful servant ever since."

"He'll put a knife in you one day," Jeralund observed.

Ellimer laughed. "I hope so! What a tragedy it would be for an old campaigner like myself to die in bed, withered and infirm! One day, when I'm tired of life, I'll invite Azar to finish our duel. He'll still be agile and strong, and I, a fat old man, so I'm sure he'll win!"

Breetan shook her head. She couldn't understand knights who were so cavalier with their lives. She'd grown up with the example of her father, and Lord Burnond never left anything to chance.

Azar returned with soundless tread. He bore a long, leather-wrapped cylinder. Ellimer dismissed him then pried the cap off one end of the case. He drew out a fistful of parchment rolls, tightly wound. Thumbing through the cryptic annotations on the end of each, he found the scroll he wanted.

Jeralund moved the dishes and goblets aside, and Ellimer opened the map over the knee-high table. With his dagger, he tapped a spot on the coast, east of Nalis Aren, where the angular shoreline bent from southeast to almost due south. "The elves will turn south here," he said.

Ellimer was convinced the Scarecrow intended to lose his bandit pursuers in the fogs and uncharted ruins and swamps surrounding the lake. The worst terrain lay between the lake's eastern shore and the coast. The land was low there, and Beryl's impact had caused a major subsidence. The north shore of the lake was treacherous, but the east was a deathtrap.

"It's not a route I'd care to take," Ellimer said, "but even changed as it is since Qualinost's drowning, it's still elf country and the most likely spot for them to go to ground."

Breetan was pleased. Gathan's huge army would be hampered by the terrain. This would allow her time to track down the elusive Scarecrow and carry out her instructions.

"I shall go to the south shoreline and let the enemy come to me."

"An excellent plan, Lady." Ellimer sat back, leaving his dagger on the map. He folded his hands across his round belly. "Don't be too sanguine about the route, though. That's perilous country. No one, neither elves nor bandits, rules there. It's infested with all manner of wild things."

"And wild rebels," the sergeant added wryly.

Ellimer lifted his cup in acknowledgment.

Fired with excitement for her new plan, Breetan was eager to depart. Declining Ellimer's offer to pass the night in his home, she declared her intention to ride on at once.

"May you succeed for the glory of the Order." Despite the formal tone of his words, Ellimer grinned widely, his eyes nearly vanishing in the folds of his skin.

Breetan frowned. How in Chaos could she judge the man's sincerity when he was so unrelentingly jolly? She took up her glass and returned his toast.

"Glory to the Order," she said and gulped down the last of her wine.

16

The bridge on Birch Trail carried the elves across the White-Rage River. On the other side, the royal guards who'd separated from the column to lead their horses up from Silveran's Way rejoined the group. Porthios ordered the bridge destroyed after all were safely across. That would delay pursuit only slightly. No more than a quarter mile north, the river was fordable enough for determined riders. Still, any obstacle they could throw in their pursuers' path, no matter how small, was worthwhile.

Birch Trail ended a quarter mile beyond the bridge. From there, on the eastern side of Nalis Aren, the land descended in giant, staggered steps, like the stairway of a colossal temple. Broken tables of stone jutted from the ground. It was not marble thrown up from Qualinost, but bedrock shattered by the tremendous impact. A single misstep meant death, and a handful of the Bianost militia were lost. Exhaustion, the exertion of combat, and the debilitating atmosphere of the region had all of them reeling. Upon reaching a stone slab more than fifty yards wide, they dared to pause and rest.

Nalis Aren was roughly triangular in shape. The White-Rage emptied it, flowing north from one of its "points." Narrow tributaries filled it at the southwestern and southeastern points. Below the elves, near the lake's southeastern corner, lay the lakeshore's lowest point. Known colloquially as the Cleft, it was shadowed by greenish yellow fog. The elves panted in the cold yet humid air and watched for signs of pursuit. Water was distributed. The wounded were settled more comfortably in their litters.

The few guards Samar had left to watch their rear came rushing in. They bore ill news: the bandits were definitely following them. Mounted humans, as well as goblin skirmishers, could be seen, but they took care not to get too close to the elves.

"The main army isn't here yet," Kerian observed. "Just the vanguard."

"They still outnumber us," Alhana said. She'd quit her litter to walk on her own.

Porthios for once was staying close. He didn't relish wandering too far in the noxious environs of Nalis Aren.

"You said the bandits wouldn't follow us around the lake," Kerian said to him. "You've miscalculated."

Porthios stood on the edge of the cracked bedrock slab—he never seemed to sit—and stared down at the Cleft. "It's good they follow on our heels," he said. "What lies ahead will strike the clumsy goblins and humans, not us."

Alhana exchanged a worried look with Kerian then asked Porthios, "What lies ahead?"

"I don't know, but there's a reason people and beasts shun this place. We'll encounter it, or the bandits will."

He stepped off the slab and dropped down to the next, and the next, gradually slipping from sight. Silence followed his pronouncement. Alhana stood, dusted herself off, and declared, "The only way to go is forward."

She and her two champions set out. The royal guards, leading their horses over the uncertain ground, came next, then the Bianost elves.

"Our leader is mad," Kerian muttered as the Qualinesti passed. They eyed her uncertainly, wondering whether they should take her words as joke or warning.

At Alhana's request, Chathendor had done a head count as they rested. Slightly fewer than two thousand elves,

Qualinesti and Silvanesti, had departed Bianost, with about four hundred horses and thirty tons of armaments and supplies. The head count revealed only eight hundred and some odd elves remained, with a hundred fifty horses and twenty-seven tons of weapons. The balance had been lost or left behind.

Casualties had fallen heavily on the Qualinesti volunteers from Bianost. Half had perished or been wounded thus far. With Theryontas slain, leadership of the volunteers had fallen to Vanolin and Geranthas. As the leading edge of the caravan neared the fog-shrouded Cleft and the angle of descent eased, the two Bianost elves came to talk with Alhana.

"Lady, we offered ourselves to fight for the freedom of our people, but so far all we've done is run away," Geranthas said.

Vanolin nodded vigorously. "Why didn't we disperse in the woodland, dividing the swords and such, each of us to raise new companies of fighters?"

Kerian slowed her pace to match Alhana's, eager to hear the answer. Alhana glanced at her then took a deep breath before replying. "If we had stayed in settled country, Gathan Grayden would have found us, boxed us in, and slaughtered us all. The days of surprise are over. Every garrison in Qualinesti will be on the alert. There will be no more easy victories."

"Then why are we here? Orexas has doubled the danger we face!"

Once more Alhana paused before speaking, weighing her words carefully. "We need allies. Nalaryn and his clan have gone into the mountains to find some. Until they rejoin us, we must elude the bandits and survive."

The Bianost elves were baffled. What allies in the mountains? Did Alhana mean dwarves from Thorbardin?

"She means griffons. Those that dwell wild in the mountains," said Porthios.

He had appeared in the mist below them. He held up a gloved hand. "We must proceed in silence now." Bits of smelly vapor drifted over them. Several coughs were quickly smothered.

Kerian could hardly believe he intended to lead them through the Cleft. No one in current memory had entered it and returned to tell of what was found there. It was dank, poisonous, and cursed. There was bound to be a price for entering it. Certainly, they had little choice now, but Porthios should never have brought them to this pass. His cavalier acceptance of the risk for himself was one thing, but he was gambling with all their lives. Gilthas would not have done this. He would have found a way that didn't endanger his people. Strange, whenever Kerian felt death coming closer, her thoughts invariably turned to her husband.

At Kerian's insistence, the royal guards braced their bows, alert for whatever might come, and a band of twelve speararmed Qualinesti was called forward. They would probe the boggy ground and test the footing. Although they looked unhappy, they didn't challenge Porthios's plan to enter the Cleft. Chathendor and the wounded Samar were as skeptical as they, but likewise raised no word of protest. Only Alhana seemed perfectly confident.

"Orexas will lead us through," she told the nervous Qualinesti behind her. "Put your trust in him."

Pale from her concussion, she moved forward without hesitation. Where she would go, Samar always would follow, and Chathendor had no intention of being left behind. If they were not completely reassured, the Bianost elves were moving.

Kerian's precautions regarding the boggy ground proved well founded. One of the probing elves lost his spear when the moss he tested gave way. In moments, his eight-foot weapon was swallowed by a sinkhole. Everyone took note. The line of elves narrowed.

Porthios came to what looked like a length of decayed log. He stepped over it. The elf behind him prodded the log. It held, so he stepped on it. Immediately, it slid sideways, taking his foot out from under him. Those behind raised a smothered alarm when they saw him fall. The "log" on which he'd trod grew larger and larger as more of it emerged from the bog.

It was a serpent, but what a serpent! A four-foot wide triangular head, supported by a body thick as a large oak, reared up. Two yellow-green eyes stared at the horrified elves. As the serpent writhed, coils broke the surface all around them. It was a hundred feet long!

Bowstrings snapped. Half the arrows skipped off the monster's heavy scales, but some punched through. The serpent stretched its mouth in a screeching hiss. Fangs as long as an elf's arm glistened in the poisonous air, and a black tongue flickered out.

In the scramble to get away from the creature, several elves left the known path. They promptly came to grief as the mire trapped their feet. The serpent, arrows protruding all along its body, glided forward rapidly. With a lightning-fast movement, its head shot forward and seized an elf, sinking its terrible fangs into his ribs. Venom worked swiftly. When the serpent's jaws opened seconds later, the elf was dead.

"Hit it in the mouth! In the mouth!" Samar shouted as the other mired elves were hauled to safety.

Arrows caromed off the scaly head. Then one Kagonesti archer coolly took aim while coils thrashed around him. He put a missile directly into the monster's near eye. The serpent convulsed, beating its head on the ground. Guards rushed forward, swords drawn. Each blow was like striking a bronze statue. Their blades made no impression at all, and two elves died when the monster's heavy, flailing coils crushed them.

Kerian snatched a spear from a nearby elf and ran at the head. Although her attack seemed reckless, she placed her feet carefully, avoiding sinkholes and the gummy loam. The snake's convulsions had dislodged the arrow from its eye, but the orb was blind. Sensing Kerian's approach despite that, it opened its mouth wide to bite its new enemy. She bored in, driving her spear into the white membrane on the roof of its gaping mouth. A fang raked down her chest. Something hot splashed on her thigh. Spurred to even greater effort, she twisted the head of the spear and was rewarded by the sound of serpent bones snapping.

The serpent was still strong enough to lift her clear off her feet when it raised its head. Flinging its head side to side, it shook her back and forth even as blood poured from its mouth. Four elves ran in beneath her and drove their spears into its body just behind its head. The monster's head dropped, and its own weight drove the Qualinesti weapons through its body and out the other side.

Kerian let go the blood-drenched spear and hit the ground with a thump. She was shaking uncontrollably, certain she had been bitten, but at least the monster was dead.

"Don't move!" Alhana knelt beside her. "You're hurt!"

Amazingly, she was not. Her buckskin tunic was sliced from shoulder to waist, but her linen underclothes weren't torn and the skin beneath was unbroken. The fang hadn't penetrated. The strange sensation on her thigh was venom. Faintly greenish gold and odorless, the venom was thick, like curdled milk, and soaked her leg. Alhana caught her breath sharply at the sight.

"Do you have any wounds on your leg?" she whispered. Kerian shook her head. The slightest cut would have allowed the poison in, but again she had been spared.

Taking care not to touch the soaked portions, Kerian shucked her ruined clothing. Alhana was so relieved, she smiled—and blushed too—at Kerian's utter lack of embarrassment. The former queen sent for new attire and a canteen of water.

Porthios appeared. He didn't ask after Kerian's health, and he ignored her state of undress. He did stop her from tossing away the buckskins, saying sharply, "Save the venom. It may be useful."

Once more, Alhana's presence caused Kerian to bite back the furious retort that rose to her lips.

With a roll of cotton bandage, Chathendor daubed at the venom. He put the poisoned cotton in a glass bottle and stoppered the bottle carefully. As a further precaution, he wrapped the bottle in two layers of leather and tied the whole bundle tightly.

An elf arrived with water and clothing. While Kerian dressed, Alhana left her and found Porthios standing over the corpse of the enormous serpent. In answer to her question, he identified it as a cottonmouth.

"But they grow no more than four feet long!" she protested.

"We are in an unnatural place. What was pest has become monster."

On her feet again, Kerian saw four elves standing nearby, watching her. They were the ones who had finished off the monster. They were ordinary-looking fellows, scribes or artisans from Bianost. She thanked them and clasped their hands in turn.

"You are my troop now," she said. "Stand by me, and I shall stand by you, always."

All four seemed overwhelmed by the battle with the monster, but each nodded as she took his hand.

The elves quickly prepared to resume their march. The belongings of the dead were collected by Chathendor. The weapons were given to others, but the chamberlain tied personal items into tidy bundles. If the deceased had heirs, they would receive their kin's effects.

While Chathendor's attention was engaged, Kerian drifted over to the cart that held his and Alhana's belongings. She removed the small leather bundle containing the poison bottle and slipped it into her waist pouch.

Turning, she realized the four Qualinesti of her new troop were standing behind her, staring. Their meager belongings were in bundles slung on their spear shafts.

"It's mine," she said stiffly. "I'll take charge of it."

They made no reply. She joined the march, and the four fell in behind her.

* * * * *

The Cleft was ten square miles of bog. It lay like an ulcer on the southeastern lakeshore. Moss and mold, in every shade of gray, black, and sickly green, lay everywhere. The stench was so bad, so much worse than the rest of Nalis Aren, that midday rations went uneaten. Spiders, biting flies, and venomous reptiles (of normal size) assaulted the elves. The swarms of flies were so vicious their attack drove several horses mad. The animals tore free of the hands leading them and galloped off to sure death in the depths of the mire.

Thorn creeper and cypress were abundant, but none grew more than waist high. As they crossed the Cleft, the elves were visible to anyone higher up on the hillside. Elves throughout the caravan, and especially those in the rear, kept looking back over their shoulders, fearing to see bandits at any moment. None were visible, but their pace quickened anyway.

The perpetual chill of Nalis Aren meant the elves had donned extra garments. In the Cleft, the opposite was true. The temperature climbed. Sweat poured, but removing clothing meant exposing more skin to the voracious insects. As the sun passed its zenith, elves began to stagger and fall. Some got back up, but others did not rise again. Alhana called for a halt. She, her lieutenants, and Kerian examined one of the immobile elves.

The deceased was a royal guard. A healthy lad, well fed until recently, he was younger than Kerian. His neck and face showed bug bites, but no more than what had been endured by the rest of them. The only oddity Kerian could find was a swollen neck. His throat had closed so tightly, so quickly, he had suffocated while walking.

They had no idea why. Toxic air, poisonous insects, evil spells—anything was possible. They kept moving.

Trailed by her quartet of Qualinesti, Kerian sought out Hytanthas. She was pleased to see he had improved in health despite the foul conditions.

For a time they tramped along in a silence Kerian considered companionable but which Hytanthas found uncomfortable. Finally, he nerved himself to speak what was on his mind.

"Commander. About Khur—"

"What about it?"

"I feel I've been derelict in my duty. My task was to bring you back to the Speaker."

"You nearly died of fever. It's a wonder you found me at all, and you think you've been derelict?" She shook her head. "I've told you, I can't go back to Khur."

"Can't, or won't?"

She glared at him, giving the young warrior a glimpse of the Lioness of legend. Hytanthas did not back down. After a moment, she returned her attention to the uncertain footing.

"What difference does it make? The Speaker dismissed me, and I found myself hurled across the world." She shrugged. "He didn't need me then. He cannot have me now."

"Would you condemn all our people in Khur to death or slavery?"

Temper flaring, she curtly told her troop to take themselves elsewhere. When they had moved away, she demanded, "Am I a goddess who can save a nation by herself? Gilthas has thousands of warriors and the combined skills of veteran generals like Hamaramis, Taranath, and Planchet. The safety of our people in Khur rests with them, not me!"

"Very well, Commander. But I must return to the Speaker. Will Orexas and Alhana forgive me if I leave once we're clear of Nalis Aren?"

"Do as you like."

To her relief, he said no more. He had the same failing carried by all the Qualinesti Ambrodels. Although resourceful and brave, Hytanthas was just the sort of soldier who'd follow an order to certain death simply because his name and honor demanded it. Kerian had no patience with martyrs, no matter how gallant they might be. The world needed realists, hard-headed, hard-fighting realists. The humans had a saying she liked: Wars aren't won by dying for your country; they're won by making the other fellow die for his.

The traverse of the Cleft claimed more lives. Seemingly healthy guards and town elves collapsed, dead. At sunset the temperature plunged. No betraying torchlight was allowed, so the terrible march continued in full dark and graveyard chill. The elves took turns climbing onto the remaining carts and wagons and napping for a short space. Kerian did not avail herself of the rest. She pulled a blanket around her shoulders and kept walking.

Alhana, clad in a white fox fur robe, moved along the caravan, speaking to everyone, and making sure all had a chance to rest in the wagons. She'd given her other furs and extra clothing to shivering townsfolk. Despite the fretting of her chamberlain, she would not stint on her self-appointed tasks.

"You must rest, lady," Chathendor urged. "And you shouldn't give away all your clothing."

"Shall I ride on velvet cushions, wrapped in furs, while they walk, hungry and cold?"

"You aren't a young girl any longer. Privation is harder at our age."

She nearly smiled. "Our age, indeed. You have a few *centuries* on me at the very least," she sniffed, returning the jest.

When they got back to the head of the column, Alhana spoke briefly to Samar, who was organizing patrols for the night. That done, she consented to rest. Chathendor led her to a wagon fitted with a canvas top. He lifted the flap at the rear of the still-moving conveyance, and she climbed inside. She reminded him to wake her in an hour. He assured her he would and dropped the flap over the opening.

She had barely settled herself next to several wrapped bundles of swords when the flap shifted again and Porthios entered the wagon.

"Peace, Alhana. It is I," he murmured unnecessarily. She'd known immediately who he was, if for no other reason than he was faceless. Porthios was the only one in the caravan whose face was completed covered.

Chathendor did not have the luxury of her better eyesight. The tent flap flew up.

"My lady! I saw an intruder enter!" he exclaimed, short sword in hand.

"Your grip and stance do you credit, sir, but you're facing your lady, not me."

The chamberlain recognized Orexas's hoarse voice. He did not lower his blade until Alhana assured him she was safe and sent him away.

Alone with her husband, Alhana lit a candle stub. She used a small incendiary stick, made by the gnomes of Sancrist and called by them a "dragon's tooth." When scratched smartly, it flared into flame. The sudden flare caused Porthios to recoil sharply.

"I have no liking for fire," he said. In the wagon's confines, he could move no farther away. "Candles and lamps can be dropped. Fires start that way all the time."

She lit a lamp with the sputtering yellow flame. "I'll be careful."

Breath plumed from her nose as she exhaled. She waited for Porthios to speak. When he didn't, she asked, "Do you believe the Kagonesti will find griffons?"

"Yes."

"And that we can tame them?"

"Yes."

She was impatient with his terse answers. "If we do find them, they will be wild adults, not creatures reared among our people. How can you be certain we can train them quickly enough to be of use?"

"I am sure." His eyes found hers in the gloom. "I was Speaker of the Sun, Alhana. I know the *tath-maniya*."

She nodded. The Keeping of Skyriders, the secret of taming griffons, was the birthright of Kith-Kanan, handed down to every Speaker of the Sun.

"I've not done it, but I know what's required," he said. "That's why I came to talk with you, to tell you—to make sure you know. It's important you believe it can be done."

He seemed uncertain, his words halting. "What's wrong?" she asked. "Something's troubling you."

"Despite the evil we have faced thus far, I don't think we've plumbed the depths yet. And I don't expect the bandits to give us up. Grayden will come after us no matter what." He reached out suddenly and laid his gloved hand on hers. Immediately, she

214

placed her free hand atop it. "But I wanted you to know . . . I wanted to tell you to keep heart. Nalaryn's people will find griffons. We will tame them. Whatever the dangers we must face on our journey to that point, remember that."

He slipped out of the wagon. The wind of his passage snuffed the candle, leaving Alhana in darkness. Her hands were still warm from his touch. She placed them against her cold cheeks.

She smiled, then she laughed. For the first time in a very long time, Alhana laughed.

17

At a snail's pace, the caravan trudged on. Short of a sojourn in a deep cavern, the elves could not imagine a darker night. The stars were barely visible, as though black mist had risen from the ground to obscure them.

After midnight they reached the river that marked the southern boundary of the Cleft and the end of the oppressive swamp. The river was choked with vines and dark green lily pads. So stained was it by black earth washing down, it looked solid enough to walk over.

"How will we get the wagons across?" said Geranthas.

"Ford," Porthios replied.

Kerian protested. "You have no idea how deep that water is!"

"Have you a better idea? Can you pick them up and carry them on your shoulders? No? Then we must ford!"

None of them had any better ideas. There was no timber with which to build rafts, and Samar had relayed the rearguard's report that sounds of pursuit could be heard, so time was fleeting.

"I will take the first cart across," Porthios declared. "We'll cut bundles of sticks and saplings, and if we get stuck, we'll dump them ahead of us to give us traction."

Such bundles could fill a moat or an enemy trench, but a river? Not if luck went against them and the river was deep.

Nonetheless, Porthios set a crew of exhausted elves to work hacking down creeper bushes and scrub willows. While they worked, Samar and Kerian conferred.

"There's someone behind us, no more than a few hundred yards out," Samar reported in a low voice. "There aren't many, and they seem unusually quiet for humans or goblins."

Spies, Kerian said. Grayden had sent his best scouts to keep an eye on them. Some rare humans could manage to be quiet in the woods. It was even possible Gathan had found renegade half-elves or Kagonesti to hire. Such things had happened. She took a deep breath.

"Let's find out who they are. I can use the stimulation."

For once Kagonesti and Silvanesti were in total agreement: Samar also was tired of fleeing, tired of creeping along with the civilians. He called a squadron of twenty mounted guards. To them Kerian added another twenty, without horses. The elves would ride double. At a prearranged moment, the riders would slow to a walk, and the extra riders would slide off silently. The enemy would hear the mounted attack coming and flee or deploy for battle. If they deployed, the elves on foot would infiltrate their line, confusing them. If the enemy fled, the riders would pursue, able to move quickly with their extra riders dismounted. It was a tactic called "Sowing the Garden" which the Lioness had used successfully against the Dark Knights.

Kerian sat her own horse and waited for a royal guard to climb on behind her. Instead of a Silvanesti, she got Hytanthas.

"You're well enough to fight?" she asked.

"Well enough, Commander."

The Bianost elves were still cutting sticks and brush as Kerian and Samar rode out to investigate their pursuers. Dawn was three hours away. Alhana saw them off, waving as they trotted past. Porthios stood on a two-wheeled cart, directing elves to roll the bundles to the water's edge. He did not acknowledge the warriors' departure.

They proceeded carefully, keeping to the path they'd probed through the Cleft. It was just wide enough for two horses abreast. A hundred yards from the rear of the caravan, Samar halted them.

They sat in absolute silence, listening. They heard the chirp
of bats on the wing, the splash of a toad into a stagnant pool,
the tap-tap-tap of a deathwatch beetle looking for a mate.

And the gentle crush of a footfall.

Samar shot Kerian a glance. She nodded. Hytanthas and
the other extra riders slid off the horses. Silently, they fanned
out ahead of the riders. Their swords were already drawn, so
not even that scrape betrayed them. Only ten feet away, they
vanished into darkness. The mounted warriors waited. Periodically, each would lean forward, silently communing with his
horse to keep the animal from growing impatient or chafing
at the noxious atmosphere.

A scream shredded the air. They'd heard no swordplay, no
twang of bowstring, just the single, sudden, heartfelt scream.
Was it human or elf?

A chorus of shouts erupted in the night. The noise was accompanied by the clang of blades. Kerian lifted her sword, and
the other elves followed suit. Despite pounding hearts, they
went ahead at a canter. No sane rider would gallop in such
darkness, with the usable trail confined to a narrow track in
a treacherous mire.

They bore right around a bend and found bodies strewn
across the path. Kerian swung down to the ground. The first
body was indeed one of their dismounted comrades. His neck
had been broken. Someone incredibly powerful had throttled
him. His sword lay in his outstretched hand without a trace
of blood on the steel.

Kneeling by the next corpse, Kerian rolled him over, and
bolted to her feet. Turning to Samar, she flung a hand at the
corpse and demanded, "Am I mad? Am I seeing things?"

Samar rode closer. He recoiled. "You're not! It's Jalanaris!
We buried him yesterday!"

The dead fellow was one of the elves who had collapsed and
died of suffocation during the crossing of the Cleft. How had
he come to be here?

A total of eight lay dead. Half were dismounted riders
Samar and Kerian had brought with them. The other half

were comrades who'd died on the march across the Cleft. All had been strangled.

The sound of a shrill whistle sent Kerian vaulting back into the saddle. She knew that call. It was Hytanthas in distress. Flinging caution to the wind, she galloped down the path, Samar and the rest following hard on her heels.

Beyond a bubbling pool of slime, a melee was under way. The remainder of the dismounted guards stood in a circle facing outward, swords drawn. Advancing on them slowly but inexorably were pale mud-streaked figures. A guard behind Samar nocked an arrow and loosed, putting the shaft through the neck of one of the stalking figures. The impact staggered but did not stop him. He came on, arrow protruding grotesquely.

"Undead!" Samar cried. "Our own people are trying to kill us!"

Hytanthas's party slashed at the walking corpses, rending terrible wounds in the dead flesh, but the undead elves simply kept coming. The horror of their existence was evident from their faces. Some had eyes open; others walked with unerring accuracy although both eyes were closed or clotted with dirt. Samar's warriors hit them again and again with arrows, to no effect. They carried no weapons, for none had been buried with them, but they would grapple with any living elf within reach. When they found a living foe, they held on with such an iron grip only dismemberment stopped them. Even hewn limb from limb, the cursed corpses twitched and heaved.

There were fifteen walking dead. With Samar's reinforcement, the elves quickly subdued them, but Hytanthas stopped the warriors from destroying the corpses. He explained why.

"They were lying in wait for us. Our fellows didn't fight at first. We thought we'd made a terrible mistake—buried comrades who were still living. Then they attacked! They strangled four of us before we could fathom what was going on. As soon as a revenant had killed its victim, it collapsed, lifeless at last."

Hytanthas said he feared the curse might work the other way, that if the undead were destroyed, then their intended victims might die as well.

Surveying the still twitching limbs and torsos, Kerian had no desire to test his theory. She wondered whether the attack was a horrible by-product of Nalis Aren, or an evil spell worked against the elves. Samar didn't care. He ordered the dismembered undead scattered so the corpses would trouble them no more.

His words sparked an idea in Kerian's mind. She told Hytanthas to find himself a horse; they were taking a ride.

"Where are you going?" Samar asked.

"If we are troubled by our own dead, I wonder how Grayden's army is faring behind us."

"A worthy question, but don't take too long in your search. Orexas won't wait for you."

His warning ended with a grunt. A severed arm had crawled across the boggy soil and fastened itself to Samar's ankle. He kicked it loose and flung it far out into the mire. Hytanthas protested his callousness. Kerian told the young warrior to get to his horse.

Leaning close to Samar, she muttered, "You'd best take care of those warriors who fell tonight too." They couldn't risk allowing the four who had died to return as undead. Their remains must be scattered.

"Dirty business," Samar muttered, grimacing.

Kerian pulled a small leather-wrapped package from her waist pouch and handed it to him. It contained the venom Chathendor had collected from the giant serpent. Viper poison paralyzed the limbs and destroyed flesh. Perhaps a dose would protect the brave, lost warriors from whatever malevolent influence was disturbing the sleep of the dead.

"Don't wait for us," Kerian said. "We'll be back as soon as we learn what we can."

The two elves rode off into the dark. They had no idea how far back the human army might be. They proceeded at a trot. Kerian was so exhausted she felt as though she wore the heavy chains of slavery again. She'd been awake and on her feet (or in the saddle) for—how long had it been? Two days? Three? She'd fought a monstrous serpent to the death. At least Hytanthas had the benefit of rest during their journey.

"Commander!" Hytanthas's hiss jerked her upright. She'd actually dozed in the saddle.

Hytanthas took over the lead. A few more miles and he reined up sharply. "Do you hear?"

The metallic clash of combat was unmistakable. It had to be Grayden's bandits. Who else would be abroad in the Cleft?

They continued more slowly. Shouts and screams could be heard, and beyond a mossy knoll they spied flickering light. The elves had forbidden fire in their caravan to conceal their position. Until that moment, so had the humans. Dismounting, Kerian told Hytanthas to hold her reins while she took a closer look.

"Let me go," he urged. "You're done in."

"I'm not that far gone."

In truth, she wanted to spare him what might lie ahead. For all her disagreements with him, Kerian felt protective of Hytanthas, as she did all the young warriors under her command. His brief brush with the undead had shaken him badly.

She dropped into a crouch and moved toward a right-angle bend in the path. On the west side of the trail was a broad mire that stretched all the way to the lake itself. The elves had lost two Bianost townsfolk in it, plus a horse they could ill afford to spare. Kerian skirted the mire's edge. The path had been rising slightly. She dropped nearly prone and inched forward to peer over the crest. The scene she beheld was drawn straight out of the Abyss.

Slightly below her was a bowl-shaped ravine containing a small pool of stagnant water. The firm trail the elves had scouted circled the rim of the bowl. Arrayed around the pool were several hundred bandit soldiers. Many brandished torches and all wielded pikes, but it wasn't Silvanesti cavalry they faced. A swarm of pale, half-naked bodies moved slowly yet inevitably forward. Scores of corpses littered the ground around the bandits' circle, some newly killed and bloody, others undead who'd perished at last after killing a victim. Horses whinnied and struck out with their hooves, terrified. Some of them had blundered into the mire on the other side of the path and were slowly sinking to their doom. They struggled, teeth bared, but the bog had an unbreakable grip. Alongside the dying animals were the banners and helmets of their riders. When a horse got stuck, its rider tried to get off and was dragged down. The weight of their armor sank them fast.

An undead attacker, missing an arm, its face and chest mutilated by sword cuts and arrows, would sidle forward or sideways, trying to unite in deadly embrace with a living victim. If it succeeded, it dragged its prey away from the rest and fell on him with grasping hands. The victim screamed for help, but none dared leave the circle's minimal protection. If Gathan Grayden didn't arrive soon, his vanguard would not survive the night.

Kerian slid backward. As she twisted round to stand, she beheld a pallid human looming over her. She drew in her breath sharply. Mud filled the man's mouth and matted his red beard. Both eyes were coated, but he turned unerringly toward Kerian as she rolled aside. Her hand fell on her sword hilt, but she did not draw. The undead man had not attacked, even when she was lying vulnerable on the ground. She stood and slipped by him, careful to keep an eye on him. He pivoted, keeping his face toward her, but did not attack.

Hytanthas rode up with the horses.

"Let's go, Commander! More are coming!"

Dozens of dead humans trailed after Hytanthas. Kerian got the stirrup and swung aboard. "Why don't they attack us?" she wondered as they turned their horses away from the terrible scene.

"We're not human."

Kerian regarded him in surprise. He was probably right. Whatever motivated the revenants, they seemed driven to slay only their own kind. Living creatures like Kerian, Hytanthas, and the horses attracted them, but the death they sought could not be had with members of a different race.

The two elves galloped away. Two of the undead humans did not move as Hytanthas's horse thundered forward. Kerian heard him murmur, "Forgive me," as he trampled the unfeeling creatures into the muck.

* * * * *

Holding a long pole, Porthios waded into the river. He pushed aside thick lily pads and prodded the dark water, searching for sinkholes or deep mud. Behind him was a two-wheeled cart drawn by Kerian's self-appointed troop, the four Bianost elves who had vanquished the giant serpent. As Porthios found firm ground, he pointed to the spot and the elves dragged the cart there. Every ten yards, they pounded a stake into the riverbed on each side of the cart, marking the path the caravan would follow.

The water quickly rose to hip height. It was shockingly cold and chilled Porthios to the bone. His teeth chattered uncontrollably, but as with all his other bodily ills, he ignored it, pushing forward methodically.

They were more than halfway across when Porthios trod on slick stones that rolled beneath his foot. He fell sideways, hitting the water with a splash. One of the Bianost elves let go the trace pole and dove after him.

On shore, Alhana and Chathendor saw Porthios fall and the Qualinesti go after him. Seconds later, the chamberlain found Alhana's elegant fur robe thrust into his face.

Scrabbling to catch it, he exclaimed, "Lady! You can't! You mustn't!"

But she was gone. Alhana waded into the river, keeping to the path marked between the poles. When she reached the rear of the cart, she eased herself around it. The three Qualinesti were clinging to the trace poles, their frightened gazes scanning the river.

"Lady, take care! There's an undertow!" cried one elf.

Here the surface of the river was free of lily pads and slow moving, but a swift current tugged at her legs, trying to pull her off balance. For the river crossing, she had donned Qualinesti-style leggings and she blessed the freedom of movement they allowed even as she shucked off her thigh-length tunic. Tossing it onto the cart, she shivered violently as the air hit her sodden underclothes.

The three Qualinesti urged her not to leave the anchor of the cart. "Obey Lady Kerianseray and Lord Samar," she said and dove into the black water.

The current was much stronger than she had realized. It pulled the scarf from her hair and rolled her lengthwise, adding to the tremendous disorientation of swimming in the dark. She kicked hard. When her head broke the surface, she gulped a lungful of air. The cart was twenty yards upstream and receding fast. She could no longer touch bottom.

Turning to look downstream, she noticed a boulder in midstream. She dove again and moments later emerged near the rock. Clinging to its smooth side was Porthios.

The surface current here was much stronger, but a few rapid strokes brought Alhana to him.

"You always were a strong swimmer," he stuttered, teeth chattering like dice rattling in a cup.

"Where's Robethan?" she asked. He regarded her blankly. "One of the Qualinesti on the cart. He went in after you."

"I've seen no one." He had trouble getting the words out, so violently was he shaking.

"You're chilled to the core. If you don't get out of the water, you'll die."

She moved around him, putting her back to the current and letting it press her even closer to him. When he objected to being touched, she told him bluntly to be quiet. He needed the warmth.

They heard voices on shore, and Alhana called out. Porthios put his face to the boulder. His shivering had eased, but the extra warmth was not worth the terrible shame that welled in his heart. That Alhana should be risking death for him, that she should be touching, even through layers of soaked cloth, the awful horror that was his body. His neck bowed further, as though he could shut out the humiliation. Then Alhana began to speak.

ALLIANCES

It was a ridiculous place to pour out her feelings, Alhana knew. They were up to their necks in a swift and icy river, and she was staring at the back of his masked head, but she didn't know whether either of them would survive to see dry land again, and she could not die without telling him what was in her heart. So she did.

She talked of their son, of the pain and loss she had endured. She described her life after learning of Porthios's presumed death, how she had never given up the search, although she had begun to think all she would ever find were his remains.

"I prayed you would be alive," she said, "so I could find you and tell you all these things. So I could tell you, just one last time, that I love you, husband."

He said nothing. Alhana thought he was fading, but she felt no fear. The cold wasn't so bad; she wasn't even shivering anymore. In fact, the motion of the river against her body was pleasant, soothing. With a little sigh, she laid her head against his shoulder and allowed herself to relax.

Porthios jerked suddenly. One emaciated arm reached up the smooth stone. Fingers stretched. There seemed to be no handholds, yet somehow he found one. He willed his frozen legs to move and managed to wedge his toes in a cleft below the surface. Slowly, he hauled himself out of the water.

The current shoved Alhana against the boulder, shaking her out of her lethargy. She tried to emulate his actions, but could find no grip at all on the slippery boulder. He extended a hand to her. With amazing strength, Porthios drew his wife up from the stream.

"How did you do that?" she gasped.

Rather than move away, Porthios embraced her, and not only to help ease her shivering. "I will not die by water. Fire claimed me, and in fire I shall perish one day."

She pushed sodden hair from her eyes and muttered, "No. You're just too stubborn to die."

Voices shouted from shore. Despite Porthios's strictures against showing a light to their enemies, torches blazed on the riverbank. Porthios and Alhana called until their rescuers located them.

The elves formed a living chain from shore to boulder. Samar, at the boulder end, held out his arms to Alhana while the elf behind him gripped his belt to anchor him. Alhana took his hand and offered her own to Porthios. The chain retracted toward shore until all were at last back on dry land. Chathendor had blankets and wine waiting.

Porthios accepted the first but shunned the second. His first words on touching land again were, "I said no one was to light a fire until we're out of Nalis Aren."

"I ordered it," said Kerian, emerging from the shadows with Hytanthas at her back. "If you don't like it, you can go back in the river."

"You'll give us away to our enemies, or worse."

"I've seen worse tonight."

She told Porthios and all within earshot of the encounter with the undead elves, painting a graphic picture of the terrible price exacted on Grayden's army.

"Gods' mercy," Chathendor breathed. "That's not a fate I would have wished on anyone."

Porthios would have argued further, but Kerian interrupted him. Fists on hips, she snapped, "Do the names Querinal, Robethan, Sanal, and Torith mean anything to you?" He shook his head. "They're the elves who accompanied you into the river with the cart. They're gone, all of them."

One by one the four had left the cart, trying to save Porthios, Alhana, and each other. None had survived the fierce undertow.

Alhana pulled at Kerian's arm, asking her to come away. Kerian didn't budge. "A leader who does not value his followers' lives is no fit leader," she said severely. "He's a gamester, moving people around like tokens on a game board!"

Samar finally succeeded where Alhana could not. After Porthios's failure to cross the river, Samar had sent scouts up and down the river, looking for a likely ford. He interrupted the argument to report their findings. Two miles south was a natural bridge, bedrock thrust up into the stream bed. The downstream side was graced by a sixteen-foot waterfall, but the upstream side was passable, the water no more than a foot deep.

Relieved on many counts, Alhana ordered that they would leave at once for the natural bridge. Porthios did not contradict her.

Weary beyond measure, the caravan turned south to follow the river. Alhana and Chathendor led. Samar and the mounted guards fanned out along the shore, while those guards without mounts marched in slow step behind. Next were the Bianost elves, still drawing their carts and wagons by hand. Wounded elves and those too weak to keep up were draped atop the precious hoard of weapons.

Last to leave were Kerian and Hytanthas. The Lioness was staring out at the black water, so calm on the surface, so deadly just beneath. Querinal, Robethan, Sanal, and Torith—she repeated the names to herself like a prayer. Four of the many who would not live to see the end of the journey. If indeed any of them would.

The last of the creaking carts disappeared around a bend, and Hytanthas suggested they move along.

"It never changes," she said.

Hytanthas didn't ask what she meant. He understood perfectly.

*   *   *   *   *

The demarcation between the area influenced by Nalis Aren and the land beyond had not seemed so obvious on the way in. The oppressive atmosphere had come up on the elves gradually. On the way out, the shift was abundantly clear. The predominant color of the landscape quickly changed from black to green, and the exhausted elves began to walk faster. Those on foot dropped weapons and walking sticks, packs and bindles, pushed past the guards on horseback, and broke into a run. The elves drawing carts and wagons let go the traces and joined the celebration.

"What ails them?" asked Samar.

Riding alongside, Alhana answered, "They smell home."

Delirious with relief, the Qualinesti threw themselves onto the greenery, stroking grass and ferns as if they were the finest silks. Tears flowed, streaking dirty faces. An aspen tree no more than six feet high was nearly trampled by worshipful elves.

Even Porthios was not immune. He stood to one side of the trail, a fern frond in his hands, pulled the feathery green leaves through his gloved fingers again and again. Only Alhana saw, and she smiled. Giving in to the inevitable, she called a halt. Since all but her guards had stopped anyway, no one objected.

A clear-flowing, shallow stream served as a bathing pool. The elves went down in shifts to wash away the filth of Nalis Aren. While Kerian was at the creek, she spotted a strange Kagonesti in the trees some distance away. None of the other bathers noticed him until Kerian pointed him out. After a few minutes, he darted away.

"Should I go after him?" asked Hytanthas.

"Why? You'll never catch him." Kerian squeezed water from a cloth onto her face. The crisp, clean water running over her skin was the best feeling in the world.

The *tonk-tonk-tonk* of a forester gourd-drum sounded. Kagonesti of the region hung large, dried gourds on a frame and rapped them with hardwood hammers to send messages over long distances. The constant noise was not a comforting sound to outsiders. Samar posted a mounted patrol around the caravan. Porthios slipped into the woods.

The drumming ceased after two hours. Before the elves had time to do more than marvel at the silence, a party of armed Kagonesti emerged from the trees. Samar's guards prepared to charge, but Kerian told them to stand down.

"Don't you recognize our Immortals?" she said, using the name bestowed on the Kagonesti by the Bianost volunteers.

Nalaryn and the rest of his Kagonesti clan approached at an easy lope. They looked fit and relaxed, a sharp contrast to their haggard comrades in the caravan.

Kerian clasped Nalaryn's arm and greeted him enthusiastically.

Nalaryn gripped her arm. "You are fewer," he said. "The black lake has taken lives."

The drums had told Nalaryn of the caravan's arrival. As he and his band were coming to rejoin it, Porthios met them on the way. "The Great Lord remains in the forest to cleanse his soul of the black lake," Nalaryn added.

Alhana came forward to welcome the Kagonesti. "Was your quest successful?" she asked.

"It was."

Alhana exhaled sharply. "Tell me!"

The Kagonesti had seen griffons in flight, as many as forty aloft at one time over the Redstone Bluffs. Nalaryn also reported no signs of elf or human intrusions. "No one has walked there in many, many days."

Alhana was ready to leave at once. However, she quickly realized she had to temper her enthusiasm. The Bianost elves needed rest. Even her own guards, and their few horses, could do with a respite. Nalaryn asked about pursuit, but Kerian shook her head. The enemy's problems were worse than their own.

The discovery of griffons put an end to Hytanthas's talk of leaving and to any thought of attacking the bandit-held city of Mereklar. They must make for Redstone Bluffs with all possible speed.

The choice of route was a ticklish one. Remaining in the forest would be safest, and Nalaryn could guide the caravan, but Alhana favored a bolder solution. The road was more direct, and would be easier going than bumping through the forest. Mereklar lay on that road, but why not skirt it, under cover of darkness? Gathan Grayden had led his bandits out to pursue the elves. He certainly wouldn't expect the rebels to return and pass directly under their enemies' noses.

Kerian regarded Alhana with surprise, and the Silvanesti queen joked, "A plan worthy of the Lioness, isn't it?"

Fatigue and the boundless relief of having left Nalis Aren behind them engendered recklessness. Alhana's plan received unanimous support. The caravan would follow the old Qualinesti high road past Mereklar on its way to Redstone Bluffs and the griffons.

"Should Orexas be told?" Samar said.

Alhana said, "No need," just as Kerian exclaimed, "No!" Alhana was certain Porthios would approve the plan. The Lioness didn't care what he thought of it.

They passed the night in the meadow beyond the shadow of the Lake of Death. After dawn the next day, the caravan rolled on. The Kagonesti Immortals were the last to depart. By the time they did so, no trace of the elves or their ponderous train remained.

* * * * *

Breetan Everride was beginning to feel she had made a terrible mistake. She and Sergeant Jeralund had been searching the province between Mereklar and Nalis Aren for more than a week, looking for the rebel army. They'd found nothing. Word arrived from Lord Gathan's headquarters of a disaster in the lake region which had nothing to do with the elves. Scores of soldiers had died from the effects of the lake's pestilential miasma, only to rise from their graves as revenants and slay their former comrades. Gathan beat a hasty retreat, convinced the elves he sought had been destroyed by that same evil.

Having found no traces of the elves herself, Breetan wondered if Gathan was right. Jeralund tried to buoy her flagging spirits.

"I've been hunting and fighting elves most of my life," he said. "They're not bound by the same laws as men. Things that sicken men and possess their bodies may have no effect on elves. I'm sure the rebels will appear."

Still, Breetan could not shake the feeling that she had erred, and badly. If true, her career as a Dark Knight would be over. There would be only one honorable course of action remaining: death by her own hand.

Then the sergeant made a discovery.

ALLIANCES

On the limbs of a hawthorn bush, he found scraps of dirty brown linen hanging as if to dry. A sniff revealed a strong stench of rot that must have come from the Lake of Death.

"The Scarecrow wraps himself in rags like these," Breetan said, daring to hope. Jeralund dismounted and prowled through the undergrowth.

"Lady! Footprints!"

They were the soft impressions left by rag-wrapped feet far narrower than a human's. Elves had come this way.

Shading her eyes against the setting sun, Breetan mused, "Heading west. But going where?"

"To Mereklar?" suggested Jeralund.

The Order's Mereklar envoy had suggested that, but Breetan still dismissed the idea. The footprints had been made since the last rain, six days past. It was only eight miles to Mereklar. In six days, the elves could have covered that distance and back again, yet there had been no attack on the city. If Mereklar was not their target, then perhaps something that lay beyond it?

Jeralund shrugged, "There's little beyond it, Lady. Forest, a few small crossroads, and mountains."

He picked his way through the brush, finding more tracks by the lone elf. Without a doubt, the fellow was headed west. As Jeralund pointed out, there was no way to know whether the tracks had been left by one of the rebels they sought. The lone elf could be nothing more than a Kagonesti out on a hunt.

True enough, Breetan admitted. Yet they had no other scrap of a lead to investigate. They would follow the tracks. If the rebels had come out of the Lake of Death, they must be ailing and exhausted. A few days' hard ride west should establish whether Breetan was on the right trail.

Beyond the need to fulfill her duty (and not disgrace her noble father), she was beginning to feel the excitement of the chase. This Scarecrow was fine game for a hunter. She would have him yet.

18

Adala sat on a small carpet, shielded from the broiling sun by a square of blanched cotton. She gripped a stick in one hand and tapped it against her leg in a quick, regular rhythm. Normally she used the stick to urge Little Thorn to move. At that moment she wished she could use it on her entire nation.

Just after dawn, a patrol of Mikku horsemen had thundered in, babbling inexplicable news. The *laddad* were gone! A broad swath of trampled sand led away from Chisel and Broken Tooth. Horsemen went to investigate the two plateaus. The first party ascended Chisel unopposed. They found only abandoned rubbish. The party that tried to climb Broken Tooth was greeted by a shower of arrows and rocks. The nomads withdrew and went to learn the Maita's judgment on the strange situation.

Chiefs and warmasters arrived, dismounted, and doffed their sun hats in deference to Adala. Chisel was empty, they told her. Tracks led away from Broken Tooth and joined up with those from Chisel. The *laddad* seemed to have departed both plateaus, so who remained on Broken Tooth?

With a sharp word, Adala silenced them all. "It's clear as a midnight sky," she said and stabbed the stick into the sand, as though spearing *laddad* flesh. "They slipped away, leaving a few of their number to deceive us."

ALLIANCES

The Tondoon chief lifted his hands. "But how, Maita? Our night patrols saw and heard nothing! How could so many escape without being detected?"

"Foul magic again, or treachery."

Despite all the changes in the world, the nomads had never lost their belief in and respect for magic. But it was her mention of treachery that upset the chiefs most. They all spoke at once, loudly disclaiming that any child of the desert could betray his people.

"Be quiet," Adala said, and they were. "We ride after the fleeing *laddad,* and this time there will be no quarter. I have been too gentle, too forgiving"—the chiefs traded looks—"but no more. The time of gentleness is past. Let every warrior carry two swords today."

Solemnly, the chiefs and their warmasters vowed to obey. Carrying two swords was an order with an especially grim meaning. In battle a nomad carried his best sword, leaving his spare in his tent. If his sword broke or was lost, honor decreed he ride back to his tent, fetch his second blade, and return to the fight. Carrying both swords meant the warriors would fight until death claimed them.

"The Weya-Lu do not go with us," Adala announced. "They will remain here and storm Broken Tooth."

The warmasters nodded sagely. It would be unwise to ride off in pursuit of one enemy and leave another unmolested behind. Adala had reserved for her own tribe the difficult task of assaulting the steep pinnacle and crushing the defenders that remained.

The men galloped away. Only the Weya-Lu warmaster, Yalmuk, stayed with Adala. He was new, having succeeded hot-tempered Bindas, who had perished fighting on Lesser Fang. Bindas had been young; Yalmuk was barely twenty. Like nearly everyone in the tribe, he was Adala's distant kinsman.

She gestured for him to sit. Yalmuk squatted with the boneless grace of youth. Adala pulled her stick from the ground and traced an aimless pattern in the sand. "Is there any sign of Wapah?" she asked.

"No, Maita." He jerked his head, tossing long hair from his eyes. "It's as if he was carried off by the wind."

She pondered that. Something untoward might have befallen Wapah. They were surrounded by dangers, and no one's life was safe. On the other hand, loquacious Wapah was a master of the desert. He knew its fickle moods, knew the many dangers that lurked in its trackless expanses. Since his possession by the Oracle of the Tree, he had been different, not as talkative and—obvious only to Adala—his staunch support of her and her *maita* had waned. Had the meddling spirit seduced him away from their people's true path? She did not like to think so.

Yalmuk was not so delicate. "Only a man who wants to disappear vanishes so completely," he said. Despite her chilly reception of his words, he did not hold back. "Wapah knew the desert like no one else, Maita. He could have led the *laddad* around our patrols."

She glared into gray eyes that were so like Wapah's. "You have no proof of that!" she snapped.

He covered his face with his hands, an act of obeisance. "That is true. I beg forgiveness, Maita, and withdraw the slur on your honorable cousin."

Your cousin, too, Adala fumed silently. Despite the words, Yalmuk's tone made it obvious he still thought Wapah had betrayed them. Yalmuk was a savage fighter, but Adala disliked him and his family. So many Weya-Lu of higher precedence had fallen that he had been left as the ranking warrior in the tribe. It was with double satisfaction she gave her next order.

"Take the Weya-Lu and storm Broken Tooth. I want that rock cleansed of its foreign taint today."

"I will spare no one!"

"Spare any you take," she retorted. "I want to learn where their people have gone."

The great mass of warriors had departed, hot on the trail of the fleeing *laddad*. It was a nearly empty camp through which Yalmuk rode to join up with the Weya-Lu.

The fortunes of war had fallen hardest on Adala's tribe. No more than three hundred fighting men were grouped together in the center of camp, and nearly all wore bandages on heads, arms, or hands. Most had the dark eyes common among nomads, but a dozen or so of the gray-eyed strain were scattered among them. As Yalmuk approached, the Weya-Lu raised a sword in each hand, showing they were armed as their Maita had commanded.

"Cousins and brothers!" Yalmuk declared. "To us has fallen a great honor—that of reclaiming the last of our ancient mountains from the foreign invaders! We ride to cleanse Broken Tooth!"

Passionate cheers greeted his pronouncement. The men had lost their families in the nighttime massacre of the Weya-Lu camp. Like Adala herself, they believed the *laddad* warriors had killed their wives, parents, and children. In their hearts burned a flame of vengeance so bright, not even the desire for survival could outshine it.

Yalmuk divided his band into three equal parts. The first part would ride around Broken Tooth and attack by the north trail. The second, led by Yalmuk himself, would storm the southeast trail, the only one wide enough for horses to ascend abreast. The last group would wait halfway between the other two and reinforce whichever seemed destined for success.

"We attack at noon," Yalmuk said. Only an hour away, the hottest time of day would be good for desert nomads and bad for soft-skinned foreigners.

Off they rode, singing the Weya-Lu war song:

> Sword to sword, we ride to battle,
> Sword to sword, we face the foe.
> Sword to sword, we fight and die,
> Sword to sword, our glory grows.

Atop Broken Tooth, Planchet heard them. He'd been expecting an attack, even after he saw the bulk of the nomad army ride away on the trail of the escaping elves. With the wind blowing their dust in his face, it was hard to see how many nomads were coming. Judging by the full-throated chorus, it must be several hundred.

He stood atop the rock signal tower. Below him were ranged his two hundred defenders. They wore helmets and breastplates whose design hadn't changed much since the days of Kith-Kanan. Each elf had sword, spear, and bow, although there were precious few arrows. Planchet had insisted the Speaker take most of their dwindling supply with him.

The spears ported on each fighter's right shoulder were an odd, tragic note, reminding Planchet again of the atrocity committed against the elves. Few had the use of their left hands, and some bore injuries on other limbs as well. Yet none had hesitated to volunteer for the final battle. He saw Qualinesti, Silvanesti, and half a dozen Kagonesti, their facial tattoos rendered nearly invisible by the dark tans given them by the Khurish sun.

He took a deep breath. "Warriors, I salute you!" he proclaimed. "The enemy is coming. To your places, as we planned."

The ordered ranks broke apart. Sixty elves trotted across the rough plateau toward the north trail. Planchet expected a two-pronged attack, with the heaviest blow coming from the north. He'd allotted his sixty strongest warriors to defend that trail.

He led the balance of his force to the southeast trail. It was heartbreaking to see how many could barely walk, much less fight. But they had played their role to perfection, keeping the nomads here, allowing the Speaker and their people to escape. They had one final gift to offer, to sell their lives as dearly as possible.

All night long they had dragged stones to the top of the trail, erecting a zigzagging, waist-high wall across the path. Tent poles, suitably sharpened, studded the ground ahead of the barrier. If the nomads tried to ride the elves down, they'd receive an unpleasant surprise.

Like the slow inevitability of death, the column of desert dust came nearer and nearer. Two plumes separated from the main cloud and streamed around the foot of the peak, heading inexorably for the north trail.

Planchet nodded. Just as he'd expected.

The rumble of hooves came from the southeast trail. The sound grew steadily louder then suddenly ceased. The telltale column of dust that marked the nomads' advance dissipated, the air scrubbed clean by the constant wind. Planchet's soldiers took up their swords and spears without a word being spoken.

"At one hundred yards, archers will draw and loose," Planchet said. His calm voice carried with surprising clarity over the barren mountain top.

A yell came from the winding trail, rising from the throats of a hundred Weya-Lu tribesmen. It started low and rose to a piercing wail.

"Ready to receive cavalry!"

Spears were lowered to hip height and locked in position. The wind changed direction, swirling around Broken Tooth and bringing a cloud of stinging sand with it. The nomads were moving again, charging up the steep trail toward an enemy they couldn't see but knew was there.

As he awaited them, a memory flashed unexpectedly into Planchet's mind: Qualinost on a summer's night. The view from his room in the Speaker's palace was green and immensely peaceful. Spread out below his window, the city was lit by thousands of amber lamps and by the clouds of winking fireflies drawn to the lights.

The nomads arrived, riding hard around the final bend. The path was wide enough to allow five abreast, and that's how the Khurs came, galloping knee to knee, screeching like creatures from the Abyss.

"Present!" Planchet commanded. The few archers raised their arrowheads skyward. "Loose!"

Many arrows fell short. The elves' injured hands kept them from drawing and holding properly. Planchet shouted for them to loose at will, and additional arrows raked across the head of the enemy column. Saddles were emptied, and the fallen nomads were trampled by hard-riding comrades with little room to maneuver. In these conditions, if a rider couldn't keep his seat, even a minor wound could prove fatal.

Planchet drew his sword and stepped into line with his warriors. Arrows flicked over their heads, so low they felt the wind of the missiles' passage. Before the elves was an awesome panorama: plunging horses in colorful desert trappings, sides flecked with foam, teeth bared. Their riders were no less fearsome, with their swords held high, teeth pale against dark beards, and their deep-voiced shouts mingling with the squeals of horses and the thunder of churning hooves.

The horsemen hit the line of elves, and it gave way at once, but the leading ranks of horsemen went down like chaff before a scythe. Following riders sent their lean ponies leaping over the fallen to land behind the elves. At once the left and right halves of the elves' line drew apart, forming tight squares against the marauding horsemen.

Yalmuk was elated. In a single charge, he'd broken the *laddad,* something his people had never done before. He called for a renewed charge against the small knots of enemy warriors. At the same time, he ordered the reserve of one hundred called up immediately to exploit the advantage.

The elves' left square threw back the nomads twice. Most of the archers had ended up with that square, and they did dreadful damage against targets almost close enough to touch. The spear- and sword-armed elves were in dire straits. Buffeted by furious horses, slashed by nomad swords, they couldn't defend themselves fast enough, and their strength dwindled quickly.

The right square, in which Planchet fought, began to back away, always a dangerous thing to do when under attack. Speaking with unruffled calm, Planchet guided them backward across the plateau onto rising ground. Their interlocked shields, bristling with spears, warded off three intense charges. By that time, Planchet found himself up against the stone signal tower. He formed his fighters in a tight circle around the pile of rubble stone. Each time an elf fell, the circle drew together, shrinking tighter and tighter.

On the north side of Broken Tooth, the sixty strongest of the crippled elves ambushed nomads trying to gain the summit by stealth. They rolled boulders down the trail (so narrow there, the nomads had to advance single file) and jabbed at the mounted men from atop tall outcroppings. The Weya-Lu were forced to retreat, dismount, and come back up the trail on foot. The fight became a hand-to-hand brawl as nomads clambered over boulders and ledges to get at their foe. The nomads' superior numbers and better health took a toll: the elves started falling back. They saw Planchet's band encircling the lookout tower, so they made for that last defensible position.

Yalmuk could not prevent the northern company of *laddad* from reinforcing those besieged at the stone tower. His lieutenants cheered that development, saying it bottled up all the enemy in one place. Yalmuk scowled and spat blood in the dust. He wanted the battle finished. Where was his reserve? They should have arrived by now!

They finally appeared, riding at a leisurely pace up the southeast trail. Yalmuk drove his heels into his mount's sides and flew at them, cursing their ancestors and their descendants, berating them for taking their time. He formed them into a dense column four abreast. While his tired warriors kept the *laddad* busy, Yalmuk prepared to smash the invaders once and for all with his fresh reserve.

Standing on the lowest step of the tower, Planchet did his best to direct his faltering command. He shifted his strongest warriors to trouble spots, shielded his weak and wounded fighters, and parried every attempt by the nomads to break his circle.

A shadow fell over the battle scene. Planchet spared a moment to look skyward. A quartet of heavy clouds had formed next to the mountains north of the Lion's Teeth. They slid south and coalesced over Broken Tooth. Planchet wondered if it might actually rain.

His beleaguered warriors cried out. Planchet saw the nomad leader slowly clearing a swath through his engaged warriors, creating a path for the final charge of his reserve.

Now is when we die, Planchet thought.

* * * * *

Favaronas was certain no one had penetrated as far into Inath-Wakenti in untold centuries. All around, the landscape was as untouched as the gardens in a painting. Each footfall broke a crust of mold undisturbed for ages, which meant he, and even the light-footed Robien, left a plain trail. Their quarry, Faeterus, had left no footprints at all. Even so, Robien followed him. Favaronas couldn't see the slightest evidence of a trail, but the strange Kagonesti went steadily ahead, never faltering, as if connected to his quarry by a string. Robien moved through darkness and daylight with equal speed.

They passed through orchards of fig and crabapple, but no fruit grew on the trees or lay rotted on the ground. With no bees to pollinate them, the trees could bloom but not bear fruit.

They left the level valley floor behind, entering the rising ground on the eastern side of Inath-Wakenti. The land began to slope up, and Robien pulled ahead of his weaker comrade. Periodically, Favaronas leaned against a handy boulder to rest. His body left a dark sweat stain on the pale stone.

Above, the slopes of Mount Rakaris were plainly visible. Its sides were terraced, the lowest step some five hundred feet above the valley floor. From what Favaronas had told him, and from the direction of Faeterus's trail, Robien had deduced that it was Faeterus's goal.

The tracker had told Favaronas a bit about his quarry—how Faeterus had been royal mage to several Khurish khans and had been responsible for calling up the sand beast that wreaked such havoc among the Lioness's warriors in the valley. Favaronas began to fear what would happen if the magician succeeded in reaching the mountain slope. If Faeterus deduced the meaning of the stones and tapped the hidden forces of the valley, their lives likely would go the way of all animal life in Inath-Wakenti.

"Hello, my friend."

Favaronas jerked. He slid off the boulder and landed on his rear with a jolt that snapped his teeth together. The shabby mage stood over him.

"You don't seem glad to see me," Faeterus said mildly.

"No, it's—I'm just not accustomed to climbing mountains."

The hood turned, looking ahead. "Your companion does not have that problem. Who is he?" The frightened archivist didn't answer, and the hood swung back to face him. Faeterus repeated the question more forcefully.

"Robien," Favaronas whispered. "A bounty hunter hired by Sahim-Khan."

Faeterus set down his shoulder sack. When the bag touched the ground, it began to squirm. Favaronas inched away from it.

"I'll deal with the bounty hunter," Faeterus said. "I do wonder how he was able to track me. Does he use any unusual implements, an amulet perhaps, a special jewel, a wand?" The archivist shook his head. He did not mention Robien's oddly colored spectacles.

The mage shrugged. "No matter. I shall find out after."

Favaronas did not ask what he meant. He feared Faeterus would answer.

The mage knelt by the leather sack, which was still moving. "I, too, brought provisions into this bloodless valley. But my victuals must be fresh."

He unfastened the clasp and withdrew a large mourning dove from the sack. As he brought the bird, headfirst, toward the front of his hood, Favaronas swallowed hard and looked away. Unfortunately, he still heard the awful crunch. The headless, bloodless bird landed between his feet. Favaronas jerked them back, wrapping his arms around his up-drawn knees.

"I thought we were to be colleagues," Faeterus said with icy sarcasm. The archivist's gaze never lifted. "For your treachery, I should serve you as I did this bird. But I won't. The culmination of my grand design requires a chronicler. Sorry specimen though you may be, you're the only chronicler I'm likely to find."

Several small stones trickled down the slope, rolling past the boulder where Favaronas cowered. Faeterus was instantly alert.

"Say nothing of seeing me. A chronicler can write as well with only a single hand or eye."

The mage disappeared. His drably robed figure blurred into nothing, and his footprints smoothed away. The headless dove, even the blood spattered around it, vanished as completely as had the mage.

Robien came down the hillside at an easy lope, stopping at the spot where Faeterus had stood. Seeing Favaronas shivering by the boulder, Robien asked if he were ill.

"The pace is too swift," Favaronas stammered, hoping his voice did not betray him. "I had to rest."

Robien extended a hand. "Come. I want to reach the first plateau by sunset."

As he drew the frightened Favaronas to his feet, Robien raised one black eyebrow. "Your hand is cold, yet you're covered in sweat. What ails you, scholar?"

Favaronas longed to tell Robien all, but Faeterus's threats still rang in his ears. He forced a weak smile and laid a hand on his stomach. "Too many roots and nuts."

The one thing that hadn't vanished when Faeterus disappeared was the mage's walking stick. Robien picked up the thick tree branch and offered it to Favaronas.

"This is just the right length. Perhaps it'll help you make the climb."

The archivist tried to decline, but Robien insisted, so he took the stick and resumed his uphill slog. After a short time, he became aware Robien wasn't following. In fact, the bounty hunter was squatting on his haunches, studying the ground by the boulder. Favaronas imagined that telltale traces of Faeterus's presence stood out like beacons to the wily tracker.

Head down, Favaronas plodded silently up the hill.

* * * * *

Thunder rolled over Khuri-Khan and caused the sandstone buildings to vibrate. The sound was so rare, Khurs all over the city paused and looked skyward. Rain hadn't fallen in Khuri-Khan in many months.

In the windy plaza atop the Khuri yl Nor, the royal palace, Prince Shobbat found the sound not amazing, but painful and frightening. His nerves seemed to worsen with each passing day. Loud noises oppressed him, bright lights burned through his closed eyelids, and everyday smells sent him into unexpected paroxysms of disgust or delight. Four days earlier, he'd had to quit a meeting early because the smell of roasting lamb made him ill.

The meeting had been a vital one, a secret rendezvous with three of the outlawed priests of Torghan. The Torghanists had long hated Sahim for his tyranny, for his lack of reverence to their god, and for the foreign *laddad* taint he had allowed into Khur.

The priests offered to put seven hundred fanatics in the streets of Khuri-Khan whenever Shobbat should need them. They would set fires and storm the souks as required. The riot would form the first stage of Shobbat's plan to bring down his father, Sahim-Khan. When the city garrison marched out to quell the disturbances, Shobbat would admit a special cadre of Torghanists into the palace. Every member of the cadre was a trained assassin who had volunteered to kill Shobbat's father.

Shobbat and the priests were discussing how best to appease the bloodthirstiness of the fierce warriors—perhaps the cadre should draw lots to determine who would have the honor of killing Sahim?—when the aroma of roasting lamb had come to Shobbat's nose from the tavern below. A hairbreadth from vomiting, the prince fled, leaving the astonished priests wondering at his sincerity and his sanity.

Shobbat wanted his father dead. His sincerity, as the sages say, was perfect. As for his sanity, even the prince himself was no longer sure.

Worse than the sensitivities to light, smell, and sound were the strange waking visions. Colors would become brighter and brighter, until they seemed to vibrate of their own accord. Every candle flame, fire, and torch wore a rainbow aura. People and animals trailed visible clouds of scent, which wafted behind them as they walked or swirled around them as breezes blew. Without warning, any of his senses could become agonizingly intense.

The sun had set, bringing twilight to the rooftop plaza. To the east, dusk made the sea a smooth, gray-blue mirror. Silent flashes of light illuminated the distant, northeastern mountains. At each stroke, Shobbat flinched as though a lash had been laid across his back.

Voices from the steps below heralded the approach of Sahim-Khan and his entourage. Shobbat panicked. He mustn't be seen in his current state, but there was nowhere to hide. Beyond the waist-high parapet at his back was a sheer drop to the coast. The sea crashed and foamed around house-sized boulders two hundred feet below.

Light was brightening the top of the stairs, light from the lanterns borne by Sahim's servants. Shobbat put his back to the parapet and froze in panic.

Sahim was arguing with the new emissary from Neraka, Lord Condortal.

"What Neraka desires is of no consequence!" Sahim snapped. "I will not send my army after the *laddad!*"

"We had an understanding." Condortal was a very tall man, his head hairless but for thick eyebrows and even thicker sidewhiskers, both the color of polished walnut wood. He never seemed to speak at any level but loud, which was not a trait that endeared him to Sahim-Khan.

The sovereign of Khur was accompanied by Hakkam, general of his armies, six guards, four attendants, and two councilors. The Nerakan emissary had his own suspiciously muscular "advisors." When the two lantern-bearing attendants turned to light their monarch's way on to the plaza, they let out twin shouts.

"Great Kargath! What is that?" Sahim-Khan exclaimed.

Next to the parapet crouched a sleek, powerful-looking animal. Five feet long, not counting its bushy tail, it was covered in red-brown fur, with pricked ears, short nose, and enormous dark brown eyes. Ivory fangs protruded from its black lips.

Six soldiers interposed themselves between the beast and the khan. At their sergeant's order, one hurled his halberd, but halberds are clumsy projectiles, and the weapon missed its mark. The sergeant called for crossbows. The animal glared at the humans as though it understood the word. It growled deep in its throat. Bowling over a soldier, it galloped the length of the plaza and leaped over the wall.

"Someone's pet, I expect?" Lord Condortal said dryly.

"Not in my palace!"

The guards ran to where the beast had jumped. The drop was thirty feet to the flat roof of the Khuri yl Nor's domestic quarters, but the creature must have survived the leap since there was no sign of it among the brass chimneys and open trapdoors.

"What was that thing?" asked Sahim.

His men had no answer. Condortal exchanged an unreadable glance with his underlings. "Some call them wolverines or red bears," he said. "In our country they're known as king martens, though I've never seen one as large as that. Do you not have them in Khur?"

"Certainly not." Sahim drew his crimson and gilt robe closer around his chest. Beneath the silk, he wore a mail shirt, but iron links seemed sadly inadequate compared to the four-inch fangs of such a beast. The look of utter, mindless hatred in its eyes would have made a lesser man shudder. Sahim-Khan did not shudder; he acted.

"General, hunt that beast down and kill it. Bring its lifeless carcass to me."

Hakkam turned to go, but his monarch's voice halted him. "Use the royal regiments, Hakkam, not just the palace guard. Issue crossbows and pikes. I want it dead tonight!"

The general bowed and departed, his face conveying none of his confusion. The khan was obviously rattled, but why? The creature was a strange-looking beast, but it had probably followed the coast looking for food, and somehow ended up here. Why such a heavy hand to kill one animal?

19

Alhana's plan was a rousing success. The caravan of elves passed by the bandit-held town of Mereklar without alerting anyone to its presence. The climb up Redstone Bluffs wasn't an easy one, but after the horrors of Nalis Aren, the physical exertion in clean, cool air seemed almost refreshing.

High atop the rocky terrain, near where Nalaryn's band had seen griffons in flight, Porthios located a suitable campsite. The caravan settled on a plateau, a semicircular table of red stone two hundred yards long and a hundred wide. Below its southern, rounded edge was a sheer, thousand-foot drop into a boulder-filled ravine. The site could be approached by only a single path, making it an admirable defensive position.

The day after making camp, the elves mustered in the predawn chill on the flats outside camp. Nearly every able-bodied elf would take part in the griffon hunt. Alhana, Chathendor, Samar, and a guard of forty warriors would remain behind with the sick and wounded. The rest were divided into smaller groups. Alhana's dismounted guard was broken into bands of fifteen to twenty. Kerian and Hytanthas divided the Bianost elves between themselves. Borrowing from the arsenal cache, the Lioness distributed bows aplenty among the teams. Even if they found no griffons, any suitable game was to be brought down for food.

Porthios was not present during their preparations. He was averse to strong daylight, and the cold was particularly hard on his damaged physique. Knowing that, Kerian still was annoyed by his absence. Leaders led by example. Whatever Gilthas's failings, he had taught her that much.

She found a thin patch of dirt and drew a simple map with one finger. The royal guards would head west. That was the largest area and the roughest terrain, but the guards were the youngest and most fit of the elves. She and some of the Bianost volunteers would head north. The balance of the elves, led by Hytanthas and including Nalaryn and his Kagonesti, would explore the south range.

The hunting parties asked her what to look for. Kerian had ridden a war griffon but had never hunted the creatures in the wild. Alhana provided the necessary information.

"Obviously, look for griffons in the air. Failing that, look for parallel claw marks on rocks, especially high peaks. You might also see shreds of animal hide, heads, or hooves—griffons don't eat those parts. A goat carcass wedged in very high rocks is a griffon larder. If the griffon isn't about, he soon will be.

"Scat is white and chalky. Castoff feathers and tufts of hair may be found around scratching rocks." She smiled at their expressions of surprise. "I was raised among griffon riders in Silvanesti. My kin includes some of the greatest griffon hunters in the land."

Hytanthas asked how to recognize griffon nests.

"They're called aeries, and they're made of slabs of stone lined with fur and feathers shed from their own hides. They build them at the highest points possible. If you find an aerie, mark the spot and return. Do not approach it. Griffons will slaughter any creature that comes within eyesight of their aeries."

"How many live in each aerie?" asked Kerian.

"One, unless there are hatchlings. Griffons mate for life, but life-mates don't share the same aerie. They're too fiercely territorial to live together."

Kerian gave her a considering look, and the former queen returned it pointedly. The description might fit Kerian and Gilthas or Alhana and Porthios equally well.

Geranthas, former animal healer in Bianost, rubbed his sunburned nose and asked, "How do we capture them?"

"We leave that to the Great Lord," Alhana said. "Our only task is to find the aeries."

Before the bands broke apart and went their separate ways, Alhana added one last warning. "These are carnivores we're hunting, predators. In their eyes, we're not much different from their usual prey. If the chance presents itself, they will carry off one of you as readily as a mountain goat."

On that somber note, the hunting parties dispersed. Kerian put the rising sun on her right and signaled her party to follow. She led them down the gravel-strewn path.

Alhana's guard walked slowly into the western ridges. Many had bows strung and arrows nocked already, and they kept eyes to the sky for swooping predators.

The last band, with Hytanthas and Nalaryn, waited until the others were gone from sight among the boulders and rock walls before setting out. Although the mountains were unfamiliar territory for the Kagonesti, they knew a successful hunt began with a quiet departure. Hytanthas was happy to follow their advice. He was a city elf, born and raised in Qualinost, although for most of the past ten years, he'd lived in the field on one campaign or another. War he knew too well, but hunting was a mysterious art.

The Kagonesti fanned out ahead of him and his Bianost followers. Periodically, a Wilder elf would pause to examine a stone or an outcropping of lichen. When one stopped, all stopped, even those not in a direct line of sight. It was a startling thing to witness. Hytanthas and his followers found themselves watching the Kagonesti instead of looking for traces of griffons.

Ahead of Nalaryn's people, a series of sawtooth peaks rose, each one higher than the last. Narrow tracks wound between the sharp pinnacles, some of the trails barely wide enough for a single elf. Hytanthas was forced to divide his followers into smaller groups, the better to filter through the rugged landscape. One band he gave to Vanolin, the second to Geranthas, and the third he led himself.

The last of the Kagonesti disappeared among the sun-washed rocks. When none reappeared immediately, the volunteers grew anxious. Hytanthas reassured them.

"They're still there. We just can't see them."

He was nervous too, but thought it better not to let the townsfolk know. He braced his bow and carried it ready in one hand. The other hand he rested atop the quiver of broadheads bumping against his thigh. That made him feel better.

An hour passed. The morning sun climbed higher in the sky, its brilliant light barely warming the high bluffs. Vanolin's band veered right around a grouping of jagged boulders. Geranthas's people paced Hytanthas until a hulking, wedge-shaped ridge rose between them. Geranthas led his party around the left side, while Hytanthas circled the other way.

With no warning, a Kagonesti female appeared in front of Hytanthas. He flinched.

Hazel eyes crinkling in amusement, she put a finger to her lips. He remembered her name was Laurel. "Our chief would speak with you," she whispered.

She led Hytanthas toward an impossibly narrow opening in the rocks. At Laurel's request, he signaled the Bianost elves to wait for him there.

Laurel entered the fissure. She moved with astonishing ease and swiftness, bending and bowing to avoid sharp protrusions. Hytanthas's clothes snagged and ripped. Dirt fell into his eyes. He felt like a great blundering human. All elves were not created equal, he decided.

Abruptly, they emerged in the open, but in deep shade cast by a ledge projecting overhead. Nalaryn and one other Kagonesti were there. Nalaryn gestured with his chin, directing the young warrior's gaze upward.

On a pinnacle sixty feet above them was perched a fortress. Slabs of stone, some as long as an elf, were laid in courses, like the logs of a human cabin. Gaps in the walls showed tufts of tawny fur and white feathers: a griffon's aerie.

There was no sign of activity. The occupants must be out hunting. Hytanthas started toward the pinnacle. Nalaryn put a hand on his chest, halting him. In the quietest whisper he could manage, Hytanthas said, "I must check. If the nest is old and abandoned, it's no use to us."

"It is not old," Nalaryn said. He lifted his nose to the wind and bade Hytanthas do likewise. "The griffon is away, but the aerie isn't abandoned."

Nalaryn never said a thing unless he was absolutely certain. Hytanthas grinned in triumph, and they went to bring the news back to camp.

* * * * *

One by one the hunting parties returned, breathing heavily from their exertions in the thin air. Kerian's group had been unsuccessful. The single nest they'd found was obviously long abandoned. The royal warriors had better luck. In the western approaches to the Skywall Peaks, they found an entire colony of griffons. Fifty-two aeries were in plain sight, and there could be more on the range behind. When menaced by a pair of wild griffons, the guards drove the animals off by clanging swords on breastplates. They saw other griffons battling in the sky, fighting with beaks and forelegs.

"Forelegs only?" asked Alhana. "That's mating combat."

The talons of a griffon's eagle forelegs were dangerous, but not nearly so lethal as the more powerful leonine claws on its hind feet. Forelegs were used for sparring, not serious combat.

The guards described the griffons as having golden-brown plumage, except for a few of the larger males, who had head and neck plumage in black and bronze. The more observant warriors estimated the beasts at eight to ten feet in length, with wingspans of twenty feet.

"Those aren't Royal griffons, but Goldens, a different breed."

The royal cavalry of old Silvanesti traditionally rode the larger, white-plumaged griffons, which had come to be known as the Royal breed.

"Can Goldens be tamed?" Kerian asked.

Alhana said, "I don't see why not. They're smaller, but fierce fighters and superb flyers. In the archives, they're said to be swifter in flight than Royals, though less hardy."

In the midst of their discussion, Hytanthas's party returned. He and Nalaryn related their discovery of the aerie. Nalaryn confirmed there was fresh evidence the aerie was being used. The news brought Alhana to her feet.

"A female! This is wonderful! She'll be in her mating season. We must capture her first. We won't need to scale every peak in the range to take more." Hytanthas asked why. Alhana blushed, and it was Kerian who enlightened him.

"We can use the female to lure male griffons into our net traps."

The ancient method of capturing griffons consisted of baiting a trap with a live goat or sheep covered in strong netting. When a griffon swooped in to take the bait, its legs would become entangled in the net. A female griffon would make even better bait, albeit for a different reason. When a would-be swain became trapped, elves would spring from hiding to rope it and tie down its wings.

"The head must be hooded very quickly," Alhana warned. "Griffons will fight to the death—their own, or yours—as long as they can see an enemy."

Among the Bianost elves were weavers and riggers. Geranthas promised to get them working on nets and lassoes. Vanolin offered to set others to making hoods. The two elves hurried away, and Alhana called after them, "The hoods must have drawstrings at the bottom. Long drawstrings!"

A shadow detached itself from between tall boulders. It was Porthios. Neither Kerian nor Alhana noticed his arrival until Hytanthas hailed him.

Alhana began to tell him what had been discovered, but he stopped her with an upraised hand. "I heard," he said. "We must capture the female immediately."

Kerian pointed out the problem. The construction of ropes and nets, even with the best will in the world, would take time.

In reply, Porthios reached behind the boulder towering next to him and hauled out a thick hank of coiled fiber. "I have rope. And a net."

Kerian stared. "How? Where did you get it?"

"I made it."

Excitement erupted. Porthios, Kerian, Hytanthas, and the Kagonesti made ready to depart, to capture the female griffon. Alhana would have sent a company of guards with them, but Porthios declined her offer. The warriors would be much too noisy for the plan he had in mind, he said.

Porthios handed Alhana a scrap of parchment, asking that she dispatch elves to locate the items listed. She assured him she would see to it, and see to the swift completion of the efforts of the Bianost artisans. Even as she finished speaking, he was moving rapidly out of sight. Kerian and the rest followed.

They covered ground quickly, slowing only when Nalaryn led them into a narrow crevice between two enormous boulders. Kerian unbuckled her sword belt and slipped sideways into the crack. At its end, she found herself in a small, oblong canyon with high sides.

Nalaryn warned her not to emerge from the cleft. The Kagonesti he had left on guard clung to the shadowed sides of the canyon like bats to a cave wall. Spying their chief, one detached from the wall and sidled over. It was the female, Laurel.

Wordlessly, she pointed skyward. Kerian lifted her gaze, and her breath caught in her throat.

On the highest prominence in sight was a massive aerie. A Golden griffon was there, asleep, wings folded over its back. Its golden-brown feathered head, with wickedly curved beak, was tucked under the leading edge of its right wing. Laurel explained it had alighted not long after her chief's departure, settled comfortably into its aerie, and slept undisturbed ever since.

A sleeping griffon was an unexpected windfall. Awake, it would be nearly impossible to approach, but asleep, they might have a chance. It must have fed heavily to be sleeping so soundly.

Porthios passed the rope and net forward to Kerian and Nalaryn. Porthios had explained his plan to Nalaryn during the journey to the aerie. By gestures, the chief relayed the plan to his clansfolk and to Kerian.

The idea was simple enough but would require not only the Kagonesti's athleticism, but every ounce of their fabled stealth. Nine of the most agile, most silent, would work their way around to the far side of the aerie. Carrying the net and rope on their backs, they would scale the pinnacle and bring the net over the sleeping griffon. Once they anchored the net on the far side of the aerie, the net would be hauled tight by elves waiting in the canyon.

"That's your plan?" Kerian gasped. "They'll be killed!"

"Only if they're clumsy."

At a signal known only to themselves, the nine Wilder elves, with Nalaryn in the lead, left the shadows and started forward. Kerian's hands, resting on the rock wall, tightened convulsively. Without realizing it, she took a step forward. Porthios had no trouble reading her thoughts.

"Go with them," he said.

"I'm not light-footed enough."

"You're Kagonesti, aren't you?"

Rather than snap back an acid retort, she simply eased out of the crevice. Nalaryn glanced at his leader. Porthios's nod was enough for him. If the Great Lord wanted the Lioness to go, then go she must.

Nalaryn and three elves attached the leading edge of the large net to the peg buttons on their tunics and started up the rock face. Three more elves, plus Kerian, picked up the net's trailing edge and followed. The last two elves flanked the group, making certain the net didn't snag on anything.

It was an agonizing climb. Despite their legendary dexterity, with the need to search for hand- and footholds, and to move in utter silence, their progress was extremely slow. Porthios had made the net from hemp line, tied with big square knots—strong and tough but very heavy. Each time an elf advanced, he or she heaved the net upward with shoulders, brought up legs, then paused to breathe, mouth wide so as to make no sound.

One of the flanking elves suddenly hissed a warning and Kerian looked up. The leading elf on the far right, moving a bit faster than the rest, had outpaced his comrades. The net went taut and tugged on the elf on his left. Caught off-balance and dragged upward, the lagging elf was pulled off his feet.

"Anchor!" was all Kerian had time to hiss before the fellow lost his footing completely. He knocked his head against a rocky outcropping and ended up dangling from the bottom edge of the net, gripping it with one hand.

The rest of the group braced themselves, absorbing the shock of his weight. After a heart-stopping instant, the dangling elf found secure footing and released the net. He was injured and unable to continue, so he climbed back down to the canyon floor. Filled with shame, he crept into the shadows.

All this took place in mere moments, and in almost utter silence.

As soon as he'd released the net, Kerian began crawling up under it to take his place. Reaching the spot he'd vacated, she took hold of the edge and started up, taking up the slack. When the rope mesh was taut over the cliff face again, the elves resumed their climb.

It was only mid-afternoon, but with mountains all around, the climbers would lose the best light before long. At their backs, the sun was going down behind the high western peaks. The east-facing sides of the mountains were darkening, silhouetted against the brilliant sky.

Nalaryn reached the base of the aerie first. The view inside was blocked by feathers, branches, and small stones that filled the spaces between the slabs of stone. He signaled his companions, and the climb resumed. When all the leading elves were poised below the rim of the aerie, Nalaryn unhooked the net from his tunic and very slowly lifted his head above the topmost gray stone slab to peer inside.

The griffon's eye, large as a pomegranate, was aimed squarely at him. The leathery red eyelid was slightly parted, revealing the pupil, black within the black iris, only inches from Nalaryn's nose.

For the stolid Kagonesti who hadn't hesitated to pledge his life to a mysterious masked leader or storm a city full of mercenaries, it finally was too much. Nalaryn threw himself backward, away from the griffon's great eye.

Kerian saw him jerk back then fall as if struck by an arrow. Her mouth opened, but she knew she mustn't make a sound, just as she knew Nalaryn was going to die on the rocky floor of the narrow canyon below. Horror turned to astonishment when she saw Nalaryn's foot catch in the net. Immediately she and the others braced themselves, but his back still slammed into the spire. His weight jerked the female elf next to him off the aerie. With an astonishing midair twist, she caught the bottommost slab of the aerie as she fell. Nalaryn was not so fortunate. The impact had knocked him unconscious and he hung upside down, foot entangled in the net, below her.

All of them waited for the griffon to spring out and tear them to pieces. It did not. Silence continued to reign over their high perch. Relieved but with hearts pounding, Kerian and the last elf with her on the aerie lowered Nalaryn to the elves below. The two of them moved toward each other, causing the center of the net, where Nalaryn was snagged, to sag down. The female elf who been pulled off by Nalaryn's fall descended with him, keeping him from hitting the stone spire.

Kerian and a Kagonesti called Breakbow watched as Nalaryn was disentangled and taken to safety. Then they climbed to the rim and carefully raised their heads high enough to see over.

No wonder Nalaryn had been shocked. But Kerian had seen Eagle Eye, her Royal griffon, in just such a pose, deeply asleep, yet with his eyelids half open.

"Asleep," she mouthed, barely making a sound.

She and Breakbow parted, working their way to opposite sides of that end of the aerie. Lifting the leading edge of the net as high as possible, they sidled forward, bringing it over the sleeping griffon. So close to the beast, they had to take even more care to make no noise, yet every gust of wind was like a slap in the face, and arms and legs were exhausted after the long, slow climb.

At last they completed the traverse. Ropes were attached to the edge of the net and sent down to the Kagonesti waiting below. Kerian and Breakbow returned to the west side of the nest, the side they had climbed, to anchor that side of the net. Once all were in position, Kerian gave the command.

"Now!"

The elves in the canyon below hauled on the ropes. Simultaneously, Kerian and Breakbow braced their feet on the cliff face and pulled on their side of the net. The griffon trumpeted in alarm. Its powerful hindquarters worked as it tried to launch itself skyward, but the net had it trapped, and it toppled forward.

"Keep pulling!" Kerian shouted. She and Breakbow released their hold while the Kagonesti in the canyon continued to pull, and the griffon's own momentum carried it headfirst over the side of the aerie. Yodeling in distress, it plunged down the sloping rock face. Elves scattered ahead of it, and it landed with a heavy thud. Kerian prayed they hadn't killed it.

They had not. Although stunned by the fall, the griffon was very much alive. The Kagonesti had wrapped it well with the rope, and Porthios was studying the captured beast as Kerian and Breakbow reached the bottom of the spire. The griffon's baleful eye darted from one elf to another, always focusing on whomever was speaking. Its unblinking attention was unsettling. The Kagonesti sidled away, out of its line of sight, leaving only Hytanthas, Kerian, and Porthios near the enraged beast.

"Very good," Porthios said. "When we have as many griffons as we can manage, I will perform the *tath-maniya*."

Kerian had never heard the term, but Hytanthas said, "The Keeping of the Skyriders? That's from the days of Silvanos Goldeneye, isn't it? The chronicle of my ancestor, Tamanier Ambrodel, mentions the rite to tame griffons magically."

"One forgets yours is an ancient and noble lineage."

Hytanthas bristled at Porthios's casually rude tone, but Kerian shot the young elf a warning glance. To Porthios, she said, "You know this rite? Why didn't you say so sooner?"

"We had no griffons. Now we do, and I am telling you."

It was the Lioness's turn to feel hackles rise. She asked whether he'd ever performed the rite. He reminded her no one had, not since the days of the Kinslayer Wars, when the great demand for griffon cavalry had made it necessary.

"Were you a scholar or a warrior in Silvanesti?" asked Hytanthas, curious to know how Orexas had come by his obscure knowledge.

Porthios could hardly say he had been much more, and in Qualinesti, not Silvanesti. His throne was lost; his identity scorched away. Orexas was as good a name as any for a walking corpse.

"I was taught the rite as a youth." Not a lie, merely an incomplete truth. "It isn't long or complicated. We're dealing with the minds of beasts, after all."

Kerian snorted. She thought a great deal more of the mind of her Eagle Eye than she did of most people she knew, elf or other.

Specific ingredients were required. The parchment Porthios had left with Alhana contained a list of them. A liquid concoction must be made, which the would-be rider and his animal must drink.

"And we must shed blood."

"Whose blood?" Kerian wanted to know.

Porthios glanced at Hytanthas. "Does it matter?" he asked in a particularly sepulchral tone.

Hytanthas began to protest, certain he was talking of sacrificing one of the griffons they would catch. Porthios walked away and Hytanthas followed, still peppering him with questions. Kerian frowned.

If she didn't know better, she would swear Porthios was teasing them.

* * * * *

ALLIANCES

The elves took the female Golden griffon (suitably pinioned and muzzled) to a convenient flat-topped spur and tied her to a stake. Hidden in ravines on both sides of the spur, camouflaged by dirt-colored drapes, Kerian and Alhana's warriors waited, ready to pounce on any griffon drawn to the female bait. In two days they caught eleven Golden griffons, ranging from small yearlings to an elder male almost as big as a Royal griffon. Kerian had feared the trap would frighten off other males once a few had been seized, but just the opposite happened. Even when airborne griffons saw the elves capture one of their kind, they came back anyway. Their ardor was so great, they ignored the danger.

Alhana suggested an alternative view, that the males were glad to see a rival taken, and came back because they were certain *they* were too clever and powerful to be caught. Kerian asked if she'd learned that from her childhood among the griffon-breakers of Silvanost.

"No," Alhana said dryly. "It's just how males think."

Still concerned by Porthios's dire pronouncement that blood was required for the taming ceremony, Hytanthas complained to Kerian until she told him to stop being so foolish.

"Alhana isn't worried, and she knows more about griffons than anyone here," the Lioness snapped. "Blood may be required, but I don't think Orexas intends to kill anything or anyone to get it."

Her reassurance was too vague for the young warrior, but she saw to it he was kept too busy to harry any of them further about it. To him, she gave the task of feeding the captured griffons. He and three Bianost volunteers tossed deer and goat quarters to the griffons every other day and made certain they had fresh water. The hunting skills of Kagonesti and Silvanesti alike were required to bring in sufficient game.

While the captures continued, Porthios prepared for the *tath-maniya*. His list of requirements included iron, copper, bronze, wine, and specific flowers. The last were the most difficult to come by, but searchers had scoured the canyons and crevices and found them all: peony, foxglove, ivy rose, and

259

bluecup, an aromatic fungus that grew in shady niches at that altitude. The Bianost arms cache provided the iron, copper, and bronze he required. For the wine, Porthios wanted white nectar, but they had only Alhana's Qwermish stock, so he would have to make do.

The metals would be used to create a sacred circle. The wild griffon and the elf who was to be its rider were brought into the circle. The flowers and wine were muddled together in a stone cup, then mixed with the blood of a griffon. The brew was fed to elf and beast. The one performing the rite (who must be of royal blood) intoned special words of command. The result was a bond that lasted the life of both rider and mount. The rite had been created by the Brown Hood mages of ancient Silvanesti but had fallen into disuse. Speaker of the Stars Sithas distrusted the Brown Hoods, during his reign a more laborious method of griffon-bonding had been favored. The *tath-maniya* faded away in the land of its birth, but the knowledge of it was preserved in Qualinesti as part of the training given the heir to the Speaker of the Sun.

When the total number of captured griffons swelled to twenty-nine, the elves ran out of harnesses strong enough to restrain them. Alhana counseled that they proceed with what they had rather than risk losing animals due to inadequate materials. After a few days' wait for the necessary moonless night, Porthios assembled the sacred circle. Chathendor assisted him. The old chamberlain had trained long ago as a priest of E'li, and he knew how to consecrate ground for many types of rites.

The first griffon to undergo the *tath-maniya* would be the eldest male Golden, by far the largest beast the elves had caught. He was the hardest to control because of his size and strength. Taming him would ease the strain on the elves' resources.

Alhana wanted to be the first rider bonded, but her reason for wanting that was precisely the reason the others refused to allow it. She mustn't be the test case. If something went wrong, she could be injured, perhaps killed. Even Porthios was against it. He spoke a few quiet words to her, and she insisted no more, drawing a little away from the rest of the group.

ALLIANCES

Kerian was surprised by Alhana's meek acquiescence and Porthios's sentimentality. As the others continued to wrangle, she went to Alhana. Before she could ask what had passed between them, Alhana told her, roughening her voice in a parody of Porthios's hoarse tone. "Save your noble sacrifice, lady. This requires a warrior."

Kerian protested, but Alhana said, "He's right." A rueful smile quirked her mouth. "Though that didn't lessen my desire to denounce him for saying it. I thought it better to remove myself from the temptation."

The wrangling had ended. Samar would be the first to attempt the bonding. Kerian did not argue. She intended to have one of the beasts for herself, but she didn't need to be first. Looking very pleased, Samar went to prepare himself.

The sun would set in a few hours. Above the eastern peaks, clouds billowed, dull purple below and roseate on their tops. Kerian wondered if they presaged rain. Her idle speculation was interrupted by a command from Porthios.

"I need griffon's blood—one gill. Fresh, not drained from a carcass." He thrust a clay cup at her.

She jerked the cup from his hand and went. As she walked away, a grin flashed over her face. Her lack of argument had so startled Porthios, he'd nearly dropped the cup.

A gill was only a quarter pint. No animal would die from losing that amount. After the nuisance Hytanthas had made of himself over it, she intended he should be the one to collect the blood.

She found him by the griffon corral. When he saw her approaching, he stood quickly. His three helpers, roused from their naps, slowly imitated him.

"It's time," said Kerian, holding out the clay cup. "Orexas needs a quarter pint of fresh griffon blood."

He stared at the container. "That's all?"

"That's all."

He took the cup and drew his sword. Before she could stop him, he vaulted into the corral—not the section that contained the smallest, yearling griffon, but the portion in which

261

resided only mature beasts. All the griffons were asleep, lying with heads tucked under their pinioned wings. The elves had hobbled both sets of their dangerous feet and tied their beaks closed with broad leather straps.

Kerian hissed at him to stop, but it was too late. At Hytanthas's abrupt entrance, griffon heads rose in unison, and the creatures watched him with predatory eyes. Disdaining the rest, Hytanthas made straight for the eldest male Golden. The male snorted deep in its chest. The sound gave Hytanthas pause but only for a moment. He lifted his sword.

"This may hurt," he advised the beast, "but it's in a good cause."

He leaned in, sword extended, intending to draw blood from the animal's neck. The griffon had other ideas. Hobbled, pinioned, and muzzled, it nonetheless resisted, butting Hytanthas square in the chest with its massive head. The young elf went over backward and landed hard on the stony ground.

Kerian stood over him. "What do you think you're doing?"

"Following orders," he gasped.

She helped him sit up. Nothing seemed broken, so he stood carefully. They both regarded the proud griffon.

A vast bowl of purple-black clouds had formed over the range where the elves were camped. Around its lower edges, blue sky showed, but overhead the cloud mass appeared solid. It shimmered with lightning, but no thunder followed. A particularly bright flash reflected red in the big griffon's eyes. Even Kerian was moved to prudence.

"Choose another," she urged. "This one's too strong."

"He's got an iron head too." Hytanthas rubbed his ribs. "But he'll bleed for me. Why shouldn't the strongest in the herd bleed for the rest?"

He picked up his sword and circled the alert beast. It lay on its left side, heavy leonine haunches lashed together.

"Don't worry, Ironhead," Hytanthas said soothingly. "You'll barely feel this."

With a single overhand swing, he made a shallow cut through the fur and skin pulled tight over the beast's thigh. Dark blood spurted. The griffon raised its beak skyward and screeched against its gag.

Hytanthas held the cup to the wound. Blood flowed fast into it. When it was brimming, he pulled it away. He called to his three helpers to tend the griffon's wound, then he and the Lioness jogged away.

When they reached Porthios, he was standing at the edge of his sacred circle, stone bowl in hand, murmuring ancient words. Chathendor, acting as his assistant, stood at his side. Alhana was present but a few yards away. She'd donned a waterproof cape, expecting rain. Against the dark gray material of the hood, her face looked even paler than usual.

Hytanthas handed the cup to Porthios. "Don't spill it," he cautioned. "I'd hate to have to bleed that one again."

Continuing his invocation, Porthios poured the blood into the stone bowl that contained the muddled flowers and wine. With a crudely formed pestle, he stirred the thick mixture.

Samar appeared in full regalia, down to spurs and a gilt-edged mantle. Behind him six warriors worked to guide a balky male griffon toward the circle. A smear of dried blood stained the animal's leg.

"Come forth, the first pair to be bonded!"

Chathendor stepped aside to allow Samar to pass. The griffon smelled Hytanthas nearby and charged directly toward him, almost trampling Porthios in the process. To his credit, Porthios stood his ground. The warriors caught the griffon's bonds and dragged him to a halt. The beast settled a bit, and the elves withdrew. Chathendor closed the circle again. Samar stood as near as he dared to the unruly griffon.

"In the name of E'li and Astarin, Matheri and Quenesti Pah, and by the grace of the Blue Phoenix, we join this warrior to this steed!" The words were punctuated by a fresh glare of silent lightning. Everyone but Porthios looked up. Even Ironhead lifted his beak to the startling display.

"Let it be done!"

Porthios put the bowl to Samar's lips. Samar sipped, eyes clenched against the incredibly bitter taste of the potion. Then, as Porthios bade him, Samar turned and slit the griffon's muzzle strap with his knife.

This was the most dangerous part of the rite. Griffons had been known to pluck the eye from a springing mountain lion. A slash of that cruel beak, and Samar would die.

Lightning flashed again. Ironhead screeched to the heavens. Seizing the opportunity, Porthios dipped a hand into the cup and flung droplets of potion into the gaping maw.

The beak snapped shut and the creature froze for an instant. Then he lunged for Porthios, ready to rend him limb from limb. Porthios darted backward, plainly shaken, and Chathendor quit the circle altogether.

"It didn't work!" Kerian cried, giving voice to the anguish on every face.

"It must!" Porthios made a fist. "The ritual was flawless!"

Samar was backing away from Ironhead. In seconds the griffon would likely slice its bonds with its beak and wreak havoc on its tormentors, or fly away and be lost forever.

Porthios felt someone draw the stone bowl from his hand. Alhana stood so close, he could feel her breath against his mask as she whispered, "You are royal, husband, but . . . much changed. I prayed you would succeed. But I am a daughter of Speakers, and I know this ritual too. You must allow me to try."

It was plain Porthios loathed the truth of her words, but he was indeed "much changed." He relinquished the bowl.

"Do you remember my words?"

"I remember everything."

Wind whipped over the plateau, tearing at Alhana's cape. Lowering her head against the gust, she advanced to the circle's edge. Samar and Chathendor both pleaded with her to keep back. Black hair swirling around her head like an onyx corona, Alhana commanded Samar to resume his place. He did so with alacrity.

Awkward on hobbled legs, but determined nonetheless, Ironhead came at Samar. Alhana commanded the griffon to halt. Its aquiline head turned, and the beast advanced on her instead.

Alhana tilted her face to the roiling clouds and repeated the pronouncement word for word.

Once again, lightning flared. Ironhead didn't salute it with a cry. He hissed at the intrepid queen.

As had Porthios before her, Alhana dipped her fingers in the potion and flung droplets into the beast's mouth. In the uncertain light, it was difficult to follow their flight, but the change in the griffon's manner was abrupt and amazing. It ceased stalking Alhana, stood immobile for a handful of seconds, then bent its forelegs, lowering its head to the ground. The proud Golden griffon was bowing to the Queen of Silvanesti.

Samar went to Ironhead but still hesitated to touch the griffon. The sound of Alhana's laughter startled him and everyone else present.

"Don't be afraid, Samar! He accepts you!" she cried. Despite the laughter, her eyes swam with tears.

Samar put a hand on Ironhead's shoulder. The griffon did accept his touch, and it was Samar's turn to laugh. He cut the creature's remaining bonds. Wings and feet free, Ironhead stood by his newly-made rider, head held high.

A joyous shout went up. Alhana turned a radiant face to Kerian. "Oh, I had forgotten! It has been so long since I *heard* them." Alhana touched her temple with one hand. "I had forgotten how wonderful it is!"

The Lioness showed her own jubilation by slapping Hytanthas's shoulder so hard, the young warrior staggered.

Only Porthios did not join the celebration. He stood silent and dazed, his arms hanging at his sides.

Frantic cries interrupted the moment of Alhana's triumph. Elves from the camp came streaming toward those gathered at the sacred circle. "Look up!" they yelled. "Look in the sky!"

Those who'd witnessed the bonding became aware of new sounds: the clash of arms, the shouts of elves, and the screams of horses. They looked up.

The great vault of clouds had grown as opaque as polished slate. Lightning flickered and danced around the outer rim, but in the center a wondrous sight had appeared. The elves beheld a battle in the sky, vivid in every detail. Horses with human riders swarmed over a small band of elves, who fought with their backs to a crude stone spire. One elf stood on the tower's steps, a few feet above the rest. Sword in hand, he directed a futile defense.

"Planchet!" Kerian cried, her shout echoed by Hytanthas and Alhana.

Kerian scanned the mad scene for Gilthas. She didn't see him, but in the chaos only Planchet stood out clearly. As the nomad horsemen pressed in, hacking with their guardless, curved swords, the elves' line grew thinner and thinner. Around Kerian, Alhana's guards were shouting encouragement and advice to the phantom combatants, but no one in the cloud-scene appeared to hear them. All any of them on the wind-scoured bluff could do was watch as the besieged circle of elves was slowly worn away.

The end was inevitable. The circle disintegrated, engulfed by the human horde and a sea of hostile swords.

Instantly, the vision vanished. Although every eye strained to see more, the dense clouds showed only occasional flickers of silent lightning.

Kerian and Alhana, Hytanthas and Samar, even Porthios, were left regarding each other in open-mouthed shock.

20

Arrayed in a long, curved line, the elf cavalry waited and watched. They were the last line of defense for the unarmed multitude struggling through the sand behind them.

The pass leading into Inath-Wakenti lay directly ahead, its entrance marked by three peaks lined up abreast. Their snow-capped tops, rising above the shimmering desert, drew the elf nation like a beacon. No one ordered them to make haste, but all quickened their steps. The injured and infirm who couldn't keep pace were carried.

For a full day after the departure from Broken Tooth there had been no sign of pursuit. The reason for that was agonizingly clear: The nomads had taken the sacrifice offered them on Broken Tooth. Before noon on the second day, however, telltale streamers of dust rose in the southwest. The Speaker, Hamaramis, and Wapah rode back to the end of the column to see for themselves.

"They're coming," Wapah said, nodding. "No more than a hundred. Scouts."

Hamaramis immediately offered to send the army to keep the scouts from reporting back. Gilthas rejected that notion. A battle would only slow their escape, and capturing the scouts would be pointless. The mass of fleeing elves was leaving a trail even the blind could follow. Scouts or no, the nomads would find the elves eventually.

Nevertheless, the Speaker did concentrate the remaining cavalry at the rear of the column, to screen it from attack. Gilthas needed Hamaramis with him, so Taranath was put in command. His orders were clear. If small scouting parties came within reach, he could pick them off, but under no circumstances was he to engage the enemy with the bulk of the surviving army.

The elves' stumbling, arduous trek continued. They swallowed meager rations on the move, not daring to pause even for a moment. At their backs, the dust cloud thickened and spread. More nomads were joining the chase. What that meant for Planchet and the Sacred Band left behind on Broken Tooth, all understood. Although some murmured among themselves, no one broached the subject to the Speaker. Gilthas's face, usually so expressive of his emotions, was stonily impassive. He concentrated all his energies on getting his people to safety. Planchet had sworn to return; Gilthas clung to that oath.

Two hours before sunset, the elves came upon an obstacle no one had expected. A wadi nearly a mile wide and a dozen yards deep ran almost due east-west. The dry riverbed wasn't on Gilthas's map (copied from an original made thousands of years ago), and Wapah confessed he'd not encountered it before.

"I thought you knew this country." Hamaramis said.

"As I know my own face."

"Then how do you not know of this enormous ravine?"

The nomad scratched his bearded chin. "Lacking a mirror, a man does not see his eyes."

The Speaker cut off the impending argument. "Find a way down, General."

Hamaramis and a small party rode away to make a quick search. They returned with disheartening news. Scores of trails led down into the wadi, but none was wider than a goat track. The elves could descend but would have to do it at dozens of widely separated points.

Even Gilthas, no soldier, knew that was bad. Fragmented in such a way, elves would become lost, and time would be wasted while they waited for the more distant parties to rejoin the whole. Worse, they would be highly vulnerable to ambush. There was of course no other choice. Wapah theorized that the freakish rainstorm that had hit as the elves left Khuri-Khan could have cut the ravine. Funneled down the mountains, rainwater would acquire torrential power. The wadi might easily run for many miles in either direction. They could not waste precious time searching for a way around.

Breaking into parties ranging from a handful to several hundred, sorting themselves by family or clan, the foot-sore, sunburned refugees fanned out along the bank of the wadi. They hacked their way through chamiso and thorn bushes, skirted cacti and the tangled debris of forgotten floods. As Gilthas and his councilors watched from atop the south bank, the first elves began to stream north across the wadi floor.

"What tribe owns this land?" Gilthas asked.

Wapah shrugged one shoulder. "Children do not own their mother, Khan-Speaker." Gilthas gave him an impatient look, and the nomad added, "An offshoot of the Mikku are its most numerous inhabitants."

The Mikku was a very warlike tribe, Gilthas knew. Their chief occupation was hiring themselves out to Neraka or the khan as mercenaries. He asked if Adala's army contained many Mikku. Wapah's solemn nod was not the answer he'd hoped for.

"Our pursuers must be delayed," Gilthas said, worried the crossing was going to take longer than he'd hoped. The desert foliage did not yield easily, and the elves had few knives and machetes with which to attack it. If the nomads caught them at the wadi, the result would be catastrophic.

He ordered the rearguard, which had been closely shadowing the great column of civilians, to head south. Hamaramis asked to lead them, but Gilthas decreed that Taranath would command. Taranath accepted the assignment and asked whether the Speaker had any specific instructions.

"Hold off the enemy," Gilthas said simply. "If we move all night, we should have everyone back together on the far side before sunrise."

It was a daunting task, perhaps an impossible one, to keep the far superior nomad force on this side of the wadi until morning. Taranath saluted smartly and rode off to carry out his sovereign's commands.

"There is too much courage here," Wapah said to no one in particular.

"I agree," said Gilthas. "Too much courage and too little compassion."

He coughed a few times, but no blood appeared. The ministrations of Truthanar were keeping his illness in abeyance.

He remained on the south bank until the last of his people descended the narrow trails into the wadi's broad bed. With him were six councilors (three each of Qualinesti and Silvanesti), a bodyguard of nine, the human Wapah, and Hamaramis. The old general would not think of arguing with his Speaker, but Gilthas knew he was furious at having been left out of the impending fight. Gilthas sympathized. His own thoughts continually strayed to Planchet and the elves left behind on Broken Tooth.

The sun lowered itself onto the western desert, painting the tan landscape in orange and red hues. The sky deepened to indigo. Stars appeared. The air cooled quickly, and Gilthas shivered. He pulled a cape on over his long-sleeved *affre*.

"How far do you plan to go with us?" Gilthas asked Wapah, standing on his right.

"As far as the khan of the *laddad* requires."

"Then I require you a while longer."

The last of the elves had entered the wadi. It was time for the Speaker to follow. His bodyguards dismounted and led their animals because the track into the wadi was narrow and steep. Gilthas led the way, pushing through thorn bushes. A branch snapped back unexpectedly and scored a bloody line below his right eye. Hamaramis wanted to inspect the gash, but Gilthas brusquely ordered the party to proceed. More than one of those accompanying him thought he appeared to be weeping tears of blood.

Half a mile away, the rearguard waited for the enemy to close. Months of fighting the nomads had convinced Taranath of one truth: however brave and bold the Khurs were, when pressed, their response was to close up together. By hitting them hard, Taranath knew he could force them to draw in all their riders, thus keeping them away from the civilians crossing the wadi.

Word came down the line that nomads were in sight on the left. Taranath ordered the crescent line of riders to re-form into a column of sixes. Haggard but disciplined, the elves arranged themselves quickly. Then, by word of mouth only, Taranath sounded the charge.

The lead riders of a Mikku patrol were picking their way through the scrub cedar and thorn trees when the elf cavalry burst upon them, as unexpected as a storm in the desert. The warriors in front didn't even have time to draw swords before they were annihilated. The trailing elements rode back to summon help.

Taranath continued to harry them, his mounted archers picking off scattered warriors. First fifty, then a hundred, then several hundred Mikku warriors faced about and cantered back to the main body of nomads, three miles behind.

Taranath left a small band to press the retreating humans, swung the bulk of his warriors in a wide loop to their right, and fell on the flank of the unsuspecting Mikku. He hit them just as the first riders reached the main body of the nomad army, shouting warnings of an attack. The result was a complete rout. Attacked on two sides, uncertain how many *laddad* they faced, the Mikku fell back in confusion. Taranath left another token force to carry on the flank attack and once more led the majority of his warriors in a loop, curving around to the left. When they emerged from a line of lordly black cedars, the whole of the nomad army lay before them, moving slowly, swords sheathed.

The Silvanesti among Taranath's troopers stood in their

stirrups and gave the ancient victory cry—*"Sivvanesu!"*—the archaic pronunciation of "Silvanesti."

Assuming a wedge formation, the elves hit the unwary nomads and smashed through, cutting off the entire Mikku contingent. Taranath's warriors rode through the confused mass of humans, swords flashing and arrows singing.

The Tondoon and Hachakee tribes, taken by surprise, began to back away from the furious assault. They weren't afraid. They only wanted to put space between them and their enemy so they could draw swords and meet the foe on equal terms, but Adala, arriving on Little Thorn, assumed the worst.

"For shame, men of Khur! The enemy puts himself in your hands, and you retreat! Where is your honor? Give them the sword!"

The warriors nearest her protested. She scorned their explanation. "A fight is never settled by fleeing the enemy. I'll show you how it's done!"

She tapped Little Thorn's flank with her stick. Guiding the donkey around the taller ponies, she rode straight at the *laddad*. Warmasters and tribesmen alike shouted for her to turn back, but she wouldn't heed them. She was a charge of one, furious, unarmed, lacking even a speedy means of retreat.

Young Othdan, chief of the Tondoon, roared, "I will not sit with an idle blade in my hands while the Maita perishes! Tondoon, follow me!"

Not to be outdone, the chiefs and warmasters of the Hachakee turned their magnificent gray horses around and spurred hard. Holding the reins in their teeth, they filled each hand with a sword.

Taranath could not understand what was happening. One moment, the nomads were ready to break; a breath later, they were thundering back, a bloodthirsty tide set to engulf the smaller elf force. It was no proper charge or calculated thrust, merely a mass of men, horses, and whirling blades crashing toward the astonished elves. On the right, the Mikku saw the change of fortune and rallied, causing Taranath to face attacks on the left and right. He stood in the stirrups and scanned the chaos, looking for a way out. His gaze fell on an incongruous figure—a small donkey, moving as fast as his stumpy legs would allow, bearing a rider clad in black robes. He didn't recognize the rider, but the mass of nomads thundering after the donkey told him it was an important person.

"Formigan!" he shouted. "Put a shaft in that donkey's rider!"

The renowned archer nocked a black oak shaft (his last missile) and drew the bowstring to his chin. All about him was utter chaos, with elves and nomads hurtling back and forth between him and his target, yet he waited calmly for his moment then loosed.

The arrow struck true. A great groan rose up from the nomads at the sight of the still-quivering black shaft protruding from their leader's chest. The impact drove the breath from Adala's body and rocked her backward, but she felt no pain, and no blood flowed. Elation sang through her veins.

With all eyes upon her, she lifted her donkey switch high and cried, "See how my *maita* protects me, even from the weapons of the evil *laddad!* Men of Khur, children of Torghan, will you fail now?"

"No!"

The thunderous roar seemed to shake the very ground beneath Taranath's horse. The general was stunned by the failure of Formigan's shot. Could the donkey rider be wearing armor beneath those black robes?

There was no more time to ponder the mystery. The nomads redoubled their efforts. Caught in a vise of human fury, Taranath looked for a way out. Left and right were hopelessly clogged with savages. Retreat was impossible since the elf nation lay in that direction. Ahead was the only option.

The elves surged forward. They cut their way through the relatively thin line of nomads in front of them and burst into the open desert. Taranath told his cornetist to blow not "Retreat," but "Pursuit." Heartened to know they weren't fleeing, the elves emerged from the human swarm and galloped away, riding due west. After some confusion while the choking clouds of dust thinned, the Khurs followed.

The only nomads who did not pursue were Adala and the Weya-Lu. Yalmuk and the Weya-Lu warriors who'd fought at Broken Tooth had ridden hard to catch up to the main army. When they arrived, they found the battle over, their people pursuing the *laddad,* and Adala Maita slumped on her donkey's back.

Fearing the worst, Yalmuk touched the Weyadan's arm. "Maita! Are you hurt?"

She straightened, and Yalmuk gasped as he saw the arrow in her chest. "I am not injured, warmaster," she said. "Can you get this thing out of me?"

Gingerly, he grasped the shaft. Adala neither winced nor swooned but told him to get on with it. He gave a hard yank. The *laddad* missile came out with a tearing sound.

"Lout. You've torn my *geb.*"

Yalmuk didn't hear her. He was examining the arrow. The sharp tip of the broadhead had snapped off, as though it had struck something hard.

"Maita, are you wearing armor?"

She parted the front of her outer robe, displaying the sash she wore underneath. Studded along its pale gray length were three flat cabochons of lapis lazuli, each as big as Adala's palm. The one in the center was cracked in half. The arrow had struck it, breaking the arrow tip and the cabochon. Adala's clothing had held the arrow in place until Yalmuk ripped it free.

She told him to keep the arrow. "It is more proof my *maita* lives and will bring us victory."

He tucked it away and asked what she desired to do next.

"The men of Khur must be brought back. Our target is the *laddad* host, not their cowardly soldiers. If so many are loose in the desert, the *laddad* must be without protection." She rearranged her clothing. "I will bring the tribes back. You will ride after the *laddad* invaders."

Yalmuk studied her closely. "Maita, are you hurt at all?"

ALLIANCES

The rib directly behind the broken cabochon felt as though it was cracked, and she felt some pain. But she cinched her sash tight to brace it, and said nothing of this to Yalmuk, only sent him on his way. Taking up her switch, she tapped Little Thorn on the flank and trotted off to find her army.

* * * * *

Clouds obscured most of the stars over Khuri-Khan. In the courtyard of the Temple of Elir-Sana stood High Priestess Sa'ida, a tall staff in her hand. At the top of the staff, a glass globe burned with a swirling white light that gave out no heat but did illuminate the loathsome creature groveling before her.

When her acolytes first came running into the sacred shrine, screeching about a monster at the gate, Sa'ida had chastised them. The age of monsters was past, she said. They were being hysterical. Yet when she saw the half-man, half-beast creature and heard it speak her name, she realized she would have to apologize to the women.

"Holy Mistress," the thing hissed. "Help me! I am cursed."

"What are you, beast?"

"Holy Mistress, it is I, Prince Shobbat!"

She recoiled in shock, and the tiny brass bells woven through her white hair jangled discordantly. The furry beast crept closer on yellow-nailed paws. The night was a warm one, and the creature's black tongue lolled as he panted.

Holding her staff in both hands before her, she commanded him to halt. "Whoever—whatever—you are, you may not enter the temple of the Beneficent Healer!"

Rising up on his haunches, Shobbat slumped against the temenos wall. "Oh, help me, Holy Mistress," he pleaded. "I am hunted through the streets of my own city. My father means to kill me!"

Sa'ida took a step toward him, eliciting a chorus of gasps and cries from the acolytes crowded in the temple doorway behind her. She ignored them.

"How do you come to be in this state?"

"I do not know! Perhaps I meddled with powers a righteous man should have shunned, but. . . ." The shrug he gave was eloquent, even if bizarre coming from such a creature.

He told her of the disgraced royal mage Faeterus and of his visit to the mysterious Oracle of the Tree, deep in the desert. The prince believed the Oracle was to blame for his condition. He told her of the grotesque images of melded humans and animals he'd seen there.

At the end of his recitation, it was her turn to shrug. "I cannot help you. I can only heal hurts, not reverse a spell of sorcery."

"At least let me pass the night here, Holy Mistress. That is all I ask."

"You must know that is not possible, Highness." Her voice faltered on the title. "You would desecrate this temple. You must go and trust in fate."

"*Maita?*" Shobbat's mouth opened and saliva dripped from his ivory fangs. She realized he was laughing. "You talk like a desert dreamer. Holy Mistress, what am I to do?"

Despite his grotesque state, his anguish was genuine. She felt a small stirring of pity for the foolish prince. "Find the one who cursed you. Only he can remove the spell," she said.

He protested the impossibility of finding the Oracle. "Yes, but there is another possibility," she reminded him. "One who is not spirit, but flesh and blood."

She was right. Faeterus was no spirit. He could be found. The thought of having Faeterus's skinny throat in his jaws filled Shobbat with pleasure. The mage would cure him or else.

Seeing the thing before her grin with unmistakable malice, Sa'ida's brief flicker of pity died. She aimed the globe on her staff at Shobbat and proclaimed, "Go from this place!"

As if shoved by an invisible hand, Shobbat was propelled backward across the courtyard and out the open gate. The gate swung shut on its own, locking with a loud clang. A luminous glow appeared above the low temple wall. Sa'ida had raised a magical shield.

ALLIANCES

Shobbat snarled. When he was khan, he would raze the woman's wretched temple flat. No, better still, he would turn the sacred shrine into a stable. Let his prized horses appreciate the beauty of that translucent blue dome.

He laughed and the sound caused a dog nearby to bark. The noise pierced Shobbat like a knife. The dog's scent came to him, and he knew it was a hound. Several other barks answered, and he remembered his fear. He was being hunted. He had to get out of the city.

Faeterus kept a house in the Harbalah, the northern district of the city still not rebuilt after the depredations of the red dragon Malys. The mage's home was bound to contain plenty of things he'd touched. From them Shobbat could get the sorcerer's scent. He would track Faeterus to the end of the world, if need be, and wring a cure from him.

As he slunk away, howls arose from every dog within a mile. Masters cursed or kicked them, and told them to shut up, unaware of the danger passing by.

21

All night the elves argued. The fantastic spectacle in the sky faded, but the fire it ignited among Porthios's followers waxed ever hotter.

The battle lines were strangely drawn. On one side, Alhana Starbreeze and Hytanthas Ambrodel were all for going immediately to the aid of their brethren in Khur. Despite their loyalty to their lady, both Samar and Chathendor were on the opposing side. Among the royal guards, those burning to avenge the elves slain in the desert far outnumbered those aligned with their commander, Samar.

The debate took place around a bonfire built in the center of the plateau. Porthios watched from a crag a dozen feet above the assembly, his robe and mask painted scarlet by the blazing fire. Kerian sat cross-legged on the ground, not far from Alhana in her camp chair.

After the vision in the sky, Kerian had removed herself to her tiny tent. Alhana sent an elf to ask her to join their discussion, but when he hailed her, the Lioness threatened to strangle him with her bare hands. Her voice was choked and hoarse. They left her alone. She eventually joined the group around the bonfire but was uncharacteristically silent. She concentrated on sharpening her sword with a whetstone, but as voices on both sides of the issue grew heated, she set the stone aside. The metallic scraping was hardly soothing to anyone's nerves.

ALLIANCES

Alhana indicated Hytanthas could speak on behalf of her faction. The young Qualinesti warrior, backlit by the fire, declaimed eloquently on the need to go to the aid of their people. "Will we allow our brothers and sisters to be slaughtered in a distant desert?"

"Yes, it is distant," Samar said. "Khur is not our land. It is no place for Qualinesti, Silvanesti, or Kagonesti. We are invaders there. No wonder the Khurs fight to drive us out."

Alhana challenged her loyal friend. "Gilthas did not lead our people there to conquer or occupy. He sought only a haven from the barbarians who overran our countries. He dealt with the Khurish khan in good faith. Now the Khurs seek to exterminate those who were their guests. Captain Ambrodel is right: How can we sit by and let this happen?"

"Khur is very far," Chathendor pointed out. "Many hundreds of miles. If we marched for Khur tomorrow, the Speaker and those with him would be long gone by the time we arrived. We'd be marching into the arms of those who destroyed a great host of our brethren. With not a thousand souls ourselves, what should we accomplish but our own doom?"

The elderly chamberlain's reasoned words carried weight. A murmur arose as those in the crowd began to take sides. There were far more voices raised on the side of caution, of remaining here, than for the position espoused by Hytanthas and Alhana. Hytanthas looked at the Lioness. She'd said not a word since belatedly joining the group, and was staring at the sword lying across her knees. He feared to ask what she thought. She'd made it plain she had no desire to return to Khur.

Alhana had no such reservations. "Niece," she said, "I must know your thoughts on this."

Kerian began sharpening her blade again: one stroke on the right side, one stroke on the left. The metallic hiss punctuated her words.

"We all saw the image in the clouds." *Scrape.* "We all agree on what we saw." *Scrape.* "My question is, was it true?" *Scrape.*

She looked up at Alhana. "Since I arrived in Qualinesti, our paths seem to have been shaped by powers greater than ourselves or Neraka or the bandit chiefs. A city garrisoned by hundreds falls to a band of twenty. We find arms enough to equip a rebellion and elude an army of thousands hunting us. And you, aunt, are saved from certain death by some means I still don't understand. Is this all common chance? Or are we being directed?"

The assembly pondered her words. The only sounds were the crackle of the bonfire and the faint scuff of Porthios's leather-soled boots as he descended the pinnacle. He came closer, but remained in the shadowy edges of the bonfire's light.

"The answer is yes," he said.

Kerian tested the edge of her sword with the ball of her thumb. "By whom?"

When he did not reply, she added, "The time has come for plain speaking, Orexas. Speak your mind."

Her meaning was abundantly clear to him. Tell the truth, or she would reveal his identity. Even at that distance, the smell of the fire, the feel of the heat on his scarred skin, was painful, and Porthios felt the urge to retreat into the cool darkness. Instead, he advanced a few steps, into the circle of firelight.

He told the story of his first encounter with the human-looking priest. He described the old man and related the example of the cicada and the ants. He told how the same priest had appeared to him the night Alhana lay dying. "The vision we beheld in the clouds was, I am certain, his latest intervention."

"Who is this priest? Why would a human do these things?" asked Alhana, mystified.

"I don't think he is human." Porthios spoke the name of the god. If the group had been silent before, they were struck dumb by this revelation.

Kerian stood and slipped her sword into its scabbard. "I believe you," she said.

His story helped explain her transportation from Khur to Nalis Aren in the blink of an eye, she said. It wasn't the work of Faeterus or some nameless Khurish sorcerer, but of the god Porthios had named.

"We must go to Khur."

And there it was, baldly stated. Hytanthas shouted in triumph. Alhana clasped her hands together, a smile of relief lighting her face. Samar glowered, and Chathendor shook his head dourly.

"Four-fifths of our race is there," Kerian explained. "To win our war here, we need numbers, but the life's blood of our people is pouring out on the sands of Khur. We need to rescue them, bring them home, and put the weapons we found in their hands."

"Which home?" Samar wanted to know.

"Here. Qualinesti. Our success shows just how weak and divided Samuval's forces are. With twenty thousand skilled warriors, I could retake Qualinesti in a year and drive the Nerakans out of the south in another year."

"You couldn't stop them before."

"Things were different before. The dragons were too strong, and Qualinesti was divided and weak. But Beryl is gone now, and the army we raise will be different. The people of Qualinesti will fight for their own."

She gestured at the volunteers from Bianost, and they answered by raising a cheer. Alhana's guard, sitting next to them, regarded them with open skepticism.

"With Qualinesti in our hands, we can gather our strength for an invasion of Silvanesti." Kerian looked to Porthios. "That's what our divine benefactor wants, isn't it? The restoration of the elf homelands?"

He shrugged. "I do not presume to guess the motives of a god. But if it was he who showed us that distant battle, then he plainly wants us to go to Khur. Both my intuition and the signs left me by the god are telling me our destiny lies there."

"How are we to get there in time to have any meaningful effect?" Chathendor asked.

Porthios looked toward the crude corral at the high edge of the plateau. "Griffons."

"We have only twenty-nine," Samar pointed out. "What can they do against hordes of barbarians?"

Kerian answered, "The nomads fight exclusively on horseback, and their horses can't bear the sight or smell of griffons. Two dozen griffons, flying just over their heads, will panic the nomads' mounts completely. A decisive counterattack at the right moment will bring us victory. Gilthas is leading our people to a valley protected by high mountains on all sides. The only way in is a single, hidden pass. With our people safely inside, we can hold off any number of Khur savages."

Samar had listened in polite silence, but when she finished, he didn't bother hiding his disbelief. "That's hardly reasonable, lady. Twenty-nine griffon riders cannot possibly defeat tens of thousands of Khurish barbarians."

"And what of those left behind here?" Alhana asked. "Gathan Grayden's army is still hunting us. How will the rebellion survive?"

Fists on hips, the Lioness declared, "Those who remain will disperse into smaller groups and return to the lowland forests, taking the weapons cache with them. They will hide the arsenal in a thousand places, and the bandits will never find it." She looked toward the Bianost elves and raised her voice, the better to be heard. "No stumbling human knows this forest better than those born to it. Until we return with the army at our backs, you will use the old ways of surprise and ambush. The bandits won't know where to turn or even who to fight!"

Her prowess in battle wasn't limited to fighting. At the end of her speech, all the Bianost elves were on their feet, vowing to do just as she said. Even the royal guards were cheering.

When the noise died, Chathendor asked, "You aren't remaining to lead them, lady?"

"With or without the rest of you, I'm going back to Khur."

Hytanthas clasped her hand, elated. His promise to the Speaker would be kept after all.

Samar and Chathendor conceded defeat. They had no arguments left and no leader to oppose the formidable combination of Orexas, Alhana, and the Lioness.

Porthios decreed they would leave at first light, and the assembly broke up in a flurry of activity. The twenty-odd warriors already bonded to griffons gathered around Kerian. Samar bowed to the will of his lady and joined the departing band. To his credit, he said nothing more of his doubts. Now that their course was set, his duty was to support Alhana.

In addition to Kerian, Hytanthas, and the other griffon riders, Porthios would go. When Alhana claimed a spot, Porthios gruffly told her she should go back to Schallsea.

Chathendor was shocked. Although he himself had been all set to protest her going on such a dangerous trek, he took Orexas to task for exhibiting such presumption. Kerian spoke quickly, glossing over the indiscretion.

"Our leader is obviously old-fashioned," she joked. Mockingly, she said to Porthios, "Women do fight, you know. Maybe you've heard of the Lioness?"

There was a ripple of laughter, and the elves went about their various tasks. Speaking for his ears only, Kerian muttered, "Watch your tongue, Orexas. Next time you can make up your own excuses."

As the griffon riders prepared their gear, one last important matter remained. The continuing rebellion in Qualinesti needed a leader. Chathendor was too old and a Silvanesti. The revolt required a local face.

Kerian suggested Nalaryn and was prepared to defend her choice, but there was no need. All agreed the Kagonesti chief would make an excellent leader. Nalaryn had been standing nearby, awaiting any orders from his Great Lord. When told he was to lead the rebellion in Qualinesti, the stolid forester didn't bat an eye.

"This is your wish, Great Lord?" he asked. Porthios said it was, and Nalaryn nodded. "Then I shall carry your sword into every corner of the land. The invader will know no rest, and his minions will run or die."

That was too much for Kerian. Nalaryn was stronger, and faster than Porthios. Why did the Kagonesti give him such unconditional fealty? Alhana, Chathendor, and Samar went to complete their own preparations, and Kerian drew Nalaryn aside. She put her question to him in her typically blunt fashion.

"Why do you serve Orexas?" she demanded. "What hold does he have over you?"

"I have seen his face," the Wilder elf said simply. "He told me his true name."

It was a brilliant stroke on Porthios's part, Kerian realized, revealing himself to Nalaryn. Nalaryn saw him as Speaker of the Sun, as Porthios had been when Nalaryn served as a scout to the royal army. The other Kagonesti were bound to Nalaryn by ties of clan kinship. Close-knit and close-mouthed, Porthios's Kagonesti were admired by all. The Immortals would form the hard core of the rebellion. Where they led, volunteers like those from Bianost would follow. Kerian could almost feel sorry for the bandits. They were in for a very rough time.

Because of the number of elves going to Khur, two griffons would have to carry a double weight. Samar, bonded to the largest animal, Ironhead, offered a place to Orexas. Kerian regarded the granite-faced warrior elf with narrowed eyes. Despite the respect Orexas had earned as a crafty leader, he still looked like a vagabond. Samar's generous offer told her he had deduced their leader's identity. Samar returned her look with one of such bland innocence, she knew she was right.

Alhana and Kerian were to ride together on the female griffon they had captured first. Although the Lioness had bonded with the griffon, it was Alhana who named the creature Chisa, in honor of Chislev, goddess of nature.

Chathendor organized the packing of supplies for the griffon riders. Kerian raided the Bianost cache for the best arms to take with them, including lightweight lances and plenty of white-shafted Qualinesti arrows. The departing warriors accepted the new weapons gladly. Kerian offered Porthios his choice, but he would take nothing, not even a helmet.

"My destiny does not lie on a battlefield," he told her. "I may walk through one or, in this case, fly over one, but I will not wield sword or shield ever again." His posture shifted. The change was subtle but noticeable. His shoulders sagged, his neck bent slightly, and he looked away from her, as though staring at a vista only he could see. "The warrior I was is dead. He perished in flames. All that remains is a mind and the means to move it about."

Kerian didn't press him further. If he wanted to drop unarmed into the middle of what might be the biggest battle on the continent, she couldn't stop him.

Working with a will, the elves completed their preparations several hours before sunrise. Porthios ordered the riders to sleep. The guards were all veterans. Despite the momentous undertaking that would begin the next day, they knew they must try to rest.

Kerian headed for her tent. She expected to be asleep seconds after settling onto her bedroll. Years of living on the run, hiding out from enemies in the wildwood, had taught her that valuable skill. However, Alhana followed her, asking, "May I have a word? It is important."

Kerian seated herself just outside the opening of her tent and gestured for Alhana to join her. Although small, the tent helped ease the bite of the cold south wind. Kerian was surprised when Alhana sat close and wrapped one side of her fox fur around Kerian's shoulders. She leaned gratefully into its warmth.

"I approve of the morrow's endeavor wholeheartedly," Alhana said very softly, "but I feel you should be wary of certain possibilities."

Royalty had a knack for calculated vagueness. "Aunt, your coat is warm, but I would like to get some sleep. What are you trying to say?"

"I do not believe he goes to Khur to save Gilthas."

Kerian had no doubt who "he" was. "Then why?"

Alhana looked away. Kerian sighed for the delay, and Alhana blurted, "He would be Speaker again."

Kerian almost laughed, but Alhana was in deadly earnest. "You know his condition," Kerian said, trying to be gentle. "He can never be Speaker again."

"If not Speaker himself, then the power behind another's throne. You don't know him as I do, Kerianseray. He was born to rule. He was always firm of purpose." Kerian snorted at the diplomatic phrasing. "But now—" Alhana shook her head. "If power comes within his grasp, he will take it. He will allow *no one* to stand in his way."

Kerian turned to face her more fully. She did not feel like laughing now. "Are you saying he would kill me, or the Speaker, if the opportunity presented itself?"

"No! I don't know! If he thought our people would benefit from his leadership. . . ." Alhana collected herself. Even in the silvery pale starlight, the intensity of her regard was palpable. "It was said of him, years ago, that he intended to unite the elf kingdoms even if he had to kill every elf in Ansalon to do it. He has not grown gentler since."

Was that Porthios's true reason for going to Khur? Kerian wanted to gather Gilthas's warriors for a great war of liberation in Qualinesti. What did Porthios want? If somehow both Gilthas and Kerian were removed, who would remain to lead the elf army? No one but Porthios.

Kerian thanked her for her counsel, adding, "You should try to sleep now."

Alhana sighed deeply. Her worries would not be easily set aside. She bade Kerian good night and departed.

Lying in her bedroll, Kerian stared at the dirty canvas three feet above her nose. Despite her own parting advice, she was unable to sleep. She kept turning over in her mind what Alhana had said.

Thank you very much, she thought sourly. True or not, Alhana's fears had utterly spoiled Kerian's rest.

Less than a mile away, two gray-clad figures moved quietly along the stony trails atop the sandstone mountains. They proceeded in an odd fashion. One would dart across open ground, hide, then signal the trailing comrade to follow. The second would then dart forward, hide, and signal. Zigzagging over the plateau, Breetan Everride and Sergeant Jeralund came within a hundred yards of the elves' camp then halted, concealing themselves beneath a pair of boulders that leaned together at their tops.

"There it is!" Breetan said, low voice further muffled by her gray suede mask.

Sergeant Jeralund grunted. He was cold and tired. They'd been bedded down for the night when Breetan shook him awake, pointing excitedly to a crimson glow over the higher peaks to the southeast. She was certain the elves were celebrating an important event. Why else draw attention to themselves with so great a fire?

With her leading, they traversed the mountains, drawn to the distant glow like moths to a candle. Breetan paused once to unsling her crossbow. She loaded it, then beckoned Jeralund onward.

Overlooking the elves' camp, they tried to make sense of the scene they beheld.

"They've got griffons!" Jeralund exclaimed, no longer sleepy. "If they mount their entire force, they can strike anywhere at will."

It was a very worrisome development, but Breetan was more concerned with the whereabouts of her target. He must be in the elves' camp. How was she to get him? Infiltrating the camp would be suicide. The elves could hear, smell, and see humans coming from far away.

"Wait," Jeralund advised, breathing on his gloved hands. "It'll be daylight in a few hours. When the camp is awake, the Scarecrow will be out and about."

"How far would you say it is to the center of those tents?"

"No more than a hundred ten yards."

She adjusted the dial on the crossbow sight. It was a fiendishly complicated device, but after regular practice, Breetan was confident she could hit an elf at three hundred yards—four hundred if the wind was still, which it seldom was at this altitude.

She sat, stretching her legs in front of her, and laid the crossbow over her knees.

"We wait."

* * * * *

False dawn flared. Like the bugle call blown to rouse human soldiers, it awakened every elf in the mountain camp. The griffons, attuned to the moods of their new riders, stood up along their picket line. They pawed the rocky ground impatiently, wings unfurling and flapping to loosen the muscles.

Under the lightening sky, Kerian pulled a quilted jerkin over her trail-worn buckskins. Weight was critical. The thick jerkin would not only keep her warm as she flew high, but would offer protection since her only armor would be a steel skullcap taken from the Bianost cache. Added to that would be her sword, lance, bow, provisions, and Alhana—Kerian began to feel sorry for her mount. The Golden griffons, smaller than their Royal counterparts, were being asked to fly several hundred miles, a much longer distance than they usually covered in one go. The journey should take ten to twelve hours. With good luck, and given the length of the summer day, they should reach Khur before sunset.

Kerian and Alhana, both experienced griffon riders, were to lead the way on Chisa. They had discussed the route and had decided to steer clear of inhabited lands as much as possible, to keep secret their acquisition of griffons. They would fly overland to New Bay, then northeast over the New Sea, avoiding both the mainland swamp and Schallsea Island. They'd thread the narrow straits of Qwermish, bisect the Inland Sea, and cross onto land again between Sanction and Thrusting Knife. From there, they would traverse the Khalkist Mountains by following valleys north and east and keeping to as low an altitude as possible. The mountains were replete with Nerakan hirelings, mercenaries, and talkative traders. Not all were hostile, but gossip would be deadly to the desire for secrecy.

Their ultimate goal was the mouth of the pass into Inath-Wakenti. Kerian reasoned that Gilthas had made a dash for the valley after being besieged on the Lion's Teeth. Good, noble Planchet had stayed behind with a rearguard to protect the main body of elves. That was the scene they had witnessed in the sky. There was no point flying to the Lion's Teeth. That fight was obviously over.

In the privacy of her tent, Kerian had wept after watching Planchet's gallant stand. Although the vision had vanished abruptly, its end was inevitable: Planchet was dead. She had grieved the loss for his sake and for what it would mean to Gilthas. None knew better than she how important Planchet was to her husband. The vision also had left her haunted by thoughts of Gilthas's looming fate. He had denied her, so she'd cut herself off from him, but their bond went deeper than politics or military matters. She missed him with an ache she could no longer ignore. If he was alive, she would make him take her back, on her terms. If he was dead—

If Gilthas was dead, someone would pay.

She decided to leave behind her bag of provisions. With Chisa carrying two riders, every bit of saved weight would be a help. Kerian could go a day without food. She would dine in Khur this night with her husband.

Hytanthas jogged up. Like the Lioness, his only piece of armor was a metal cap to protect his head. His face was flushed. He looked happier than at any time since he'd turned up in Qualinesti.

"The riders are mustering by the corral! Hurry, Commander!"

"They won't leave without us," she replied grumpily. His enthusiasm was sometimes refreshing, but after a sleepless night, she found the bright-eyed vigor of an elf only a few years younger than herself extremely tiresome.

The elves staying behind were arrayed in a great semicircle behind the corral. Kerian surveyed their faces, one and all, from the pale-eyed good looks of Alhana's Silvanesti guards, to the smaller, darker, all-too-ordinary elves of Bianost, who had risked everything to join the rebellion. In the center of the group, Chathendor and Nalaryn seemed polar opposites—a Kagonesti scout from the deep forests of western Qualinesti and a life-long courtier of Silvanost—but they stood shoulder to shoulder, like brothers.

Kerian swallowed hard. Deliberately avoiding an emotional scene, she turned away from those staying behind and studied the flyers. One was missing. Before she could mention his absence, Porthios arrived.

He came slowly, tying twine around his wrist. He'd wrapped the twine around his arm to keep his loose sleeves from catching the wind and was trying to finish it off at his wrist. Tying knots one-handed was difficult work and he struggled with it, but not for long.

"Let me."

Alhana took the loose ends of string and tied them off. She asked, "Too tight?"

"No." His voice was barely audible, but she heard him well enough. She held out a hand for another length of twine. Wordlessly, he gave it to her, and she began binding up his other sleeve.

Although she never once looked up at him, Porthios's gaze did not leave her all the while she worked. She was clad in a riding tunic of deep blue suede, trimmed with white fur, and gathered at the waist by a belt of woven silver. A slim dagger was thrust through her belt and a quiver of arrows slung over her shoulder. She was good with a bow, he remembered. Better than he with moving targets. Better than he with all targets now. Her hair was covered by a scarf that matched her tunic. Her eyes, reflecting the tunic's color, were the dark purple of the late-evening sky over Qualinost.

He moved abruptly away from her to stand by Samar and his griffon. She'd only just finished tying the twine around his wrist. She looked at him curiously. "Did I hurt you?"

One shake of his head and he concentrated on the Lioness, climbing a rock prior to addressing the riders. Far better to put his attention there than to think of Alhana or dwell on the upcoming ride. Porthios had not been astride a griffon since his own was blasted from beneath him by dragonflame. There was no time for fear or hesitation, however. He must go to Khur. Griffonback was the best way to get there. Nothing else must matter.

After outlining the route she and Alhana had chosen, Kerian said, "We've had no time to practice, so keep everything simple. Stay together. If anyone gets separated, make your way to the valley."

"What formation do we use?" asked Hytanthas.

"Like a flight of geese. Alhana and I are on point. Samar and Orexas will fly behind us on the left. Hytanthas, you're on my right." She went on, specifying each rider's place.

From her hiding place, Breetan could see her hooded target but didn't have a clear shot. Elves kept passing in front of the Scarecrow, and he kept moving through the crowd. When he finally stood still, while an elf woman fixed his tunic, the female was squarely in Breetan's line of fire.

"I could shoot her then get him with a second bolt when she falls," she whispered.

"No!" Jeralund hissed. "The first strike will alert them, and you'll never get another chance! Be patient, Lady."

Be patient, she repeated silently to herself. Be patient. Breetan sighted the front ring on a spot directly between the elf woman's shoulder blades. As soon as she moved, the target's chest would be exposed.

Unfortunately, the Scarecrow moved first, and he placed himself behind yet another elf, a warrior with a weathered face.

Breetan murmured an obscenity.

Kerian finished outlining their flying formation and asked if anyone had questions. One of the riders wanted to know what they should do if separated from the group and forced to land somewhere other than Inath-Wakenti.

"Tell no one who you are, where you've come from, or where you're going."

There were no other questions. The riders looked at her expectantly. It was the time a commander would say something to bolster their courage and prepare them for the great adventure ahead. The sun was just peering over the eastern peaks. Its light washed Kerian's helmet in gold. She drew a deep breath.

"Keep your seats. Let the griffons do the flying. We go to bring our wayward cousins home from Khur."

"Sivvanesu!" shouted the guards.

Hytanthas, not to be outdone, cried, "For the Speaker of the Sun and Stars!" The Bianost elves cheered.

Accustomed to her much larger Royal griffon, Kerian had no trouble vaulting onto Chisa's back. She wrapped the reins around one gloved hand and checked the straps of her makeshift riding harness. All were tight. She told Alhana to climb on.

The former queen ducked under the griffon's partially unfurled wing and put her foot in the rear saddle brace. She sprang gracefully onto the griffon's back, landing lightly.

"You've done this before," Kerian joked.

"Since before you were born," Alhana shot back.

She tied herself to the saddle, and Kerian offered advice on how to ride pillion. Alhana chuckled suddenly.

"I suppose you know all this already too," Kerian muttered.

"I do, actually, but that's not why I was laughing. It's Chisa. She's very"—Alhana hunted for the right word—"proud of herself just now. Smug."

"Why?"

"Because she has *two* riders. Only she and Ironhead can claim that distinction!"

It was time to go. Kerian cried, "Ay-hai-hai!" Chisa spread her wings and ran forward three hopping steps. On the third bounce, she took to the sky. Despite her formidable dignity, Alhana let out a whoop of joy as the ground fell away. Hytanthas's griffon, Kanan, sprang down the slope and took off. Samar turned Ironhead's mighty head and snapped the reins. Unlike the short, bounding run taken by the first two, the big male griffon reared up on his hind legs, crouched, spread his wings wide, and launched himself skyward from a standing start.

All Breetan could see was pounding wings, rising griffons, and bobbing riders. She had four bolts before she must reload. The Scarecrow was on the largest griffon, sitting behind a warrior elf. With four arrows, she could bring down their griffon. If the fall didn't kill the target, she would reload and finish the job.

She began to stand, to track the flying beast, but Jeralund grabbed her sword belt and dragged her down again.

"What are you doing?" she cried. "He's getting away!"

"Don't be foolish, Lady! You'd never hit him now! And if he is alerted by your shot, you'll never get a second chance." The target was quartering away from them at a speed greater than that of a horse at a full gallop. Adding to the impossibility of the shot were sweeping wings and the other griffons still rising from the plateau, crowding the target.

In her anger, Breetan saw none of that. "This is mutiny, Sergeant! Let me up!" She struggled, but the heavier man kept her from standing. "I'll see you hanged for this!" she raged.

"As you wish, but if I'm to be gutted by a mob of furious elves, I would at least like the satisfaction of having succeeded in killing their leader."

The griffons passed high overhead, and the two humans hid beneath the overhanging boulders. Jeralund put his lips next to Breetan's ear. "He may be gone, but where he goes, we can follow."

Her teeth were bared in a hiss of fury. "How can we follow flying beasts?"

"Think," he urged the impetuous knight. "We can find out where he intends to land." He pointed to the elves in camp, all staring rather forlornly after their departing comrades. "All we have to do is get one of them and ask."

As usual, the sergeant's tactics were sensible. "You get one. I'll ask the questions."

When the griffons had circled away, Jeralund released her and raised up to peer down at the elves' camp. Immediately, he felt the cold edge of Breetan's dagger on his throat, just below his knotted kerchief.

"If you ever lay hands on me again, I will kill you."

His voice was maddeningly calm. "My life is yours, Lady, for the duration of this mission."

He slipped out of their hiding place and crept down the shadowed side of the promontory to waylay an elf from the camp. Leaning against a sun-warmed boulder, Breetan trembled with anger and more than a little hunter's fever.

22

The elves walked all night, across the wadi and up the opposite bank. There they waited while the various groups trickled in. Dawn was just brightening the eastern sky by the time the last of the stragglers arrived and the nation was once more a single great column. They had made it across the obstacle. No nomads had attacked. They began to congratulate themselves.

Their relief was premature. When the first blood-red sliver of the rising sun cleared the eastern mountains, the nomads fell upon them.

The Mikku, familiar with the wadi, had ridden hard and crossed it at a low point farther down. They caught the elves with their backs to the dry riverbed. Of Taranath and the rearguard cavalry, there was no sign, only more and more Khurs. Like ants converging on a dying serpent, riders emerged from a screen of low trees and charged. Only forty yards separated them from the elves, so they hadn't room to gain much momentum. They were counting on swords, rather than the impact of their galloping horses, to drive the *laddad* nation to its death over the steep side of the wadi.

Gilthas, at the head of his people, had just cleared a stand of juniper and seen the pass into Inath-Wakenti ahead when the sounds of battle reached him. Joy evaporated in an instant. Despite all his people's sacrifices, the nomads had caught up with them.

He dodged among his frightened people, shouting for any with weapons to get to the front. An elderly female was knocked to the rocky ground in front of him. Gilthas picked her up and passed her to an elf running in the opposite direction.

Hamaramis had no more than two hundred warriors on hand, and all were on foot because of the shortage of horses. Without hesitation, the old general led his warriors out of the disorganized mob, hoping to draw the nomads' attention, but the humans rode around his well-armed company to attack the civilians. With cooking pots, sticks, and pitifully few spears, the elves fought desperately to fend off the nomad horsemen. The weak and old were gathered in the center of defensive squares and circles. While the women labored to build barricades from baggage, stones, windfall tree limbs, and anything else to hand, the males drove Tondoon and Mikku riders back with rakes and shovels. Keen-eyed elves of both sexes emptied more than a few saddles with well-aimed stones.

Gilthas moved from square to square, comforting the frightened and urging the fighters to greater efforts.

"Taranath and the warriors will return soon," he assured them. "Take heart! I have seen the entrance to the hidden valley. It is just ahead. We're almost there!"

The elves knew the nomads would not follow them into Inath-Wakenti. The nomads considered the valley the last home of the gods before they departed the mortal plane. As such, it was taboo. If the elves could reach the valley, they would be safe. If.

Hamaramis marched his soldiers back to the Speaker. The warriors moved with shields locked, presenting a fearsome hedgehog of spears. Several tribes feigned thrusts, but none dared close. The humans had learned just how hard elven blades could be.

"Great Speaker!" Hamaramis had taken a hard rap and the nasal of his helmet had cut his nose. Blood trickled down like a crimson mustache. "The enemy is not yet here in full strength! I estimate five or six hundred."

That meant many thousands of nomads were still to arrive.

"We must get the people moving!" Gilthas declared. "Immediately! Inath-Wakenti is just beyond those trees!"

He raised his voice, exhorting the people to follow him. "Our journey is almost over! The valley, our safety, is beyond that grove of trees! Follow me there!"

The elves could see only the fierce tribesmen milling beyond the reach of makeshift defenses. None moved. Gilthas redoubled his efforts, pulling at arms, clapping backs or shoulders. A few dozen elves struggled to their feet, but the majority stayed where they were, too tired and too fearful to comprehend the desperate truth the Speaker was telling them.

Gilthas coughed. Dust clogged his sickly lungs, and the illness the healer's potions had eased came roaring back. Hamaramis saw him double over and ran to him. Blood stained Gilthas's chin. The old general cried out, but Gilthas waved him away. When he could speak, Gilthas asked, "Where is Wapah?"

Puzzled, Hamaramis said, "With the head of the column, I think. Why, sire?"

"I must find him."

Gathering his strength, Gilthas walked to the outside ring of elves, still anxiously watching the nomads. The riders would circle, attack small bands of elves who dared move, and circle again. Unfortunate elves marooned when the lines broke apart were ridden down and mercilessly put to the sword. The horrible spectacle so captured the elves' attention, they didn't react at first when Gilthas approached. He began tugging them apart to make his way through the crowd. Ingrained respect for the Speaker finally penetrated their terror and they complied. Only after he was through did the elves realize he was leaving the protection of the circle.

Hamaramis yelled for him to stop. Others took up the plea. A few dared take his arm or grasp the back of his tattered *geb*.

He looked coldly at the hands gripping him and one by one they fell away. Head high, he strode onward, in the direction of Inath-Wakenti.

Several Mikku saw him break the circle. Shouting, spurring their mounts, they rode at the lone *laddad*.

Hamaramis broke into a run, bawling at his warriors to protect their sovereign.

"The Speaker! The Speaker!" The cry went up from dozens of throats. Warriors and civilians alike ran after Gilthas. Rather than try to hamper his progress, they formed a double wall between him and the advancing nomads, with warriors on the outer face and civilians on the inner. As he moved, the walls moved with him. Elf warriors and Mikku riders collided, and a skirmish began. Tondoon warmasters mustered their men to join the attack on the pocket of elves walking from one square to another.

Gilthas reached the next defensive circle. Its near side opened to allow him to pass. Sheltered within, a tiny blond Silvanesti child regarded him with frank curiosity. "Where are you going, Speaker Pathfinder?" she asked.

He smiled. "I'm going home, little one. Will you come with me?"

The girl left the cover of a pile of baggage and came to him. Without hesitation, she took his hand.

He kept walking. Soon hundreds of elves had joined him, walking alongside and behind their Speaker. Nomads sallied in, hacking at the fringes of the moving crowd, but were driven off when the elves swarmed around them, attacking from all sides. Not even the best swordsman could defend against thirty or forty foes armed with farm tools and a great deal of determination. The elves were fighting not only for their own lives, but for the life of their Speaker. Fear for his safety outweighed fear for their own.

Gilthas gave his tiny companion over to her father and walked faster. Every strike of his heels against the stony ground shook his whole body. Every rapid breath burned in his chest like fire. But he smiled and waved jauntily at his astonished people. His route encompassed circle after circle, until the entire front half of the nation was in motion. Word was passed back to the rear. Not yet under attack, the remainder of the elves picked up their bundles and came on.

At the last circle, Gilthas found Wapah standing with sword bared in the midst of hostile and worried elves. The circle opened and Gilthas entered. He hailed the nomad. Wapah doffed his sun hat.

"Greetings to you, khan of the *laddad*. You bring your nation on your heels."

"They only want a leader to show them the way, and I need a scout to show me. Will you enter the Valley of the Blue Sands?"

Wapah's chin lifted. "If the Speaker so orders."

He returned his weapon to its brass scabbard. Side by side, Speaker and nomad headed for the juniper grove. Mikku and Tondoon riders followed, not engaging but staying always within sight. Gilthas wondered what they were doing.

"Some stratagem of the Weyadan's," Wapah told him. "Beware, Khan-Speaker. My cousin is a shrewd woman."

Beyond the gnarled junipers, the distant, blue-gray slopes of the Khalkist Mountains rose. These were the first real mountains the elves had seen since coming to Khur. The elves walked faster.

Wapah had ridden into the pass years earlier, although of course he'd not entered the valley proper. He explained the pass was like a funnel, narrow at the near end and wide at the valley end.

Gilthas pushed low-hanging juniper branches out of his way and stepped through to open air. Wapah emerged a few steps away. When human and elf beheld what awaited them, both stopped dead.

"Merciful E'li," Gilthas whispered.

The bulk of the nomad army was arrayed in a vast semicircle a hundred yards away. Thirty thousand warriors faced the thunderstruck Speaker. All seven tribes of Khur were represented, although the coastal Fin-Maskar tribe had sent only a token presence and even fewer of Sahim-Khan's Khur tribe had joined Adala's venture. The men sat motionless and silent, morning sun glinting off the swords resting on their shoulders. Their horses, trapped in the colors of their rider's clan or tribe, were bright as a rainbow. Positioned in the center of the line was one member of the vast army mounted on a small gray donkey.

"The Weyadan."

Wapah's identification was unnecessary. Gilthas recognized the black-robed figure of Adala Fahim.

Hamaramis and his small band of soldiers came crashing through the trees. The general uttered an oath when he saw they'd fallen into a trap. He urged the Speaker to come away. Gilthas ignored him. The nomads' horses snorted, pawed the ground, and switched their tails, but the men did not move. "What are they waiting for?" he asked Wapah.

"*Ifran.*"

"What?" Hamaramis demanded.

"The single moment in time when a thing is destined to happen. The Weyadan is mistress of the *ifran.*"

"I'll ask for a parley," Gilthas said, but Wapah shook his head.

"There will be no more talking."

A cry rose from the Khurish host. It began low then grew and grew until it seemed the nomads might beat the elves back by the very power of their joined voices. The roar cut off abruptly, and in the sudden silence, over the ringing in his ears, Gilthas heard Wapah murmur, "*Ifran.*"

Swords were lifted high. The line of horsemen lurched forward.

Hamaramis formed his warriors into a double line to protect the Speaker's position. Desperate, the general pleaded with his sovereign to withdraw. Gilthas tore his fascinated gaze from the onrushing horde and retreated a few yards into the shelter of the juniper trees but would go no farther.

"Not another step in retreat," he said. "Here we win, or we die."

ALLIANCES

With weary familiarity, the elves aligned themselves to receive a charge of horsemen. The closely growing trees made a natural barrier that would break the force of any headlong attack. The gaps in the trees quickly sprouted spears, staves, and farm tools as the elves got into position.

While nomads charged from the front, the several hundred who had been shadowing the elves' left flank also attacked the column south of the juniper grove. The straggling line of elves thinned and broke as they once more hurried to form defensive squares.

The shouting Khurs smashed through the column, cutting it in two. The larger portion, thousands of confused and terrified civilians, backed away from the nomad assault, seeking more defensible ground.

Where Gilthas stood, in the juniper grove, all that could be heard was the thunder of hooves, the deep-voiced shouts of the nomads, and the answering cries from the elves. A few arrows flicked out of the grove but not many. The Khurs pressed on and slammed full-tilt into the junipers, losing many to the hedge of sharp points and many more to collisions with twisted, sturdy trees. There were so many nomads that, for a long, blood-drenched moment, it seemed the impact would carry them through the grove, obliterating the elves within. Yet Gilthas held true to his defiant vow. He did not retreat a step. A horse and rider were upended in front of him and crashed at his feet. Wapah ducked, but the Speaker of the Sun and Stars held firm.

When it became clear their initial attack was not going to destroy the elves, the nomads withdrew. Along the edge of the juniper grove lay the bodies of Khurs and elves. Intermingled among them were dead and dying horses.

At seventy yards the nomads turned around and came roaring back. More penetrated the grove, galloping among the startled elves, sabering all within reach. Hamaramis's warriors moved from point to point, applying their skill and weight to each crisis until the encroaching Khurs were dead or evicted.

"Next time they back off, we counter-charge!" Hamaramis said.

But the nomads didn't withdraw. They kept fighting. Knocked from their horses, or with their horses killed beneath them, they rose and continued the fight on foot. Their vigor and unusual tenacity began to tell on the trail-weary elves. The Khurs penetrated farther and farther into the trees.

Behind the grove, the main body of elves was in dire straits, but fresh plumes of dust rising in the southwest heralded the arrival of Taranath. The elf warriors had had to ride completely around the lengthy wadi to rejoin their comrades. Horses blown, the cavalry nonetheless fell on the several hundred nomads harassing the column. They were routed in short order. Taranath immediately rode to the aid of those in the juniper grove, but by then the wings of the nomad force had lapped around the grove. Taranath tried to fight his way forward, but the Khurs stubbornly refused to yield.

Fighting closed around Gilthas. Sweat poured down his face. He was cold but perspiring at the same time. It was only a matter of time before the nomads overwhelmed his exhausted people. His bodyguard was engaged. Hamaramis had taken a place in line. Even the Speaker's councilors were fighting. When Wapah drew his weapon, Gilthas asked, "Will you fight your own people?"

"There are no roads in the desert," the Leaping Spider sage replied. "Any way that gets you where you're going is the right way." He shouldered in behind Hamaramis, trading cuts with a mounted Tondoon warrior.

Gilthas dodged a slash aimed at his head. He felt the nomad's blade snag the loose fabric of his *geb*. The sword ripped free, and the Khur was knocked flat by Hamaramis and Wapah.

More and more nomads streamed out of position to join the battle for the juniper grove. More and more fell, slain or wounded too badly to continue fighting. Adala watched impassively. "No respite," she told the warmasters gathered around her. "Keep on them until they break."

"And if they don't?" asked Yalmuk.

She rubbed the broken lapis cabochon, the one that had saved her from the *laddad* arrow, as if to extract every bit of power from it. She'd tied her sash on the outside of her black widow's *geb* so the broken cabochon would be visible and could act as a sign of her *maita*.

"They will break. I know it."

Fighting raged all day. The sun was low in the west when Hamaramis received a stunning blow to the side of his helmet. His sword spun away, and the old general sagged to his knees. Two nomads spurred their horses at him. Gilthas was unarmed, but couldn't stand by and see his old comrade killed. He snatched up two hefty stones. He hurled one, hitting the nearer nomad's horse. It bucked, throwing its rider. Before he could throw the second, something slammed into his back, knocking him flat.

The nomads have killed me, he thought, struggling desperately to draw breath. "Kerian," he managed to say, although no one could hear him.

As the Speaker went down, dark shapes appeared overhead, emerging from the low clouds shrouding the setting sun. No one engaged in the battle spared a glance at the sky, but the rear ranks of nomads, trotting forward to join the fray, found their horses suddenly seized by a strange madness. The animals balked, planting all four feet at once and refusing to go ahead. No amount of spur, riding stick, or cursing would induce them to move. The madness spread to the horses in the next wave. They reared and snorted, bared their yellow teeth, and bit each other and nearby riders. Hundreds of men who'd learned to ride before they could walk were cast to the ground and trampled.

The source of the madness was revealed when a high, ear-shredding screech split the air. Griffons were a rarity in Khur, but the nomads recognized the winged creatures swooping down upon them. Mounted on the flying beasts were *laddad* warriors brandishing lances and bows.

Kerian and Alhana led twenty-two griffons down from the heights. Two of their number had been lost crossing the mountains when the griffons flew into cloudbanks and never emerged, and five were swallowed up by a storm over the New Sea. Wind-burned and saddle-sore, the remaining riders had completed their grueling, amazing flight.

They skimmed low across the line of nomads, relying on the horses' innate fear to disrupt the charge. It worked. The desert ponies panicked. With the wave disrupted, Kerian told Alhana to unsling her bow.

"I'll steer for the trees!" Kerian added. The juniper grove was where the main battle was raging.

Hytanthas, Samar and Porthios, and the rest of the sky-riders fell in behind Chisa. Alhana leaned far to the side, drew back her bowstring, and loosed. A Khur wearing the brown-and-blue striped *geb* of a Mikku threw up his hands and fell from his horse.

Following Alhana's example, the griffon riders rained arrows on the nomads. They could hardly miss. The mass of humans below was so dense, their horses so uncontrollable, the elves barely had to aim.

Soon enough, the remaining nomads quit the juniper grove and galloped back up the slight rise to Adala and the warmasters.

The panicked horses didn't stop there, but stampeded past, all but knocking Little Thorn over. Adala shouted at the men, but they couldn't control their animals. The last of twenty thousand thundered by, leaving her enveloped in clouds of choking dust, colored red by the fast-dying sun.

The air stirred violently, and the dust was driven away by the downdraft of beating wings. Seeming to materialize from the blood-red air, the agents of the nomads' catastrophic reverse alighted in front of Adala. She glanced back and saw her warmasters and chiefs returning to her. They'd given up trying to urge their beasts back and were hurrying forward on foot. Curiously, Little Thorn seemed unaffected by the griffons. He dropped his head and cropped a tuft of saltbush. A single figure swung down from one of the lead griffons and approached her on foot.

The griffon rider appeared unarmed. Below a metal skull-cap, the figure's face was covered by a dust cloth. When the dust cloth was pulled down, Adala recoiled in shock.

"By what magic do you appear to me alive?" she exclaimed.

"A god's magic, it seems," the Lioness replied.

Adala glanced over her shoulder again. The main body of her host had recovered control of their horses and were drawn up several hundred yards away.

"You came back in time to perish!" she said.

"I've come back to take my people into Inath-Wakenti." Kerian gestured to the griffon riders behind her. Two more dismounted and came to stand by her. She introduced them.

"This is Alhana Starbreeze, once queen of Silvanesti. And this is Orexas, leader of the elf army of the West."

Adala's expression settled into hard lines. "It doesn't matter who you bring against us, *laddad*. We will not yield. If it costs every life we have, we will not yield!"

"You see?" the Lioness said to Porthios. "What can you do with such a fanatic? Reason doesn't work. Nor fear. The sword is all she understands."

"Must we wade through blood to find peace?" asked Alhana.

"Yes!" Adala said. Her chiefs and warmasters had struggled through the churned-up sand to stand on either side of Little Thorn, their swords drawn. Adala added, "The battle will resume. Flying beasts or no flying beasts, you will not pass!"

"I think we will."

Porthios stepped forward and addressed Adala. "I was once like you, proud, defiant, certain of the rightness of my cause. I faced enemies far more powerful than you without hope of victory because I knew I was destined to win in the end."

"Every foolish warrior in the world thinks that," Adala said, dismissive. "I am not a warrior. I am a woman, mother of my people, and Those on High have granted me the gift of *maita*. How can the destiny of a single *laddad* compare to the fate promised me by the gods?"

She had asked a similar question of all her opponents. The humans had joined her or been struck down by her divine *maita*. The *laddad* had been delivered by it into her hands.

Porthios was silent for a moment, making a decision, then he said, "*Maita* means 'fate ordained by the gods,' I believe. Perhaps you do have your gods' favor." His hands dropped to his waist, and he untied his ragged sash. "Or maybe you've just been lucky." He loosened the gray cloth winding around his neck.

Kerian realized what he meant to do. It was brilliant and terrible, matchlessly brave and utterly selfish. For the first time during their endless, arduous trek, she admired him.

His hoarse voice went on, unstoppable, impossible to ignore. "Let me tell you about fate, you insolent barbarian. I once ruled the greatest, most civilized nation in the world. I was married to a queen who was as good, honest, and brave as she was beautiful—and she was very, very beautiful." A tiny sob escaped Alhana's lips, but Porthios went on, remorseless. "We had a child, a son to rule our combined nations. He was handsome, intelligent, and courageous as only a prince of elves could be."

He dragged the scarf away from his neck. The flesh was mottled red and scarred like the skin of a lizard. The Khurish chiefs muttered. Adala blinked a few times, but held firm.

"All this greatness I lost. My son threw away his life on a false love and an evil cause. My wife never forgave herself, or me, for his death." He pushed back his hood.

"Oh, my love, don't," Alhana whispered brokenly.

His gloved hands halted for an instant, and he glanced at her. "I must, beloved. It's *maita*."

He spoke to Adala again. "No mortal being should have survived what I survived. You speak of your divine fate. You know nothing! I *am* divine fate. It is all that keeps me alive, and I will not be denied."

In one motion Porthios drew off the cloth mask. Nomad and elf shrank back in horror. Kerian had seen this once before. Although she looked away, she saw it still. The image was burned into her memory. Only Alhana did not recoil or avert her eyes. She looked full upon the ruin of her husband's face, and she did not waver from his side.

The dragon's fire had burned Porthios's flesh down to the last layer of skin. Flame-red, it covered a head devoid of ears, nose, and lips, the eyelids retracted to nearly nothing. Almost as if to mock what was gone, a fringe of long hair remained on the lower half of his skull, but the hair was dull, dead gray. His face was a skull, covered by crimson muscle and slashed by harsh, white scar tissue.

He turned his head stiffly toward the shocked warmasters and several dropped to their knees. "We *will* enter this valley, and you will do nothing more to stop us. Go!"

The apparition before them was horrid enough; to hear it speak was the final straw. The chiefs and warmasters fled. Even Adala's fortitude wasn't proof against the sight. She did not flee, but she lifted her dust veil over her eyes.

"Abomination," she gasped. "You should not be!"

The lipless mouth moved in an awful parody of a smile. "I agree. But here I am. Do you really want to match your fate to mine?"

He stepped forward and slapped the donkey's flank. Faced with the wall of elves and griffons ahead, the donkey snorted and jogged back toward the men and horses he knew. Adala clutched reins and wiry mane to avoid being pitched off. She did not try to halt his going.

Porthios could not move. He had bared his shame to the world, and he could not turn to see the horror in the eyes of those behind him, especially one pair of violet eyes. A hand, clutching his mask, appeared at his side. He turned to find Alhana standing close by. Her eyes brimmed with tears, but there was no revulsion on her face, nor even pity, only love. He replaced the mask, raised his hood, and began to wind the long cloth around his neck again.

"Get the people moving," he said. "If the humans think too long, they may try to fight again."

Kerian climbed onto Chisa. She expected Alhana to follow,

but the former queen stayed by her husband. Porthios told Samar to go without him.

"You're staying here?" Kerian asked.

"What are a few thousand humans when you've bathed in the breath of a dragon?"

The Lioness saluted. It was not a gesture she performed often. She had a Wilder elf's inbred distrust of authority, but at this time and place, a salute seemed proper.

Porthios returned the gesture, then Alhana linked her arm in his.

*　*　*　*　*

Gilthas awoke. Only one eye would open. He lifted a hand and felt a thick bandage crisscrossing his forehead.

He was lying in a litter, being carried. Night had come and around him were the voices and footfalls of his people.

He must have spoken his confused thoughts aloud, because the elf holding the rear poles of the litter said, "No, sire. You're definitely not dead."

"Hytanthas! When did you—?"

"I carried out your orders, Great Speaker," said the young captain. He nodded to the elf carrying the front of the litter. Gilthas strained to see with his good eye.

"You look like the dog's dinner," Kerianseray told him. Her voice broke, betraying her true feelings despite the crude human expression. "Why were you in the middle of a raging battle without arms or armor?"

He could not credit the evidence of his eyes. Her presence was a miracle such as the gods might have bestowed on a long-ago hero. He remembered having fallen during the battle, but in his muddled mind something else seemed of greater import.

"Your hair!"

She shrugged. "It's a long tale."

They told him all of it, from Kerian's plunge into Nalis Aren and the participation in the rebellion, to Hytanthas's arrival in Qualinesti and the capture of Golden griffons. Gilthas found it impossible to fathom. Yet the griffons wheeling overhead, keeping watch over the mass of refugees beneath them, were undeniably real.

"Where are we?" he asked.

"Inath-Wakenti. Where else?"

He pushed himself painfully up on one elbow. It was true. They were enclosed in the tree-shrouded embrace of the mountains. Gilthas inhaled deeply, filling his ravaged lungs with balmy air. They had done it. They were here.

He lay down again. "I am glad you came back."

She thought how best to answer him. "I'm glad too," she finally said. "We'll be at the creek soon. It marks the boundary of the valley proper, and the strange things that go on inside it."

He asked no more questions. The Speaker of the Sun and Stars had slipped, aching but contented, into slumber.

* * * * *

Robien sniffed the wind. "They come," he said.

"May the gods help us all," Favaronas murmured.

* * * * *

At the mouth of Alya-Alash, Adala sat on Little Thorn. She'd sent her faithful followers away and was alone at the doorstep of the sacred land, pondering the meaning of fate.

A horse and rider appeared, shimmering in the morning mirage. The *laddad* had all passed through the night before. Who was coming back?

The rider finally resolved into her cousin, Wapah. A ferocious frown twisted Adala's face.

"Traitor! You betrayed your people."

He pulled his horse to a halt by Little Thorn. "I betrayed you, cousin. You are not Khur."

With that he rode away, into the sacred valley. Adala listened until his horse's hoofbeats were lost in the sighing wind. She stared at the ground, trying to understand what Those on High wanted of her. The foreign killers were in the valley. What was she to do next?

A few feet from Little Thorn's left front hoof lay an unusually shaped stone. It was of common composition, but rectangular, with sharp corners, as if worked by a mason's hand. Adala slid off her donkey, an idea taking shape in her mind.

The stone was three feet long and two wide, and she could barely shift it, but she finally got it aligned across the entrance to the pass. It was perfect. More would be needed, of course, many more. Yet it was a start.

The united tribes of Khur had a new task before them.

THE NEW ADVENTURES

A Practical Guide to Dragons
By Sindri Suncatcher

Sindri Suncatcher—wizard's apprentice—opens up
his personal notebooks to share his knowledge of these
awe-inspiring creatures, from the life cycle of a kind copper
dragon to the best way to counteract a red dragon's fiery
breath. This lavishly illustrated guide showcases the wide
array of fantastic dragons encountered on the world of Krynn.

The perfect companion to the Dragonlance: The New
Adventures series, for both loyal fans and new readers alike.

Sindri Suncatcher is a three-and-a-half foot tall kender,
who enjoys storytelling, collecting magical tokens, and
fighting dragons. He lives in Solamnia and is currently
studying magic under the auspices of the black-robed
wizard Maddoc. You can catch Sindri in the midst of
his latest adventure in *The Wayward Wizard*.

For more information visit www.mirrorstonebooks.com

For ages ten and up.

ELVEN EXILES TRILOGY
PAUL B. THOMPSON AND TONYA C. COOK

The elven people, driven from their age old enclaves in
the green woods, have crossed the Plains of Dust and harsh
mountains into the distant land of Khur. The elves coexist
uneasily with surrounding tribes under the walls of
Khuri-Khan.

Shadowy forces inside Khur and out plot to destroy the elves.
Some are ancient and familiar, others are new and unknown.

And so the battle lines are drawn, and the great game begins.
Survival or death, glory or oblivion — these are the stakes.
Gilthas and Kerianseray bet all on a forgotten map,
faithful friends, and their unshakable faith on the
greatness of the elven race.

SANCTUARY
Volume One

ALLIANCES
Volume Two
August 2006

Volume Three
June 2007

For more information visit **www.wizards.com**

A NEW TRILOGY FROM MARGARET WEIS & TRACY HICKMAN

THE LOST CHRONICLES
Dragons of the Dwarven Depths
Volume One

Tanis, Tasslehoff, Riverwind, and Raistlin
are trapped as refugees in Thorbardin, as the
draconian army closes in on the dwarven
kingdom. To save his homeland, Flint begins a
search for the Hammer of Kharas.

Available July 2006

For more information visit **www.wizards.com**

FOLLOW MARGARET WEIS FROM THE WAR OF SOULS INTO THE CHAOS OF POST-WAR KRYNN

The War of Souls has come to an end at last. Magic is back, and so are the gods. But the gods are vying for supremacy, and the war has caused widespread misery, uprooting entire nations and changing the balance of power on Ansalon.

AMBER AND ASHES
The Dark Disciple, Volume I
MARGARET WEIS

The mysterious warrior-woman Mina, brooding on her failure and the loss of her goddess, makes a pact with evil in a seductive guise. As a strange vampiric cult spreads throughout the fragile world, unlikely heroes – a wayward monk and a kender who can communicate with the dead – join forces to try to uproot the cause of the growing evil.

AMBER AND IRON
The Dark Disciple, Volume II
MARGARET WEIS

The former monk Rhys, now sworn to the goddess Zeboim, leads a powerful alliance in an attempt to find some way to destroy the Beloved, the fearsome movement of undead caught in the terrifying grip of the Lord of Death. Mina seeks to escape her captivity in the Blood Sea Tower, but can she escape the prison of her dark past?

AMBER AND BLOOD
The Dark Disciple, Volume III
MARGARET WEIS

February 2007

For more information visit **www.wizards.com**